DINER OF LOST SOULS

Book Two

By

Graham Diamond
&
Hedy Campeas

Copyright © 2023 by Graham Diamond and Hedy Campeas

All rights reserved. Including the right to reproduce this book or portions thereof of any sort whatsoever without written permission of the authors.

Lion Press, New York

Table of Content

ONE	1
TWO	11
THREE	18
FOUR	27
FIVE	43
SIX	57
SEVEN	67
EIGHT	75
NINE	91
TEN	102
ELEVEN	122
TWELVE	129
THIRTEEN	153
FOURTEEN	163
FIFTEEN	171
SIXTEEN	181
SEVENTEEN	196
EIGHTEEN	213
NINETEEN	235
TWENTY	248
TWENTY-ONE	259
TWENTY-TWO	278
TWENTY-THREE	292
TWENTY-FOUR	318
TWENTY-FIVE	334
TWENTY-SIX	346
TWENTY-SEVEN	376

ONE

"I'm in the weeds!" called the frantic waitress.

Cora looked over her shoulder to see the overwhelmed server delivering food orders to a round table crowded with raucous customers celebrating a happy occasion. She snapped her fingers and manager Eddie Coltrane and another waitress hurried over to assist. The diner was busier than usual for a rainy day. Eddie quickly indicated he would get matters under control. "No worries, Mrs. Gus," he told Cora. "Take your time."

"I'll have to help out in a minute," she told her brawny guest sitting opposite.

Solerno nodded, picking up the demitasse cup of Greek coffee and sniffed the aroma. The smell was strong and good. A bricki, a little pot with a long handle and spout, sat on the table directly in front of him. He took a single sip, then another.

"Well?" asked Cora.

He gently placed the cup down into the tiny saucer and smiled, showing a gap between his two front yellowed teeth, a testimony to many decades of smoking. "You never fail to deliver," he said in his raspy voice, obviously pleased. His narrow eyes focused on his fingernails, recently coated with a clear polish at a local salon he dutifully visited once a week. Solerno was fastidious about his nails and his white hair, growing thinner, it seemed, by the week.

"You teach your kitchen staff well."

"Thank you." Cora knew Solerno rarely gave compliments.

"Go on, finish your business. Then explain what happened."

Cora nodded. She eased out of the booth beside the window. Raindrops streaked more heavily across the glass now. She quickly assisted Eddie until the bottleneck had been cleared and service was running smoothly, eager to return to her important guest.

Solerno was watching as she went about her work. He mused that she struck an appealing figure, scrutinizing her shining sable hair and alluring almond-shaped dark eyes. Cora exuded femininity and authority, and the Greek owner of the Athena Diner's charisma never failed to fascinate him. He knew no more than anyone else about her life before her sudden arrival in America several decades ago. Like many others he wondered if some of the malicious rumors and gossip might be true. Since his own past was a carefully concealed business, he was not about to try to delve into hers.

"The first contact came less than a month ago," she began after she lithely slid back into the booth, resuming the conversation.

"At first I thought the guy on the phone was joking," Cora continued, her gaze meeting Solerno's. "He asked directly for me. Knew my name, and casually mentioned a couple of things about the diner that customers or passersby wouldn't be aware of."

"Like what?"

"Like a good guesstimate on how much money comes in on a typical week. About how much we normally spend on necessary supplies, basic costs, amounts in taxes. Things like that. He was well informed regarding this type of business."

A frown crossed Solerno's thick lips. "A shakedown," he said.

Cora shook her head. "Worse. When he said he wanted to set up a face-to-face meeting with me and his interested local 'investors,' I assumed he was some crank." She paused, pushing a few strands of hair from her face. "I laughed and told him I'm not interested. Then I hung up. We got busy and I forgot all about it."

"Until?"

"Until about ten days later when this letter came in the mail." She reached in her pocket and pulled out a folded envelope, passing it across the table for her confidant to read. Solerno put on his reading glasses. His body tensed, his lips pursed. The noise of nearby customers chatting and laughing didn't distract him. The letter was handwritten, sloppy, and difficult to make out in a few places. When he was done he passed the letter back, and she quickly returned it to her pocket. "This isn't from a nut job. It's menacing."

"That's why I contacted you. I wanted your opinion and advice."

Solerno was reputed to be a retired mob figure. He had been arrested several times but avoided conviction. He was not so prominent in his family that he posed a major threat to anyone. And even though he had stepped away years ago, Cora understood he still maintained a net of complicated connections to the inner 'family' circle. Still, she never questioned him concerning personal matters.

"That line they wrote about not wanting to see your business suffer a decline…"

"I considered it a veiled threat."

He nodded in agreement.

"Things stayed quiet for a few weeks after that. Until the recent phone call. Again, they asked for a meeting. Nothing at all was mentioned about this letter I received." She didn't hide her anger. "Then the other day Eddie opened up extra early and he found several trash cans overturned, garbage bags spilled behind the restaurant. Garbage pickup isn't until dawn."

"Sounds like they're escalating. Tell me again about the last call."

"It was brief and to the point. You'll get a fair offer, the voice said matter-of-factly. Take it while you can."

"That's all?"

"That's all. They didn't even wait for any kind of reply from me. Just a hang up."

Solerno lifted his demitasse, leaned back, and consumed it all. Cora reached for the bliki and refilled his cup. "Not too much to go on," he said candidly. "Have you discussed any of this with your police friends?"

"I only spoke with Jonah Hunter. The detective I've worked with before."

"Yeah, I'm familiar with Hunter. You know there's been gossip about you and that detective…" It was more of a statement than a question.

Cora flexed her wrist dismissively. "People can say whatever they like. Doesn't affect me one way or the other. But you know that. Whatever I may do with or without Hunter isn't anyone's business. You know that too. And you also recognize I keep links on all sides. I don't play games."

Solerno listened and didn't disagree. He had first met the independent owner of the Athena a number of years before, while Gus Karos still owned and ran it until he passed away. Afterward the neighborhood diner was turned over to his young wife, Cora, still known today to most by her popular nickname, Mrs. Gus. The older Gus had taken the new immigrant from Athens under his wing, and it was no secret that he quickly fell in love with her. Gus was a patient man, and never tried to rush Cora Drakos into anything. It was a shame he developed a serious heart condition, and that when they married their years together were limited. Solerno had liked Gus, a no-nonsense businessman who understood the way the world worked. If on rare occasion Solerno's people needed something the restauranteur might provide, Gus arranged it. No questions asked. And vice-versa, if ever a special service was required. Cora Drakos now played by those same rules. No favorites, no games, no hitches. Favor for favor. Solerno had no issue that Cora kept beneficial connections among the local police, just as she also maintained contact across the neighborhood community and far beyond. Contacts, some of which might be considered questionable by some. One hand washes the other. That was the rule. She was smart like that. And truthfully,

Solerno felt if he were twenty years younger he might have envied this Detective Hunter.

"So, what was your detective's take on this?"

"To take it seriously."

"Right about that. The Ukraine war propelled money transfers to safety in America hand over fist. Russian money especially, but other currencies as well. It upset the whole world balance." There was a hint of bemusement in his voice. "Hard thing to hide half the cash available in the world. How many mega-yachts can these oligarchs buy?"

"Dirty money," Cora added. "Looking for somewhere to hide in plain sight. You think that's what this is all about?"

Solerno shrugged and put a toothpick between his teeth to help subdue his desire for a cigarette. "Possible. Someone looking to find safe shelter. Keep low key, strong-arm the reluctant, frighten current owners. Begin by making a decent offer to the owner, maybe even adding a little cash on the side. Meanwhile, scare or disrupt you enough so they wind-up buying a business on the cheap. A diner won't arouse that much notice in a working-class neighborhood like this. Your place, Cora, could conceivably provide an excellent location to hide loose foreign cash as it flows in. Maybe drug money too, and maybe also payoffs owed that finally got collected and need a temporary legit home. They won't care if this particular diner makes or loses money. They might even decide to purposely run it into the ground. So what? It's still an opportunity to own a legitimate business to use as a cover for whatever else you're doing."

"Like what else?"

He grinned. "Like procuring a few politicians to look away while you traffic drugs from Central America, maybe. Or seek potential partners who are desperate to get the hell out of whatever country is after them. You'd be offering a convenient shelter available for a nice amount off the top. The whole trade works like an international spiderweb. It's not as hard as you think to find some bigshot business types looking to hide buried monies. Go try to figure where one-piece fits into the other, which country next moved their cash cargoes to another…and they're all eager and ready to pay to play."

Cora dismissed the idea with a sneer. "Well, I'm not ready to play in that game." The thought of it depressed her beyond measure. Solerno held out his palms. "Hey, I'm not the one trying to muscle my way in. Just throwing a few likely schemes your way cause you asked."

Her eyes looked down at the table, staring at the salt, and pepper shakers. She didn't like the direction the conversation was heading, but she realized Solerno was dead-on. "I'm sorry. I didn't mean to take anything out on you. But the Athena Diner isn't for sale to anyone, no matter who or what. Period."

"We live in a dirty world, Cora. I don't need to remind you of that."

"And I've gotten my own hands dirty more than once, but not that way."

"I know you have," Solerno said cryptically. Her reputation for getting entangled in situations she had no business with was no secret.

"Just be aware this time you might be dealing with people who play in a very different league. A tougher league than you've ever encountered."

She shuffled uncomfortably on the seat, trying to camouflage a creeping feeling of vulnerability. She'd dealt with enough coarse, dangerous types before. Street pushers and gangs, situations that included rape, intimidation, even attempted murder. It was also true she maintained a few mob contacts, and willingly spread a little money around in necessary causes. She'd first met Solerno during a brief mafia family encounter. Nothing major, but once things were settled she noticed him coming into the diner from time to time. Back then she assumed she must be under some sort of surveillance. It turned out she was wrong. In reality, due to scarred lungs as well as numerous decades of loyalty, Solerno had been allowed to 'retire' from his family duties. He was out.

Actually, he found himself occasionally frequenting the Athena because of his curiosity about this strong-willed owner. She had risked confrontation with thugs demanding unusual payments for special truck deliveries. Expensive, imported exotic foodstuffs added as essential to enhancing her menu. Demand for increased payment was strictly business, she was informed. Special products, special pricing. That's the way it worked.

She gauged her options. Was this a form of extortion? Of course, it was. She refused and held out for a while, and Solerno was impressed by her gritty resilience. No threats, no violence ensued. Just somehow these valuable products got delayed, and soon were becoming lost during deliveries. Everything was accounted for at shipping, but somehow not reaching its destination.

Cora realized she wasn't going to win this one and reporting it to her friends in law enforcement would likely create far more trouble. At the finale of her valiant refusal, they finally came to an agreement. Cora recognized that before refusing to deal with people she considered thugs, she'd better think twice. She wasn't aware of it at the time, but several of the crime family lieutenants actually had a modicum of admiration for her bold stand amid subtle and not so subtle pressures. Foolish, maybe, but it taught a great deal about her character. It was said her own past in Athens before coming to America was questionable, to say the least. Speculation and rumors circulated whether she might have been involved in the murder of a hated professor responsible for her fiancé's death. Perhaps it could be true. Perhaps not. In any case it placed Cora Drakos in an atypical status, a respected status.

Solerno liked that. So, gradually over the years they became friends. He was close to twenty-five years her elder, so for him it wasn't going to be anything romantic. His respect grew even stronger as he came to know her better, and at this point she became almost like one of the children he'd never had. From time to time she still called on him for advice, and he gave it, willing to open up regarding things about life in a mob family he knew he shouldn't. Cora understood his rules. She never spoke of anything he said to anyone—ever. So, in time he came to trust her. And she him. That mutual understanding was what brought him to visit the diner today.

"So where do you think I stand? If you're right, I mean. And I'm aware these people are a ruthless crew, whether from overseas or not."

"Too early to know for sure." He scratched at a nagging itch at the side of his head. "Look, here's how I see it. For now, you continue business as usual. Next phone call, and there will be, agree to have a meeting. Not here, but somewhere safe and in public. Daytime. If you want, I'll trail you." She nodded enthusiastically. He smiled, then threw his head back and drank to the bottom of his cup. "*Aux kaliterous kafes*!" he exclaimed in Greek. "The best coffee."

Cora laughed. "*Gia senna panda*! For you, always!"

TWO

Cora stared at her bedroom ceiling, watching the streetlight shadows of tree leaves and limbs dancing in the wild winds outside. In fact, she'd been awake, surveying them for hours. Yesterday's talk with Solerno had caused disturbing memories to surface. Acid churned in her stomach, inching its burning way up her throat. Most of the time, she kept the anguish of Dirk's death submerged in the recesses of her of her mind. But the fierce flashes of lightening glowed red inside her eyelids, and sharp cracks of thunder triggered recollections of a gunshot. She rarely thought back to her mindless determination, the bizarre thoughts and irrationality that upended her former life in Greece. Was she ever going to be able to end this recurring nightmare?

She doubted it. With hands to her face she cried for a time.

She rose from bed. No point in trying to sleep now. Another day was beginning.

*

The Weather Channel predicted a soggy, windy, and most unpleasant morning, so Fiona Sweeney dressed for it. Despite the gloom outside, she was in a cheerful mood. Tuesdays had become her favorite day of the week. Rather than heading to her dreary, minimum wage restaurant job, today she was headed to Queens College, Studio Art 101, Drawing. Despite the fact she always drew all over her high school notebooks, and adored painting since kindergarten, this was her initial authentic art class. Everything about it excited her, from the oversize newsprint sketchbook to the boxes of pencils, charcoals, and even the oddly named paper stump tortillon used to blend shadows. Plus, a class filled with fellow artists, new people to meet and friends to make.

The class was paid for with money she earned, and now became her gift to herself. She made a face at the mirror as she pulled on an outgrown childish yellow rain jacket and hood, stuffed her art supplies into a small protective plastic bag, and shrugged on her backpack. Four full hours together with creative young people like herself, and now with a teacher who really knew something about art. "*I got rhythm, who could ask for anything more?*" she happily hummed the old film ditty as she danced her way to the front door and outside.

Grinning, she wrestled with a strong wind gusting outside her apartment building. She mused that if Robbie, her wayward boyfriend, didn't call or come home from his so-called 'visit' to his mother by the end of the week, he'd find himself tossed out permanently. And this time she really meant it. No way was he going to remain with *her* anymore. Deep down, she knew she'd had enough, even if she wasn't yet ready to admit it. In fact, if matters between them continued the way they had been recently, they'd wind up despising each other. And then another reality struck home. She really couldn't picture a world, a life, without Robbie. For all his drama, she did love him, and maybe this time, he would finally shape up.

The rain slashed fiercely, and Fiona ducked under the awning of a nearby shop. Long, cold drips of rainwater spilled off the awning's edge, drenching her hair and neck. She muttered a few choice words under her breath and hurriedly moved away.

It was a slog to reach the busy bus stop on the broad boulevard backed up with traffic, and she amused herself with thoughts of painting colorful reflections of stoplights, streetlights, and neon signs reflectively punctuating the wet streets, and avoiding thinking about the restaurant and strife at her job. At length, she reached her destination just in time to view the bus driver slam the front door closed, shouting out, "This bus is full. The next bus will arrive in about five minutes. Have a nice day."

Fiona groaned. At least the bus shelter would keep the rain off her face, trying to give the awful spring climate her best spin. She waited patiently as a line of umbrellas behind her overflowed the bus stop's defined space and strung out like a sea of bobbing mushrooms along the sidewalk. All these colorful umbrellas reflecting in the rain also might make an interesting painting, she mused.

Fiona squinted down the street. Surprisingly enough, the next bus was coming, and within the promised five minutes, too. Other commuters spotted it as well and began to gently push their way forward. Everyone reached into pockets, wallets, and handbags to pull out their convenient MTA cards. Fiona kept hers ready on a thin strap dangling from her neck. As the bus neared, she gathered her art supplies with her left hand and held out her METRO card in her right. The bus tires pushed waves of dirty cold water splashing over the curb, **drenching waiting riders. Fiona shook water from her legs, approached** the curb and made toward the oncoming bus. She felt a sudden strong blow at her back and a powerful shove. She barely had time to open her mouth to scream. The bus driver, a veteran of fifteen years, instinctively slammed down on the brakes. The girl tumbled directly in front. The full weight of the slowing bus slammed against her. Fiona saw a brilliant flash of light. Her retinas tore, and then she knew no more.

Her body vaulted forward into the air from the full momentum of the thirty-three-thousand-pound machine. The driver's body hit the steering wheel hard, then whipped rearward against the plastic divider.

Standing bus riders were tossed backward and pitched forward during the swift, harsh stop, grabbing for anything they could. Seated passengers swayed and knocked against seatbacks and poles. Umbrellas, pocketbooks, and briefcases flew through the air.

Oh my God, have I killed the pedestrian? the driver gasped.

Dazed, she shook her black and gray cornrows, desperate to clear her chaotically confused mind. Fifteen years of spotless driving without a single accident were precipitously ended with an abrupt disaster, the disoriented driver realized. It wasn't her fault, she insisted herself. The figure in front appeared out of nowhere.

In addition to that horror, there might also be severe injuries among the many passengers. Well trained in the MTA's protocol, she quickly radioed the local dispatcher, who in turn contacted central dispatch in East New York. They requested immediate medical support, aware the cumbersome dispatch service might encounter delays during this ghastly bad weather. Dizzily she searched for alert passengers, zooming in on a single regular who appeared uninjured, asking him to immediately call 911. Others inside had already begun calling. Lives were at stake. Oblivious to the stream of blood running down the side of her own face, the driver stood up shakily and sought to assist wherever help was needed.

The 911 calls went out quickly to first responders. Local hospitals, police and traffic control were immediately alerted. Within several minutes of the calls ambulances, squad cars, EMTs, and a fire engine converged on the scene. There were multiple injuries aboard the bus, but few seeming serious except for the body lying motionless in the wet street. Because of the police precinct nearby, Detective Jonah Hunter joined two squad cars and hurried to the accident scene. From hearing emergency radio dispatches, he realized there was a potential fatality.

Arriving at the scene he ran an experienced eye over the chaos. Two EMTs were making their way throughout the bus, triaging a number of injured riders. Amid the downpour two uniforms aptly redirected traffic towards the nearest side street. Traffic grew near a standstill. Several other policemen were hurriedly marking no-entry zones with yellow tape. The front of the bus had withstood dents and shattered glass from the hit. A number of medics leaned over the stilled nearby body, frantically searching for signs of life. Hunter looked away and shook his head at the grim scene. In her yellow hooded raincoat she resembled a schoolgirl.

Ambulances weighted down with passengers were preparing to pull away, sirens whooping, headed for trauma one medical centers. The bus driver was already being debriefed by one of Hunter's detectives, Michael Chin, whose demeanor would be both soothing as well as competent in his questioning. The dazed, traumatized driver seemed oblivious to the EMT who was standing over her trying to staunch bleeding from the back of her head and a severe cut on her chin. An MTA representative was also on the way to assess the accident, as well as deal with a fast clean-up, getting traffic moving again, and limiting any liability to the agency.

Satisfied things were being professionally handled, Hunter walked in pools of water over to the area in front of the stalled bus. The victim had been taken away, replaced by a watery chalked outline on the black road surface. A wide area was splattered with water-soaked blood, some running off with rainwater toward a sewer.

A torn backpack flapped in the wind and rain, revealing broken pencils, wet paper, and crushed charcoal sticks as well as an artist's pad. Likely it all belonged to the victim. He needed to learn if she had been called DOA or was still clinging to life. He knelt down and lifted the cover of the art pad with his pen. Perhaps there something inside that would help identify her. He turned over pieces of heavy water-saturated paper and saw a realistic sketch of a woman wearing running apparel. The signature on the right-side bottom was signed, "F. Sweeney".

Sweeney, Sweeney, the name seemed more than familiar. Hunter went through his mental rolodex, and finally connected the surname to someone working at the Athena Diner. He made a mental note to speak with Cora Drakos, proprietor of the commonly named Diner of Lost Souls, to ask if this victim, F. Sweeney, was employed there or could possibly be a relative of one of Cora's employees. Grimly, he continued to sift through the soaked backpack.

He found a Queens College ID in a tiny purse with a little cash and a New York driver's license. Hunter sighed. Valuable information about Fiona Sweeney could undoubtedly be discovered now. He glanced around at the morbid scene. Rain was still pelting. Was this a horrid accident? Had the young woman somehow slipped in the rain? Or might it have been a possible suicide? Unlikely.

He dreaded at the prospect of a potential homicide, the young woman being pushed. But these were all possibilities that couldn't be discounted at this preliminary stage of investigation.

Wiping dripping rain off his face, Detective Jonah Hunter made a quick call back to his office requesting someone begin the laborious task of creating a contextual folder on the background of this unfortunate girl.

THREE

Sara Sweeney's blue eyes were bloodshot, sore, and swollen. Soggy tissues overflowed the trash bin. Cora sat with her in her small private office, gently keeping her arm around the girl, stroking gently, attempting to provide a physical anchor for Sara's shattered world. She looked up at Cora with a mixture of confusion and heart-rending disbelief.

"Is Fiona going to die?"

"We don't know yet. She's unconscious. Anything is possible, but it doesn't look good." Giving encouraging news was pointless, Cora understood. If Detective Jonah Hunter's brief call was a harbinger of what actually happened then any type of hopeful outcome appeared slim at best.

Cora had met Fiona a number of times but didn't know her well. She seemed serious, well-mannered, and appealing. It was obvious that Sara Sweeney was proud of her artistic sister, and how she had managed to turn her life around. In high school Fiona had become involved with a rough group of kids. Her life became turbulent, marked by drugs, booze, and other self-destructive behaviors. One night she deliberately overdosed. When she awoke twenty-four hours later, Sara was standing over her, sobbing. Fiona realized how close she had come to dying, and how much her death would have hurt her sister. Right then she resolved to change the direction of her life.

She decided to stop clinging to or depending on friends or family to be there for her anymore. She shut out her mother and began therapy, attended AA meetings every day, and gradually managed to turn her troubled life around. During recent months Fiona had kept her promises to herself, enrolling in art school, working steadily in an Italian restaurant. Sara witnessed her sister's glow of determination and deserved happiness and became prouder of Fiona than she'd ever been. Living clean and sober, and maybe best of all, no longer as overly concerned regarding her on-and-off troubled boyfriend, Rob Perry.

Sara's own life hadn't been easy by any means either, Cora was well aware. Their father was physically abusive before he abandoned the family. Their alcoholic mother was chronically depressed, endlessly berating her daughters as if her despondent life was somehow a fault of theirs. No wonder Fiona became a picture book example of an unhappy young woman from a dysfunctional home and acted out the part.

Unlike her pained younger sister, Sara was old enough to escape her unfortunate homelife, wedding her high school sweetheart, and striving to begin a good life of her own. She had now been working for the Athena Diner for the past several years. Serving as part time hostess, cashier, handling phone orders, and generally filling in wherever needed, she worked hard and presented herself with a cheerful mien. She remained eager to please her demanding boss and offered an attractive pleasure for customers to look at with her bright freckled face, engaging smile, and quick repartee. Everybody liked her. Everybody. Some perhaps a little too much. More than once, Cora had to admonish an eager staffer from hitting on the good-looking young woman. Sara didn't mind the attention, though. She took all admiration as a compliment and was always glad to get home to her adored husband, Marty, a nice young man who gave her the love and attention she so badly needed.

Knowing something of her difficult past, Cora had watched Sara flourish in these roles with sympathy and pleasure. The unhappy girl of a few years ago had blossomed into a fine young woman. She hoped it might be possible soon to move Sara into a new trainee managerial position, allowing Cora more time for her own extracurricular work. Between Eddie Coltrane, her Jamaican right-hand and full-time manager, and also Claude, an exceptionally reliable chef, the king of her kitchen, the restaurant was already in outstanding hands. A bit of supplementary support from Sara Sweeney was going to provide icing on the cake.

Until now.

Whatever the circumstances of Fiona's accident, things for Sara would forever be changed. Cora continued to clasp the girl, biting her lip, and assessing intensely, hoping against hope that her fears that there was more to this accident in the rain would prove mistaken.

The cellphone rang. It was Hunter again, calling as he promised he would. She held the phone close to her ear and listened.

"It's bad, Cora. My detective waiting at the hospital informed me that Fiona Sweeney's currently on life support. That damn bus slammed directly into her. The docs are trying everything they can to keep her going."

"I understand." She said, holding the phone in a way that Sara couldn't hear what he'd said. "Thank you…"

"I'm so sorry. I'll get back in touch as soon as I have more information. Me and a couple of uniforms are starting to interview people who were waiting at the bus stop. It all happened in an instant, a total calamity. The driver's still in shock. She says the victim appeared out of nowhere. Local streets were already flooded when she hit the brakes. Sewers backed up. It's still a chaotic scene out here."

A tear welled as Cora gathered her energy. She set her jaw in with determination, dark eyes tightened. She felt certain that although Sara didn't overhear their conversation, she undoubtedly sensed dire news.

Thunder rumbled loudly outside. "Thank you again, Hunter. I appreciate your personal help with this. I have her older sister Sara right here with me now. We've got our fingers crossed, and I'm trying to keep Sara soothed."

"Sara's lucky you're there. Talk later." He hung up.

As Cora put the phone down there was a knock on the small office door. "Yes?"

"Anything we can do for you out here?" asked a worried Eddie Coltrane.

"Eddie, a nice pot of strong black coffee would be good. And some slices of dark toast on the side. That's all."

"You got it, Mrs. Gus."

Sara stirred from her morose posture. She gave the impression of being a decade older, face drained, complexion white as chalk, lipstick smeared and her whole appearance diminished in a suddenly surreal atmosphere. Cora wasn't able to view subconscious pain, but she could clearly sense the gut-wrenching fear and dread the girl was experiencing. Not unlike the helpless hurt which she had also experienced those years ago back home in Athens.

Sara cleared her throat, and spoke in a soft childlike voice, "When can I go to the hospital?"

"Soon. We'll get a car."

"Can't I go now? I want to see my sister. I *need* to." She squeezed Cora's hand. "Please, Mrs. Gus."

Cora listened to her plea, wiping the formed tear from the corner of her eye. "The doctors are working on Fiona now, doing everything possible. She isn't conscious. There's nothing we can add by being there now. Traffic is jammed everywhere in this horrible weather. When the winds ease up, and the streets clear, I'll personally take you." She stared at an empty glass of water on the table. 'Can I get you something else? Something to drink, to eat?"

The girl demurred. "I know you're trying to be helpful. That you really are worried too, Mrs. Gus. But…"

"Do you want to try phoning your husband again?"

"I've tried so many times. He's been working on this jobsite upstate for the past three weeks. It's been difficult to get ahold of him, but he's due back Friday for the weekend." She sniffed, heaved a breath.

"We'll be able reach him soon, I promise. Find the number for the contractor, maybe we can reach an onsite foreman."

Ricardo, normally a chatty waiter knocked lightly and brought in the coffee and toast. He moved silently, placing the tray on the table, and noiselessly left. Cora held the cup with both hands and stared down at it.

Sara put her slender hands over her face and sobbed again.

The wind abated, the slant of the rain halted. It descended straight now in a momentary torrent, then a steadier hard pattern. It provided an opportunity to go.

Cora took Sara's left hand tightly while holding the umbrella in a tight grip as they rushed from the cab and dashed from the sidewalk through the glass revolving doors. Queens Central Hospital had been under renovation these past few years, its large new lobby looking now more like a space-age movie set than the grim, bleak unwelcoming site of the past. The lobby was filled with visitors and wet pedestrians from outside waiting for the rain to subside.

At the long reception desk at the end of the hall Cora asked where they could find Fiona Sweeney, the emergency patient recently brought in from the bus accident. The receptionist dialed ER first, then redialed seeking better information from an OR location.

"I'm sorry, you'll have to go to the waiting room on the seventh floor."

"I'm her *sister*," protested Sara. "I have the right to see her."

The receptionist listened professionally and made another quick call, speaking in a low voice. "Go up to the seventh floor," she said as she hung up. "Someone will meet you at the elevator bank."

"Over here, Mrs. Gus."

Cora looked sideways to see a tall, balding broad-shouldered man holding a wet raincoat over his arm. She recognized him immediately. It was Hal Capps, a seasoned detective from Jonah Hunter's precinct and squad.

"Good to see you, detective. This is Sara Sweeney…"

He introduced himself and started to put out his hand but quickly took it back. One glance at the younger woman's dejected appearance was enough to recognize her dismal emotional state.

"There's a couch over this way," he said, pointing halfway down the hall. "We can sit and talk better over there. Follow me."

They walked past a number of pots containing artificial trees, and colorful prints of landscapes hanging in an even line along the wall. The visitors' couch was placed between a number of cushioned chairs. A television on the wall played soundlessly, tuned to a local news station discussing the day's weather in the tri-state area. Nearby were several vending machines offering a selection of chocolate bars and potato chips. There was also a coffee machine.

"What can you tell us, Hal?" Cora asked as several nurses quietly hurried by toward a set of closed double doors in the distance.

The detective spoke without emotion. "The patient has a number of broken bones, I'm told, but the main concern are her multiple head injuries. They're trying to reduce the swelling. Her skull was fractured in various places, I was told. They said something to me concerning a craniotomy, to try and reduce the cranial pressure. Allowing the brain to reduce inflammation, drain the hematoma before operating on damaged blood vessels."

Sara gasped as he talked. "But she's going to be okay, right?" and broke into tears. Cora quickly cradled her tightly against her wet raincoat. "Shh. Let the doctors finish their work. They're doing everything possible. They'll be coming out and telling us what's going on as soon as they can."

The detective met Cora's gaze. He'd said too much, he realized. The best thing he could do now was shut up. Pointing to the vending machines he got up and walked away. Cora ran her hand through Sara's moist hair, saying nothing, breathing in and out slowly, trying to regain her own composure.

Several relatives of other patients came through the swinging doors and headed for the elevator. They spoke softly among themselves, faces projecting a hint of their own grief and fears.

A few moments later a solitary surgeon, still wearing scrubs, came out and looked over at Cora and the girl she embraced. His demeanor was stoic. Detective Capps shot a glance at him. It seemed apparent the news was not good.

"I'm Fiona's sister," Sara said, girding herself. She tightened her grip on Cora's arm. She was shaky, and Cora held her close. The detective came over but remained discreetly a step behind.

"I'm Dr. Rossi, one of the team of surgeons. Your sister is critical and unstable, but we've been able to stop the bleeding," he said in a low tone, "and we managed to relieve some of the pressure on the brain."

"Is she going to make it?" said Sara, her wet mouth open, fighting to hold back more tears.

The doctor thought for a moment, then answered without a flicker of expression. "We can't say anything for sure yet. Her head hit the ground hard. She's had several life-threatening fractures to her skull, and a few blood vessels were seriously damaged. We're doing our best, I promise. But her trauma was severe, and additional surgery may be required. Her heart is strong, though. As of now we've put her in a medical coma and will be watching carefully for any possible complications. We expect to know more hopefully by tomorrow, and then we can take another look and reevaluate."

Sara listened numbly, hanging onto any hint of hope. "Thank you," she whispered. The doctor met her gaze and nodded both to Sara and Cora before he turned back toward the swinging doors.

Cora made meaningful eye contact with Hal Capps. They both understood the outcome could go either way.

FOUR

Rose Perry Mograbi jerked awake at the pounding at her front door. Her blackout curtains shielded the room from any outside light. A dog barked frantically next door. Rose was now a single woman living alone in a nice suburban development of Raleigh, North Carolina. Grimly, she grabbed her cell phone. It was almost 3AM. She started to dial for the police but at the last moment hesitated, leaving the forefinger of her left-hand hovering above the final digit. Without turning on a light, she fumbled for her robe and covered herself over her flimsy pajamas. Next, she seized a heavy old wooden bat that resided under her bed. The banging on her door continued as she made down the stairs of the stucco two-story home.

Pulling aside a sliver of curtain, she peered through the window. A big man was standing on her stoop, untidy and disheveled. He continued knocking. Rose positioned herself at the side of the door, bat at the ready.

"Get the fuck off my property right now or I'll blow your head off!" she called to the intruder. "The police are already on the way."

"It's me, Ma! Robbie. You don't need to call any cops." Weary, hungry, and scared as he was, he admired his mother's gumption. Her strong-willed personality hadn't changed a bit since he was a child.

"Robbie? That you?" The voice was uncertain.

"Yeah, Ma. It's me. Open the door, please." Rose hastily undid her multiple locks and yanked the door wide open.

At the sight of her son, she threw her arms around him and then narrowed her gaze at the unshaven, scruffy, youthful face. He look bad with long uneven hair on the sides and back. She pulled away sharply. "What are you doing here in the middle of the night? Why didn't you phone you were coming? Give me some notice?" She babbled on, staring at his condition. She lowered the bat and tossed her phone on a table. He followed behind into the hallway. "Look at you, Robbie. Your clothes wet and filthy like a beggar. You've been walking in this rain? You smell, too. You look awful. Anyone would take you for a homeless vagrant. What the hell happened?"

"Ma, it took a couple of days to get here from New York. I'm exhausted. Haven't slept. I'll answer all of your questions, okay? Just let me in to rest up for a while."

"Where's your car?"

"Don't have it anymore, I had to get rid of it."

"What? Get rid of it? Why?"

"I'll explain later." He held a hand to his groin like a boy. "I need a bathroom. Badly. Please, Ma. Just once, give me a break."

Without missing a beat, she led him inside her spacious home, switching on a light. "I'll bring you some fresh clothes. Go take care of yourself and clean up."

There were plenty of her last ex-husband's clothes tossed in a closet she quickly found and sorted.

Robbie used the toilet inside the downstairs guest bathroom, then stripped off his sullied clothes. He went into the shower and savored the fresh hot water gushing over his fatigued, sturdy body. His back and knees were aching after all those unpleasant hours squeezed into his narrow seat on the bus. Rose quietly opened the door to drop off fresh underwear, black slacks, and a blue linen shirt that her recent ex Amos Mograbi would never use again. She heard Robbie call out amid the steam, "And Ma, listen to me. It's important. Don't tell anyone I'm here. Understand?"

As she tidied up the guestroom bed, her mind worked furiously. Robbie's last comment told her the state of things. He arrived without transportation. He had no luggage, and likely no money either. Her oldest son was in some kind of trouble—again, she knew, and she admonished herself for prior over-indulgences for him over the years. His efforts to befriend and ingratiate himself among New York's wannabe rich and famous frequently paid off through his good looks, manners, glib talk, and hollow boasting. Obviously something went amiss this time.

She showed him the guestroom, and he plopped onto the welcoming queen-sized bed. He fell asleep before she could open her mouth to question him further, so she left him alone, aware of his utter exhaustion. There would be plenty of time to talk in the morning.

It was almost noon when he awoke and meandered into the kitchen, feeling protests from virtually every muscle and joint in his body. He picked up the note his mother had left on the kitchen table.

It clearly displayed her distinctive left-handed print. "Good morning. Go eat something," it read. "There's plenty of food in the fridge. I have an important real estate meeting this morning. Stay home until I get back. We'll talk everything out in a while."

In spite of her bossy and irritating nature, Robbie felt a little warmth creep into the black despair he'd been feeling for weeks. Without any explanation whatsoever, it was obvious his mother intuited his current situation was dire. Rose loved him anyway, he knew, no matter his wild energy and unbridled lifestyle. For at least the moment he felt safe, and he had someone who might be able to help him in his current situation.

He toasted a few slices of rye bread, and found a block of cheese, cutting the muenster into small chunks. Then, slouching at his mother's dinette kitchen table, he ate. His usually impeccable dark hair stuck up in random spikes. His handsome features remained pallid, expressive eyes red and visibly irritated. He chewed slowly, pensively, and without appetite. He drank a quart of milk from the carton, elbows on the table, his head sunk into his hands. Events of the past week flooded his thoughts. He groaned, wondering if there was anything to be done he hadn't already contemplated.

He was more scared than he had ever been in his life, and he was flat out of options. There weren't any juicy anecdotes regarding feuds and friendships to relate to impress his mother today. No tales of mingling at parties with celebrities, or social climbing efforts paying off due to his pricey wardrobe, smooth conversations, and exaggerated name dropping.

Robbie rarely phoned and seldom visited his mother since she had married the so-called scholar from South Africa and left New York with him, selling her house. It was her third marriage since leaving Robbie's father, first hooking up with a known Norwegian international architect who soon dumped Rose and now reportedly resided in California with a too young model, fully enjoying beach life in La Jolla.

Next in line came the international scholar. A mismatch if there ever was one. A lecturer at Duke University with a noted reputation, hence Rose moving south to North Carolina to be with him. Not too long after the scholar split academia, broke his teaching contract and returned home to Cape Town, halfway round the world. Robbie's mom now found herself stuck with a stack of bills and in need of robust earnings in her new home and state. Rose was like this, he knew. Impulsive, reckless, always on the hunt for some elusive, perfect partner. As usual she wound up stepping into an emotional and financial mess in addition to getting hurt in the bargain. Robbie's biological father had been no winner either. An educated, successful businessman, he was abusive to her and him, so much so Robbie was thankful when in the middle of night she quietly packed them up in Chicago while dad was high and snoring, took off and brought the small family to New York City. And there they remained.

These days Rose was wounded and angry at her son's lack of contact, but she did a good job of hiding it, realizing that any display would likely push her errant son even further away. Instead, she generally tried to ease her irritation with an ironic motto she'd read somewhere. *If I don't hear from my kids, I know they're fine. When they need help, they'll call.*

It was barely afternoon when Rose returned home, harried, and profoundly concerned about what was going on. Since Robbie arrived without so much as a brief phone call, she correctly speculated his predicament this time was greater than usual.

She masked her irritation with opening casual chatter and if nothing else, was sincerely glad to see him. It had been several years, after he had decided to drop out of college. At that time, her questions had drifted past him heedlessly. Robbie had been doing badly in school as usual. She knew he smoked a lot of pot and maybe drank too much with his supposedly sophisticated friends, but he had sworn to her he never used hard stuff, and she had no reason not to believe him. Rose was savvy enough to recognize those signs. While attending public schools the expensive shrinks had told her he was acting out because of the divorce from his father, and possibly her other relationships. But Robbie was a bright kid, and with luck and therapy he could turn his life around and do something beneficial with his life.

In these past couple of years, though, she didn't have to wonder if he was fucking up. He was. Her son also liked to gamble. It started during high school. Blackjack, poker at private all-night games with classmates who could afford playing for high stakes. Some of the sports betting had been going on for a long time. Pro football on Sundays, college ball on Saturday. Big games of every type. College bowls, World Series, world soccer championships. Several times he'd asked her to lend him money, honest enough to admit he needed cash for betting debts. Feeling guilty about her indiscretions and neglect while trying to deal with her own issues, she acquiesced in an effort to shed a bit of that blame. Fortunately, her talent as an exceptional real estate broker dealing with higher-end properties allowed her to keep him out of any serious trouble. He was young. He was smart. He'd see the light after a while, she believed. Until she didn't.

Soon he scarcely paid attention to anything else, she saw. His decision to return to school this past year seemed such a good thing after the series of jobs he never kept. Either he quit because the work was 'beneath him,' or got fired for arguing with bosses. Sometimes he just didn't show up. It became a downward spiral leading him nowhere other than trouble.

Much more than that she didn't know. And maybe didn't want to know.

Before he pounded on her door this morning his life had become a secret from her. She didn't even have an address for him. He stopped staying in touch except for occasional unexpected calls for a little money, and an idealistic promise to do better. Three or four times she'd sent money to some girlfriends' address, bailing him out. Those female relationships had also come and gone like everything else in his life.

Rose cooked up three eggs, sausage, bacon, and home fries with gravy without saying anything. She set a plate in front of him, and a smaller one across the table for herself. The bacon was still sizzling.

"Go on and eat," she said. "If you don't have a car anymore, how did you get here? Hitch rides? I hope you didn't steal a car."

He ignored her sarcasm. "I took a Greyhound bus," he muttered, stifling a yawn.

Rose winced. This was unexpected. "A Greyhound? All this way?"

"No, I had to *walk* from your bus station. In this drizzle and humidity. Okay?"

She sighed at his typical mockery. "Go ahead, eat. Then we'll talk."

Reluctantly, he picked up his fork. After a couple of bites, he discovered he was actually quite hungry. Except for the toast and cheese he hadn't eaten a meal since escaping New York with just the clothes on his back and the hundred and thirty dollars of Fiona's money in his wallet he'd 'borrowed.' Nor had he dared to take a direct route to his mother's house. After taking a bus from Port Authority in Manhattan he changed to the long-distance Greyhound line in New Jersey.

The thugs who were hunting for him would be searching high and low, growing angrier with every unsuccessful lead. Taking no chances, he'd tossed his iPhone into Flushing Bay, and a burner phone he kept somewhere inside a Manhattan trash bin. "My mother didn't raise any fools," he thought at the time, thinking it funny. It wasn't funny anymore.

The current mess he found himself in came crashing back into consciousness. "Shit," he muttered, shaking his head slightly, puffing his cheeks and exhaling slowly. He'd been stupid this time. Really stupid.

His mother noticed the grimace, his sincere discomfort. She grabbed the coffee pot and poured each of them a hot cup.

"Think you may be ready to talk to me?" she asked. "Come on. Go for it, Robbie. I'm all ears, and eager to listen. What did you get yourself into this time? And please, no lies or excuses." She knew her son well.

Their gazes met. That's the drill, he understood. If there was any hope of getting her support, he'd have to do some explaining. "I'm in trouble," he muttered, averting his eyes from her intense glare. He drummed his fingertips against the table.

"In trouble *again*," Rose prompted, leaning back in her chair, putting the coffee cup on the table, slipping off her heels. "Go on, tell me."

"I got in over my head again, Ma. I'd lost some money in a couple of all night poker games with these high roller friends. I borrowed what I could…"

"And then you used the borrowed cash to play some more?"

He faltered. "No, not exactly. See, I tried to double down to get my losses back. There was this big football game Sunday before last. Patriots against the Jets. The Jets had homefield advantage. The spread was big. Ten and a half points. So, on my credit I took the underdog. I maxed out with my bookie and another guy he works with. He knew I always paid up, sooner or later, so I was good for it, anyway. I mean, how could the Jets, having a bad season as usual, how could they come out losers with so many points given? And New England's top wide receiver was questionable for the game because he'd sprained an ankle. The Patriots were already hurting with other injuries."

"I don't understand this jargon. Stick to the facts."

He stopped talking and looked down at his plate. He'd eaten the bacon, but the rest of the food was left untouched. His appetite disappeared, and he suddenly felt the urge to retch. His anxiety was real and bad, she saw. Worse than usual. She shifted in her seat, preparing herself for what was coming next.

"So even with this large spread you ended up losing, I assume." Rose was fighting hard not to let any anger show. Revealing herself would only stop him from telling her everything she needed to know.

"They lost by eleven. *Eleven*! Half a fucking point, Ma. Final score 24-13. They tried for a touchdown in the final two minutes. How stupid is that? They could have tried for a field goal. They'd have won with the spread." He covered his face with his hands. Rose noticed how dirty his fingernails were. This unhygienic attitude was very unlike her son. He tended to be fastidious about his appearance, always looking and behaving like a real gentleman, at least before getting drunk or high with his foremost affluent friends.

A heavy silence filled the void between them. She let him wallow in his misery. How many times had she bailed him out? Yes, she did earn a good living. Yes, she liked to buy things like jewelry and classy business suits. But it was honest money she earned. Worked hard for. To Robbie she had become nothing but a bank dishing out loans he never repaid.

She scrutinized him carefully. He knew his mother's game; she liked to wait, bide her time. Let him almost have to beg before she agreed to give him anything. But she was in the driver's seat, they both knew.

"I never expected to come to you for money again," he said at last with an irritated undertone. His bloodshot eyes opened wide. There was a slight tremble in his normally deep, seductive voice as he spoke. "Listen, I was warned that my bookies were fed up. I wasn't playing with astrologers or gurus. I was given a week to pay up. I asked everywhere from Manhattan to Montauk, but I wasn't able to pay back more than a few hundred bucks on my losses. Pennies on the dollars. I've got to do something fast before it's too late, you can understand that, right?"

"Right," Rose said. "Tell me more."

"About what?"

"About your poker losses too. You said the reason you went all out on this damn football game you couldn't lose on was to pay your poker debts." She couldn't help rubbing it in a bit. Her son deserved that and a lot more.

Here his reluctance grew. He seemed to be staring out into some faraway place.

"They're bad people, Ma. The kind you don't want to mess with."

"I never did mess with these sorts. Obviously, that's all you do these days."

"I'm sorry, Ma. Somewhere along the line I recognized I was being too ambitious. I tried to borrow all over the place. My hotshot friends turned their backs, didn't want to know me. I'd already taken all the cash my girlfriend could get her hands on. She even borrowed from her sister to help me."

"The same girlfriend you had last time or another? I can't keep track. I think the previous one threw you out."

"That's unfair, Ma. Those other girls weren't exactly innocent ingénues. They all loved me when I was a winner. But no use to hanging with me when I lost my stake when I'm flat broke. Eating gazpacho with caviar and sea bass in the Hamptons is great. But not without money to back you up. I made bad choices, you don't have to tell me. These worthless, highbrow snobs love their coke when nighttime comes. Party time. All night. Jesus, I could write a book. They soon become too good for someone like me especially when my standard of living takes a dive during dark days."

"Oh, Robbie. And this latest girl of yours?"

"I met her at a restaurant."

"Some politician's daughter?"

"No. She works there."

"Your girlfriend works in a restaurant?" That was a genuine surprise. "She fell for your hard luck line?"

"She's real, Ma. Working class. A really nice kid. Yeah, she also had some troubles, but she cleaned up her act a long time ago. She works, goes to school. I did mention her the last time I called. I told you she was more serious."

"Oh yeah, right. Is that the artist girlfriend? A waitress? I almost forgot. Naturally, I never met her."

"Someday I'll want you to," Robbie quickly said. "I really think you'd like her a lot."

"Why? Because she also helps pay your debts?"

"That isn't fair." He narrowed his eyes and sniffed. "She's been great for me. More than I deserve, I know. I had to leave her apartment a few days back. I didn't want anyone coming around looking for me and wind up bothering her. You know, I said these were rough people. These guys are capable of anything."

Rose winced. "What does that mean?"

Rob realized he'd frightened his mother and tried to hastily make up for it. "I keep Fiona away from my outside business. She has absolutely nothing to do with anything I've done. I promise you, Ma. You have my word on that. Fiona is a good person with a big heart."

"Okay, okay. I believe you. Just give me the details. You took a Greyhound bus all the way from New York. Got rid of your car…"

"I sold that piece of junk months ago. It cost more to repair than it was worth, believe me. Besides, the happy city of New York would have impounded it. I owed money there too. Mostly for outstanding parking tickets. Petty stuff that the city like to hound people for. It's a minor offense."

"Just bottom line everything for me, Robbie, alright?" Rose said this with more than a hint of growing impatience.

He swallowed hard. She saw his Adam's apple bob in his throat.

It was difficult to tell her the truth he promised. "I owe twenty-five thousand to these bookies. I know how that sounds, but you gotta understand."

"*Twenty-five* thousand dollars?"

He nodded, hands still on his chin, arms up tightly against his chest, looking as if he were protecting himself. Against one of his father's drunken blows.

"Wow. I don't know how much cash I can raise quickly," Rose mused, half to herself.

She could sell some stock, she knew, but the market had been down lately, and she was already losing money on her investments. Paying a penalty maybe she could tap into her retirement fund. That was a possibility. Robbie could tell how hard his mother was tinkering money figures in her mind. He didn't mean to stop her, but he had no choice. "Plus, remember there's the money for the poker losses. I gotta come up with that, too. I gotta."

Rose snapped out of her calculations. "What?"

"The reason I took the chance with the football bet was because of the card games, Ma. Remember, I told you."

"Double the loss? Are you telling me you owe this crowd fifty thousand dollars, Robbie? Is that what you're telling me?"

"Yes." His voice was a whisper, embarrassment mixed with shame.

Rose struggled to take all of this in. "You've never been in this kind of mess before…"

He bit his lip hard. The welling tears were real. "I know, Ma. It's crazy. Stupid. I took on way more than I could handle and got bit in the ass for it. I'm in a stranglehold. I admitted everything to my girlfriend. She couldn't believe it, either. She lambasted me, saying I'd finally gone nuts. She said she didn't want any part of me anymore, too. She was right."

"You act like this was only some small lapse in judgement."

"No. Listen, these goons, they've been out looking for me, to collect. For days now. Some old friends must have informed on me, blabbed where my girlfriend lives. That was the only place I could keep out of sight. She lives out in Queens, in a nondescript neighborhood. I don't know what to do. They're dodgy people, these collectors. Capable of anything, and their tentacles spread everywhere. My girlfriend gave me all the cash she had. Hardly a couple of hundred bucks to pay for the bus ticket here and get me far away from New York. The cash was everything she had, her whole pay from the restaurant where she works."

"Then she's as big a fool as me. Maybe bigger." Rose glowered, breathed in sharply, and breathed out several times to manage to calm herself, the way she learned at yoga. Matters were more out of control that she realized. She was almost afraid to ask her next question. "These *people* after you, will they try and hurt you, Robbie? Is that what you're inferring? Is that why you needed to run away from the city?"

He tightened his lips together, kept his eyes closed, dreading to contemplate his actual circumstances and complications. He didn't want to expound on it even more.

"The thing is, I need to keep my head low, and I gotta keep Fiona out of any trouble. Really, I take responsibility for everything. I know all of it's my own fault. I could always handle things before, but this time I got screwed. Involved with real a badass crowd. Connected types. Honestly, I didn't realize how deep. Fiona warned me. She knew their reputation, and what they were capable of. I didn't take it seriously. She said these people don't give a shit who gets hurt."

Rose stared in shock. Her son was a worse addict than she ever dreamed. Addicted to gambling, a fast life, and usually able to smartly talk his way out of countless situations, but this time was different. This time she believed every word he said.

FIVE

The morning was sunny and bright with a mild breeze. The foul weather of yesterday was gone, the storm moved out over the ocean. Only a few trivial streams of water still trickling into New York's sewers left a tiny reminder of the horrendous storm that had caused so much agony a few hours before.

Cora brooded, staring mutely from the diner's remote window near the kitchen, sensing somehow today was likely to produce even more change. *Each day begins life anew*, Mama used to say whenever Cora or her sister Lyra appeared troubled. Cora wished she could see her mother now to remind her of that optimism once again. However, she well grasped that we're all at the mercy and whims of external cause and effect, and she wished she knew some tactic to help ease the pain and struggling Sara Sweeney was suffering. The difficulty in accepting the cruelty of real life. It was the best anyone could do.

"Hey Mrs. Gus," stuttered Harry Benzel, her grizzled regular, coffee cup in hand, bending over and sitting on his customary stool at the far end of the counter.

Cora offered a modest smile. "How are you today, Harry?"

As the waitress refilled his mug he turned toward Cora. "Still drying myself out from that beastly blast. Hell of a mess. Ouch."

"It sure was," she commented, not in the mood for pausing to chat with anyone.

"And I heard about that awful accident with the bus," Harry continued in a quiet, solemn tone. "Is there any news yet how that poor girl is doing?"

Cora shook her head. "Our Sara's at the hospital now with her sister. I'm waiting for her to phone with an update."

"Please let me know if there's any news."

"I will, Harry. Enjoy your morning." With that she turned and made her way toward the front and the cash register booth, wiping her hands along the sides of her apron. Annie Munoz was covering for Sara's shift today, collecting last night's late receipts, and playing hostess to incoming customers. The mood among all the staff remained cheerless and somber.

The ICU allowed visitors for only ten minutes each hour. Sara went in hesitantly, aware of disinfectant, and gaping in shock when she entered Fiona's room. She stood by the bed rail. Fiona's head was swathed in bandages. Her beautiful red hair had been shaved, while staples ran like railroad tracks across her scalp. An oxygen mask covered her nose and mouth. Her neck was swollen and bruised with purple blotches. Her right arm was attached to numerous IV's and monitors, and mysterious tubes with perplexing fluids flowing from underneath her hospital gown. Sara reached for Fiona's limp left hand, needing to be close and hoping for some sign of awareness. Fiona didn't react to the touch. An unsteady beep followed by an alarm brought a nurse rushing to her bedside. Sara immediately let go of Fiona's hand.

"My name is Brian," Fiona's male nurse said gently in a low voice as he checked on the patient. "You might want to trying talking to her. Often just the sound of a family member's voice can be very soothing to the patient. Hearing sometimes remains intact and you never know what might get through to her." The nurse shut off the alarm, fiddled with numerous screens, and carefully double checked IV drips. He nodded to Sara as he left and went to respond to another patient in a nearby room.

Sara bent her head close to Fiona's ear and spoke melodiously.

"I love you, Fiona. You're my sister and I need you with me. You know I'll be right here for you whatever comes next. So, you damned well better not die on me. You're a real fighter and give it everything you've got. Remember, us Sweeney's never give up." Not knowing what else to say, she kissed Fiona's hand, stood teary-eyed for a minute, and then left the room.

She called the diner as soon as she returned into the hallway. Cora answered, and Sara's lips quivered as she strained to speak. "I could hardly recognize Fiona with all that equipment so close and those heavy bandages wrapped all around her head. I'm petrified she's in really bad shape, Mrs. Gus. And I'm worried when she gets out of there she's going to have to deal with brain injuries. A long, long rehab for sure, and God knows what else. Honestly, I don't know what to do. I'm feeling so alone in the world and scared."

Cora did her best to comfort Sara, but there really was no comfort to be had. "You're *not* alone, Sara. I'm here for you. You have my keys, right? Go back to my house, okay? Wait for me, I'll be there as soon as I can get away." The lunch rush was beginning, and Eddie Coltrane signaled for her assistance. Cora held up a single finger. "We'll talk more in a while. For now, say a few prayers. One for me too."

"Are you sure it's okay to stay with you another few nights?" Sara sniffed.

"Of course, it is. Your husband's coming back for the weekend, right? Just look forward to that. For now, the doctors are in charge, so let them do their jobs."

Sara's lips twitched briefly in acknowledgment. "Thank you so much for being there," she managed to say before bursting into tears again as she headed towards the elevator bank. The swinging doors of the ICU closed behind.

Cora put her phone down as if it had burned her fingers. Memories of her own painful past flooded over her. She fought to shake them off, and quickly strode over to greet a waiting group of lunchtime guests.

After an exhausting hour and a half, the diner finally quieted. Several of the staff sat tired and quiet at the counter, unhurriedly eating their own lunches. Most of the team were also working tonight's dinner shift and needed this free time to recoup.

Cora took off her apron and started to take a seat. Then the diner's phone rang again. She picked it up with trepidation, sensing it wasn't a delivery request. The cracked and grieved voice on the other end was barely recognizable. "Sara, I can hardly understand you…"

"They just called me. I'd only just left and reached the street. The hospital. She…Fiona. A hemorrhage they said, Mrs. Gus. Heavy bleeding. Oh, God." Then even more tears welled up from somewhere deep, a wailing voice that sounded almost like an animal cry. "She died, Mrs. Gus. Scarcely minutes ago. Fiona's dead."

*

Things kept going round and round in Cora's head like a revolving carousel of jumbled thoughts and images. Was there any way to make sense of the disarrayed pieces of information? It felt wrong, unjust that there was no reasonable explanation for Fiona's death. She couldn't think of a single reason why this vibrant young woman lay on a slab in the hospital morgue instead of being busily working at her job today. Everyone was aware she'd died because she was hit by a bus on a stormy day, amongst a crowd of restless, cold, and frustrated commuters. But Cora needed facts, hard facts, and professional opinions about the cause from someone more objective than she could be right now. She picked up the phone and pressed the name.

"Detective Hunter here."

"Hi. It's me. Bad timing?"

"I've been expecting your call," came Hunter's deep, familiar voice. Cora could hear the smile behind it, a tone she knew he reserved exclusively for her. Hearing his voice and calm tone released some of the tension building in her stomach she hadn't even been aware of before.

"She died. The girl at the bus stop. Only minutes ago, I'm told."

"I know, Cora. Detective Capps informed me just before your call. He'd been praying for her at the hospital's chapel."

"Can I talk these things out with you? I really need to."

"Listen Cora, I'm up to my ears in paperwork and meetings all afternoon. Would you like to meet someplace this evening? Maybe at Zeke's Inn on Jamaica Avenue? We can both relax unwind, maybe talk a little shop."

Cora agreed. Zeke's was a popular local spot also close to the elevated train. She hung up with a feeling of relief and anticipation.

"Sounds good. I'll be able to make it by 7."

Trains rumbled above, screeching into and out of the frayed station. Rush hour was coming to an end. The approaching dim red neon of Zeke's was a welcome sight. Cora slipped inside and looked around. Lights were dim, serene music played from hidden ceiling speakers. A cozy and welcoming atmosphere. The fixtures above the bar lit the bottles, glasses, and rich wood. At the rustic tables, each light hung low and tight, illuminating the patrons 'faces in muted, reflected light. The environment was unobtrusive, people conversing in soft tones intimately with one another. Cora squinted and scanned the tables. Hunter was already there, sitting at a nice table towards the back, a plate of buffalo wings and a soft drink in front of him. He smiled as she drew closer and rose to greet her. She looked put together in her slacks, yellow collared shirt, and dark blazer even after her exhausting day.

He gave Cora a peck on the cheek, not exactly what he wanted to do, but good enough for now. "Sorry if I'm a little late," she said with a modest smile.

"Hey, I know how the Athena works. I'm just glad to see you."

"Me, too," she answered honestly. Her nascent friendship with the smart cop had been developing in recent times. Was there ever going to be something more? Well, that was still a question they both had pondered. However, there always seemed to be a hint of sexual tension whenever they spent time together. They both knew it, felt it, but tried to ignore it, keeping things casual for the time being.

"Hungry?" he asked.

"Famished. I rushed out without even grabbing an apple."

Hunter moved the plate of wings toward her. "I figured as much. Eat a couple of these before we order. Spicy, the way you like Greek food."

She gave him a sideways glance. As their eyes met they both broke into laughter. They took their time surveying the menu. As Jonah Hunter eyed her he noticed she was trying to subdue her restiveness.

"How have you been feeling, other than the news today? It's been a while since we last caught up."

Cora blew a stream of air from her mouth. "Moody. Fidgety, especially after I heard. Trying to keep myself from growing sour or bitter, fed up with all the shocks of this world. It's like no matter what I do the ground keeps shifting under my feet. And today…" She sniffed and ran her index finger under her eye, trying to wipe away a budding tear. He pretended not to notice. "I'm sorry, Hunter. Ignore everything I just said. This has been a difficult afternoon. What I really wanted was to enjoy a good, fun evening with you."

"Life gets in the way. Look, we'll deal with whatever's needed."

"Thanks for being so understanding. You're always so damn understanding."

He laughed, but he also realized tonight was going to be a heavy conversation. She ordered a soft drink too, then they gave their entree orders to the smiling young waiter and continued sharing the remainder of the wings.

"So, tell me Hunter, what's the latest news with *your* life? How about your custody fight over your kids?"

"New day, same old crap," he said with a shrug. "I'm grateful for AA, as always. They keep me on track." Hunter had never been a heavy drinker, but the war, and then his marital woes had taken a toll. He knew he'd been drinking too much. Joining AA two years back had been a life saver.

"I'm glad you're keeping up. You're so much better."

He gave a small hollow laugh. "You really want to know about my kids, too?"

Cora looked at him intently. "You know I do."

He sighed. "Well, the annoying thing is that we had a pretty amicable divorce. We both wanted to make it as easy as possible on the kids. Actually, I don't care that she remarried. Whatever. It didn't bother me."

Cora listened without a response, knowing that wasn't quite true.

"But lately things are getting completely ugly," he continued. "Everything, and I do mean everything, is becoming a fight. Kids' camp. Kids' schooling. Even dumb things like the cost of new shoes or haircuts." He groaned. "She argues over what time to pick them up for visitation. I kid you not. I feel like I'm being marginalized."

"Stupid fuss over nothing." She reached over to touch the top of his hand.

"Luckily, the kids are doing okay in spite of it. They're still at their regular school in Deer Park. But get this, my ex's nasty brother-in-law, the hotshot-lawyer, is filing motions to have me declared an unfit parent. Because I'm a cop, I'm too brutal and insensitive to meet my own kids' needs. Go figure. Probably the only reason he didn't accuse me of being a racist pig is that we all belong to the same race. Including the judge. What a bastard that guy is. I'm afraid they'll be in high school before he runs out of dirty tricks."

"And every court appearance costs you time and money. I get it. This clown needs to be sidelined." She thought for a moment, eyes darting among the diners at various tables. "Maybe the sanest thing I can suggest is to deal directly with your ex. Explain if they don't stop harassing you there'll be a hefty price."

"Like what?" He saw the mischievous look in her dark Greek eyes.

"What I feel like saying is, threaten to kill the bastard. You do 'menacing' really well. I've seen it." Her deadpan face looked serious.

Hunter nearly choked on his soda. He laughed out loud. Cora serenely touched her napkin to the corners of her mouth. A swift thought passed through Hunter's mind. Did she actually mean what she said? The Athena's owner was a difficult study. Her sweet and charming public persona covered a shrewd and insolent side, he knew. Was any of the continuously rumored gossip about her true? He would love to know the reality about her life in Athens during the years prior to her coming to America. Loose talk claimed she was involved with some spy who was killed. That she may have sought revenge on the man behind it in cold blood, going into hiding before beginning her new life here. If true that would take quite a woman.

Cora could be cold when necessary. Like a frozen winter when needed. He saw that with some of her own investigations when she asked for his help. When they last worked together she found herself necessarily pointing a gun at an intended killer of a homeless man. Would she actually have shot him, he wondered at the time. Killed him? He wasn't sure then, and he wasn't sure now. What he was sure of was that she fascinated him in every respect.

The food arrived and he shook these meandering thoughts off.

They ate their dinners of medium burgers and curled fries with few words passed between them.

After several minutes Cora couldn't help but sound out Hunter about Fiona Sweeney's death.

"I hate to bring this up, but Sara Sweeney is walking around amid grief and trauma. She's shattered. I can barely watch her stumbling in such pain." The image depressed her beyond measure. "She staying with me until her husband returns from upstate this weekend. I told her to take time off, but she insists on coming to work, keeping her mind busy."

"Makes sense. I've encountered that numerous times."

"There's also a pall of gloom that settles over the diner staff when she comes to work. She's trapped in the 'Why me? Why Fiona?' stage of mourning. Of course, I can't blame her. She has to work out whatever needs to be worked out, but she tells me she can't stand being alone with these morbid thoughts pounding in her head. And now that her husband is finally coming home, damned if he doesn't have to go back out on the job Monday morning."

Listening, nodding, Hunter said, "Tough going. Poor kid. I need to go over the case, read the reports again that Hal Capps has been filing. Plus witness interviews, then get the city's official account on the condition of the bus, especially regarding any wet or damaged brakes. Check the driver for drugs and the like. Still too many variables at this point. It's early, Cora."

"I understand. But so far what do *you* make of it? What I mean is, what's your gut telling you?"

"Jury's still out on that one." Hunter speared his fork into a few fries, skimmed them through ketchup and crunched. "We're running all the scenarios, but we still can't rule anything out. Sure, she could have slipped in some puddle and accidentally fallen forward right into the bus." He leaned toward her and spoke in a low tone. "One of my detectives, Kasey Cosgrove, has been talking to her employer and their staff. I understand Fiona had been under a lot of stress recently. So, we can't rule out suicide yet."

Cora sighed. "Yeah, she wasn't just the happy-go-lucky art student the news portrayed. But she wasn't taking psych meds, or illegal drugs for that matter. She was reportedly clean, and glad to be moving on with life."

"I asked for a special blood analysis on that, but yes, it appears she was off drugs and booze for a while now." He wavered. "As for being purposely shoved, there's no evidence or motive for murder. Seems she outgrew her teenage troubles and was doing fine. She even broke up with her boyfriend, tossing him out on his ass, I'm told."

"That's an angle that keeps bothering me. Sara says he's a real sleaze. A low life drinker, gambler, taking her pay and blowing it. I did meet him once. Believe it or not, he dressed nicely, had manners. Smiled for me and acted social. But his face was blotchy, eyes dilated. I know it was a good act from everything I saw."

"We're looking for the boyfriend now." Hunter answered. "He seems to have disappeared a few days before Fiona's death."

Cora cursed under her breath. "Blown town. Not surprising. Sara told me he was deep over his head in debt."

"That's a possible reason she could have been made a target. The creep went into hiding so they figured they'd teach him a lesson through her."

"Kill her?" Her brows rose in surprise.

"Maybe that wasn't the plan. Rough her up a little. Try and force him to come up for air. Conceivable they wanted to push her in front of the bus, so she'd get hurt."

"But not murder…"

"Right. People get hit in traffic all the time. Moreso in bad weather, and that storm created hell all over. Multiple injuries on highways and streets. Lots of broken ribs and bones. Bruised drivers and pedestrians flooded hospital ER's. The idea may have been to harm, but not planning her death."

"Murder by accident," she said faintly, biting her lip and debating possibilities. It made sense, Cora thought as she went over the facts as she knew them. But Hunter was right. Rushing to judgement was the worst thing they could do. "My gut says this wasn't a suicide. No way. Fiona had really climbed out of her hole. I believe Sara with that much."

Hunter nodded in agreement. They were on the same page.

"And your gut says, Detective?"

"My gut is leaning in the same direction."

Both declined dessert. On the way out, Hunter helped Cora with her jacket and put his arm around her shoulders to guide her out the door. She leaned back ever so slightly against him. "I'm on it, Cora. Don't worry."

"So am I. I don't care how long it takes or how much effort. I owe it to Sara." She kissed him briefly and turned to walk back to the diner. Streetlight glow cast shadows of her attractive figure.

Hunter allowed himself a smile. It had been a satisfactory dinner on all fronts.

SIX

Cora set the diner's night alarm, then keyed in the numerals for the outer door lock.

She felt sleepy, sweaty, and mentally drained. She ruminated on the long miserable day, finally allowing her shoulders to slump. Her concerns and worries seemed bottomless. On a small note, she was thankful that Sara's husband Marty had finally returned home for the weekend, and Cora would be alone in her own apartment. She realized she desperately needed time to unwind, clear her mind, put the past two days' events into some semblance of order and sense. A brisk walk along the late-night Friday crowds along busy Jamaica Avenue might just fit the bill.

She sauntered along the brightly lit street in the general direction of home. Swarms of people, mostly late-dining adults were exiting the numerous local restaurants while teenagers continued linger even at this late hour. The odor of weed wafted from a huddled knot of nearby youths energetically whispering and laughing among themselves. Cora felt a mild headache developing. She trusted her walk would do her good, and she always enjoyed the crisp nighttime air during late spring. It wouldn't be long before summer and the next autumn revealed itself.

The converging neighborhoods of Kew Gardens, Richmond Hill, and Forest Hills now merged seamlessly, with recent immigrants from virtually every location in the world moving in. As she strolled she listened to English being spoken with lilting Jamaican cadences similar to Eddie Coltrane's Haitian patois, interspaced with Spanish dialects, some Russian, and occasional Korean, as well as several more she didn't recognize. The kaleidoscope of communities with their colorful clothing faded as she turned into quieter residential side streets. It was dimmer here, with isolated pools of light coming only from widely spaced streetlamps. Cora could feel her mood plummet.

Sara's deep grief stirred echoes of Cora's own suppressed memories of her hidden past. She reflected on the sudden loss of the one she loved most, a life cruelly cut short. In an instant, the promise of a happy future extinguished. It was an unfair, meaningless, unacceptable rent in the fabric of her life and its expectations. Without meaning to, Cora's thoughts returned to the events that transpired home in Greece that had sharply divided her life into a 'before' and 'after.'

The face she pictured though wasn't Fiona's but Dirk Bonneau's. Cora had lost her fiancé under inexplicable circumstances. The planned and orderly lifetime of marriage, children, career, and home had all vanished. Nowadays, it seemed like the inevitable end to an ancient Greek tragedy. Cora had set out on a quest to avenge the man she lost, and to end to the source of the evil that had consumed Dirk. During this time of agony and vengeance, she had all but lost her sanity, her morals, her family, and her home country. In that short, brutal, and agonizing time, Cora mislaid everything that composed her very identity. She became lost in a bottomless hell of impulsive madness.

She had retained fragmented memories of that awful time; bright sunshine illuminating the embassy meeting room where she learned of Dirk's sudden death. The aggrieved look on his friend Brian's face when he revealed to her the awkward truths about his partner's hidden life. Then, feeling her own life had become worthless, the fetid smell of the abandoned warehouse where she purchased an illegal weapon. And afterward, the bright hue of splattering blood.

The color red. For some time that's all she ever saw during her gruesome thoughts at night, her tormented dreams. Sprays of red everywhere in that lobby in Athens. The rebound of three rapid gunshots. The smell of gunpowder.

When she came back to the here and now, Cora found herself leaning against a thick tree trunk, heart racing, breathing deeply and hurting still from that time, tears running down her face, spilling off her chin.

She was back in Queens. New York City. America. Safely restored to the here and now. She ran her hands over the tree's rough bark, anchoring herself to the present. Gus, her late husband, had taken her in, enabling her to build a new life, a new identity. She became 'Mrs. Gus' to those at the diner. Her heartbeat normalized as she took slow deep breaths. It had been a long time since an agonizing flashback like this struck her, although it was never long enough. These acute panic attacks would never totally disappear, she knew. Cora wiped her face on a sleeve, and slowly made her way home, feeling completely drained and wanting nothing more than to sleep a dreamless sleep. Maybe even an endless sleep. No hurt, no ache, no feeling at all.

If Mrs. Gus was a bit subdued at work over the weekend, no one remarked on it. Cora hustled, refusing to let straying thoughts detract her. Starting early, staying late, she helped cover breakfasts, lunches, and dinners. Sara Sweeny remained at home with her husband. That was a good thing—at least for the time being. When Monday arrived, Cora checked on incoming deliveries and conditions in the kitchen, and then kept herself busy by chatting with customers.

The diner's phone rang. Cora picked it up with the standard greeting. A rough, slightly accented voice said, "Time is running out, Ms. Drakos. I warned you in our last conversation…"

"Fuck off!" She hit the phone on the counter.

Eddie Coltrane stared at her. "Everything okay, eh, Mrs. Gus?"

She forced a weak smile his way. "Some jerk who keeps calling, wanting to buy us out. No worries, Eddie."

But there were worries. After lunch hour she'd have to do something. It was time. Discuss it with Hunter? That was her first thought. She decided against it. He had so much on his plate. Better if he'd focus on the witnesses to Fiona Sweeney's death. She knew his conclusions would be objective, and she was hoping to soon hear some information on these conclusions. That was more than enough to take on. Besides, another point of view wouldn't hurt.

She decided on speaking with Solerno.

*

Arriving on the scene, the fire engine pulled up sharply into the alley. Huge flames erupted from the dumpsters filled with combustible material roared higher than the diner's roof. Fire hoses deftly aimed at the base of the flames, pounding heavy streams of water, aggressively attacking the mushrooming orange and yellow flames. Dancing sparks shot chaotically over the predawn sky. Black smoke billowed into clouds above the diner. The screaming siren of a second fire engine blocked out the multiple shouts of on-scene responders directing hoses and necessary water pressure to extinguish any dangerous substances. Behind the dumpsters several piles of large compacted black garbage bags also ignited, and their chemical fumes were posing a secondary danger to the five-story apartment house mere yards away from the rear of the restaurant. Residents peered fearfully behind windows, watching embers arc like fireworks in bombarding flashes too close for comfort. Several firefighters shouted orders to the crew of the newly arrived engine.

"Connect to the hydrant," instructed the firehouse captain.

Within moments new strong water streams were gushing in unison with the first engine aimed at the flammable roof, aware that the smallest sparks could create multiple new fires.

A squad car with lights flashing pulled up and stopped close to the standing highest-ranking responder. Sgt. Molina kept the engine running and lowered the driver's window. The firefighter leaned over and explained the situation. Arson for sure, most likely some punks from the area had purposely set the dumpsters ablaze. The smell of kerosine was obvious. Molina listened, nodding his head. When the talk was done he jotted a few notes for his report and then called it in to the station.

Fortunately the fires had been quickly contained, leaving an acrid smell spreading from the alley into the nearby streets. The first fire engine backed up slowly, as its crew scrambled on board and exited slowly.

Cora woke up with Molina's phone call. She hurried from her apartment and quickly scurried the half dozen blocks to the diner. Dawn was breaking. In the distance she could see a concoction of rising black and white smoke climbing toward the sky, staining the panorama of early morning's orange and pink clouds. As she approached the scene she studied the breadth of the horrid mess. Green metal dumpsters were transforming into blackened, badly scarred hulks. The heaps of searing garbage bags created an awful toxic stench. She held her nostrils, shaking her head with dismay and ire. As far as she could tell the restaurant itself appeared intact, save for some possible glass damage from the adjacent flames and smoke. The cleanup would take time, with new dumpsters needed to be ordered quickly, scorched windows inspected for damage and possible replacement. It would take prolonged days to put everything back in running order.

"You all right?" asked the voice on her cell phone. It was Hunter.

"I received another one of those damn threatening calls the other day," she said.

"Why didn't you call me?"

"I knew how busy you are. Besides, I didn't take it that seriously."

"Well, you'd better start taking them seriously." There was more than a hint of annoyance in the detective's voice. 'These people can hurt you or any of your staff and customers."

"Can we talk about this later? I've got to get some sense of the damage, deal with the firefighters while they're still putting out the blazes."

Hunter confirmed by saying, "Sure thing. Also, I have a few things to tell you regarding Fiona Sweeney's death."

Cora wiped her forehead with her sleeve. "Later," she said, clicking off.

This calamity could have been worse, she told herself as she walked dazedly amid a smoldering debris of food bones, cans, and Styrofoam.

"Be careful of hidden embers," said Eddie Coltrane, hands on hips, peering.

She turned in surprise. "How did you know about this…?"

"I didn't," said the handsome Jamaican in his patois accent. "I had to take my little brother to the train early to show him the way into Manhattan. He's just flown in from Kingston. Applying for a New York culinary school."

She touched his shoulder lightly. "I remember you telling me. Sorry, Eddie. This trouble has thrown me off balance. Thank you for showing up early again."

Eddie looked again at the burnt damage, a stern mien crossing his face. "The first deliveries are due pretty soon, Mrs. Gus," he reminded. "I'll have everything brought through the front and into the kitchen. Let the trucks park all along the curb. Don't you worry about anything. I'll take care of it all. You go inside with the fire official and check on what we need to fix."

Cora felt a heavy weight lift from her shoulders, knowing she could trust Eddie with anything and everything. "You're the best. I'm lucky to have you."

"Maybe you'll remember that at Christmas bonus time, eh?" He smiled widely, his large white teeth adding to his broad grin.

"Maybe I will," she retorted, walking toward the entrance, wiping her face, digging deep for renewed energy. The fire captain, a very tall burly middle-aged man joined her along the way.

"We're gonna check for inside damage now. I hope to file an initial report by later today. Luckily for you, it doesn't look like you'll need any extensive renovation. You have good insurance?"

"We do."

"Smart."

He peered consciencely at the seared windows. "Heat causes glass to expand. And stress causes it to crack. I'm thinking we got here in time to prevent much loss. If a single pane is broken you'll have to replace the whole window. That's code. We'll have to check it out. Meanwhile, spray all your windows and let them air-dry. When you open your place up make sure you keep this entire side facing the alley closed." He gestured toward the far side of the building, then drained a water bottle in seven big gulps. Thirst satiated, he wiped the back of a hand across his mouth.

"No chance this was some kind of freak accident, I suppose?" Cora asked. "Something in a dumpster somehow accidently ignited?"

"Not in my opinion." He grimaced, calloused fingers scratching a stubbled face. "Purposely done, maybe just for kicks. Could be area kids thinking it fun, or maybe could be some homeless drunk flipping his lit butt. Or even druggies wandering the streets, searching dumpsters for anything of some value." He vacillated. "But…" Kris Hughes looked down, regarding Cora's unmistakably distressed face.

"Or what?"

"Do you have any determined enemies? Anyone intent on doing you harm we don't know about? Some people who don't like you, would want to see you put out of business? Have you had any threats made?"

She dismissed his question. "Let's hope not," she replied, finding herself seized with a sickening feeling but not willing at this point to mention any of the recent intimidating calls.

Fire Captain Kris Hughes was smart.

"You prevented a much worse disaster from happening, Captain. You saved my diner from disaster. I can't find enough words to thank you and your crews."

"Just doing our jobs." He took another brief look around. Some embers glowed, and the stench of burnt food leftovers and trash assailed his nostrils. "I'm satisfied with everything out here. It's time for us to safely go inside and inspect your business. We don't want any ugly surprises."

Inside, the long flank of side booths facing the alley were closed off to upcoming diners. Eddie Coltrane made sure that everything appeared normal as possible, as well as making the diner able to open up on time. He directed morning staffers on what to do, what to avoid, and above all not to bother Mrs. Gus today. To bring any issues directly to him.

Thankful, Cora remained sequestered in her modest office for the time being, busy making a distinct phone call of her own.

SEVEN

"I was getting ready to call you," Hunter said, holding his phone between his ear and his shoulder. His hands nimbly continued writing on the computer keyboard.

"Are the witness interviews all done?" Cora asked.

He made a sour face as he corrected several misspellings. "Yeah, we're done finally. No point in flogging dead horses. It was a real chore trying to put together a coherent picture of the scene of Fiona Sweeney's last moments at the bus stop."

"Lots of different versions of what happened?"

"Too many to enumerate." He took the phone with his right hand and put it on speaker. "My team has done all it can. Hal Capps will stay in charge of that angle for now. I'm tackling the rest."

"Do you have any concepts yet?"

"A number, yes. But I still have to have to have a thorough and detailed talk with the sister, Sara. I need to fill in lots of missing pieces."

"That's why I was calling you, too. Listen, Sara Sweeney is back with me again for a while. Her husband returned to his upstate job."

"I still need to talk to her ASAP."

"Would it be possible to do your interview over here? She's staying again for a while at my place. She shouldn't be alone. You can come over any time you like. But I do have a favor to ask. Might it be possible to allow me sit in during your interview?"

He smirked at Cora's request. "Kind of killing two birds with one stone? Looking to obtain info for your own investigation, I assume."

"I won't deny it. You know me quite well, detective. What do you say?"

"You've got to promise not to interfere in any way, shape, or form. This is official, serious business."

"Whatever you want."

Sara Sweeney was listening intently to the conversation. As Hunter half-heartedly agreed with the request, Cora gave Sara a thumbs up with a smile. "You have my word, Detective Hunter. My mouth will remain closed shut."

*

Eclectic residence, Hunter thought as he surveyed the apartment. Cora led him down a short hallway into a bright sunlit living room with large windows along the far side. This was the first time he'd been inside Cora's home. He was impressed. A dark, center medallioned, patterned authentic Persian rug lay in front of a handsome leather couch, slightly worn but in excellent shape. Several Victorian antique lamps stood atop quality chestnut side tables. A number of large colorful panoramic oil paintings of Athens and sunbathed Greek Islands adorned both sides of the wide side walls.

Opposite, sitting on an oversized settee, Sara Sweeney peered pensively and inquisitively at the arriving senior detective. She'd noticed him come to the diner on occasion, and realized he was a good friend of her employer. Hunter was interested in her boss, she was sure, but wasn't certain if Mrs. Gus felt the same about him. Much more than that regarding their relationship she didn't know. Normally Sara kept an instinctive avoidance from the police, a mistrust brought on by her own recreational drug use.

Cora brought bottled water for them all, quietly taking a seat slightly away from the direct view Hunter and Sara had of each other.

"It's nice to meet you outside of work, Sara," Hunter said, hunching his shoulders and breaking the ice. "I believe we've casually met before at your work. My name is Jonah Hunter. I'm a senior detective at the local precinct—"

"Yes, I've noticed you in the diner a number of times."

Hunter assumed a relaxed pose, hoping to make Sara Sweeney feel comfortable. "And I need to inform you I'm just here to ask some questions, helping me try to put together exactly what happened to your sister. This isn't any kind of interrogation, and nothing we talk about is being recorded or written down, okay? Just an informal chat. Let me start by telling you I'm so sorry for your loss."

Sara shuffled on her cushion, playing with the edges of her hair. Her nervousness was evident to both Jonah Hunter and Cora. "Thank you, detective. I…I still can't believe any of it." Her eyes met his and then looked away and down at her hands resting in her lap.

When he spoke his voice was soft and reassuring. "I do understand, Sara. May I call you by your first name?"

"Yes. Certainly."

"Let me explain. My job is to help you find out *how* this frightful thing happened and try to learn *why*. So, I need to go back in time a little bit and discover as much background as I can." He crossed his legs and took a sip from the bottled water. His eyes focused on her. "Do you recall when was the last time you saw or spoke to Fiona?"

Sara took her time, interlacing her slender fingers. Her legs were tightly crossed, and one foot swung slowly back and forth. "I talked with her on the phone the night before…Marty, her husband, was away. He's a builder, you know. He works in construction and has this gig up in the Hudson Valley. It's a good, well-paying job, but it's too much to come back and forth every day, so he stays over at a motel."

"I already know about Marty's work, Sara. He sounds like a good guy. Can you recall your conversation with Fiona at all? Anything you remember might be helpful to me, to us assigned to this case."

Sara shut her eyes, put the fingers of her right hand above the bridge of her nose and pinched. Her breathing seemed laborious as she sought to recollect. "Small stuff. I think we were discussing my husband Marty, making plans for an upcoming birthday party. His sister's turning twenty-five soon. Fiona offered to paint a portrait of her as a present. She's good at that. She can make a good sketch of anyone. She did this beautiful color pastel of me last year…" The memory made her sniff. Cora reached over with a handful of tissues. Sara took them gratefully and blew her nose.

"What about Fiona herself? Anything about her own life these past weeks?"

"She mentioned to me that her boss offered her more hours. Some good shifts. They like her at the nice Italian place she works. La Luna."

"I know it. Good reputation, good food."

"They were aware Fiona was back at school, art school, and were really nice to her. She just about made her own schedule according to her classes. Not many bosses do that, do they Mrs. Gus?" She looked at Cora and tried to smile.

"No, they don't," Cora responded.

"How about more personal things?" Hunter asked. He was obviously trying to keep her thoughts on track. "Did she ever talk about money? How was she getting by financially?"

At that the girl paused, her mouth turning down into a small frown. "She wasn't behind on her rent or anything. But she did complain to me a little. See, she has this on-and-off boyfriend. I don't know. She met him a while back where she works…worked I mean." Sara blew her nose. "He acted like a real gentleman when I met him a year ago or so. He was kind of sweet. A nice smile has good manners, please and thank you, that sort of thing. But you know…" She bit her lower lip, tensing up, Hunter noticed. "Go on please, Sara."

"I…I think he's a phony."

"How do you mean?"

Sara took her time drinking water and thinking before answering.

"Well, he's nice, he's clever, dresses good. Knows how to impress people. On the outside, know what I mean? But then he disappears. Makes all kinds of promises he doesn't keep. So many times he left Fiona sitting at home alone all night waiting for him to show up. He likes cards, playing poker. Forgets the time, gets involved. If she gets angry and refuses to answer his calls, he comes to the door and begs her to forgive him. He's sorry—again. It happens a lot. He got caught up in another of his damn card games. He's a real gambler, this guy. Loves high-stakes games. Plays above his head, too. Thinks he's a hotshot and like games with big payoffs and rich guys to play with. Upper class jerks he hangs out with, trying to impress. They drink, get high. Play all night. You know."

Hunter cast a quick glance at Cora.

"So, with this, um, tumultuous relationship, do you know if they were still together? As a couple, I mean."

Sara rolled her eyes with disgust. Waving her hands, she said, "Fiona broke up with him so many times. Took back the keys to her apartment. Refused to see him or talk to him. Nothing worked for long. He pleaded, promised, as usual. I told you he is charming when he wants to be."

"He ever hit her?" The question was unexpected.

"Oh no. Robbie's not like that." Sara shook her head. "He's a user. I mean, I think he really believes some of the things he says. He vows he won't gamble, drink, or do any drugs anymore. Sure. Then a week or two goes by. He can't help himself. There are lots of guys like that. I warned Fiona he wasn't good for her. She knows that. *Knew* that I mean. But she loves the guy, what can I say? And in his own way, I think, maybe he does love her, too. He keeps coming back, doesn't he? No matter what. And sooner or later she takes him back every time. Even giving him money to help pay his debts which happened a lot."

Hunter's attention piqued. "She gave him money often?"
Sara nodded. "Lots of times. I told you, he plays for big stakes with bigshots. He's dropped thousands in a single game," Sara confided. "He 'borrows' from her, other sleazy friends. Of course, they charge interest for loans. God knows how much he may secretly owe. In fact, Fiona said he'd been in some real big game maybe a week before…before the bus…" She started to cry.

Cora got up and put her arms around her. "Take your time, hon," she whispered. Again, she and Hunter exchanged looks.

"We have his name as Rob Perry. Is that right, Sara? His real name is Rob Perry?"

Sara used another tissue to wipe her tears. "Yeah, as far as I know. Everyone calls him Rob or Robbie, I think. His mother is some kind of go-getter real estate broker. She moved from New York a few years back. Fiona says she got married again. And divorced again. Robbie stayed here. He likes New York."

"We'd like to speak with Robbie. Any idea where we can find him now? Is he staying at Fiona's apartment?"

"Oh no. Last week, the last time I saw Fiona, she told me Robbie was going away for a while. Another bad loss, I think. He was concerned, and Fiona said he acted concerned for her too."

Hunter's eyebrows rose. "Oh?"

"I told you he wasn't reliable. Coming, going, like that. What a jerk."

"Do you know what his mother's name is? Where she's living now?"

"Rose. She's Rose Perry something or other. A strange name, foreign sounding. Married for a while and divorced again. A few years back she moved to the South. Not Florida," she thought for a moment. "Carolina, I think."

"North or South?"

"North, I think."

"Thank you, Sara. You've been very helpful. I've got enough to start." He turned to Cora. "Thank you, too. I appreciate your hospitality. I'll be in touch soon."

Cora was fully aware of what Hunter was thinking. Odds were her own thoughts were practically identical.

EIGHT

"Did you know that Louis Armstrong lived in Corona for a long time?"

Cora looked at her companion with surprise. "No, I didn't."

"It's true. They turned his house into a small museum. It's become an historic landmark." Solerno pointed directly across the street. "See over there on the far corner? That was where the famous Lemon Ice King was. People came from all over Queens and the city to buy their famous Italian ices. The place was always buzzing, lines would be going out to the curb."

"That I do remember," Cora said, with her own recollections of the celebrated shop. "They made terrific ices in lots of flavors. Lemon was my favorite. A real shame when they closed."

Solerno frowned, white stubble on his unshaven face prominent in the sunlight. "Yeah, I was just a young guy in the neighborhood back then. Thought I was tough. You know, looking to make my mark, make a name for myself. Trying to impress some of the local connected guys. You know, people who said they knew the right people." Here he chuckled. "Like anyone was going to tell me anything."

"I bet you were a hit with the girls, too."

"I tried to be."

They strolled slowly along busy Corona Avenue, the main street. It looked like a father proudly showing his daughter all the neighborhood sights, past and present. "Later Corona became a big center for immigration, especially Hispanic, and Latin American food restaurants spread all the way from here to Northern Boulevard. More establishment than you can count. Good food."

They paused by the tiny William F. Moore park, a landmark. "I loved to watch the crazy old guys playing old-fashioned, Italian-rule bocce ball in this little court right here. I remember people gathering in crowds to watch and make bets on the outcome. Some of these players were real pros. They'd wager among themselves, too. Summer evenings were packed with the public gathering along the streets, wandering up and down, enjoying cooler evenings after the daytime heat. There were big firework displays on the Fourth of July. What a mob would show up. Corona was almost exclusively Italian back then. But with time most of the younger couples moved out, the older generation remained, staying in place. These days you got people sleeping on the benches in this little park. It ain't the same, but I suppose nothing is. I guess I've just turned into another of those old guys I've been telling you about." He laughed at his poor attempt at humor.

"You still look good. In shape. I bet lots of older ladies are still interested."

At that his amusement deepened.

Cora had contacted Solerno yesterday, informing him of the fire in the diner's alley and her growing concerns. She asked him to meet with her at his convenience, and he readily agreed, giving a time and place. She took the bus from Queens Boulevard down 108th Street and got off at the Long Island Expressway underpass. Her elder friend stood patiently waiting on the opposite side of the street and waved when she got off the bus. "Let's take a walk while we talk," he said to her. "Let me show you Corona, I mean my Corona, the old haunts, places where I grew up."

She'd been uneasy on her way to meet her retired shady friend, but now she found she was enjoying herself as he played the role of expert tour guide.

"Down that way," he pointed, "is where my sister Rosalie lived. Raised four girls in the same house for fifty years until she passed a little while ago. Her kids are all over the map. I sold her little house for them a while back. Nobody wanted to deal with it anymore."

She touched his arm. "I'm sorry about your sister…"

"History now. She's in a better place. Gotta be a better place that this world."

"My father used to say that." Cora said, remembering. "We live in a world overflowing with endless wars, corruption, diseases."

"Sounds like a very smart man to me." They continued strolling for a while without speaking, Cora tried not to dwell on her elderly dad and family back in Athens. She missed him so much, her mother and sister Lyra, too. It had been so long since she had been home. Sometimes she felt like an exile, unable to return, although that wasn't literally true. Maybe one day. Maybe. Fighting away these memories she focused instead on making note of all the colorful foods for sale from the numerous shops enhancing every block on both side of the active avenue.

Solerno noticed her interest. "Like all the different aromas around here, huh?"

"Spices. I really enjoy the spices." Her nostrils flared with the multitude of odors.

"Down at Corona Plaza there are dozens of vendors selling there every single day, everything from tacos and grilled meats, fruits to jewelry and underwear."

"Glad they're not my competition."

Solerno grinned. "No, they can't match the Athena Diner." He turned and faced her, addressing her in a serious tone. "How much damage is there from that fire the other night? How much out of pocket money, you think?"

"The insurance people haven't tallied it yet. My guess is around the five thousand insurance deductible I'll be hit with. Luckily our glass windows didn't break."

He sucked in a breath. "Bastards. Just enough to scare you, let you know they're determined. That your place can be hit anytime they like."

"That's what's troubling me. This time the message hit home."

Standing at rest in the shadows of Our Lady of Sorrows Catholic church, Solerno pursed his lips and grew deep into thought. The look in his eyes became cold and angry in a way Cora hadn't encountered before.

"What did you tell the police?"

"Very little. I played dumb. A fire captain questioned me, but he didn't push. I answered only questions regarding fire damage."

"Good."

"At some point I'll have to tell them more, though."

"Listen. Cops like to be objective. They don't care who's in the way as long as they think they'll solve their crime. Maybe they can use informants to rat out who or what kind of gang lit that fire…But they won't learn who's at the top, I mean the very top. Those kinds of people they won't be able to touch."

"You think my diner's so valuable?"

"For someone, apparently yes. You gotta be very, very careful, Cora. Hear me?"

She bit her lower lip, unable to reconcile her trust in both Solerno as well as Hunter. Two opposites, yet in some ways so similar. She swallowed hard and then said, "I'm here with you, aren't I?" There was a brief silence.

"Okay. What are you asking me?"

"I'd like for you and some of your former colleagues to try to discover who's behind all this. At the top, as you say. I'll pay whatever required."

Solerno scoffed. "I don't want your money. But I can't say everyone I may contact will feel the same. There could be a fee. And I can't promise no one won't get hurt, understand? You've been around. You know how these things work."

"I don't care who you have to strongarm. I won't stand around and be terrorized. Whatever people, whoever they are, wherever they come from."

"It could be South American drug cartel pressure, maybe Russian money needing a cozy place to park, even a hungry local big business, there's no shortage of human roaches crawling everywhere…"

"It doesn't matter, Solerno," she snapped. "I've faced formidable trouble before. And I've suffered for it, believe me. When I've confronted parasites I've dealt with them."

She spoke with a venom he hadn't encountered from Cora, nor did he doubt a word she said. Again, he wondered if the gossip about a gruesome murder she may have committed in Greece were true.

He nodded. "I'm well aware you're a resilient lady, Cora. I respect that."

"When necessary, I've had to be. That's the way the world works, isn't it? I learned those lessons very well, a long time ago back in Athens." She stopped there, not wishing to divulge matters better left unspoken.

"And I have your word the police will be kept out of this? My associates won't like it if you plan on keeping any of your friends informed. Including your detective buddy Jonah Hunter. I know you're close, don't deny it. That's a personal choice. However, it could make things turn ugly if you involve him. This isn't a warning. This is business. I'm telling you for your own good—and safety."

Her face hardened, she matched his own rigid look. "Hunter has nothing to do with this at all. He's out, you're in. You have my word," she said whole-heartedly. "It's between me and the scum trying to intimidate me. I want them gone forever, no matter what. With your support, of course."

"All right, Cora. I hear you loud and clear. Give me a little time. I'll see what I can do." They walked to the nearest bus stop. A bus was coming. "Go back to work, take care of your business. I'll be in touch soon." He put out a calloused hand to shake, but to his surprise she reached up and kissed him briefly on the cheek. "Thank you, Solerno. Perhaps one day I can return the favor."

*

"Detective Hunter asked me to call," Detective Hal Capps said dryly. "He's stuck sitting in on a high brass meeting, but he wanted me to let you know he'll still try and meet you on time."

"Thank you, Hal. I appreciate the notice. I'll be waiting." She put down her cell phone and drummed her fingers on the desk. Her cup of Greek coffee grew cold as she debated how best to work closely with Hunter regarding Fiona Sweeney's death, while keeping him remaining at bay regarding questions he would surely have regarding the fire. The two of them together would be like kindling waiting for a match.

Hunter arrived at the diner an hour later. Eddie Coltrane quickly guided him to her small office near the kitchen.

"Sorry for being so late," he said as soon as he saw her. His smile was perfunctory as he dropped into the chair near her desk. It was obvious to Cora that the meeting with his top brass had not gone well. Likely he was being hassled by the mystery of what had actually happened at the bus stop on that horrid stormy day.

"Can I get you something?" she asked while he took off his sport jacket. His tie was askew and there was sweat under the armpits of his beige shirt. The detective was clearly agitated.

"How about a sandwich? Coffee? Something cold?"

"Cold water would be fine, thanks."

A minute later she reappeared with a fresh bottle of water and a bowl of potato chips and pretzels. He smiled weakly at the gesture, finding himself reaching for the pretzels. "Rough day," he began. "The pressure's on from the Department. Top brass won't budge. Budgets are through the roof. Overtime, sick leave, staff shortages all over the city. Blah, blah, blah. Not a single precinct up to par. The rookie trainee I was supposed to get for my unit has been postponed for now." He sighed. "Again."

"And your Detective Kelley is going on a maternity leave soon, right?"

"Right. She'll be due in a few months. We're already shorthanded. They gave me a Third-Grade replacement. Detective Cosgrove. Meanwhile, uniform cops resigning still aren't being replaced on time, and these new kids need guidance. They're rookies.

Our captain is freaking out and I don't blame him." He sulked. "Screw it. I should hand in my own resignation."

"You love your work too much, Hunter. You won't quit."

He tossed a few pretzels into an open mouth and crunched. "Imagine your diner losing a bunch of your best people. That's how my unit is going to have to operate."

"Sorry to hear all this. The city's in another crisis. I wish I could be helpful."

He took several long drinks from the water bottle. Then he took out his phone. "Never mind that for now. I made some notes I wanted to discuss. Witness material from the bus accident."

She listened without interrupting. Hunter gradually caught his breath and eased into a semi-relaxed mode, ready to talk with Cora and also feeling pleased to see her. "We looked at the scene over and over," he began. "From every possible angle. Hal was a great help. I couldn't have done it all without him. So many witnesses, so little info to compile. Almost everyone was holding an umbrella, and most of what everyone saw were bodies stacked side by side and other umbrellas tightly held in a strong wind. One small piece of luck. A closed-circuit camera outside a nearby fruit store caught part of the bus crowd waiting in the rain. We blew up the pictures and went over the timeframe moment by moment. Extremely carefully. Pausing every few frames. It wasn't great, but it provides the best on site information we could find. Slow and tedious, but hopefully there'll be some kind of clue."

Cora tensed. A camera doesn't make mistakes and doesn't lie.

"The angle wasn't great. Skewed, and the lens got wet with dripping raindrops, affecting the clarity. Nevertheless…" He took out his iPhone and opened the notepad. He took his time glancing briefly over the summaries. "The lens caught the front of the bus approaching the bus shelter. People were already beginning to move both toward and from the curb. Amid this slow surge we could see a figure moving forward at a slightly faster speed than any of the others. And then there's a sudden movement I would describe as an acceleration. Our lab is examining this unexpected rush. Frame by frame. The figure seems to stumble, loses balance, then falls forward at about a twenty-degree angle right into the path of the bus. Remember, the tumbling figure is tightly surrounded by other passengers also stirring. I'm waiting for the opinion of a couple of experts at this stuff. Backup for my own theory."

"But that falling figure is definitely Fiona Sweeney, right?"

"Right. No doubt. The bus slams—" He stopped speaking.

"And your own theory?"

Hunter was momentarily uncomfortable. He didn't like the idea of possible conflict coming from other places in NYPD. "Between us, Cora, it's not one hundred percent…"

"Of course, I understand. Please, share your personal view with me."

He gestured with his hands, trying to simulate the movements the camera caught. "She's here, surrounded by other waiting passengers.

Slowly she moves forward, obviously seeing the oncoming bus. Then," here he bent his hand sharply forward. "She appears to be propelled by something. A push, a shove, something hard."

"Does it seem to be accidental, like someone's elbow pushing to move her or anyone else out of their way?"

"Nothing is certain, at least yet. I want corroboration."

"But your gut, Hunter. Tell me what your gut says."

"My gut," he offered slowly, "tells me she was shoved purposely. With force. Someone was standing directly behind her, waiting for some opportunity, and when the bus got closer she was chucked directly in front of it, deliberately and with malice. That's my conclusion based on the camera."

Cora's dark eyes widened. His words were head-spinning. "Oh my God. Then you think the intention was to kill her?"

He waited, thinking her question over. "I didn't say quite that. It's conceivable the intent wasn't to kill Fiona, but certainly to injure, to maim her, to create serious injury. Dying, though, could have been unintended."

A silence fell between the veteran detective and the diner's resourceful owner. Cora felt a tightening in her abdomen. She'd feared this conclusion all along and now it was in front of her face. Fiona had been marked. Selected by some sick fuck among those standing at the bus stop. If she was targeted, why? For what purpose? Tears started to well in the corner of her eyes and she was unable to stop them. She had trouble clearing her throat to talk. Hunter noticed but didn't say anything.

"Who would do something like that?" she muttered, partly to herself. "For what reason? Some psycho eager to watch someone die? Hear them scream in fear, or them crying out in fright? Or is it something else? What?"

"We don't know—yet. But this investigation is only beginning, remember."

"I have some thoughts on where it can start."

Hunter respected Cora's instincts, her proven aptitude to take apart an incident and analyze it from every side and aspect. Her countenance at this very moment assured him she was already dissecting every thought he'd shared.

"I'm going to pick Sara Sweeney's brain for every detail, every contact Fiona had, I promise. Her coworkers, anyone she'd dated or drank with back in the day. Even students in her art classes. See of someone was or is jealous of her…"

"That takes a lot of legwork and effort, Cora. Your diner might suffer."

"I can't just let this go."

"Why not just leave it to us this time? I know the way you think. Your compassion and need to right these wrongs. But I already gave you my word how seriously we're tackling this case."

"I do know. But I can't just stand by, you know that, too."

"You can't interfere with our work, either. We're the police, not you."

His words dug at her, and she stared at him with a hint of confusion. "Are you saying I should totally keep out of this?"

"I'm only saying that you already have so much going on. Helping Sara Sweeney is a really good thing. You more than anyone could assist in bringing her shattered life back to health. Meanwhile, let me run the inquiries regarding Fiona."

"I can't step back, Hunter. I gave Sara my word."

"Do what you can, of course. But what about those other issues?"

"Which other issues?"

He regarded her with perplexity. "Our precinct also received the FD report on the fire you had in the alley. They think it remains suspicious."

She took a few breaths, trying think on her feet on how to keep her detective friend from involving himself with that. "I'm letting our insurance people take care of this mess. Probably some drunk with a lighted cigarette or punks thinking it was fun."

He viewed her with genuine surprise. "You don't think it might be related to those phone calls you told me about? Those ominous 'offers' to sell this place?"

She waved a hand with indifference. "I thought about it. But right now, I'm not letting that bother me. At least for the time being."

Her flippant answer didn't sound like her at all, and he knew Cora well enough to not believe any of it. Not when her most personal interests were involved. "You're telling me someone set fires right in your alley and you're willing to let the matter be handled by an insurance company?"

"I pay them enough, don't I?" she huffed.

"What are you up to, Cora? What's really going on?"

"I don't know what you're referring to."

They looked at each other for a long moment. "You wanted my help before…"

"Please Hunter, don't press me on it. I need my mind and energy in shape to focus on Sara and this possible gruesome murder. That's the number one concern."

"So, if you come to the diner tomorrow and find glass smashed all over the street, or the restaurant has mysterious power outages ruining business, you won't worry. You're telling me you'll let the insurance companies take care of it."

She shrugged. "I'll deal with whatever happens when it happens."

"Okay, Cora. Have it your way. Just one question, though, and I need an answer. Have you been in touch lately with any of your underworld friends?"

She regarded him blankly. Anyone other than Hunter asking something as banal as this she would have tossed out into the gutter and never looked back.

Hunter studied her, realizing her glacial bearing. He felt as though he was suddenly facing a cold brick wall. "You have been in touch, haven't you?"

"I have no underworld friends." That wasn't an answer they both knew.

Hunter leaned over, gritting his teeth, not trying to hide his antipathy. Not an eyelash flickered, not a muscle moved on his face. "So, you're thinking of having mobsters help you out with this affair? Killers, murderers. The worst of the worst, like that old Mafioso, Solerno?"

Cora held her tongue. Hunter didn't, couldn't understand. As much as she cared, as close as they were becoming, she wouldn't, couldn't, break her promise. It was her word, her moral compass. "Keep Solerno out of this. You have no right. He's long retired, doesn't work for any of those individuals you're describing."

"You know that doesn't matter with them. He's *connected*. Always and forever among mob families. Dead is the only way out for these people. Once unleashed, if they do a favor, they *own* you."

"No one owns me." She threw back her head. "No one."

He shook his head slowly from side to side, sensing an unstable situation ahead.

"What you're doing is irresponsible and dangerous. And there'll be a price." There was no hint of delicacy in his panting voice.

She put her hands over her face and rubbed hard. Her mind was racing with the punishing events crashing down on her, and she steeled herself as best as she could, ready for come what may.

There was a quick knock on the office door. "Mrs. Gus, we need some help out here." Eddie Coltrane's plea broke the intense mood.

Cora stood up and looked over her shoulder. "Be there in a sec, Eddie." Then turning to Hunter, "Thank you for all your help today. I mean it. I appreciate what you've done more than I can ever express." Her eyes treated him with sincerity.

Hunter stood up and put on his sport jacket. The bulge of his holster and gun were evident. "Take care of yourself, Cora. Take good care. I hope I didn't misjudge you, and you know what you're doing."

That stung. Hurt more than she wanted to admit. She stiffened and looked at him. Then she opened the office door and walked out, imposing a wide smile at a growing group of customers waiting to be seated. Hunter nodded a curt goodbye at Eddie Coltrane and hastily left the diner.

NINE

It was almost dinner hour. Cora refused to give in to the continued knotted, sinking feeling in her stomach. She busied herself prepping vegetables for Claude in the kitchen. She instructed two new hires, Allison, and Stavros, in the specifics of the Athena's procedures. Both were experienced pros in the hectic world of restaurants and diners who caught on quickly. Allison was eager to learn everything, and Stavros was especially good at dealing with patrons. In his mid-twenties, studying economics at night school, the Greek youth reminded Cora of happier times and old friendships in Athens. These few nostalgic moments of her lost life gave Cora the strength to confront the implications of her melancholy meeting with Hunter.

Their friendship had grown gradually, as she frequently requested the detective's advice on various probes of her own. Both became aware of an unspoken sexual attraction. Their relationship was, or had been, on the verge of moving to a deeper level. Recently, he had even personally helped on several of her own investigations. It would be a terrible loss to have to cut him out of her life. At the same time, she knew he was an ethical man in a world known for its corruption and visible prejudices. His police work duties might never be reconcilable with her need to keep contacts and friendships with a few people she knew who lived on the wrong side of the law. While some maintained that cops and criminals were two sides of the same coin, she knew the difference. She'd been on both sides of the coin herself and appreciated from bitter experience that occasionally the Athena Diner required her to operate in some very gray areas. So did her efforts to help others when needed. That's just the way it was. The diner had become her life since coming to America. If it hadn't been for Gus taking her in, her world would have been much grimmer and more problematic. She closed her eyes and sent a silent "Thank you," out to Gus.

Later, back in the privacy of her office, Cora's shoulders slumped. Sometimes the weight of her world pressed too heavily. Worry about unknown malignant forces trying to take over the diner, the urgent need to find Fiona's killer and the reason for her death, and now a rupture in her relationship with the one person she valued most. Cora struggled to keep things in perspective, but now she was feeling overwhelmed.

She jerked when her office door pushed open. Sara burst inside frantically waiving her phone at Cora, exclaiming, "It's *him*!"

Cora jumped up.

"Cover for me," Cora said, sticking her head out to nearby Eddie Coltrane, and hurried back inside, shutting the door behind.

Sara's phone was on speaker. The voice on the other end sounded strong, hints of candid concern obvious. "Sara, are you there? Who are you talking to?"

"Yes, I'm here, Robbie." Cora stood behind her, a finger telling Sara not to divulge anything yet.

"What's going on, Sara? For days I've been calling your sister. She doesn't answer her cell. I left so many messages it's filled up. The landline keeps on ringing. Why won't she pick up? I even tried calling her job, but they hung up on me. I also phoned your mother, but no one answered there, either. What's going on?"

"Where are you, Robbie?"

His sigh was loud. "Far away. Fiona knew I had to leave for a while. I explained everything to her. She said she'd expect my calls…"

Sara looked at Cora, unsure what to say. "You're at work," Cora mouthed silently.

"I'm at the diner, Robbie. Working a late shift. My boss asked me to stay late."

"Listen, I'm worried. Really fucking worried. Why isn't she answering?"

"You shouldn't have left like you did, Robbie. Fiona needed you. Badly. I…we have to talk, go over some terrible things."

They could feel the sense of apprehension at the other end. "What's wrong, Sara? What's going on?"

Seeing Sara was about to cry, Cora pointed at herself.

"I…I can't talk now. Here. You can speak with my boss."

"Your *boss*? Mrs. Gus? Why?"

Cora took the phone in her right hand, holding it so Sara could hear everything said. "Don't hang up, Robbie," Cora said in a strong husky voice. "You know who I am, right?"

"Sure. You own the Athena, where Sara works. I've been there and seen you a few times."

"Then you know I'm also Sara's friend."

"I guess so. What's this about? Why isn't Sara talking to me? Can you tell me what's going on? I need to talk to Fiona. It's important. *Very* important."

"You can't speak with her, Robbie. A lot's happened in the past days since you disappeared. Sara tried to call you dozens of times. You ditched your phone, didn't you?"

"Yeah, I did, but I didn't disappear. I'm using a cheap prepaid burner I bought. I had to split from the city for a while. Fiona knows. She can explain it all to you."

"She can't explain it. She can't explain anything."

"What the fuck are you talking about? What do you mean she can't? Just tell me what's going on, okay?"

"Okay, Robbie. Take a deep breath and listen carefully to everything I'm saying. And listen well." A pause. "Your girlfriend had a terrible accident on her way to school. A tragedy. I'm sorry to say she died. It just happened. Fiona is dead."

There was a profound silence on the other end. He might have heard Sara's muffled sobs in the background while Cora was speaking.

"That isn't funny. Look, I know she's really pissed at me. I get it. And maybe I deserve it. But stop this shit, okay? I need to get in touch with Fiona right away. Is she staying with Sara? Or maybe with her mother? Where is she?"

Cora said dryly, "She's at the morgue."

This time the silence lingered. "Please," he said. "Someone, tell me what's happened." This time there was genuine anguish in his voice. Bewilderment mixed with fear.

"Hear this and hear it good. As I told you, she was on her way to school early in the morning. On her way to her art class…"

"I'm listening."

"Fiona was waiting, standing at the bus stop in the rain. Then as the bus was coming either somebody pushed her, or she stumbled and fell. The bus couldn't stop in time. She was rushed to the hospital, and they tried to save her, doing everything possible, but the damage was too much. She died the next morning."

"Sara, please tell me if this is real or bullshit."

Sara cleared her throat. "It…It's real Robbie. She never regained consciousness. Fiona's gone." Her tone of desolation was more convincing than words.

"Where are you, Robbie?" demanded Cora. "Don't try and lie about it. This call can be traced. No anonymity anymore, not even on a burner."

"Look, here's the truth. I've been staying for a few days with my mother, okay? She lives in Raleigh, North Carolina."

Cora exchanged glances with Sara. Before Cora could say anything, Robbie said, "Look. Please. Don't play games. Tell me. Just tell me." The cracking in his voice sounded earnest. "Was it some freak accident? I heard about the bad weather in New York. She fell you said? An accident?" Here again he hesitated. "Or was it…"

"Or was it what, Robbie?" Sara cried through her tears.

"Was it…something else?"

"Robbie, you need to come back to New York. Right away. The police are looking for you." Sara gathered herself and added, "We both know it's possible one of your contacts might have done this."

"My contacts? Are you nuts? You think anyone I know might be responsible for this? That's crazy."

Cora put the phone closer to her lips. "Now you listen, you little prick. We all know about your gambling debts. Your card games. Your rich friends and their drug parties. And your boozing. I can dig up lots of dirt, buddy. Don't test me. The police would be delighted to know where you are."

"I know you, Mrs. Gus. You have a reputation too. I care about Fiona. You have to believe that. I never would wish her harm."

"Then prove it. And don't doubt it for a second. So, unless you want cops banging on your mother's door in an hour just follow my instructions."

"You can't do that. My mom doesn't have anything to do with my life, or what happened. Keep her out of this, please."

"You think I care? Fiona Sweeney is dead. Local cops will detain you and her until my New York cops get a court order and show up themselves to escort you back here. You don't believe me, you, and you repulsive gambling friends? Then go ahead and try me." Cora's anger was rising, and she was wholly serious. Even if she had to beg

Hunter for help now she was willing. Go to him herself and plead. And she'd be sure to follow through with her threat.

"I'm listening to you," Rob Perry said in a quiet but clearly timorous voice. "I need to know the whole story. I want to find out too, and I want to help."

"I think you can provide insightful information that will be helpful to finding out what happened. Maybe if you're serious we can put two and two together, come up with some answers, even solve some things. I need honest answers and names. Your friends, connections, these trashy bookies. And I need you to provide them."

"You think I don't care about Fiona and what you're telling me? I'll let you in on everything I know." There was emotion in his voice now. "I do care, no matter how may stupid things I did in the past. Look, I ran because I was afraid these people were hunting me. I never dreamed it was possible they might come after Fiona. She's totally innocent—" His voice started to crack.

"I believe you *can* provide good info, Robbie. But I won't hurt you like your so-called friends will if they locate you where you are. I promise I can keep you out of sight and harm's way."

"You can trust her, Robbie," Sara burst out. "She's good like that. She won't turn on you. You've heard some of the stories how she's helped people in trouble."

He quickly thought the offer over. "Fiona means a lot to me. She's the best thing that ever happened. Please believe that. If you can go after anyone that tried to hurt her—"

"They've already hurt her, Robbie."

The words seared into his mind. It took long moments for him to gather himself. "Alright. If I agree, what do you want me to do?"

"Get to the Raleigh bus station right away. Don't even pack. Get on the first Greyhound back to New York. You'll be met at the Port Authority Bus Terminal by one of my people, not cops, I promise. I'll have Stavros there awaiting your arrival. You have my word. I'll vouch for your safety. Stavros will have my car, drive you directly to me. Then you and I will talk alone and try to figure some things out on our own. Together we might even find answers sooner than later. Just keep your word and give me all the information I require. Understand? No arrest if you give me names. Then afterwards you'll be free to do whatever, go wherever you want."

"How do I know I can trust you, Mrs. Gus?"

"You don't. You said you know my reputation. I keep my word. But don't try to play me. I promise you, Robbie, if you're not back by tomorrow morning the police in every state on the eastern seaboard will have an APB, an All-Points-Bulletin, for your arrest. And I won't be there to help you."

He believed her on that. "I will be there. I'll phone you again with the number of my bus and its time of arrival."

Cora closed her eyes in a thankful prayer. Maybe there really could be some justice. "Good. I'll be here and waiting."

Stavros kept a watchful eye, and with Sara's description was able to recognize Robbie as he walked off his bus near the 8th Avenue exit.

He signaled, and Robbie nodded, slinging his backpack over his shoulder.

The car was waiting in a paid garage across the street, within an hour they had maneuvered through midtown traffic, driven through the Midtown Tunnel, and arrived at Cora's Queens apartment.

Rob Perry was taller than Cora had pictured, she saw as he and Stavros came into her living room. He was a good-looking young man, late twenties. Cheekbones elevated, a furrowed brow with eyes deep set and intense. He carried himself well, head held high, amiable, and poised, arms clasped behind his body, with a well-heeled look despite his shaggy, worn clothes. Cora immediately recognized how he would be eye-catching, even striking at first glance. His mouth was wide with thin lips, a jutting chin. He needed a shave. His dark cheeks enhanced the look with several days of stubble growth.

She turned towards the young Greek with a relieved expression. "Thank you, Stavros. You did a great job. Please, go back and check on the diner for me."

Her young employee appeared reluctant to leave Cora alone with Rob Perry. He was aware and disturbed his employer was overloading herself by taking on the case of Fiona Sweeney's death. "You're sure you'll be alright?"

She nodded. "I'm sure, Stavros. I appreciate you picking him up and bringing him to me."

"No problem." At that he turned around and left quietly. When the door closed behind Cora, she turned her full attention to Rob Perry, standing before her, clearly trying to hide his edginess.

"Put down your backpack and take a seat," she told him in a convivial tone. Then she went into the kitchen and brought out bottles of cold water. She handed one to her guest, who took it eagerly. He thanked her and gulped almost half the bottle in thirsty gulps.

"You look pretty beat up."

"Long trip," he muttered. "Lots of stops. Crowded bus."

"Your mother aware you left and came back here?"

"I left a note. She was at work showing houses."

"Have you eaten anything?"

He shook his head. A mess of hair fell from the top of his head as far as his eyes. He surveyed the unfamiliar room with quick, curious glances.

Cora placed her bottle of water on a small three-legged table beside her armchair. Placing her hands together in a pyramid, elbows on her knee, she said, "Take your time, Robbie. We're in no rush. Consider yourself my guest."

"Will I be staying here for the night?"

"Several, I expect. There's a lot to go over."

"I'm okay with that."

"If you'll forgive me for saying, you don't look the way Sara talked about you."

"Oh? That good or bad?"

"Good, but we'll see."

Cora crossed her legs, swiftly sitting up straight, maintaining eye contact, and purposely trying to assume a serene, composed posture. In no way did she want to display how exhausted and worn she also was, nor make her guest feel more uneasy. She had full faith in Eddie Coltrane's ability to manage everything at the diner, but she wasn't so sure Sara Sweeney would be able to handle herself at work yet. She had asked a newer waitress, Allison, to watch over her, and knew Stavros would lend a hand also if needed. So unless some new disaster occurred perhaps now the real work could begin.

TEN

Hunter dropped his two kids off at his ex-wife's on Sunday night. Thankfully, she just waved them inside without starting a conversation. With all he had to juggle right now, he didn't need any gratuitous arguments from her adding to his distress. He needed time to think, clear his cluttered mind, and he often thought best while driving. When he reached the Long Island Expressway, he took the ramp east, toward the far end of Long Island. He cracked open the window, hoping the fresh cool air would assist in clearing his head. He was well aware of what was bothering him most. Cora, of course.

What was he to make of his good friend, the owner of the Athena Diner, Cora Drakos? This fascinating woman who was also a seeker of justice, a doer, not a whiner or a braggart like so many others. Cora walked the walk. She had a long record of aiding kids in trouble, adults in need, and working to help those caught amid uninvited trouble. He knew this for a fact, from his own experience. Yet she was thoroughly familiar with using a handgun when necessary, and unafraid to use it. Able to think quickly on her feet, she was also an excellent tactician and problem solver. At the same time, there was her peculiar friendship with a known gangster, a mafioso, supposedly retired. A real bond that existed which he didn't understand. Moreover, Cora had totally disregarded his strongly worded advice to keep her distance from this man.

Always lurking in the background were also these persistent gossipy rumors regarding her supposedly murky past in Greece. So many stories had developed it was all but impossible to separate truth from community blather.

His own friendship with Cora in recent times had begun to grow deep roots, he knew. He also was sure that they both valued it, and he was certain he wanted it to grow more. Was Cora now having second thoughts? Were his own feelings just wishful thinking? Perhaps he need to back off.

Hunter was very aware of the failure of his first marriage. He recognized the damage his PTSD and drinking had done to his kids and his ex. His military years and the war in Afghanistan had cost him far more than time. He could be considered damaged goods. He needed to be cautious, for himself as well as his kids. It would be disastrous to push himself into a relapse. Unaware of time, he had reached Orient Point nearly a hundred miles east of the city, a lovely rural hamlet located at the end of Long Island's North Fork, where Long Island Sound meets the Atlantic Ocean. The fresh sea air was exhilarating. The silent streets, dark barns and quaint houses, fishing boats, the scent of saltwater and mud flats all soothed his turbulent thoughts. Behind him the sun was waning, low down near the western horizon. He would talk to Cora about his concerns, he decided, but not tonight. He slowly turned his car around onto Sound Avenue and began the long drive back home.

His phone rang. Annoyed at being bothered by work just as he was beginning to manage his stress he answered tersely, "Hunter."

"Detective Hunter, a report came through from the Fiona Sweeney autopsy. It was written hours ago, so somehow it got delayed. But I thought I'd better give you a head's up."

"What does it say?"

On the other end Detective Kasey Cosgrove, a recently promoted newer member of the detective bureau hesitated. "It says that she…Fiona Sweeney was pregnant. About eight weeks they estimate."

Hunter's jaw dropped. "She was? The family hasn't been informed yet, have they?"

"Not as far as I know, sir."

"Good. Thanks, Kasey. I'll swing by the squad room on my way home. Leave the report on my desk if you go."

"You got it, Hunter. I'll be here."

The third-degree detective smoothed out the jacket of her pantsuit and stood up as her senior supervisor walked in ninety minutes later. She was tall, used little makeup, and had her chestnut hair pulled back neatly into a ponytail. In her early thirties, she had been a member of Hunter's Crime Scene Unit for barely a year, working with the handful of precinct detectives. Everyone in the squad room recognized her as a quick learner and eager to get every task accomplished. Ambitious, too.

Chips in the green wall paint faded in the dim light of a few computer screens and desk lights scattered around the darkened second story room. The Sunday night skeleton squad staff looked up at Hunter, nodding hellos, trying to seem unsurprised to see him at this late hour.

Detective Cosgrove waved a paper. "I have the lab reports here," Kasey said, holding several printed sheets. Hunter took them, slumped into the swivel seat at his desk, rubbing tired, reddened eyes. It was true, he saw; Fiona Sweeney had been pregnant at the time of her death. He felt a vexing twinge in his gut. This startling news meant he had to rethink all their theories regarding Fiona Sweeney's case.

"I phoned you the moment I read the report," Kasey said, aware of how much this unexpected piece of information was bothering him.

"Glad you did," he said through a clenched jaw. "We need to pay a visit to the mother in person, Moira Sweeney. She needs to be told, but as gently as you can. No telling how she'll react to this additional loss, but it's bound to be sensitive information. And it's also important to get in touch with Fiona's sister, Sara." Hunter's eyes scanned the report again. "They estimate she was about eight weeks into the pregnancy. She would have known by then, right?"

Kasey's demeanor remained calm. "I'd say she most likely would have known by then."

"No point in withholding anything now," Hunter decided. He clasped his hands placing his elbows on the desk. He didn't bother turning on his own computer. For a time, he fell into deep thought, evaluating all the implications. He observed that his young detective was still standing there and spoke in a soft tone, "This information is going to definitely upset the family. I think it would be better if the mother was informed by a woman. I'll speak with Sara Sweeney. No phone discussions, Kasey. Do it in person, okay?"

Kasey lifted her head, "Of course, sir. Isn't Sara Sweeney staying with her boss, Mrs. Gus?"

Hunter nodded. "Sara's being taken care of while her husband is away. It would probably be a good idea to keep Cora Drakos in the loop as well. I'll also handle that one."

Kasey nodded. "Consider it done." She deftly turned off her computer, slung her purse over her shoulder, and swiftly left the detective squad room. Hunter watched her go, heard her footsteps going down the stairs. He remained at his desk, for a few long minutes, fiddling with a pen, wondering how the latest news would affect Cora's own investigative efforts. He thought it best to speak with both of the women at the same time, to better see how each woman handled the news. He shoved his chair back, walking tiredly down the stairs, taking out his phone to let Cora know he'd be coming with disturbing news.

Kasey Cosgrove surveyed Mrs. Sweeney's building with interest. It was an old brick rental building in transition, similar to numerous others in the neighborhood. The lobby was renovated and gentrified, with pseudo-marble tiles and a fake fireplace in the wide lobby. Every apartment had been upgraded as each tenant left, allowing landlords to raise rents accordingly. Long-term tenants made do with outdated original kitchens and bathrooms, now almost seventy years old.

Kasey's guess was that Mrs. Sweeney was one of the older remaining tenants.

The elevator was slow, but nicely appointed with mirrors. She strode to the apartment at the end of the hallway, following the faded carpet, seeking the right number for Moira Sweeney. When she reached the door she rang the buzzer. There was a noticeable silence, then the sound of laborious shuffling steps approaching the weighty door. Moira Sweeney peeped through the peephole. Kasey's held up her police ID. Moira Sweeney eyed it carefully.

"I'm Detective Cosgrove, Mrs. Sweeney. Kasey Cosgrove. May I come in to talk with you for a moment?" Moira unlocked three strong locks and bolts, then grunted as she opened the door wide. Kasey flinched as she crossed the threshold. A dank, musty smell assaulted her nostrils. The entry hall opened into a dim, cigarette smoke-filled living room cluttered with assorted bric-a-brac, and dark furnishings that were outdated and shabby.

"You can sit yourself down," she said with a throaty smoker's voice. Moira was a short, thin-haired, stout woman with a ruddy face, dressed in an old plaid robe, whose lit cigarette bounced between her thick lips as she spoke. The smell of alcohol was strong on every breath. She waved Kasey toward a threadbare couch, and unsteadily sat herself down on a recliner that faced a dusty flatscreen TV. Crammed ashtrays, empty glasses and abandoned liquor bottles scattered across several side tables.

"I'll stand if you don't mind."

"Suit yourself."

Kasey took a deep breath. "We received some new information regarding your daughter, Fiona."

Moira Sweeney sat, crossed her legs, and drew a deep drag on her cigarette. "Can't you let the poor child rest in peace? What kind of new information? She's gone."

"I'm so sorry, Mrs. Sweeney," said the detective, honestly regretful about what she was about to say. "Fiona, your daughter…The last report we received informed us that she was newly pregnant. Maybe about eight weeks."

"What? Pregnant? No, no."

"I take it that she didn't talk with you about it?"

The mother's rounded, baggy eyes grew disbelievingly wide. "How dare you imply my daughter didn't talk to me…" Then she became tearful, scratching her hands against her thick arms. "Is it true? Oh, my baby," she stuttered with surprised upset. "God in heaven, my baby was going to have a baby…"

"I'm sorry to have been the one to tell you. We thought it important, and of course you have the right to know."

Moira's lips quivered. She stubbed out her filtered cigarette harshly into an overflowing ashtray. Her cheeks visibly reddened as she began to grow angry. "And what are you doing about what happened to my little girl? Smearing her reputation when she can't defend herself? My daughter's dead. Killed by a damned bus, you all say. And you're doing what about it? You said you're a cop!"

"We're truly sorry for your loss, Mrs. Sweeney. It's an awful tragedy. And we're working hard to discover how it happened and—"

"Who's the damned father? Just tell me that much."

"We don't know yet."

"You don't know who the baby's father was?"

"Not yet, not at this time. We'll be looking into it."

"That's all you have to say? That's bullshit! Get the hell out of my house!" Moira Sweeney stood up abruptly, trembling from head to foot. Her arm shakily pointed to the front door. "You cops are worthless. Go. Get out!"

"We can try to help you, Mrs. Sweeney, but you have to work with us."

"Help me? Help me with what? A little too late for that, don't you think? Come on, get the hell out of my house."

Kasey put her card on the edge of the frayed coffee table. "Please call me if you change your mind. I would like to be helpful." Then she turned and walked to the door, closing it behind her as softly as she could. Despite the tirade, Detective Cosgrove felt sorry for Fiona's mother.

*

Cora was surprised to get Hunter's call so late in the day. "Hope this isn't a bad time at work," he said with a tinge of hesitation.

"No worries. What's up?"

"It's important for me to speak with Sara Sweeney. It won't take long. I assume she's still staying with you?"

"Most of this week, yes. But we're still finishing up, getting ready to close for tonight. Should I put her on the phone?"

"No, no. In person. It...It's something she should be told in person. Of course, you can be there, too."

It was evident that their recent scrap regarding her underworld connections was disturbing him. "Do you want to stop by for a few minutes now?"

"If it isn't going to keep you at the diner..."

"It's all right, Hunter. See you in how long?"

"I'll be there in just a few minutes."

"Okay, I'll unlock the front door."

She smiled when she saw his car pull up. "Come on in. We're not quite ready to mop." Behind her Stavros and a busboy were carrying water buckets and mops.

"Let's step outside."

Hunter followed as she and Sara moved under the awning.

The detective looked straight at Sara's eyes. "This isn't easy for me," he said. Cora stood ready to brace her young friend if needed. She had no guess as to what Hunter was about to say.

"I received news from the coroner's report just a while ago. We should have learned this before..."

"Please just tell me."

He nodded, placing a hand on her shoulder. "Your sister Fiona was pregnant."

It took long seconds for the gut-wrenching news to sink in. "No, it isn't possible. I mean, Fiona would have told me."

"It was an early pregnancy, Sara. Approximately seven, eight weeks. It's possible she didn't know it for sure herself."

Sara shook her head, refusing to believe. "You're wrong. It must be someone else mixed up in the report."

Hunter kept his gaze and voice steady. "No mistake, Sara. Please believe me."

Cora eyed Hunter and squeezed Sara's shoulder. "I think he knows what he's saying. This isn't something they'd get wrong."

Tears streamed down the young woman's face. As Cora hugged her tightly she whispered to Hunter, "Is it still possible to get DNA from the fetus? Find out who the father was?"

She was reading his own thoughts. Was the child Rob Perry's? Most likely. But if not…? "I'm on it. I've been having a few ideas of my own to check out."

"I'll take care of Sara," Cora said. "Go home, you look exhausted."

"I am. We'll talk soon." Within seconds he was back in his car and gone. Cora heaved a sigh. She had not yet said anything to Hunter regarding Rob Perry being back in the city, let alone sleeping now in her apartment.

Rob Perry was awake and sitting in the corner of the settee. He'd been tossing and turning on the small bed Cora had set up for him. Despite having not had much rest since returning to New York, his mind had been so jammed with feelings and memories of Fiona that no matter how tired he was, sleep didn't come. He looked up when he heard the key in the door, watched it jerk open. Sara came in visibly distraught and hurried into the bathroom. He turned toward Cora as she came inside. He had a quizzical look on his face.

"We've got to do some talking," Cora told him matter-of-factly.

"I've answered all the questions you've been asking…"

"And now there's a lot more." Cora rubbed at her tired eyes, puffing her cheeks, and blowing out the air. She sat down heavily on the couch opposite. The bottle of sparkling water on the coffee table was flat but she drank deeply from it, deciding the best way to tackle the latest news. They both heard the toilet flush several times in the bathroom, Sara coughing loudly and blowing her nose continuously. "Robbie, are you purposely avoiding telling me intimate details about you and Fiona? Personal stuff? Keeping anything hidden?"

"I've been completely honest with you about everything. I don't need to hide anything. I told you, Fiona was the only person in my life I could be myself with. She knew everything about me, my bad luck." He looked straight into Cora's eyes, then lowered his gaze to his clasped hands. His lanky frame leaned forward. "Ask anything you want. I keep telling you. What's happened has me sick. I offered you my help and I meant it. Right now I'm scared for my own life."

"This bookie who always lets you owe money, what's his name again?"

"Troy Finley, he's called. An older guy who furnishes the odds. He's well known in the betting world. Mostly deals with upscale types. Bigger bets, high rollers, regulars. He's been taking bets for a long time. Has lots of clients…"

"But he took you on."

"I keep saying, he only took me on because of a couple of my poker buddies."

"And who are his people who come to collect?"

"They come and go. One I've encountered is called Marcus, he's muscle. Another is this smaller guy, Leo. Tattoos all over. Big threats, scary. A third I've encountered is known as Melissa. She handles smaller amounts, women gamblers. I told you this. I don't know if any of their names are real or what. It doesn't matter. They work for Troy. Collect for him. None of us players know who backs Troy with the money. Maybe it's drug money, maybe anything. But I already said, most of my real losses came from playing poker. If I want to bet a game, he's there."

"We'll go over that. Your games are with familiar players?"

The sound of Sara vomiting caught both Cora and Robbie's attention. "She okay?"

"She will be. The news upset her terribly. It upset us both."

"What news?" Robbie looked concerned, apprehensive.

In a low monotone, Cora said flatly, candidly, "We found out Fiona was pregnant. But then you knew that. She did tell you, didn't she?"

He stared, frozen, eyebrows raised high. "She *what*?"

"Come on, don't say you didn't know" Cora purposely spoke in a casual, routine way, acting as though Fiona's condition was common knowledge.

Robbie shook his head vehemently. "I…I had no idea. She never said a word."

Cora leaned forward, looking directly into his eyes. "Before you ran out on her, fled New York for your safety, you're telling me you had no idea? Fiona never told you, said anything?"

"Not a thing. I swear." There was a slight stammer in his voice. "We'd been fighting lately. Arguing every time I showed up. She was really pissed at me. You know that. I'd been playing a lot, losing, borrowing wherever I could. She said she couldn't deal with it anymore—couldn't deal with me. That I should take my things and leave, that I was hardly there anymore, anyway. She was crying and shouting. I was concerned she'd go back to drinking and I didn't want that to happen. She didn't deserve that old life. She'd worked so hard to overcome so much."

"But you hadn't moved out, right? You had keys to Fiona's apartment. You still lived together."

"Keys, sure, but I was gone so much. The only reason I came back before leaving New York was to warn her. Tell her to be careful, keep her safe. Tell her some goons may come looking for me, and I didn't want her involved in my mess. I didn't want them to know where I could be found. Who knows what these crazy fuckers could do? I was flat broke and being threatened by Troy. He told me I was out of time and out of luck. Twenty-four hours was my limit to pay up my losses. Period."

"So you were frightened of this guy Troy, what he might do, but not concerned about the woman you say you loved?"

"I did love Fiona. I still do." He voice was compelling and adamant. "And of course I was concerned. She was the only one who ever believed in me, didn't judge me. I could openly spill my guts and not be blamed. Before her the others didn't want to know me, they threw me out, tossed me aside and treated me like a leper. Fiona, she *understood*. Really understood, I mean. She'd talk for hours about her own story, how she struggled so hard to overcome alcohol, and not become like her mother. Stopping drug use, and slowly climbing back on her feet despite setbacks. She attended AA meetings, kept in touch with her sponsor daily, and eventually managed to clean herself up. Sara can vouch for what I'm saying. I was so proud of Fiona. And when I came home after an all-night game, broke and in debt, I cried and she'd hold me, trying to soothe me with her acquired strength. God, how she tried to give me confidence in myself. No one ever did that before. You don't know how good she was to me, you'll never know."

"And you repaid her by running away." Cora remained cold, goading him.

"I tried to keep her protected" he protested. "Inform her what was going on with the people I owed, cautioned her to be careful with phone calls, answering the door, looking out for strangers at work coming and asking about me. Before I had to leave I even offered to take her with me if she wanted. Come to North Carolina. She said no. She couldn't just pick up and leave like that. Her job, her art school, her new life." Robbie sniffed, his voice suddenly cracking. "She got her handbag and gave me all the cash she had. Tips, salary from her job. I didn't have enough to pay a bus ticket. She was angry, sure, but she still wanted to protect me, no matter how pissed she got. Keep me safe. Oh God, a baby?" He buried his head in his hands.

Sara had come out of the bathroom and was standing there, looking, and listening. "So you fucked her, got her pregnant and now you're sorry? Sorry for what? That she can't hand you any more money?"

"You don't know anything about the bond we had," he said, looking up.

"I know my beautiful sister is dead. I know she was carrying your kid."

"Fiona…" He took a deep breath. "Fiona and I weren't having much sex for a while. She was really turned off lately. Refusing to sleep with me. I never forced her, ever. That's the truth."

"So when was the last time you had sex with her?" Cora asked frankly.

He hunched his shoulders. "I…I'm not sure exactly. It's probably a couple of months more or less…"

"So you still could be the father."

He shrugged. "I suppose so. Yes, I could be."

"Trying to throw that blame on someone else, Robbie?" cried Sara, infuriated. "Poor Robbie. Can't help himself. Can't control his betting impulses. Excuses for everything, huh?"

"No Sara, of course not. I only meant—"

"Stop this both of you," Cora demanded. "Your arguing gets us nowhere. And your sex life doesn't interest me in the least, Robbie. We just need to figure out a timeline. So, tell me again, you did sleep with Fiona sometime in the couple of months?"

"In the past couple of months, yes." He looked away, reluctant to continually discuss his intimacy.

Cora looked over at Sara. "Come and take a seat. Let Robbie explain his side of how things got so out of control."

He fought stuttering again. "I...I keep saying how much I appreciated Fiona. I know I'm the kid's father, I accept that. But what does this matter now?" His face appeared distressed and contrite. He was expressing himself with genuine sincerity, Cora judged as she turned to Sara. "What do you say?"

Sara looked away, biting her lower, quivering lip. "There is something I just thought of," she finally said in a quieter tone. "A few weeks back Fiona did reluctantly mention something about her boss. The owner of the fancy place where she's been working. Her boss. His name is Enzo."

"I know who Enzo is," said Cora. "Enzo D'Amico. He's a member of the chamber of commerce for Kew Gardens and Forest

Hills. I've seen him a few times. He's been negotiating expanding his place and was asking me a few things regarding the Athena."

Sara looked glum. "Yeah, him. This guy, Enzo. He…he's been harassing Fiona. You know, touching her when and where he shouldn't, making a few no-so-quiet advances when others weren't in sight. She refused of course, but she told me he wouldn't stop. I think she wanted to quit, but this wasn't a good time. Enzo's a game player, a sleaze who already has a family."

"A large family," Cora added. "Are you sure it was him bothering her?"

Sara nodded. "Positive. He hinted at a promotion, special favors, making more money. But she wasn't going to play along. She wasn't looking for trouble."

"Did you know anything about this, Robbie?"

"Not a thing. She never said a word." He was unmistakably upset.

"She wouldn't have told him," said Sara. "She knows how angry and out of control Robbie can get."

Robbie shifted restlessly, surprised, and clearly not wanting to listen to what he was hearing. Cora quickly switched the topic. "Going back to the trouble you're in now, what were you planning to do about it?"

"Look, I can get some of the money I owe. My mother gave me her word. She knows about my debts, and why I had to get away, go down to Raleigh, and remain out of sight."

"Leaving my sister alone, and—"

Cora cut her off. "This isn't getting us anywhere," she said. "Right now we're on the same side. We need answers to what happened. What I need from you are names. Real names of people you deal with. All of them. And I especially need to find out what you know about Troy's goons, the ones who do his collecting. Write down the phone numbers for your bookies and other gambling contacts. Make me a list, text it all to my phone. And also include all your so-called buddies you play poker with on a regular basis. We need to narrow things down. Get answers and solutions."

"Are you planning to go after them or something?" he asked dubiously.

Cora regarded him coolly. "No, not me, Robbie. *You* are."

"What? These guys are dangerous! You think you or me can sit down and deal with them? You have no idea…"

"No, Robbie. *You* have no idea. The police are investigating this whole damn thing already, understand?"

"Why? Why?" He was shaken by Cora's steely look and relentless questioning.

"Her death is an open question. It's looking less like an accident and more possible she might have been pushed."

His jaw dropped. His moved his head sideways, glancing from Cora to Sara. His mouth opened but he had no words.

"What we don't want is to jump to conclusions," Cora said. "But it is possible someone wanted to send a message…"

"What kind of a message?"

"Using Fiona as a pawn because you couldn't be located. Possibly teaching a lesson originally meant to frighten *you*."

"Frighten me by pushing Fiona into a bus?"

"They couldn't find you, right? You disappeared off the face of the earth owing big money. Fifty thousand? Your bookie friends knew you had a girlfriend. Knew who she was and that you'd likely been staying with her. She was already implicated whether you admit it or not. What better way to convey a message to you?"

Robbie dropped his head, slumped with his hands between his legs. He suddenly appeared pale and disheveled, all traces of charm and bravado vanished. He was scared. Fearful like never before. Conflicting scenarios of what might have happened danced through his thoughts. "The baby has to me mine," he muttered.

"Listen to me, Robbie," Cora said, regaining his attention. He looked up.

"We can find out exactly what went on and then deal with it. Learn the facts. The coroner's report is inconclusive, but my police contacts believe this was likely a purposeful act. If you're not the father of Fiona's child, DNA will tell us. Which opens up another possibility. Maybe Fiona confronted the real father who worried that concerned that she might expose him. A sleaze like this Enzo D'Amato might have wanted to scare or harm her, or maybe try to strong-arm her into getting an abortion. Maybe he or someone close to him played a part, concerned she might decide to go public. Humiliate him. Or even blackmail him."

"You think Fiona would actually blackmail this pig?"

"I'm only speculating on possibilities. Again, if we can get the child's DNA that will eliminate some questions." Robbie winced the word 'child.'

On the other hand," Cora continued, "There's still a good chance that one of Troy's collectors was following her, planning to teach you a lesson, Robbie. Show if they can't reach you they can reach those close to you."

"By killing her?"

"They may not have planned it that way. The weather was horrible that morning, roads slippery because of the rain and high gusts of winds."

Fearful eyes looked at Cora. "It was an accidental murder?"

"I'm not saying that. We don't know anything for sure. But we're going to find out." Cora's voice was flat and matter of fact. She tilted her head slightly. "So as I said, we need names from you, Mr. Perry. Now. Can we count on you or not?"

He didn't hesitate. "Of course I'll help. I want to. You have my word."

"All right. Now let's get to work."

ELEVEN

Dawn in an urban environment is a patchwork quilt of light and foggy shadow. The tops of tall buildings light up first. In the faint reflection of that light, Eddie and Claude met to prepare for the early morning deliveries. Beyond grunts of greeting, no words were necessary; each knew the steps to this routine perfectly. Claude pulled out the keys to unlock the kitchen back door.

"Ah, fuck!" he yelled. Eddie quickly raced over.

"What? What happened?"

Claude pointed. Eddie stared at the door, and felt a sickly sensation overtake him. Hanging from the doorknob was a large dead rat. A foul-smelling, bedraggled brown sewer rat strangled with an electric cord. Both men struggled against the impulses to vomit.

With a shaky hand, Eddie phoned Cora. From the sound of her voice Eddie could tell she had been fast asleep.

"We got trouble, Mrs. Gus. Bad stuff."

"What's happened?"

"There's a dead rat hanging from the outside kitchen door. It's been strangled. Do you want me to call the cops?"

Cora struggled to pull her thoughts together. Could this be simple vandalism? Unlikely. The tactic smacked of gangster TV shows and movies. Should she inform Hunter? And what about the due deliveries?

She pulled herself to sit at the side of the bed. "Don't do anything yet, Eddie. If a delivery comes, try to unload the truck by the curb, out of sight of the kitchen door. If you have to, tell the driver that we're having some door problems and the locksmith is on the way. Hang tight, Eddie. I'll be there in 10 minutes."

She parked her car to block the view of the view of the kitchen door. Eddie and Claude were busily helping a driver's helper unload a delivery of fresh beef. Steeling herself, she walked around her car to examine the damage. When she saw the hanging rat slowly twisting in a breeze she struggled to suppress a queasy mixture of fear and disgust. This wasn't the work of teenage vandals. It was an intimidating threat. Time to call Solerno.

Cora and Solerno met at a vegetarian Chinese restaurant on the boulevard a day later. Solerno had been placed on a heart-healthy diet by his doctor, much to his disgust. The restaurant chef had promised him a low salt version of their traditional menu. Solerno was now a regular. Cora was unfamiliar with the hole in the wall eatery, and she looked around with professional interest. Hanging red paper lanterns, travel posters, and a chalk board for a menu. The specials were listed in Chinese characters and English. The cooler was full of unrecognizable drink cans and bottles. In spite of her anxiety, the place piqued her interest.

For a few minutes, they focused on their cups of soup. Cora politely inquired about his family's health, and they discussed a political race. But Cora was too anxious to discover what, if anything, Solerno had learned about the incident with the rat to waste much time on small talk. Solerno chuckled at her impatience and got down to business.

He sipped at his tea and covered his mouth when he belched. "You're right to be taking this seriously. I already warned you that people gunning for your business are dangerous, and this episode tells me they're escalating. Getting impatient."

"Do you have any idea who's behind this yet?"

"I may." He leaned forward, darting his eyes to be sure no one was close was paying attention. "Here's what I think is going on. Several years ago, the FBI and an alphabet soup of national and international agencies decided to go big time after a consortium of technocrat top bosses found working out of Brighton Beach, Sheepshead Bay, and Coney Island. Syndicates with fast-growing operations. Their business was dealing in cash currencies, and they weren't a hedge fund. They liked to use fancy words like management and public relations in overnight worldwide dealings. A tough bunch to go after."

"What was the result?"

"The feds succeeded somewhat in breaking it up. Some at the top were caught, others disappeared with international warrants still out for their arrest. A couple of their people went to trial. Conspiracy to commit every crime under the sun and surprisingly some of them stuck. A few got time, but others were found not guilty because of a lack of evidence. So, the syndicate pie got cut up into smaller pieces. What's remaining is a mixed bunch thick with expatriate Russian tattooed racketeers, money launderers, heroin traffickers, extortionists, suspected gangland murderers. They'll even do low-level loansharking and gambling if it's worth their time. The names at the top running the operation now are mostly East European types. Maybe throw in a few South Americans who can't go back to their former associates."

"Sure you didn't leave anything out?" Cora said with sarcasm. "Haven't the feds come after these people too?"

"Sure. There have been some arrests, and probably countless ongoing extradition charges. Just try to find those wanted, let alone prove it in court." Solerno paused to let it all sink in. Cora sipped at her tea, aware of what she was facing.

"Look, some of these people are sophisticated, cosmopolitan, rich, and smart. Their hands still remain in everything from Wall Street to international currency manipulation, as well as crypto currency fraud. Even a couple of health insurance companies were investigated for fraud on one end, and on the lower end embezzling to old-fashioned hustling drugs. If they take over a gas station they can skim gasoline taxes. Occasionally a few of these people approach working with the established Five Families. Mostly though, the mafia has kept away, preferring to remain low profile. But if the money gets big enough someday, who can say? Look, you don't need to hear all this crap. These bloodsuckers are all over the place, that's the bottom line."

Cora sighed and made a sour face. "So where does all this leave me?"

"First, keep in mind that those going after you are probably lower-level types looking to likely fast-track some laundered European or Middle Eastern money. These people aren't international big bosses who could take you out like that." He snapped his fingers. "That leaves you with the choices you already know. Take their offer, or—"

"Or clash with this specific crew playing me," she offered.

Solerno tried to hide the slightest of smiles. She understood well. He wiped his mouth with a napkin. A gold tooth glinted slightly. "Yeah. These are independents, breakaways, seeking to penetrate new territory. I'll tell you this much: no genuine godfather would risk rotting in prison over a neighborhood diner. Those bosses collect their slice no matter what. But don't for a minute underestimate the damage some ruthless underlings can do."

"Right. I get it. Do you have some names of who I'm dealing with? You do know who these subordinates are, don't you?"

"I know of one, somebody recently buying up retail businesses in Queens and Brooklyn. Decent money, take it or leave it. Also lately there's been a spate of other suspicious fires that put a few good people out of business, and a couple more mysteriously run down by cars while walking dogs or crossing a street after dark. Those small business owners bolted New York, too."

"You're telling me I'm in danger?"

"I'm telling you these are bad people. If you've decided to tackle them, you gotta be prepared."

"Any suggestions?"

"Gotta cover your ass. Beef up staff security. Harden the diner's protection with new CCTV cameras all over. You'll be getting another call from these people soon enough. They'll be eager to see if the hanging rat made enough of an impression. They're gonna keep the threats coming until they get their way."

Softly, Cora said, "I keep a licensed gun."

"Good. Have it handy. How about that strong Greek kid you hired?"

"Stavros."

"He trustworthy? Someone who can back you up, rely on?"

She nodded. "I do. He's already helping me with another matter."

"I see. Still playing detective, huh? Okay. Tell him the score cause he deserves to know what you're up against. Double his pay if he's willing to take risks. Keep him close enough so they'll assume he's personal security."

"And when they phone me?"

"Minimum words can have maximum impact. When they call, be willing to set up a meeting. Let them believe you're worried, scared enough to deal. Listen to any offer and say as little as possible. Don't go to meet anyone someplace they suggest. Agree on somewhere neutral, public." Here Solerno tensed, tightened his gaze, and scrutinized his companion, speaking with an aggrieved expression.

"And you keep your cop friends away, right? That especially includes your detective friend. Involving them will complicate things, not help. My contacts will about-face. So be careful. Meanwhile, I'll do whatever I can from my end. No guarantees though, understood?"

"Understood."

"I gave you my word and I keep it. So, now you can get outta this eyesore and let me enjoy my lunch in peace."

She pushed herself away from the table and got up, taking a few fried noodles from a bowl. "Thanks, Solerno. You know how much I appreciate—"

"Just stay careful, Cora. Hear me? They're gonna squeeze you hard. Keep your eyes open, and your head clear."

TWELVE

Cora studied the men on ladders installing new state-of-the-art CCTV cameras. Customer service was appallingly disrupted inside the diner, but today it couldn't be avoided. Camera image sensors would now cover virtually every inch outside, from the small parking area on the north side, covering the front, back, and vulnerable alleyway.

Onlookers from nearby shops and passersby stared at the ongoing work. The day was grey and chilly, and Cora reflected how the gloomy weather matched her mood. Back at her apartment Stavros was busy keeping an eye on Rob Perry as he communicated with people to whom he owed money, claiming he was returning to New York in another few days, and enquiring who would be collecting his debt. Meanwhile, she found herself also tensely waiting for the call Solerno predicted, mindful of its potential repercussions. As she watched the technicians finish up the cameras her mind was racing with questions about how she might effectively deal with these dodgy people, and she wondered if her own defenses would be good enough to deter them. The thought of her not sharing what she had learned from Solerno with Hunter nagged profoundly. Was it a mistake promising she wouldn't tell the police of the formidable danger she was in? Was she as capable and self-reliant as she assumed or was this pending threat far greater than she supposed?

"Good morning, Mrs. Gus."

Cora looked down from the top of the entrance steps. "Morning Allison. Everything good with you?"

"I'm fine, thank you. Any particular instructions for me today, Mrs. Gus?" The youthful, bright-eyed freckled waitress held an umbrella under one arm and a book in her hand. A shoulder bag was slung low over her shoulder. A graceful recent hire, Cora had high hopes for mannered Allison speedily becoming a valuable addition.

"Just be prepared for some irritating disruptions. They'll be finished soon enough. Eddie will assign your tables and help out with any questions."

Allison nodded with an upbeat smile, viewed the new camera staring from high above the entrance, lowered her eyes, and walked inside. Needing to do some work herself, Cora followed. She had to stay focused, put her qualms and suspicions aside for the moment.

Cora studied the men on ladders installing new state-of-the-art CCTV cameras. The shrill sound of drills, banging hammers and yelling workmen drove most customers to take out their meals or eat elsewhere. Today's disruption couldn't be avoided. Camera image sensors would now cover virtually every inch outside, from the small parking area on the north side, to covering the front, back, and vulnerable alleyway. Smart locks with passcodes and fingerprint IDs were set to be installed tomorrow.

Onlookers from nearby shops and passersby stared at the diligent ongoing labor. The day was grey and chilly, cool for spring, and Cora reflected that the gloomy weather matched her disposition. Back at her apartment Stavros was busy keeping an eye on Rob Perry as he communicated with people to whom he owed money and markers, claiming he was returning to New York in a few days, and enquiring who would be collecting his debt. Meanwhile, she found herself also tensely waiting for the call Solerno predicted, mindful of its potential repercussions. As she watched the technicians finish up the cameras her mind was flooded with questions about how she might effectively deal with these dangerous people. She wondered if her own defenses would be good enough to deter them. The thought that she hadn't shared Solerno's information with Hunter nagged profoundly. She knew Hunter would feel hurt and betrayed by her silence if he learned about it. And had it been a mistake to promise that she wouldn't tell the police of the formidable danger she was in? Was she as capable and self-reliant as she assumed or was this pending threat far greater than she supposed?

"Good afternoon, Mrs. Gus."

Cora looked down from the top of the entrance steps. "Morning Allison. Everything good?"

"I'm fine, thank you. Any particular instructions for me today?" The young, bright-eyed waitress held a furled umbrella under her arm and a book in her hand. A leather bag was slung low over her shoulder. She looked curiously at the frenetic activity around the diner.

"Just be prepared for a little disruption. Eddie will assign your tables and help with any problems."

Allison nodded, viewing the newly installed camera staring from high above the entrance, smiled, and walked inside. Cora soon followed. She needed to clear her head, put her qualms aside, and focus on the moment.

The lunch crowd was handled better than expected. Once again asking Eddie to cover, Cora decided to pay a brief visit to La Luna, the posh dining restaurant owned and run by Enzo D'Amico and his wife. She crossed Jamaica Avenue just as the screeching El train came to a stop at the nearby station. Riders dressed in drab coats ran down the high staircases and swiftly scattered. The ambient chill made her bury her hands deeply in her pockets and turn up her jacket collar.

It was a ten-block stroll from the Athena when she saw the sign. The façade of Enzo's La Luna wasn't fancy, given the limitations of the attached buildings on either side. It initially struck her as cozy and unpretentious. From the dark front window Cora could make out white linen tablecloths and elaborately folded cloth napkins on the tables as she entered its impressive entrance. The restaurant was preparing to open, LED dim lighting flowed from above, creating an inviting mood. She was quickly greeted by a young woman hostess. "Hi, I'm sorry but we're not open for another half hour. Would you like to take a seat in our waiting area?"

"Sure," Cora answered. The hostess turned to lead her toward a shallow area furnished with a small, cushioned bench and picturesque murals on the walls.

Nearby, Enzo was busy in conversation. He glanced over at the newcomer with surprise and smiled widely. "Cora Drakos!" he exclaimed, holding off his discussion with the employee. He hurried over with an outstretched hand. "What brings you to our little establishment?" he asked, eyes looking straight into Cora's.

Cora studied Enzo with new eyes, evaluating him now as a woman rather than a business colleague. He was nearly a half head shorter than she, with too-shiny thinning black hair and a receding hairline. His features were even and symmetrical, though the tanned skin on his face was visibly beginning to sag. There were several thick gold rings on his fingers, Cora noticed. Dressed in an expensive dark suit, light blue shirt, and dark blue tie, he gave a successful appearance despite his burgeoning beer belly. Black well-shined shoes completed the picture of a middle-aged lothario who seemed unlikely to appeal to twenty-something Fiona. Especially considering how she had found unconventional, almost bohemian Robbie to be her primary choice in men.

Enzo bustled with joy at his unexpected visitor. He squeezed Cora's hand, looking over at his hostess with displeasure. "You should have called me right away, Denise."

Denise cast her gaze downward. "Sorry, Mr. D'Amico. I was just about to."

"Well, never mind." Denise slipped back to the hostess station. "Welcome, Cora. How lovely to see you again. To what do we owe the honor?"

"Nice to see you again also, Enzo. I didn't mean to intrude. Forgive me for not phoning first. Mainly I came today to offer condolences regarding Fiona Sweeney's death."

"Oh, dear God. Poor, poor child." He made the sign of the cross. "Thank you for that. She is sorely missed by all of us," he added as an afterthought, "May her beautiful soul rest in eternal peace."

"Amen," said Cora, not changing her expression.

"Come, come sit down." He pointed to a quiet quality teak table far from the kitchen where the chef and line cooks were vigorously preparing. A busboy hurriedly set napkins and cutlery at their places.

"Sit, please, Ms. Drakos. Allow me to serve to you a cup of our finest Italian coffee. And let it prove for once and for all that Italian coffee is better than Greek coffee." His eyes danced with humor.

Cora laughed lightly and agreed to the test he proposed. Enzo held out her chair in a polite gentlemanly fashion. They settled and were silent as a pitcher of fresh ice water was brought while waiting for the coffee.

"I heard about that bad dumpster fire at the Athena," Enzo said with a scowl. "Vicious bastards. These loitering punks need to be taught a good lesson, eh? Back in my hometown of Genoa, and yours of Athens, these things wouldn't happen, would they? If our own people didn't beat them half to death the police would do it for us. I am so sorry to have learned this. Anything you need or want, please ask. I'll accommodate. Consider me your friend. After all we are rivals in business, no?" He winked.

"Thank you, Enzo. I appreciate the offer, and I'll keep it in mind."

The coffee arrived, hot and fragrant. A dark roast Arabica, its quality indicative of how La Luna gained its reputation. The busboy carefully served them both. "Cream or sugar, ma'am?"

She shook her head. "Black is fine, thank you."

Enzo said with pride and self-satisfaction, "You'll taste a delicate note of caramel blended with orange blossom. Considered the finest of any medium roast."

"I can tell it's superb. Kudos, Mr. D'Amico."

He gleamed, and they sipped and exchanged a few more pleasantries. Then Cora abruptly said, "Back to why I came. I think you're aware that Fiona's sister Sara Sweeney works for me. Needless to tell you, she's shattered. I've been caring for her while her husband is working upstate. I'm sure you realize how the family is devastated."

"I can well imagine." He spoke softly, setting his jaw.

"So, the family asked me to come by and talk to you, perhaps also some of your staff. We have some questions about Fiona's state of mind lately, and what was going on in her life during the final weeks before she passed. You do understand?"

Enzo listened and nodded. "Of course I understand. Allow me to help if I can."

"Again, thank you. A few things have cropped up these past couple of days. Just unanswered questions we can't quite answer. We want…The bottom line is we need to rule out any chance of foul play."

"Foul play?" he repeated. "I thought she died in an accident?" Enzo's voice rose in query, his brows turning down inquisitively.

"Yes, she was hit by a bus, thrown. All of it happened so fast during that horrible storm. The family is trying to learn more about what might have been going on in her life over the last few weeks, maybe keeping her distracted that day. Is there someplace where I can talk to you and your people more privately?"

"Certainly. Come into my office." Looking somber and concerned, Enzo led Cora down past the well-stocked quartz countertop bar to a wide, decorated door. As he opened it, Cora saw a well-groomed woman dressed to hide middle-aged spread sitting behind a hefty desk in front of a large-screen computer. Her dark blonde hair was frosted and newly blown out, contrasting with her tanned tight facial skin hiding a few wrinkles and a mole on one cheek. Her nails were acrylic and so long that Cora wondered how she managed to accurately use the keyboard.

"Ah, Vera, I almost forgot you were working today. Cora, let me introduce you to my wife Vera, who we couldn't live without. She's our chief bookkeeper for sales, payroll, expenses. The whole enchilada. She's amazing. You of all people know how complicated running a restaurant is. We couldn't survive without our Vera." He kissed his wife briefly on the lips. "I believe the two of you met once briefly at some Chamber of Commerce annual. Vera, let me introduce the well-regarded Cora Drakos, known to most as Mrs. Gus, the owner of the popular Athena Diner."

Vera D'Angelo looked Cora up and down, as though she were evaluating her like a pedigreed dog for sale, or perhaps an upcoming potential rival. Apparently, Cora passed muster because Vera stood up, smiled fully, and held out a hand to shake. "A pleasure, to see you again, Ms. Drakos."

"Likewise, Ms. D'Amico."

Enzo swiftly explained the purpose of her visit today. "Oh, is that right?" Vera visibly stiffened, mistrustful that La Luna might somehow be blamed for something. "Yes, a horrible, horrible tragedy."

"It certainly was an awful shock. I'm only here to ask a few things of importance to the Sweeney family during their time of grief."

"Yes, a terrible situation for any family to be in. The police have already been here several times," Vera informed, tapping her pudgy fingers on the edge of the keyboard. "They were very thorough with their questioning. And very polite. I believe they spoke with every single employee we have. Enzo and I readily gave as much information as we could. Detective Hunter was such a gentleman. And his assistant, Kasey, I think her name is, was efficient and thoughtful. They were most tactful with our staff. Very professional."

Cora was well aware of police investigative tactics. "They're good people. I know them, too. But please bear with me. I'm here strictly for Sara's sake. And especially the mother…"

Enzo and his wife shared a look at the mention of Fiona's mother.

"Did Fiona seem unusually happy or unhappy in the days or weeks prior to her death? Did she ever discuss boyfriends, family, or something at her school? Anything in particular you might recall?"

"Such a gifted girl," Enzo said. "I've seen some of her art. She would bring in her portfolio sometimes. I promised I'd hang up one of her paintings in the dining salon. She was talented, but I really I knew so little about her personal life. She was a good worker. Always willing to fill in when needed. And loyal. Such a misfortune, no one deserves something like this. I will miss her. We all will."

"The poor girl had her whole life in front of her," Vera D'Amico added.

"She never seemed unusually upset or worried about anything?" Cora asked. "Did she ever talk to you or others about her boyfriend? They'd been together on and off, and I was told there were some problems lately. Frictions."

Enzo averted his eyes from his wife's stare, clicking a pen on his desk. "I only know he treated her badly. Sometimes she cried about it. He hurt her. A loser if there ever was one. A gambler. But she loved that son of a bitch, no matter what." He shrugged, continuing to click his pen. Vera sat impassive, as if she were totally unaware of any of this and didn't care one way or the other.

After a few minutes of casual banter Cora had enough. She wasn't going to learn anything further from Mr. and Mrs. D'Amico. "Thank you both for sharing your observations. You've been helpful." She peered at Enzo and the old-fashioned clock on the wall. "I know how crazy your place is going to get in a few minutes, so I'll be leaving. But would you mind if I asked a few of your staff about their knowledge of Fiona? I won't take long. Would that be okay?"

Enzo looked at his watch. "Sure, Cora. But please, we're almost ready to open." He turned to his wife. "Let's let her use the cloakroom for a few minutes?"

Vera D'Amico agreed. "Why not take a seat up front? Enzo, why don't you send Veronica Labrano over to see her. I think that girl was a friend and talked to Fiona often. They shared shifts, often covering for each other. Perhaps Veronica might be able to provide you with better details than we can." At that she looked away and returned to her computer screen.

"My wife keeps so busy with her eagle eye, checking everything twice and points out any issues. Where we've overspent. Splurged. Left out. She's a good accountant." He almost seemed embarrassed as he gave Cora that tidbit.

The cloakroom was right at the front, left of the entrance, not within earshot of the private office where Enzo and his wife might be continuing the conversation between themselves. They were so closed mouthed at this point Cora figured she was pretty much wasting her time, but since she was already here she'd give it a shot. Again she thanked the owner profusely, shaking Enzo's hand as he led her to the dim hallway. "Don't be a stranger, Mrs. Gus," he said with a grin, his eyes now glancing at Cora up and down, admiring her nice feminine shape.

Cora lifted her head and smiled. "Please come visit us at the diner. Let's see how good my Greek coffee compares. Then we'll vote to see who won." She winked and Enzo laughed heartily.

"You have my word, Cora. If I can be of more help in anything..."

She waved and turned, saying, "I'll only take a few minutes at the cloakroom. Thank you again."

Enzo D'Amico signaled to one of his waitresses. As Cora passed the tables to reach the front she barely notice the freckled brunette dressed in her black uniform following behind. There was a cushioned chair in the cloakroom, but Cora pushed it aside. The waitress was quick to slip inside, stand beside the thick rack of empty hangers.

"Hi, Mrs. Gus. I'm Veronica Labrano. I was asked to speak with you."

"A pleasure to meet you, Veronica." The room was diminutive, the air close, the women standing practically face to face. "I'm told you were a friend of Fiona."

"Oh. You're here about Fiona?" Her blue eyes widened, wide and attractive, body nicely curved in all the right places. Cora easily pictured Veronica as someone a man like Enzo would zealously hit on.

"Yeah. It a hard time for everyone, I know. I'm trying to learn how Fiona had been acting during those days leading up to her accident. To find out if anything was wrong. I mean, was she being her normal self or acting unusually upset about things happening in her life?"

Veronica appeared anxious and averse. "I still can't believe what's happened," she murmured in a low voice. "It was devastating to all of us. Awful. Horrible and frightening. And especially now. Not when…"

"Not when *what*?" Cora repeated in a whisper, putting a hand to the waitress's shoulder. "You can trust me. Please, be frank, be straightforward with me. No need to be frightened of anything. Look, I'm working together with Sara Sweeney, Fiona's sister. Searching to learn what was happening. I would like for you to tell me what was going on in Fiona's life those preceding days. We're trying to learn all we can. Put the pieces together. Gather any and all information, intent on learning the truth."

The attractive woman wiped her nose as she sniffed. "I've met Sara Sweeney, yes. Several times. Oh lord, I can't imagine how broken up she must be. Especially now, when…" She wavered in her sentence. "You did know, right? I mean, you *do* know…"

"Know what? Are you talking about the baby?"

Veronica nodded. "Yes." She was holding back tears and glanced outside the tight coatroom into the dimly lit waiting lounge. A few diners arrived for an early supper and sat waiting on the tufted entryway bench.

"I know you can't talk freely now," Cora said hastily. "Listen," she pulled a small notepad from her pocketbook and scribbled a number. "Call me after your shift, okay? I don't care how late. Sara told me some things regarding Enzo I need to learn about. We can meet somewhere to talk without worry of any prying eyes, I promise."

Veronica nodded without speaking, and Cora squeezed her arm briefly. "Believe me, Veronica. You'll find me to be a reliable friend. You don't have to be nervous that I'll gossip about you or Fiona or anyone who works here." Then with a small smile she hurried out, repeating, "Call me."

On the way back to the Athena her phone rang. It was Rob Perry.

"I've been making calls all day," he began in a hurry. "I finally did get ahold of Troy Finlay. He's fucking furious. Didn't even want to hear me out. He says he can have every bone in my body broken if he wants. His flunky Marcus has been looking for me for days, he said. That tough, muscular joker, the dirtbag strongarm I told you about. Troy didn't admit anything about Marcus going to Fiona's apartment, but he hinted it was an option. He was about to make more threats when I told him I got the money I owe him. Some of it, anyway, in jewelry. That I'd be back in New York in forty-eight hours. He didn't believe me, but I think I convinced him when I said I stole these jewels off my mother. Gold bracelets, diamond ring and more. That seemed to mollify him for the moment. I've stolen stuff to pay up before, he knows. We set up a place to meet…"

Of all Robbie's gambling contacts this bookie Troy seemed to play the most important role. "This Troy has no idea of your location now, right?"

"Of course not! As far as he's concerned I'm likely still hiding out in North Carolina."

"Stay put, hear me? We don't want you spotted on the street. I have to return to the diner to meet with someone later. Is Sara with you now?"

"Don't worry about that. She's standing over me like a hawk this very minute. If looks could kill I'd be dead." Cora heard Sara agree in the background.

"Good. Believe me if you try playing games, Robbie, I'll kill you myself."

"I won't leave the house, Mrs. Gus. My word."

*

Cora received the anticipated call from Veronica that night. They arranged their meeting at the library on Lefferts Boulevard, a location halfway between the Athena and La Luna. The library was full of life with a mixture of students and local seniors using the rows of available computers and reference books. When Cora arrived she quickly saw Veronica browsing the racks of new books near the front. Out of uniform of white shirt and black slacks, she was wearing faded tight jeans, a rich grey pullover sweater, and black high-heeled boots. With her hair still pulled back in a ponytail and her pocketbook slung over her shoulder, she appeared quite attractive. Several men seated at various tables ostensibly occupied with newspapers were adroitly giving her the eye.

Motioning to Veronica, Cora made her way to an isolated table near the back. It was piled high with a jumble of books and technology magazine. Veronica delicately took a chair and placed her pocketbook on her lap.

"Thank you for meeting me so soon," Cora said. "I appreciate it."

"No problem, Mrs. Gus. I'm glad to do it. Enzo knew you wanted to talk to me, so he let me out early. La Luna is usually quiet midweek nights and there's enough staff to cover." She smiled. "So here I am, ready to answer any of your questions."

"So, as I was explaining, Sara Sweeney asked me to help out with the investigation of what happened, and how things happened. I heard you were a friend of Fiona, as well as a co-worker at La Luna. I'd like to get to know what life was like during these last few weeks for Fiona. If anything unusual was taking place, how was her state of mind, those kinds of things. Will you try to help me out, Veronica? Please."

"Of course I will, Mrs. Gus. I've heard a good deal about you. Fiona said her sister often talked about you. Bragged what a great boss you were in comparison. So, I'll do whatever I can. Ask away."

Cora initiated slowly, hoping to have Veronica talking in her own way, from her own point of view. "These were tough times going on," Veronica began. "I'm sure you're aware that Fiona was under all kinds of unpleasant pressure. She usually kept pretty cool, able to take things in stride, ya know? She was good that way. She'd been through so much with her own drug and alcohol issues and fought like hell to get out of that mess and regain herself. It's no cinch for anyone, but she did it. I saw her pull her weight at La Luna as good as anyone. Better even. She was serious, always ready to fill in when needed, and to me always trying to be a friend despite all the craziness I have to deal with in my own life."

"And what about Fiona's private life? Outside of La Luna, I mean?"

Veronica raised one eyebrow with distain. "Sara must have filled you in with some of her high drama."

"She did. But, please, I'd like to hear it from your point of view. How you saw things going on with her. Here, up close."

It took a few long moments before the waitress reacted. "I suppose her biggest problem has always been this on-and-off rotten boyfriend, ya know? One day here, next day gone. You know that kind. Sure, people think he's cute and charming when they meet him, and he seems like such a sweet guy. I saw him a few times. But at home he was making her life a living hell. You know about his gambling habit, right? He'd disappear for days at a time. Once he vanished for more than a week. No calls, no texts, no answer when she phoned him over and over. Sometimes poor Fiona showed up beside herself, worried to death maybe someone sent him to the hospital because of his debts, or worse." Veronica shuddered with the recollection. "Always telling her lies, making vows he couldn't keep. Worse, he'd come home pleading for money. A 'loan,' he always called it." Veronica made quotation marks in the air with her fingers. "Just for a few days, until after the next rich card game. He was gonna win and win big next time. He guaranteed it. Sure he was. What a loser. And then he'd beg for forgiveness, cry, and she'd take him back, forgiving him, all the while knowing and riding this carousel…"

Cora nodded with understanding. She was familiar enough with poker rules and successful playing characteristics, like managing your stake, focus, controlling emotions. Behaviors Robbie evidently lacked. "And these last few weeks, right before the accident? Anything different?"

The waitress scoffed. "She threw the parasite out again, I know that. Good fucking riddance, I told her. Of course, he tried turning up again. She'd let him stay a few nights mostly out of pity. I don't know all the details. But she was so much better off without him. He stifled her, ya know? I mean, at least she was able to breathe and not be worried out of her mind." Veronica hung her head, shaking it from side to side, and her voice cracked. "She was so *happy* returning to school. Fiona had *ideas*. Plans, dreams. She may have become a great artist, she also had dreams for opening her own business." She paused to breathe and recover her equilibrium.

"Take your time. No rush," said Cora, aware that Veronica was spilling out her guts in a torrent of passion.

"And what about the bus driver, huh? Did they arrest the damn driver for killing her?" She looked at Cora with tears forming and beginning to fall on freckled cheeks.

"It wasn't the driver's fault. Not with the weather as bad as it was. But the case is still open. The cops are looking at everything, I promise you."

Veronica took a few tissues from her bag and blew her nose. "I'm sorry, Mrs. Gus. Please excuse me. I just can't wrap my head around her death. Really, Fiona and I had become like sisters." She wiped away a few silent tears.

"No need for apologies. I only have a few more questions."

"Sure. Anything I can do or help you with. I feel so bad for Sara Sweeney."

"Sara was crushed. But she's strong too and beginning to accept it. And between us, I'm doing my own private investigating independent of the police. I promised Sara."

"That's wonderful to hear. How can I help?"

Cora drew a breath. "Listen, my mission is to look at all possible angles. Not discounting anything, including Rob Perry's slimy friends. But how about the restaurant? Anything going on there to trouble Fiona? Anyone who might have been stalking her, like some weird customer? Or some guy who thought he could make it with Fiona?" Delicately, she added, "Including Enzo."

Veronica laughed bitterly. "Yeah, I'd say she did have a stalker. Right there at work. So, you know about Enzo, right? He's a real piece of work, that guy."

"Why don't you tell me about him? Please. Any information could help, and your name would never be mentioned. *Never.*"

"Where do I begin, Mrs. Gus? His eyes are darting everywhere. Every woman from fifteen to eighty gets the once over. If you're halfway decent he likes to check you out. Even occasionally some new customers. It's his pastime. He tries out cute little remarks. Maybe offers a free glass of wine or hors d'oeuvres. Sits with a lonely woman eating by herself, the pig."

"Tell me about the staff, too. How he treats them and how they react."

"I've only stayed at La Luna cause tips are good. Especially on Fridays and Saturdays. I know a few girls who did quit, who wouldn't put up with this nonsense. But the bottom line is everybody needs money, right? I mean, we all have bills, kids to support. Enzo D'Amato knows exactly who he can play and who he can't. Except when his wife Vera is around. Then he turns into a perfect gentleman." She chuckled. "You could say he's as innocent as a newborn. Smiles and laughter, loves telling stupid jokes as he walks up and down between the tables greeting diners, trying to make everyone happy. Vera's got an eagle eye. But when she's not there, he'll corner someone in quiet places like the cloakroom, or the hallway outside of the kitchen. Maybe even in his office. First come the compliments. Then he'll promise the best shifts, some paid time off, whatever, while he brushes a soft hand down your back, a pinch on your cheek. His voice becomes deep and sexy. Some girls play along, ya know? They can't afford to lose their jobs. Tease him with vague promises. Cause Enzo has the power to make your life miserable."

"A boss always has the power," Cora ruminated, recalling incidents that had happened to her long ago, going back to when she worked as a translator at the American Embassy in Athens. "How was he with Fiona? You said he practically 'stalked 'her."

"Oh, he had a hard on for Fiona, all right. Pretty, with the most beautiful smile. Good figure, fast with answers when she was asked stuff. I noticed Enzo practically drool while Fiona was hurrying her way between her tables and the kitchen. She told me more than once he offered her the best shifts on the weekends..."

"If she'd agree to sleep with him?"

"He was careful with words. Maybe ask you to come in early on Sunday, use some trite excuse like helping with inventory in the basement before opening..."

"Meet up also outside of the restaurant?" Cora asked.

"Oh, Fiona was clever about that, I can tell you. She knew how to handle him, fend him off, maybe offer to think about it. I really don't know. As I told you, tips are good, and people need to get paid. Enzo has a small getaway studio apartment nearby, I've been told. For so-called emergencies."

"And stays over alone sometimes, during bad weather or extra late hours?"

"Bingo! His house with Vera is up in Westchester County. So he misses the last train and can't get home." She sneered.

Cora and her companion shared a knowing look. "I assume he invited Fiona and a few others sometimes. Did she ever agree to visit?"

"We didn't talk about those things, Mrs. Gus. It's all too painful, even hurtful. But the bills have to be paid, the landlord wants his rent money."

Cora knew exactly how this foul game was played. A mixture of promises, intimidation, and never quite knowing where you stand. Her previously low opinion of Enzo D'Amico sank further.

"I can tell you this," Veronica added. "I noticed Fiona had a couple of quiet meetings with him in his office. When Vera wasn't there. And she didn't seem very happy when she left. I once asked if anything was up, but she brushed me off, saying everything was okay. It was like, this isn't your business. Don't ask. So I let it go, ya know? It's not for me to interfere in anyone else's dealings at work. I've got trouble enough of my own."

"So these secret meetings were how long ago?"

Veronica pursed her lips. "Recent. Maybe even the week before Fiona's accident."

Blood drained from Cora's face. Was it possible Enzo had somehow twisted Fiona's arm or threatened her in some way? That if she refused to have sex and threatened to expose him to his wife or the public, would he be willing to do anything to keep her quiet, shut her up? The thought was frightening, and maybe exaggerated. After all, the bottom line was that Enzo D'Amico was a highly successful and respected businessman. If he was desperate enough might he consider doing something irrational like pushing Fiona in front of a bus? Her pregnancy was certainly problematic. The very thought made her feel like the ground was shifting under her feet. Farfetched perhaps, but right now nothing could be ruled out.

"Veronica, since you've been at La Luna, has Enzo been after you, too?"

She ran a hand to brush a tangle of hair from her face. "No, he hasn't been badgering me for some time. Our head chef's been obnoxious for a while. Tony G. He runs the kitchen like a warden, and brazenly told me he can make my life at La Luna hard or easy if he wants, depending on me. His way of hinting I better play ball. The bastard."

Again no surprises for Cora. She knew she was fortunate in having a man like Claude running the Athena's kitchen. Too often men in charge in various powerful roles treated their female staff as potential sex toys. There was nothing new in that.

It was quiet between them for a time, the only noise coming from some nearby students sharing a joke near the computer stations.

"Is there anything else you want to know from me, Mrs. Gus?"

Cora surfaced from her melancholy thoughts with a start. "You've been a wonderful help, Veronica. More than you know. Thank you." Then as an afterthought she added, "You know where you can find me. Don't hesitate to contact me if anything new comes up, or if you need me for something."

Veronica Labrano smiled fully, and they shared a brief hug. Cora left the library first, her new friend waiting a few minutes before following behind. New information, new leads to follow. Cora felt it was still most likely that someone among Robbie's shady circle was most likely behind the push that took Fiona's life, yet it nagged at her that it was possible, even if unlikely, that Enzo D'Amato or one of his cronies could have been involved.

THIRTEEN

"We still don't have a conclusive DNA report on the fetus," Hunter said, his voice lacking its usual warmth. "We're waiting for the morgue's final findings. And potential matches. Meanwhile we're going through the video frame by frame from every CCTV camera anywhere near the bus stop." Hunter switched his phone off speaker. His thoughts continued to race.

"Every hour feels like a day," Cora said glumly. "Thank you for filling me in."

The colorless tone of his voice made it obvious the detective was still perturbed about Cora's dealings with Solerno. Her misplaced trust in the charming side of the retired gangster was preventing her from correctly assessing the risks to herself and to the diner. Keeping him and the police in the dark was stupid. And bringing Perry into her apartment was unadulterated folly. Lives could easily be lost that way. Hunter's brows met in a deep frown. His cheeks were sucked in, looking almost hollow. He ground his teeth. Looking down, he saw his hands clenched, and his thighs ready to spring. He was ready to attack. That hadn't happened in a long time.

Consciously, he clenched and relaxed his muscles. Realizing that his fear for Cora was driving his thoughts, he ruthlessly suppressed his feelings to examine later. He decided not to bring up controversial subjects, at least not for now.

Hunter was unaware of the prolonged silence on the line. Cora found the silence unnerving. When, she thought, had she last been uncomfortable speaking to Hunter? This was awful.

"I was able to gather a few names of local bookies," Cora said, also avoiding difficult topics. "Sara remembered a few from things her sister had told her."

"How is Sara doing?"

"She's trying hard. Came to work the last few days. She's still with me. Her husband Marty calls every day. He's willing to quit his job upstate, but I suggested to Sara to let him stay for now. She knows I'm here for her, and he's earning really good money right now. She agreed, reluctantly."

"You're a good friend, Cora. She's lucky to have you. We also know a number of the street runners who work the gambling circuit. Hal Capps has tracked a couple of these lowlifes down. No good leads, at least yet. I've contacted Major Crimes in Manhattan. They've offered to do some work too. They've got informants all over."

"That's great, Hunter. I have one name I'd like to share. Troy Finlay. I'm told he sets his own odds, deals with street people, and works cash only. He's said to have a few cronies who collect and use muscle when necessary. One may go by the name of Marcus."

"Troy Finlay sounds familiar. Thanks. I'll have him tagged. I'll let you know as soon as we get that DNA info."

"I appreciate it, Hunter."

He hung up. Cora sighed, put her head in her hands. It was increasingly difficult to keep Hunter at a distance. She missed the camaraderie, bouncing ideas back and forth, the jokes that they shared. Hunter had come to mean more to her than she wanted to admit, she knew. For the first time now, ever since Athens, ever since the death of Dirk, the man who held her heart for so long. Gus had been a good man and a good husband, but their love was not the instantaneous giddy passion that she had experienced with Dirk. It had grown over time, out of mutual respect. Their interactions had clearly marked boundaries, experiences they chose not to share. There were fewer dramatic highs and lows, more constructive understanding of each other's needs. She owed him so much, and she celebrated and honored him for his care and careful role in nourishing her broken heart and spirit. In many ways Gus had given her a whole new life after her aching loss, and Cora was sure there would never be more romantic love in her life after Gus's passing almost ten years ago. However, in recent months she wasn't so sure.

Having made friends among the police at the local precinct was a good thing. Important, naturally, for any local businessperson. And gradually developing an association with the leader of the detective squad wasn't breaking any rules and was clearly a welcome bonus. In the past year or so that alliance had deepened to perhaps more, although she couldn't pinpoint exactly when it began. She knew Jonah Hunter had begun to have feelings for her, and she couldn't deny that some of it was reciprocated. But mixing business with pleasure posed its own convoluted problems and risks.

The cup of Greek coffee in front of her had grown cold. After a brief knock on her office door, a voice said, "Sorry to bother you, Mrs. Gus. It's me."

She looked up and smiled at the friendly face of Stavros, impatient and concerned, holding a phone. "What's up? Allison taking care of things okay out front?"

"Alison's on top of everything. But listen, we just got a frantic call from Sara. It's about Robbie," Stavros lowered his voice and looked behind to be sure he was out of earshot of any customers or staff. "Sara says he left the apartment. Wouldn't listen, said to tell you he was going to meet with Troy Findley."

Cora was taken aback. "He *left*? Damn him! He gave his word." She fumed with swift fury. "He's putting Sara in danger, he know that. And he's putting us all in danger."

"Maybe I can still find and stop him. Bus stops, check the subway platforms…" He offered his phone to Cora.

"Don't waste your time. I can have the police out looking with a single phone call of my own. I should have notified Hunter right away, not believed Robbie when he pleaded with me. God knows what he's capable of exposing to this cunning bookie. I gave him a chance, a safehouse. Now what's to stop him for exchanging his own neck at Sara's expense--and maybe mine too?" She slammed a hand on her desk in disgust at herself for trusting Robbie in the slightest.

"He swore he'd return in a few hours. He said the jewelry he grabbed from his mother will be enough payment to pacify Troy for a while. And he thinks he might be able to learn some of the truth about what really happened to Fiona. He promised me."

Cora stood and struggled to compose herself. She bit her lip in an effort to take her emotions out of it. "And why are we supposed to believe a single word this conniver says?" She turned away from Stavros, staring into the distance, the phone between her ear and shoulder.

"He told you he planned to use the jewelry as payment," Stavros reminded. "He openly said he'd try to barter it in exchange for some deal or promises, you know that."

"Don't even try to predict what this liar will do," Cora said with a grimace, waving her hand with frustration. She knew that Robbie was too devious to be found standing anywhere he might be spotted. Trying to locate him now would be futile. She hastily spoke into the phone. "You there, Sara?"

The girl answered quickly and anxiously. "I'm so sorry, Mrs. Gus. He sounded desperate on the phone this morning. You know he'd been frantically calling nonstop all over the city, trying to reach any his so-called friends. I have no idea who he may have been trying to reach. He was cursing about how no one would return his calls. After a while I think he finally did locate somebody, and then just got it into his head to leave and go meet someone somewhere. I warned him not to go and reminded him he'd given you his word to stay put. But he didn't pay me any attention. He mumbled something about finally managing to get in touch with this guy Troy. He said this was the chance he'd been hoping for. He was adamant he could make things 'right.' I tried to stop him, but he brushed me aside..."

"Not your fault, Sara. He's a loose cannon. Smug and phony. Did he tell you anything about where this meeting is supposed to take place? Or how he'd come up with all the money he owes?"

"He stuffed a small bag into his jacket pocket on his way out, promising he'll be back soon, that's all I know. There was no way to stop him. He flew out the door and ran down the stairs."

Cora looked at Stavros. "I bet you're right about him bartering the jewelry." She drew a deep breath, rubbing a weary hand over the stiffness at the nape of her neck. "Let him go. It'll take a lot more than luck to convince this scumbag Troy he raised enough to repay everything he owes. If he can't, then he'll probably…"

"Wind up dead." Stavros finished the sentence for her. "Think we should inform the police? Notify your detective friend?"

Cora considered and shook her head. "No use, no. Robbie's already long gone. And I avoided telling Hunter I'd located him, let alone that I was hiding him in my home."

Moreover, Cora realized that Robbie trying to placate the notorious bookie was a very stupid, dangerous thing to do, and wondered exactly what he might be up to. "Something about this whole thing doesn't sound right," she said, half to herself. "Yesterday he acted so terrified of Troy, and today he's not afraid to meet with him? What's the game he's playing? Rob Perry is smart enough to realize that by openly surfacing he just upped the ante."

*

Kasey Cosgrove gave it barely a moment's thought, then made the call. "Hunter? He's here. In front of the train station at Queen's Plaza, waiting, pacing. He seems uneasy. I followed him here on the train. Shall I pick him up now?"

"No. Wait for his contact to arrive. We want them both. I want them both."

The young detective was tired, worn from her long, exhausting hours of surveillance. She'd been following Cora's movements continuously for the past several days, sharing the work with an equally weary Hal Capps.

"I sat parked in my car since just after dawn. Saw your friend Cora Dracos leave early for the diner, but following your instruction I remained here, watching her building for visitors. Your instinct was good, sir. Rob Perry had likely been staying there. She must have kept him together with Sara Sweeney in her apartment. When he left the building, I recognized him immediately from the file photos."

Hunter listened with a twinge of validation and equal disappointment. He'd felt sure Cora was holding back on her knowledge regarding the whereabouts of Rob Perry. Today his intuition was paying off, but simultaneously making him lose a little of his trust in Cora.

"I followed Rob Perry to the subway, got on the next car," Kasey went on." I saw him exit when the train pulled into Queens Plaza, so I got off too, mingling with the rush hour crowd, walking up from the platform on the opposite side of the street."

"Can you see him now?"

"Very clearly." The active plaza straddled Queens Boulevard where it met with Northern Boulevard, two major streets crisscrossing elevated subway tracks, roadways clogged with traffic entering and exiting the Queensboro Bridge. Tall newer office buildings, apartments, and several notable hotels increased the neighborhood's density.

"He went into a donut shop, came out with coffee. He's trapsing up and down in front of the shop now."

"And he can't see you?"

Detective Cosgrove shook her head. "Absolutely not. "Right now, I'm standing between a couple of busy street vendors, steps away from traffic leading to the bridge. I assume Troy Finley or whoever else he's meeting should be showing up any time now."

"Nice work, Kasey. I'll have two squad cars stationed along the side street waiting for your signal. Leave it to the uniforms to pick them up, keep them separate. I'll have them brought here for questioning. You stay out of sight. I don't want either of them to see you. You're my concealed eyes and ears on this case."

"No problem, Hunter. They won't know. Afterward do you want me to go back to keep an eye on Cora's building?"

"Won't be necessary. Take a break, then come back here."

Kasey Cosgrove smiled, savoring her success. The long hours of the past few days were paying off.

Within a couple of minutes, a chunky medium-height man with thinning hair and a stubbled beard approached from the train station. Kasey thought him an ungainly sort, dressed in a fashionable light leather jacket and baggy dark jeans. Broad shouldered, beer-bellied, he ambled his way toward Rob Perry as he caught sight of the youth apprehensively awaiting nearby. Robbie saw him coming, and they moved in tandem toward each other.

Kasey called Hunter again. "He's here."

"Leave them alone until they begin to move away," came the reply. "Backup's being notified. Identity available?"

The two men greeted one another inconspicuously, exchanging a few unheard words. Robbie maintained a calm veneer acknowledging his companion, nodding as his acquaintance gestured which way to walk.

"Fits the description I have of Troy Finley," said Kasey at length. She took a number of photos of the men with her phone. "I've got eyes on them both. They're heading to the north corner."

"Good. We don't want to risk endangering any passersby. Hold your location, Kasey. Troy has several minor warrants outstanding, including one for speeding, then missing court appearances. Misdemeanor stuff, but enough ample excuse to pick him up. And

Robbie also has a few trivial infractions outstanding. Just stay put and wait for them to get picked up."

Listening, Detective Cosgrove stood nonchalantly observing and ready for any new directive.

A waiting NYPD squad car slowly turned the corner and paused. Robbie saw it first and nudged his companion. Appearing startled, Troy Findlay turned toward the far corner and began walking fast, Rob Perry following right behind, aware of the situation.

Within moments an unmarked police vehicle approached from the other side. Plain clothes officers exited quickly. Badges flashed.

Within seconds it was all but over. Amid surprised onlookers along the street Finley was hustled into one car, Rob Perry into the other. Robbie tried to protest being taken, while Troy stood casually, remaining composed and silent with sneer on his lips.

When he received word of the successful apprehension Hunter exhaled with satisfaction. Finally, some serious questions and answers could be asked. At last, a chance to dig deeper into the puzzling death of Fiona Sweeney.

FOURTEEN

Hunter met Rob Perry's gaze evenly. "You're not under arrest. I had you brought you here to answer some questions, that's all."

Robbie stared back, unfazed. "You had no right. I haven't committed any crime."

"Those necklaces, rings, especially the one with the large diamond, they belong to you?"

"I'm holding them for my mother. They belong to her. Rose Perry Mograbi. She's in North Carolina, okay? They're not stolen."

"We can check on that. But that's not my concern, at least yet." He looked over at Hal Capps who was sitting quietly across from Robbie. "Bring us something to drink, please, Hal. Just water for me." He regarded his difficult visitor. "Want coffee instead? A soda?"

Robbie declined. "Can we get this over with? I want to leave."

"What's the rush, Mr. Perry? Robbie, can I call you Robbie?"

"Sure. What the fuck."

The room was small, a camera set up on the far wall recording the conversation. This wasn't the precinct's main interrogation room. That was down the hall, where Troy Finlay currently sat stewing by himself.

Right now, Jonah Hunter really wasn't interested in the expensive jewelry, stolen or not, nor anything else his uneasy person of interest was involved in other than the nagging unanswered questions related to Fiona Sweeney.

Robbie sat with his arms folded, eyes looking down at the wooden tabletop. He paid no attention as Detective Capps returned with several bottles of spring water. Hunter opened his and drank slowly. "So, let's see what we have here, Robbie," he began, scanning his computer screen. "You and Fiona Sweeney had been together for about two years. On and off. I understand she threw you out a few times, took you back a few times…"

"Yeah. She was good like that."

"So, I understand. When did you see her last?"

Robbie gave a half shrug. "Probably a few days before…" He stopped. You must know this stuff. I mean, you had conversations with Sara, right? She would know everything that was going on."

"Maybe, but I want to hear it from you. When did you return to New York?"

Robbie avoided the question. "I visited my mom for a couple of days. What's the difference anyway? Why aren't you out looking for answers to what happened to her? Why am I here sitting with cops questioning me? I loved Fiona. I still love her. So go do your jobs. Find out." The more he spoke the more annoyed his tone became.

Hunter listened to his tirade, remaining composed, sipping his drink. "Where have you been staying since your return?"

At this he hesitated. He had sworn to Cora Drakos not to say anything regarding his being given sanctuary at her apartment. He knew she'd already be pissed and ready to kill because he broke his word and left. He didn't want to add to that.

"What's the difference? I'm here now. And I'll do anything to help in finding out how she died. If anyone meant to harm her, or if it just an accident."

"You seem to know a lot for someone who's been out of town."

Robbie took several breaths and puffed his cheeks. "Sara. We talked, okay? She told me there are questions. Bad stuff may have happened to Fiona. Sara's scared out of her wits. Look, you know all this. I know you know."

"And we know about you, Mr. Perry. Your gambling problems. The money you owe. The games you play. Borrowing, stealing, lying, cheating. I'm sure with just a few words with your pal Troy sweating in the other room we'll get reasons to hold you. Maybe make an arrest after all. Perhaps you'd like a lawyer? You're entitled—"

Robbie fidgeted, looked at the camera, at Hal Capps, then turned his face back to Hunter. Gathering as much courage he could bluff, he said, "I know I have rights, too. Like am I being charged with something or not? You said I was here just to talk to you."

"Talk yes, Robbie. Not bullshit me, understand?" Hunter narrowed his eyes and glared. "We know where you stayed these past two days, okay? You've been very lucky to have someone like Cora Drakos looking out for you."

Hunter saw Robbie's distress at the name and noted it, letting it sink in and make him well aware they weren't going to be duped or misled, no matter how smart or charming or wily he could be.

"I'm sure you'd really like a joint to smoke about now, but weed isn't allowed here. Sorry."

"So, you know it all, okay. What the fuck do you want from me?"

"Facts, Hunter replied dryly. "You owe big money, not just to a lowlife creep like your buddy Troy, but also to other trash who took you at poker. Like who's this joker Marcus, the collector? The muscle man who'll break some bones. What's he capable of?"

"Why ask me? Ask Troy. He works for Troy and others. Gets a percentage of what he collects."

"We know that Robbie. But this thug, this punk, you ever hear of him going further than beating someone up? Not only threatening, bullying, coercion."

"Like killing someone?"

"Yeah. Like murder. We know how frightened you were. How you fled the city scared for your worthless life. How Fiona turned over her pay and tips in cash to help you run, despite how much you'd hurt her. Fucked her and then left to play and have fun, only coming back when you needed her for something more. A pretty nice world you had in your pocket. Until things really got hot, and you rode a bus to get away as far and as fast as you could. Back to mommy. Taking her money now. All the while leaving Fiona alone at home, frightened and left to pick up any pieces, and in the end maybe even losing her own life because of you."

His jaw slackened. It was a blistering rant, and it took Robbie time to recoup and resume his hard-edged attitude. "It...It wasn't the way you say it."

Hunter's thick brows rose. "Oh? Then tell me how it really was."

A glimpse of pain was clear in Robbie's eyes. He crossed his arms tightly, stammering as he searched for words. "She...Fiona, that night when I returned home, I told her what had happened. How I messed up. She's the one who told me to get out of town. She gave me her cash, all of it. She was afraid for me, not herself. I warned her it was possible someone like Marcus could come looking. She was strong, she said. She wouldn't answer any doors or unknown phone calls. I offered to take her with me right then and there. Keep us both safe. She said no. She had school, her job, wasn't going to screw up anything she was building for herself. She said after living through her own hell she now could handle herself. Fiona was stronger than me, you know? I mean that. She still loved me, she said. No matter what. I should get some money from my mother. She's a top-selling real estate broker. Come back when it's safe. We'd stay in touch. She told me to go. No car rentals, just a bus ticket. Buy it in New Jersey, not here. No one would be able to track me. That's what she said. I swear, man. That's what she said." Robbie dropped his head low to his chest. Hunter saw his lower lip tremble, his shoulders shaking slightly. Robbie was trying not to cry.

"These people in your world, would they kill if they didn't get their money?"

Robbie's head rose slowly. There were hints of red in his eyes. "I owe fifty thou. Half to other gamblers, half to Troy Finley. He's a real bastard, Troy. Doesn't care who gets hurt. But he's smart, too. You know, cunning, has lots of ways to get what he wants. He has a good thing going. A good life. Do I think he would murder somebody, or pay for someone to do it? I don't think so. If he wanted to make an example, he'd hurt me for sure. Break my hands so I couldn't play cards, maybe. Scar me with a knife, even threaten to cut off my balls. But I don't think Troy would allow Marcus or any of his muscle to commit murder, chance life in prison. Not murder, not that." There was fear now in his face.

Hunter had to mentally agree that in his experience homicide due to unpaid gambling debt was rare. These people were professionals. Being owed twenty-five thousand dollars was not worth the risk of 20 plus years in the penitentiary. He recalled a case some time back where some hired gambling muscle burned up cars to collect, even cutting off a few fingers. Threatening to go after the loser's family with the intent of killing was one thing maybe, but never actually doing it. There were always enough suckers around to make up losses. It seemed more likely to him that Fiona's death might have been unintentional. An inadvertent shove meant to knock her over, hurt her, certainly send a strong message to Rob Perry, but not purposeful homicide.

There was silence in the small room for a time. When Robbie spoke again it seemed his thoughts were on the same track as Hunter's.

"Marcus or someone might have followed Fiona. Intending to scare me by pushing her so she'd fall by the bus. You know, like an accident. The bus was rolling to a stop. Maybe she'd get some bruises or something. Letting me know I'd better get their money or else…"

Hunter exchanged aggrieved looks with Hal Capps. "Of course, they wouldn't have known she was pregnant when it happened," Hunter said slowly, looking to see what kind of response he would get. "Look, Robbie, to rule you out of any wrongdoings, I'd like you to give a sample of your DNA. A few swabs in your mouth, okay?"

"What for? What am I accused of?"

"Just procedural, Robbie. It'll make both our lives easier, believe me."

Again, Robbie seemed lost for words, but Hunter's no-nonsense approach told him it was best to agree. "I didn't know any of this. I swear. You're saying Fiona hid it from me? She was having my child? Why wouldn't she tell me…?" He bit his lip. "You know, it was Cora Drakos who told me. Sara was there also telling me it was true. I was shocked to find out. I had no idea I was going to be a father…"

The young man wasn't trying to deny it. Claim the child couldn't be his. In any case, a strictly enforced DWI from several years back had suspended his license for six months, but as a first-time offender, it hadn't been a felony charge. It did put him into the records. Hunter had already obtained Robbie's DNA from their search of Fiona's apartment. There was plenty of it. From toothbrushes, to combs and bed sheets. Robbie's willingness now to provide a sample supported Robbie's story, but Hunter wasn't going to share any of the news.

The awaited fetal DNA report had finally arrived that morning, and to Hunter's great surprise it indicated that Rob Perry was not the child's father.

FIFTEEN

Cora reached for the vibrating phone. To her surprise it was Jonah Hunter on the caller ID. She frowned, she was already on overload, and didn't have the energy to manage their fragile relationship at the moment.

"Hi Cora. How are you?" If his voice was as warm as usual, at least it wasn't angry or cold.

"Good. You okay? What's up?"

"Crazed, overworked, underpaid. The usual. But yeah, I'm all right. Listen, I've come across some new information I think you should know..."

It was good hearing his voice, Cora had to admit. Meet him halfway, she thought. Don't say anything to trigger the raw, devastating emotions that characterized their last meeting. "Please, tell me..."

"This isn't something we should discuss on the phone. Any chance we can meet for a few minutes? Can you spare some time?"

"Sure. The lunch rush hasn't started. How about we meet at the new pocket park?" It was a small irregularly shaped nearby area roughly halfway between the diner and the police precinct. An unexpected garden of diffused light with airy trees surrounded by neat patches of grass, a wide walkway with benches on both sides, it was literally a breath of fresh air. Formerly a garbage strewn vacant lot, it offered a small but pleasant diversion from the clogged traffic, crowded retail stores, and rushing pedestrians. Instructing Eddie

Coltrane to take over for an hour, Cora made her way towards the park. She found Hunter had already arrived, sitting on a bench with his legs crossed, face held up towards the sunny blue sky.

"Hello, Detective."

He turned. Cora looked at him and smiled. She was wearing a knee-length dark skirt, matching jacket, colored blouse, and low heel black shoes. Her hair fell alongside the rims of her sunglasses.

"Good to see you, Cora," he said admiringly. The sight of her made his heart skip a beat. "You're looking good."

She sat next to him, not too close, but not far, and made herself comfortable. "Good to see you too, Hunter." *Damn*, she thought to herself, *I really did miss this guy*. An elderly lady sitting on an opposite bench smiled at them as she opened a sandwich wrapper and made herself comfortable.

"How are things with the diner?" He was careful with his words, not wanting to bring up anything that might be misconstrued as referring to their last difficult conversation.

"Breakfast, lunch, dinner. Breakfast lunch, dinner. The story of my life I guess." She shrugged, following his polite lead. "Just being here now for a short break is a blessing. "Here," she offered him a hot coffee from a paper bag. I made it the way you like it." He took it appreciatively, carefully removing the plastic cover and blew several times on the cup's rising steam. Closing his eyes, he sniffed at the satisfying aroma. It was a rich dark roast. "Thank you."

She took out her own cup from the bag. "It's a blend. Arabica. You'll like it."

He gingerly took a sip, keeping his gaze on her. Both took this rare opportunity to relax.

A young mother pushing a baby carriage passed by. The baby was giggling loudly and waving his chubby arms and legs as the woman leaned over and tickled the infant. Mother and child laughed.

"Boy or a girl?" asked Cora.

"Girl," the mother said, her innocent face beaming as she pushed the carriage toward the corner.

"Cute baby," offered Hunter.

Their gazes followed the mother until she reached the corner of the park, waited for the light to turn green, and crossed the busy street. A bus spewing exhaust went by. "What a different world that mother lives in, "Cora remarked, brushing hair aside that had been tousled by the breeze.

Hunter agreed. It reminded him of his own kids as happy toddlers, when he was king of their world. The world before his divorce, before hasty weekend visits with his two growing children, the pointless arguments still continuing with his ex, and her ongoing threat to take them with her new husband to move to Florida, which would effectively deny him any meaningful time with the almost-grown boys.

Cora knew something of his past too. A soldier during the war in Afghanistan, the PTSD he suffered after returning from his tour, and his damaging reliance on alcohol to ease his anguish. It had cost him that marriage, and almost his career until he sought treatment and overcame his addiction.

Hunter knew more than most about Cora's background in Athens. He was aware of her own trauma over the death by terror of her American fiancé, her life turned upside down, and leaving her work at the American Embassy, finally coming to America to begin a new life. But there were still secrets, things she had never revealed except to her deceased husband, Gus Karos. Things she had thought about sharing perhaps someday, but not now. Definitely not now.

Several minutes passed without talking, each far off in thoughts and memories, and each wary of inadvertently damaging their budding relationship.

"So, I have updates regarding Fiona Sweeney," Hunter said, putting the coffee cup down beside him. "We were able to track down Rob Perry. We caught him together with his bookmaker Troy Finlay at Queens Plaza."

Cora listened and nodded, unsure when to provide her own information.

"We had him followed. I had a hunch he'd be in touch with Sara when he couldn't reach Fiona. Can you help me with that?" He approached the topic carefully. "No crimes were committed..."

Cora's brows drew pensively together. She knew she need to be candid. "Sara was in my place when he called. Your hunch was right. He was frantic because he couldn't reach Fiona. He was already scared and shaken when he learned what happened. I told him he had to come back…"

"I know. He told me. I understand why you offered to give him a refuge."

"It was the only way to lure him back."

Hunter nodded. "It was good you talked him into it. But I wish you'd told me."

"I was going to, Hunter. Please believe that. He was frightened, so I told him he could stay for a few days, to try and contact anyone who might help him keep himself safe. I recognized his lies and manipulation. I ordered him not to leave my place. I wanted him there for you to pick up."

The detective smiled, dismissing her worry. "I guess we think too much alike. As I said, I was certain he'd contact Sara. I figured she was with you, and because of that he'd go directly to your home. Luckily, I was right. So, the rest was easy. I had your apartment building watched. The next day Robbie took off and we followed."

Cora showed her surprise. He put his hand over hers, adding, "No broken laws. As I said, I'm glad you found a way to get him back. He was wanted for questioning, and sure enough he provided me with good info on several fronts. We'll be able to charge this worm Troy and probably a few of his cronies. However, this still leaves serious questions regarding how Fiona died."

"I have a few things to share with you. Disturbing stuff. Things I never expected."

Hunter regarded her with anticipation. "From Robbie?"

"No. As a matter of fact it came from Sara. Apparently what happened may have other wrinkles no one could anticipate."

"What are you talking about?"

"Sara told me that the boss at La Luna, this guy Enzo D'Amico, seemingly had the hots for Fiona. He's known for chasing skirts, and Fiona had caught his eye some time ago."

"Go on." Hunter put a hand over his mouth, watching Cora intently.

"I took a walk over to his restaurant. I came in about an hour before they open for dinner. Enzo knew who I was, he recalled me from a couple of local Chamber of Commerce meetings."

"I'm aware of Enzo D'Amico. He likes to play hot shot. Donated to police charities a few times."

"He was very surprised to see me, but he was quite polite. He showed me around. His place is impressive. Expensive, best wines and liquor at the bar. He even took me into his private back office, introduced me to his wife Vera. She works there a few days a week. Bookkeeping, it looked like. My guess is she does a lot of the money handling while he's the front man, greeting big spenders." Here she paused, mentally reviewing everything she'd seen. "The restaurant functions like a well-oiled machine. Around Vera he was a perfect gentleman. On the floor, not so much. He flirts, ogles his staff. Almost entirely female, good-looking women. I noticed he looked me up and down a couple of times, but I ignored it."

"So, he's a pig. There are lots of them."

Cora laughed. "So true. But again, this particular one had been after Fiona Sweeney for some time. She was a very lovely young woman, remember. He gave her the best shifts without seniority, and Saturday night dinners for the best tips."

"He can't be arrested for that."

"There's this waitress, Veronica Labrano. She's been at La Luna for a long time. She talked to me on quietly before I left. I met with her later at the library. Enzo used to hit on her too, she told me. But she never responded and after a while he gave up. He went after a few others, and one or two quit because of his hassling them. He never does it when Vera is there. Only when she's gone. According to Veronica he acted overfriendly from the day she was hired, offering her the top shifts, days when she could make the most money. Maybe give a little 'bonus' now and again. She thinks Fiona refused his fawning time and again. It didn't seem to matter. It got bad at first. Veronica said found Fiona crying in the restroom several times."

"And he never stopped?"

"With time he eased up, sure. She needed the job, and she was good at it, so Enzo stepped back. Things may have calmed, but when Enzo learned of her problems at home with Robbie, he started stalking again. I think he gave her some extra cash as a gift, for her art supplies, maybe a little rent help. A young woman alone, and now him trying to become a nice guy who sincerely wanted to help. After a while she seemed to accept these gifts. Maybe she thought she could pull off taking offers while still keeping him at bay. Again, after a time, who can say?"

"You're saying Fiona Sweeney might have been in a sexual relationship with this Enzo?"

"I'm not saying that—yet. But it seems he did have the hots for her. Enzo owns a small studio apartment near La Luna. He keeps it for when he can't catch the last train home to Westchester County. You know, when closing is late, or the weather is really bad, he prefer to stay overnight near the restaurant."

"So, Enzo owns a little love nest, you think?"

"Possible. What really caught my attention was when Veronica said that in recent weeks she noticed Enzo and Fiona having some quiet talks in secluded places. More than usual. And lately some of those talks had turned explosive."

Putting his hand to his eyes, rubbing at the corners, Hunter said, "So you think it's possible he might be the father?"

"All I can tell you is that Fiona told Sara she finally wanted to get out of her relationship with Rob Perry. She was done with him, even if deep down she still may love him. His lifestyle was too destructive. She'd had enough. And they weren't sleeping together very much anymore." Cora leaned back with a long sigh. "Or so I've been told."

Hunter thought it over carefully and decided that this was the proper time to reveal his own news. "I haven't told you yet why I phoned today. The DNA from the fetus arrived. My people had already examined Fiona's apartment several times. While there we took DNA samples. Toothbrushes, combs, cups, and bed sheets. Rob Perry had a couple of misdemeanors. Speeding, one DWI, so his DNA was already in our files. We compared it with the fetus. Cora, The lab indicates Rob Perry has been ruled out as the father." A cloud covered the sun as he said that.

"Oh my God."

"So now we have to learn who the actual father is."

"I might know where to begin," Cora said, contemplating Enzo's thrill at the power he relished dangling over his employees. "Did you inform Robbie during your questioning?"

"No. My judgement is to let it rest for the time being. I don't know how he'd react. So, after he gave the names and locations of people I've been looking for I released him. He told me he planned on trying to learn for himself if gambling muscle may have played a role regarding Fiona. I had no legal reason to hold him and allowed him to leave. But I strongly warned him about getting into trouble. And I requested him to keep in touch with me. He gave his word he would, which of course we all know is worthless."

Cora sniffed. "I just hope this guy doesn't get himself killed. But look, how about if I go and pay another visit to La Luna. Try to get myself close to Enzo, and hopefully get a DNA sample for you."

"Be extra careful, Cora. This case is turning so dicey it may not be worth the risk. You can be sure Enzo has his own unsavory contacts. If he gets a clue what you're up to he may decide to make you a target."

"A target for what?"

"For linking him to this case, or possible ties to this pregnancy." Hunter frowned. "Let alone anything whatsoever dealing with her death."

SIXTEEN

Cora crossed Jamaica Avenue and stopped in her tracks. In the bright sunshine in front of the diner she saw Eddie Coltrane, Chef Claude and his assistant Diego standing still and silent at the bottom of the Athena's steps.

Eddie caught sight of her, waved, and determinedly walked her way. Cora took a deep breath and picked up her pace. There were no lights showing from inside the diner.

"I was just about to call you," Eddie huffed, out of breath.

"Power outage?"

He rubbed his hands together, shaking his head with anger. "It's not a neighborhood outage, just us. Look." He pointed to the bodega across the street. A few customers were leaving. You could easily see the ceiling's fluorescent light in shade reflecting off their heads.

"I've already notified Con Ed," Claude informed, referring to New York City's utility company. "They're on the way now, they said."

"Have any of you checked the kitchen yet?" Cora asked, concerned about spoilage. Anything longer than about a four-hour outage would mean food in the freezers would immediately have to be thrown out. This was every restaurant owner's nightmare.

"Not yet," answered Eddie. Passersby stopped to see what was happening. A white and blue NYPD patrol car pulled up to the curb. Sergeant Molina, local and no-nonsense NYPD veteran, rolled down his window and stared. Another problem.

"Everything okay?" he asked. Cora and Eddie walked over to talk to the officer. Grimly Molina told them, "The security cameras might be helpful if they weren't knocked out too. Everyone should stay outside. We'd better notify FDNY. I'll go in first, the rest of you stay here until I tell you otherwise."

"I'm going in too," said Cora. "I'm the owner…"

"Sorry, Mrs. Gus. You also gotta stay till things are cleared, okay?"

The sergeant swiftly called dispatch. Next he carefully walked the perimeter, looking for signs of a break-in. None were obvious. Eddie unlocked the back door for Molina and one of his uniformed men. The inside of the building was unnaturally quiet without the hum of motors, fans, neon, and florescent lights. The empty restaurant looked abnormal, like a waiting movie set. Deep shadows contrasted with bright sunlight on orderly tables neatly set up for the breakfast crowd.

The storage area was intact. Molina cautiously entered the kitchen, his hand lowered toward his weapon. There were no signs of anyone hiding. All the equipment was shut down. No hum of freezers, refrigerator, air conditioning, or lighting.

Outside, Cora was already anticipating a grim picture. This disruption of electricity meant she'd have to contend with refrigerators and freezers full of food that now had no motor to keep them cold or fresh. The backup generator wasn't large enough to accommodate the size of her equipment, let alone providing light, cooling or other possible power needs.

What could be salvaged from this mess? She slowly walked up the steps, opened the front door and shouted to Molina.

"Sergeant, how bad does it look?"

"You can come in by yourself and draw your own conclusions, Mrs. Gus. Looks like the big freezer isn't cold at all."

Cora walked trancelike, groaning as she entered the open kitchen area. She sniffed at odors already beginning to permeate the air. The meat was turning bad. Poultry. Fish, too. It was obvious the exhaust system had stopped working due to the outage. Within a short time, the whole place would be reeking. The power had definitely been out more than four hours. Much longer than her initial guess.

Sergeant Molina looked at her with sad eyes. "I'm no expert, but I'm afraid you've lost just about your entire food inventory. He sniffed a rainbow trout, made a sour face, and turned away. "It stinks. All of it."

A Fire Department truck wailed from nearby. Cora stepped from the kitchen and looked up at one of the newly installed cameras. It was off. Everything was off.

Eddie Coltrane came beside her. Cora had tears in her eyes, and he squeezed her cold hand. "We'll get back in business soon, Cora. I promise you."

"I know," she muttered, looking at Eddie. "We don't know how long this utility interruption may last. But we need to be prepared in case we're shut for days. No point in trying to put together an emergency menu. We can't do anything until Con Ed inspects and approves, and…"

"I'll deal with those bastards. I'll also take care of what we need to resupply. Meanwhile Claude, Diego and me will start the bagging and tossing this smelly stuff out into the dumpsters. We'll have to have a special pickup arranged."

"For sure. Take photos of everything, Eddie. We'll need some acceptable proof."

"Sounds good, Mrs. Gus. Why don't you take care of calling our insurance and start making claims. This will cost us big time."

"Thanks, Eddie. That would be helpful. We need an adjuster to show up fast so they can see for themselves." There were tens of thousands of dollars' worth of spoiled foodstuffs, she knew. That hurt. That hurt a lot, even with the spoilage coverage included in her policy. And Cora also knew she'd need all the help she could possibly get.

Sara Sweeney had come to work and was now also standing outside. Cora also saw Stavros park his car at the far end of the parking lot. The fire truck pulled in front. Amid their comings and goings she saw Allison, looking confused and slightly scared. Cora indicated for them all to gather around.

"Okay everyone. As most of you know we've had a serious power outage. Seems to be a total one. But listen, we'll spend today sorting, cleaning, doing whatever we can. Everyone will get paid, so don't worry. Listen to the Fire Department's instructions, the police, and do whatever they ask. Con Ed should be coming out here soon too.

Maybe with luck I can get an insurance adjuster. All the food is bad or turning."

There were groans of anger and frustration.

"The fruit still looks good so far," she continued, "so eat as much as you want, take some home, scrap the rest. Same goes for all leftover bakery goods. I don't know how long we'll be closed, but count on a few days at least, depending on how fast we'll be able to get new deliveries."

The morning shift crew were eager to help. Within moments they were busy at work. Cora showed herself to be capable and ready to take charge. No one knew that inside she was crying and shaking.

"What could have caused this?" she asked the Fire Captain after he finished his initial look around. "Blown circuits is my first guess. Somehow they all got tripped. Luckily I don't see any immediate hazards. But I can't understand why your small backup generator didn't kick in. It should have, unless..." He stopped speaking.

"Unless what?"

He wiped his brow. Traffic was clogging because of the firetruck, and frustrated drivers were beginning to honk their horns. Early rush hour was underway.

Harry Benzel, the early morning regular who always sat at the far end of the counter, ambled along, and looked on in dismay. "What the hell?"

"No coffee this morning," Cora said as he approached, his jaw opened and his eyes wide. "I'm sorry, Harry."

The retired stockbroker scratched his head. He'd been a daily customer for years, remembering Cora as she learned from Gus Karos, back in the day. "What in the world is going on around here, Mrs. Gus? You've had fires, dead rats, and now this?" His eyes moved slowly over at the chaos all around. "Seems to me someone is out to get you."

Cora put her hand to his shoulder. "You may be right, Harry. You may be right. Listen, stick around, okay? Keep an eye out for me while I make some calls to the insurance company. Tell me if you see anything out of the ordinary, strangers watching, things like that. Can you do that? Once we get up and running, and we *will*, you'll get free coffee for a month. As much as you can drink. A deal?"

Harry gave her a mock salute. "You can count on me, Mrs. Gus, you can count on me."

Cora took out her phone and walked away for some privacy. Of course, Harry Benzel was right. This was sabotage. Another warning from her would-be buyers. How, though, did they manage to pull this off? Get the power shut for almost the entire night? Making sure that almost everything in the diner would be ruined.

She shuddered with her thoughts. The fires were started from the outside. The fucking rat was hung from the outside. This was different. What nagged her most now was what the fire chief said. Why hadn't the backup generator worked? It was on a separate, devoted line. It made no sense. All going out at once? *At once*?

As she stood amid the disorder, confusion and clattering noise around her she felt a virtual kick to her solar plexus. She appeared to stare into an abyss so deep no light could escape. She came to a dreadful conclusion. The thought came rushing before she could stop it.

It could only have been an inside job.

It took a full day to dispose of the rotting foods. While Eddie and Claude inspected everything, Cora spent her time dealing with deliveries, utility inspections and ongoing issues regarding cleanup. She felt too depressed to start adding up the losses. It wasn't only because of the power outage but the cost of the fire, new cameras, window replacements and who knew what else might be found. She knew it would come to a considerable amount, even after any insurance payments. The business alone wouldn't have enough cash in the checking account, she was certain. Money from her personal savings and retirement accounts would need to be tapped.

Solerno had warned her that these people were serious opponents and would throw anything they could her way. Hunter had offered his help in investigating, but Cora felt surer than ever that someone at the diner had thrown the switches. She said nothing to any of her employees, not even the most trusted ones like Eddie or Claude. She made a list of names: current staff, full-time and part-time. Then a second list of those who had been temporary in recent months. No names stood out.

It occurred to her that a customer could have been responsible, someone with a knowledge of restaurants. But how could they have played with the circuit breakers without being seen? How did they know where things were located?

Sara Sweeney entered quietly and handed Cora a cup of takeout coffee that she brought from across the street. Miguel Fuentes, the bodega owner was being a great help, sending over a couple of his own workers to assist with the heavy loads, as well as supplying a constant stream of fresh sandwiches from his small deli counter. Several other retail shops also lent a hand, for which Cora was immensely grateful. Even several regular customers came to help, including Harry, who suddenly seemed to be on watch from morning till night. With luck, fresh food deliveries could begin soon, and the Athena might open for business the day after tomorrow. In spite of her upset and ire Cora felt the genuine caring from the community supporting her. It was a good, warm feeling. People actually were concerned, and her appreciation left tears in her eyes. She sniffed and blew her nose as her phone vibrated.

It read, 'Possible Spam', but she picked it up anyway.

"Good day, Cora," came the voice on the phone.

Cora said nothing, not even hello.

A woman's voice spoke on the other end. Accented and harsh. "My friends wanted me to check up on you…"

"I'm good. Never better," she responded in a calm voice. "How are my friends who have a concern?"

There was a slight chuckle on the other end. "You have a good sense of humor. That is refreshing. Very nice, Ms. Drakos."

Cora tried to recognize the accent. Eastern European was the closest she could guess. "What do you want?"

"To meet with you, that's all. A chat. A friendly chat in a public place."

"And what shall we discuss?"

"Terms. Good terms, Cora. I think you might be pleased after all you've had to contend with in these past weeks."

Cora struggled to keep her voice steady and cool. "And which of my new friends will I be meeting?"

The voice softened slightly. "With me, Cora. With only me. I speak on behalf of these friends, believe me."

"And you are who?"

"You may call me Ursula."

"All right, Ursula. I'm pretty busy today. But maybe tomorrow…"

There was a bit of hesitation. "Today would be better, Cora. Perhaps this evening works for you? Our discussion can be brief."

"Too much going on, nope."

Cora heard a long sigh on the other end. "You are an obstinate person, Cora. Tell me, were you this way when you worked as a translator? A translator at the American Embassy in Athens? I forget, what was the reason you quit such a good position?"

Inwardly Cora fumed. Ursula was adept at manufacturing disorienting questions, and she was determined not to fall into that trap. She countered by saying, "I detect a soft East European accent, Ursula. Not Russian, not harsh. You must also know that I was proficient in Russian too, at the embassy, right? Maybe a bit more Central Europe, I suspect. Is it Czech, perhaps?"

"When tomorrow then?" was the only reply. Cora had scored. Touché!

"Ten AM sharp. At the Starbucks near the movie theatre on Queens Blvd. How will I recognize you?"

Ursula didn't skip a beat. "I am tall, with short blond hair. I will be wearing sunglasses. And you?"

Cora faked a laugh. "Oh, I'm sure you'll recognize who I am. See you then, Ursula."

The Starbucks was crowded. Cora arrived precisely at ten and stood in a short line to place her order. She kept her eye on the door, watching other customers hurry in and out, more women than men, but saw no overt sign of Ursula.

The day was cloudy and cool. A tall woman wearing an expensive open raincoat entered. She appeared genteel in her expensive shiny brown boots and gloves matching her blouse and skirt. But it was the sunglasses and short blond hair, nicely quaffed that assured Cora who it was. She indicated to the newcomer with a slightly raised hand.

Ursula caught her gesture and nodded.

"Would you like coffee?" Cora asked.

"Yes, please. Black with a single sugar. Small size. I limit my caffeine." She was polite and acting as though they were actual friends meeting up for a nice morning chat. Her accent was precise, clipped, and soft. Maybe not Czech after all, Cora thought, trying to place it. Bulgarian?

Ursula offered a ten-dollar bill which Cora immediately rejected with a wave of her hand. "My treat, Ursula."

"Thank you. I'll find us a table." And off she went. Tall, her back straight, her chin lifted high. The only thing to remark on was a slight limp, her right leg slightly impaired. Ursula very much reminded Cora of typical upper-class businesswomen of the variety she knew back home in Greece. Daughters of society. There definitely was something patrician about her manner. Not quite what she expected of some predictable shakedown, mob-connected felon. And not at all what she anticipated after Solerno's lecture on mafia-style muscle.

An older man with a rolled-up magazine was leaving a small table near the front window. He took his cup and napkin in his hand, wiping away a few crumbs from a muffin. Cora noticed Ursula smile and thank him for leaving the table neat and clean.

Cora ordered two of the same coffees and brought them over. Ursula had taken off her raincoat and made herself comfortable, her posture perfect, legs crossed neatly at the ankle. Her eyes bright blue and clear when she removed her quality, classic sunglasses. While Cora couldn't name the specific designer, Ursula's dress was clearly high quality and expensive.

Ursula removed the lid and watched the steam rise, blowing lightly on the brew. "You chose our meeting place well," she said, removing her light gloves. Her fingernails were painted a dark, subdued red, her hands slender and fingers long.

"I'm glad you approve," Cora replied, sitting straight, and mirroring her demeanor. "Shall we get down to business? Why we're here now."

Ursula's wide smile showed perfect white teeth, a testament to some expensive dentist's superior work. This was not at all the type of person Cora expected to meet. Ursula seemed anything but a thug.

"Certainly, Cora. My associates, those who have an interest in the Athena, are people of impeccable business experience. Experts, you see. It may not seem this way to you, but you might be flattered that they wish to purchase your diner. Land, also. Equipment. And everything you have."

Cora sat back, studying her companion once more, carefully analyzing every word, memorizing every gesture. Cora raised an eyebrow and asked, "So, am I supposed to feel lucky?"

"Fortunate, yes." Ursula's face remained impassive. It reminded Cora of diplomats trying to impress one another while lying, cheating, and plotting to stab each other in the back. "It's a pity you've been having issues at your business." She said curtly.

"Nothing we haven't been able to handle," Cora retorted with a back of the hand motion. "And naturally the police have been most helpful."

"Good to hear. These problems do so quickly have an impact on a property's value." She sipped and waited.

Ah, this woman wants to turn this into a pissing contest, Cora thought, her face an expressionless mask. "Our weather's a bit chilly today, don't you think?"

"Yes, for New York. Actually, I am used to colder climates, so this doesn't bother me."

"Do you miss Europe, Ursula? Where did you say you come from?"

"Only occasionally. America has so much to offer, I'm content. And my work takes me to many places." She obviously avoided answering.

"Oh?"

"I only recently returned from viewing several properties in Los Angeles."

"Ah, so real estate is your occupation? Buying, flipping with fast cash?" Cora knew she was annoying to her interlocutor, and she enjoyed every second of it.

Carefully, without batting an eye, Ursula answered, "I dabble in many professions. My friends put their trust in my opinions. They are very pleased with my work, I'm happy to say."

"That must be very gratifying for you." Cora allowed herself a slight smirk. Evidently that stung Ursula's pride.

"You apparently have very little experience with larger investing properties. My principals have interests throughout the world. I travel everywhere. My most recent recommendation to my colleagues was regarding a casino in Macao. I actually don't understand interest in such a mature enterprise. Imagine. And I don't like so much humidity. Did you know the best place in the world to see rainbows is Hawaii? It's true." She chuckled artificially. "However, I don't question their whims. My task is to show sellers where their best interests lie." She paused, glancing at her raincoat, which was neatly folded on the nearby chair, then looking boldly into Cora's eyes.

"My friends requested me to present you with a generous offer. Of course, the offer is a bit lower than they originally had in mind, due to the recent difficulties you've had being able to keep your diner open." Ursula drew a folded piece of paper from her raincoat pocket and slid it across the table. Cora accepted it. She turned it over, opened it and glanced down briefly at the handwritten number written in the center.

Then she turned the paper face down. "No, thank you."

Ursula displayed a flicker of surprise. "Considering location, age, environmental issues, we consider our offer more than fair. Of course, I could bother my friends to find a few dollars more. But these people don't like being inconvenienced with minor matters. Especially when dealing with cash. It's more of a nuisance."

"I expect they wouldn't be pleased with me anyway, Ursula. However, do convey my message to your friends if you would. They'll understand." She pushed her chair back slightly and started to rise.

Ursula looked up at Cora's face. "I'll convey your answer expeditiously."

Cora's mouth widened into a tiny smile. "A pleasure meeting you, Ursula. By the way, you have a spot under you right eye. Your cheap mascara is starting to run down your face."

Cora turned and left, not looking back as Ursula sat fuming.

SEVENTEEN

Vera D'Amico twisted her plump body while Enzo leaned over her shoulder and stared at the laptop screen. He squinted his eyes as Vera handed him his reading glasses. "The numbers look pretty good to me," he said, running his gaze up and down the columned spreadsheet.

"These numbers suck," Vera retorted, her mouth turning down, heavy-lidden eyes staring at her husband. "This year so far is down from last year. And during last December—"

"Holiday time. What do you expect? Prices have been going up." He made an elaborate show of lighting a fresh cigar, a once-in-a-while treat. "Don't worry. We'll work it all of it out. It's just part of the game."

"Get that damn thing out of my face." She waved away the smoke. "This isn't a game to me, Enzo. I've busted my ass to keep expenses—and you—in line. Don't think I don't notice all these unnamed entries. A little bonus money here and there? You're spending more. Too much more."

"We're in the black. But if you want I can skimp round the edges on some smaller items. No one will notice or care."

She glared at him. "*I* care."

Looking to avoid further argument and placate his accounting partner, Enzo said, "We'll go over the books tonight if there's time."

"Don't try that bullshit on me. You have an engagement party of twenty-four coming tonight, remember? And put out that cigar in the restaurant."

"That family will spend a lot. I guarantee it. They like fine wines and liquor. Both sons love to drink, and the old man won't spare anything to make his daughter happy. I'll handle everything, Vera. You'll see. You'll be pleased."

A strong knock on their office door turned their attention. "Yes?"

"A visitor for you, Enzo," came a husky voice.

He shared a look with his wife and shrugged, his expression telling her he wasn't expecting anyone.

"Who is it, Barry?"

"She's waiting at the bar, drinking a sparkling water. It's that owner of the Athena Diner, Cora Drakos."

Enzo looked genuinely puzzled, then recalled. "Ah yes. She called. Wants to talk about something."

"You didn't make her any promises?" Vera hissed.

"Promises? Of course not. You met her."

"I did. And I saw you eyeing her too." She grated her teeth. "Go ply your silver tongue on that Greek woman. This one won't fall for your stupid games. I know her reputation."

"Look, whatever brought her here, whatever she wants, I'll get rid of her fast, okay? Stick with your counting."

He left the office, looked over to the dimly lit bar. Elbows on the counter, face looking at the selection of wines, Cora was sipping her water through a straw. She was wearing a business suit, her legs crossed. Her slightly tanned countenance appeared patrician to Enzo. A well-shaped, well-heeled, and mature woman, she reminded him of a Renaissance painting portraying lovely Greek and Roman goddesses. He casually ground out his smoldering cigar in a convenient ashtray.

"Nice to see you again, Cora," he said, his eyes looking straight into hers. He held an outstretched hand. She took it firmly as they shook.

"I hope I'm not inconveniencing you, Enzo…"

His smile was wide, shaven face clean, thick dark brows close together above a wide nose. "You could never be an inconvenience." There was a mischievous twinkle in his eyes. Then he swiftly turned solemn, saying, "I heard about your misfortune the other day. A total power outage, a tough one. Not even a back-up?"

"It's been a mess. In fact, the reason I stopped by, I mean I hope I'm not here at a bad time…I want your advice on an idea."

"Don't mind this cigar. Sure, we don't open for lunch for a half an hour yet."

A tall good-looking waiter came to ask a question. Enzo shooed him away with a frown. He turned back to Cora.

"How are you doing with your clean-up over there?"

"We're just about done," she sighed. "Now we're disinfecting and restocking. We hope to be up and running, maybe as early as tomorrow." She crossed her fingers.

"Wonderful news! You're very efficient under the circumstances. We were shocked at your bad luck lately. So, what brings you here today? Do you have any news regarding poor Fiona Sweeney?"

Cora knit her brows together. "Nothing new to tell you about that, unfortunately. It's a horrid investigation."

"Well, you called me. What is it I can do for you? Need some help?"

Cora eyed the nearby ashtray with the barely smoked cigar. It would be perfect to give to Hunter for DNA. She began to plot ways to get a hold of it.

"No help at the moment but thank you. Unfortunately, it's all become strictly a police and FDNY matter now. But as a matter of fact, I had this idea and a few thoughts I wanted to run by you."

"Let's hear it, please."

"I lost a pretty big bite out of my reserves," she began. "Other places may have had to shut down. So, I came up with this thought I'd like to get your views on."

"You're flattering me, but of course."

"Listen Enzo, we all know you're something of a bigshot with the local Chamber of Commerce. I've heard the way they listen to you and your ideas."

"Well, I'm not so sure about that…" His eyes were still smiling, but he liked the factual compliment.

"Come on, you're not that modest," Cora said, sharing a laugh. "And I didn't say it to flatter you. But hear this out," she let her fingertips ever so lightly touch the back of his hand. "They all respect you. I've been thinking of proposing to the Chamber a new special fund raised to assist local retail businesses who've run into tough financial issues beyond control. I've certainly had some bad luck, but we all know these unexpected hazards could happen to anybody."

"Of course, you're right," Enzo said, inspired and feeling slightly turned on by her gentle touch. Was it intentional, he wondered? "I count my blessings every day. Please continue, Cora."

"My idea could give a sense of optimism and hopefully security to every shop owner in this area. Monthly or quarterly contributions carefully put aside, invested. Beyond any meager insurance company payout we all pay for. Individual owners could decide to be covered by the Chamber or remain out. Nothing compulsory."

"A Chamber of Commerce fund. I like the concept. Keep talking."

"So, at the upcoming Chamber conference I was wondering if you would be willing to second the proposal if I made a motion for consideration. I believe the whole neighborhood would benefit. Remember how during the worst year of Covid the city was so unprepared? If there had been available funds back then so many businesses might not have been forced to shut for good. Especially restaurants. Federal grants certainly helped but weren't enough. This is dealing with private money, capitalized, and invested with realistic oversight. A business matter that would be akin to friends helping out friends."

"Yes, that sounds like a good slogan. Go on."

Cora continued. "So, here's an opportunity making sure no one will suffer on their own in the future. After my proposal is brought to the floor I hope we can discuss the idea, and hopefully with your backing we can bring it to the full Chamber committee for serious consideration. I wanted to get your input."

Enzo listened and nodded. "I'm not sure we'd get enough support, at least initially, but of course I'll be pleased to look over an outline and offer your self-insurance plan my support for deliberation. Excellent thinking, Cora. You have a sharp mind. Everyone knows it. I am impressed. Please, feel free to come to me with initiatives like this or any others you may want to discuss."

She met his gaze and nodded appreciatively. "Thank you so much, Enzo. I was told you're somebody who knows how to get things done. Making friends in all the right places." Her smile was warm, engaging.

"And I hope you and I can become friends, Cora." He leaned in closer.

His clumsy attempt to get familiar was so obvious it almost made her chuckle. "I think I can call you a friend already." She shook his hand and shifted on the barstool and made ready the leave. How to grab that cigar without Enzo seeing?

"Oh, and I also want to thank you for introducing me to Veronica Labrano."

"You talked with her here, right?"

"I did. She was a really good choice you made. She was supportive in helping me understand Fiona Sweeney better. We even met outside for a longer chat. Is Veronica coming in today?"

Enzo lowered his gaze. "A shame, but no. I'm afraid she won't be here with us at La Luna anymore."

Cora showed surprise. "She certainly seemed quite good at her job. Experienced. Knew her way around the trade better than most. A seasoned pro, in fact."

"Yes, she was a good waitress," he admitted, making a sour face. "But she has a fresh mouth that can't be controlled. The other day she argued with me publicly and refused several of my directions. I couldn't let the other staff see such insubordinate behavior happen without severe consequences. We're a team," Enzo nodded piously to emphasize his point. "I told her to collect her pay for the week. And I asked my wife to give her an extra week's pay as severance…"

"You *fired* Veronica?"

"I did. I had no choice, you see. An employee can't publicly belittle her boss, can she? It opens the door. You understand that."

Somehow that didn't seem to fit, Cora thought. Veronica Labrano seemed too smart and understood her boss very well indeed. She was too much of a veteran in restaurant work. "Oh, I'm so sorry to hear this, Enzo. But I'm sure you'll have no trouble filling her shift."

"None at all. I've already interviewed several for the position."

As she thought of how she could get in touch with the waitress La Luna's air conditioning kicked on. It made Cora sneeze. She held a hand over her nose and mouth. "Excuse me, I have a dust allergy. Happens every time."

Enzo was quick to pick up a napkin from the bar counter and give it to her.

"Thank you." It was perfect. His fingerprints would be all over the napkin. She pretended to blow her nose into it.

"Here, give that dirty thing to me. I'll throw it out."

Cora deftly moved her hand away, putting the napkin into her jacket pocket. "No bother. I'll probably need it again."

"Here's another. Take a fresh one."

"Ah, my allergies are really acting up. Thank you, Enzo." She took the napkin gratefully. More DNA gifted to her. She couldn't ask for better. The troublesome cigar was no longer needed.

"I need to leave. Please do give my regards to your wife. I'd love to say hello."

"Vera will be happy to hear that."

She thanked him again for his time, got up and turned toward the door.

"Good luck with your opening tomorrow, Cora. May I phone you to learn how it's going?"

"Of course, Enzo. Let's stay in touch." She waved, beaming fully, passed adroitly by several arriving waiters, and then hurried from the door.

She swiftly turned back to the diner, more than pleased with the ease of acquiring Enzo's DNA sample. As she walked she noticed a woman eyeing her from across the street. Nicely dressed, but it certainly wasn't Ursula. Cora purposely crisscrossed from one street to the next. Just as she began to feel comfortable approaching the diner she noticed the same woman again, this time pausing at a shop window, talking on her cell, and laughing. It hadn't been a long walk from La Luna and back, and there were plenty of other pedestrians hurrying here and there on the way, still it troubled her. Were all the problems piling on top of her making her too suspicious? A touch of paranoia? Or could someone affiliated with Ursula and her international buyer 'friends' be watching?

Two delivery trucks were busily unloading. She saw Stavros and Eddie assisting the truckers and showing them where to put their boxes. The sight gave her comfort. She recognized the utility inspector from Con Edison and breathed a sigh of relief. The power was back, and if the inspector gave his approval they were certainly back in business.

Stavros saw her and waved. The strong young man was smiling from ear to ear. Cora waved back, felt for the napkins in her pocket, and set aside any mistrust.

Harry Benzel seemed to appear out of nowhere. "Been looking for you, Mrs. Gus."

"Hey, Harry. You been here long?"

"Long enough." He grinned so widely that a gold tooth that Cora had never noticed before showed. "I think I'll be getting that free coffee pretty soon."

"Hopefully tomorrow, Harry. Thank you so much for your help."

He winked at her. "Always at your service, Mrs. Gus."

Stavros put down a box, stretched his back and approached. "Glad you're back. Come have a look around."

"Things going well?"

"As good as it gets these days." Then his mouth twisted in disgust saying, "Guess who came by looking for you?"

"Hunter? Hal Capps from his squad?"

"Nope. Our friend Robbie. Mr. Perry."

"Robbie showed up here?"

"He was a sight. He babbled about how the cops pulled him in, how your friend Hunter threatened to arrest him, how he gave the police as much information as he could. Names and numbers, and finally they released him…"

"Anything regarding Fiona Sweeney?" She was concerned if he knew anything about the pregnancy.

He shook his head. "Didn't mention her. He wants to speak only with you. He gave all kinds of apologies for breaking his word, how he meant well trying to manipulate his mother's jewelry for a down payment, blah blah."

"I get the drift. Any idea where he went?"

"He asked to borrow my phone, called Sara Sweeney. He asked Sara if he could come back…"

"To my place?"

"Yours or Fiona's, I guess. They only talked for a few moments. He returned my phone and split."

Cora heard her name called. She looked up to the top of the steps. The utility inspector beckoned. "No water contamination," he began by saying. "That was my concern this morning. Your electricians replaced a lot of burnt wiring. In fact, the amount of burning almost took down this whole place. You're more fortunate than you know." He pulled a small piece of bent and blackened plastic from his pocket. "This came from your PCB…" Cora didn't know what he meant, he realized.

He explained, "Your printed circuit board. It doesn't get melted like this without intense burning." He showed her the twisted, melted piece. "Component failure? It's possible. But your PCB had a high voltage protective diode. That's good surge protection. It's needed, due to all the power the diner uses. In this case," he spoke with his hands, "with surge protection removed, something was done to trigger multiple circuits to blow simultaneously. Possibly it became exposed to flame, follow me? One circuit right after the other tripped, and boom," he threw his arms wide, demonstrating an explosion. "Something's clearly off about this."

"You're saying a flame of some sort initiated the outage? What does that tell you? It wasn't that any of our equipment was overloaded." The inspector was reluctant to answer with certainty. "Your capacitors were spaced out properly, which decreases likelihood of component-failure burning. But we'll make a PCB failure analysis. And it obviously wasn't some freak lightning strike...Based on that and a few other things, I do think this possibly was an intentional outage."

"Set on purpose?" Cora cringed. Her worst fear was being confirmed. "Someone deliberately caused the outage?"

The inspector looked miffed. "I can't prove this, but I think it calls for a criminal investigation. I know the police have already looked around, but I don't know if they determined anything. My final report hinges on our own conclusions, and we'll be sending a copy to the proper authorities."

He looked around at the bevy of busy workers stocking the scrubbed freezers and refrigerators. "I'm really sorry about this, Ms. Drakos. You need to be on guard. Anyone in your life angry at you enough to do this kind of disruption or damage?"

"I didn't think so."

He wiped his mouth. "Someone with just a little knowledge how to disable an electrical system could accomplish it in a very short amount of time."

"You're saying anyone could have done it? No special instruction?"

"Virtually anyone with a rudimentary understanding of how electric systems work could. However, if someone burned down their own house purposely, we'd discover it fast."

Cora thanked him and walked inside her tiny office. The computer screen monitoring the cameras was functioning. She could view the alley and dumpsters, the front where Eddie and Stavros were handling a shipment of new supplies, the street view, and the parking lot. The power was back. The hum of kitchen appliances sounded like music to her ears. Thank heaven, she thought. Then she called Hunter. He was waiting to have Enzo's DNA samples examined as quickly as possible. And he also wanted to know the inspector's findings.

*

"Well, well, Mr. Perry," said the man in the shadows.

Robbie heard a deep, nasty voice and turned. The stranger was a brute of a man. Instinctively Robbie spun around and started to run as fast as he could. Within seconds the enforcer caught up. He grabbed Robbie by the shoulders and threw him to the ground. With a grin he stared at the frightened figure squirming on the sidewalk. It was dark, no one directly around. A low kick from the toe of a heavy boot hit hard into Robbie's soft belly. His victim cried out; hands moved to protect his soft middle. "Please," Robbie sniveled. "Don't. I'll get the money." Another hit with the boot and his face twisted in pain. He tried to roll and curled into a fetal position to protect his vulnerable organs. The attacker momentarily paused, looked around to make sure no one was nearby. He kneeled, and with a grin pounded Robbie's face with his fist. Robbie felt and felt the blow reverberate through his head. After an interminable amount of time the assailant stood up. He swung one more kick into Robbie's supple belly saying, "And this one is for talking to the fucking cops."

The pounding at the door stopped Cora in her tracks. She walked over and listened, putting a finger to her lips to keep Sara Sweeney from making noise. There were low groans from outside, following by a cracking voice.

Cora barely cracked open her door. She gasped at the sight of Rob Perry on one knee, his bloodied bruised face, blood running down the side, spilling all around his jacket and shirt. "Please," he managed to say with a sibilant sputtering noise, looking up furtively at a startled Cora. "Please." He extended a hand seeking her help.

Cora opened the door fully, Sara looked on gasping and staring at the beaten, forlorn figure barely able to stand. Together they managed to bring him inside, letting him lie beside the Persian rug.

They put cushions under his head. "Who did this? Marcus, Troy's thug?"

Robbie shook his head. "Some—someone else I didn't recognize." One eye was nearly shut with swelling, the right worse than the left. His clothes were bloodied and damp. Cora glanced over to the kitchen. Sara, unspoken, dashed to bring wet dishcloths and cleaning rags. She also brought a bottle of water and offered it. Robbie wanted to drink but was unable to properly swallow. He spit most back up like an infant. "My stomach hurts," he whispered, rocking, his arms wrapped around his aching midriff. Cora deftly felt his arms, legs, and chest in a search for broken bones. There didn't seem to be any, and that at least was a good sign. But she was also concerned about any unknown internal bleeding.

"Let's get these clothes off and clean him up," Cora said, pointing a finger towards the bathroom. "And lots of warm water and soap." Robbie had been unable to control his sphincter, and the stench of it was vile. "I…I'm sorry, Mrs. Gus…"

They worked slowly and carefully, meticulously removing everything little by little. His shirt, pants and underwear were caked with a reeking mixture of vomit, body fluids, and feces. Holding her nose Sara threw the rags into an unidentifiable black plastic bag. She tied it in a tight knot and shoved it down the garbage chute in the hallway. They found a clean shirt and underwear in the backpack he had left behind. Cora meanwhile wiped away blood and snot from his face. Soon his bruises would change color and shape, and the swelling would balloon. She knew he needed to be cleaned before that happened.

"Should we call an ambulance?" Sara asked.

Robbie groaned shook his head as hard as he could manage and refused. "No hospital. Please…" He began to cough. There was a little blood in his spittle. His mouth was bloody, lip swollen and the sharp edges of two broken teeth made talking difficult.

"One of my neighbors is a nurse," Cora said. "I'll ask her to come take a look. Meanwhile let's keep him clean, feeling if his ribs or other bones are broken."

It took an hour before they were able to help him dizzily stand and stagger onto a bed in the bedroom where Sara had been sleeping. Robbie was passing in and out of consciousness, fighting it, but aware that he couldn't control anything. Sara knew it was just short of a miracle he was able to reach Cora's building in his condition. She surmised he might have been on his way here when he was waylaid.

"The fucker caught me by surprise," Robbie groused, gasping to catch breath.

"Don't try to talk. You'll pull through." Sara fought back tears of her own, surprised that she suddenly felt sympathy for this man she loathed.

Meanwhile Cora phoned her nurse neighbor.

Kim, a critical care nurse at Queens Hospital Center, came over at Cora's request. She took a severe look at the injured man and evaluated Robbie. "He's a mess, but probably lucky he doesn't have broken bones. He doesn't realize how much worse it could have been. Usually we expect multiple fractures in these circumstances, broken ribs, legs, arms." Kim turned back toward Robbie.

"And you'll need to stay put out of harm's way and focus on healing for the next week or more." She gave him two pills for pain. "These will keep take the edge off for now so you can sleep."

The bedroom door closed behind Cora and Kim.

"That'll keep him sedated for a while," the nurse said softly, quietly passing Cora a handful of painkillers.

"Can he heal here without needing to be taken to the hospital?" asked Cora. "I think he might be better off ..." Her glower at Kim spoke more than words. Kim had witnessed numerous victims of deliberate violence, and she looked back at Cora with understanding.

Rob Perry, whoever he might have angered, might not be secure anywhere outside of a safe house.

"I bandaged him up, but it'll take a while to heal. However, he's certainly going to need a good dentist for those broken teeth."

"He can stay," Cora said with resignation, realizing her limited options.

Kim smiled sympathetically, and offered, "He's lucky to have you. I can provide a few phone numbers for good home care," she said as she washed her hands.

"Thank you." Cora said, thinking, *that's all I need, having this loose cannon stuck in my house.*

Kim checked again on her neighbor's patient, who was already fast asleep.

"I'll text you those numbers," Kim smiled and left.

Cora nodded, sighing deeply. What else could go wrong?

EIGHTEEN

"You're pushing yourself beyond your limits."

Cora looked askance. She was not eager to get into another dispute with the man who had become her closest friend and ally. "At least we're up and running at normal speed. Regulars cheered, and business hasn't fallen at all."

"That's certainly good news to hear," Hunter replied. "Nevertheless, you know I worry…"

Cora returned her gaze directly at the detective. "I know you mean the best for me. But right now, my life feels squeezed between the devil and the deep blue sea. What with this negligent jerk hobbling around my house, and me waiting for your results on Enzo's DNA."

"I all but begged the lab to have it rushed. The official Office of the Chief Medical Examiner is always backed up, even now with the newly expanded database. Naturally I've relied on a couple of friends to push it along. But this isn't a criminal investigation, just my request, plus Enzo didn't give permission, not to mention you obtained it illegally. So that's where we stand. Do I have to continue?"

Cora licked her lips in an effort not to laugh at the absurdity. "No need. You should have seen how eager Robbie's been to please. I mean it's almost embarrassing."

"You underestimate your sex appeal, Cora."

"I'll take that with a grain of salt, Detective. But thank you."

"Listen," he took her hand and held it in both of his. "We have no clue on who did this to Rob Perry. Troy Finley is being held for old, lesser warrants but he'll be out on bail before evening. This Marcus guy, Mr. Muscles, is somewhere in hiding. Maybe fled to Hawaii as far as I know. So, this new unknown guy could have killed Robbie if that was his intention—"

"But he didn't. I'm thinking he was careful not to break any bones. Just hurt him enough to send a message. He could have crippled him forever."

"Send a message to who?" asked Hunter. "Anyone besides me taking the time to look deeply into how Fiona met her death?"

"I don't know. Maybe this was a straight-out warning Robbie, get that money you owe. It's all still speculation. And now you're doing what you accuse me of: jumping the gun." She grinned. He started to protest but she stopped him, adding, "Is it possible they weren't trying to harm Fiona, after all? It's something else?"

"How much more danger are you looking for, Cora?"

"No more than usual." She kissed him lightly on the cheek. "Gotta run. The diner's waiting. We've got new early dinner specials starting today. Come on over and have a good meal. You look like you need one."

Hunter got up from the bench. "Give me a raincheck, okay? I'm swamped. As soon as I hear any DNA news I'll call."

"You'd better." She blew a kiss and walked away from the pocket park that was becoming a regular meeting place.

It had only been several days, but Robbie was rapidly improving. His strong young body got him out of bed, able to walk slowly with the assistance of the home aide Kim had suggested. He could speak better, but mostly kept quiet, inwardly seething at his incapacity, Cora could tell. Eager—too eager—to get back out and search for any of his contacts who could provide information on anyone who had considered using Fiona as a substitute for him.

In retrospect it was easy for Robbie to hate himself for running away, leaving Fiona alone and vulnerable. Because of that, he now felt ready to march blindly into worse danger seeking to unearth any possible culprit.

It was a preposterously stupid idea, yet a part of Cora sympathized with his personal rage. Cora recalled all too well her own blind hatred long ago after Dirk Bonneau, her fiancé, was murdered. Nothing could have made her think clearly then, nor prevent her seeking revenge. Why would Rob Perry be any different?

Cora was willing to do whatever she could to get information from her own street sources, but the investigation into Fiona's tragic death was mired in confusion. Was it really because of Robbie's debts? Or a warning to Robbie that turned heartbreakingly catastrophic? Add into that Fiona's surprise pregnancy, and the question if that might have played a role. Was Enzo or someone else the baby's father? How would Robbie react when he learned that? Or could it be the real father learned of the pregnancy and didn't take the news well. Could that scenario be what led to Fiona's fatal accident? The case was long on hypotheses and short on answers.

Cora could only think of one thing to do now: find the fired waitress, Veronica Labrano. She might provide some insight into Fiona's mysterious life and death.

*

"How did you find me?"

"It wasn't that difficult," said Cora. "Come on, let's walk." Veronica was surprised at the phone call she'd received barely a few hours before.

"I heard about your argument with Enzo. I'm sorry. What was it about, why did he go and fire you?"

With a sniff, clearing her throat, Veronica answered. "It wasn't an argument, really. Just call it a difference in ideas. You know…" There was a tinge of regret in her voice as well as resentment.

"Did you really insult him right in front of the staff?"

"Ha. Is that what he said, the horny, lying bastard?"

They took a leisurely walk along the boulevard near the bustling Queens Center, several expanded and updated malls featuring hundreds of shops, restaurants, and various big box stores. Close to Forest Hills, it was a couple of miles west of the Athena. To avoid Enzo's involvement, Cora found several phone numbers and addresses for Veronica through her own contacts at other nearby restaurants and personnel. A number of managers knew Veronica well, and a few had different addresses for her. It took a handful of calls for Cora to finally reach the waitress. To Cora's surprise

Veronica seemed somewhat uneasy when she phoned and appeared reluctant to meet. After some coaxing, Veronica reluctantly agreed.

"Enzo didn't go into much detail. Only that whatever you said was said was in public, leaving no choice but to let you go."

"I'm so sick of that squirming worm. The scumbag owes me." Veronica was adamant and angry. "You don't know, Mrs. Gus. We all realize he's a hotshot, big-talking fool. Money is like a toy for him. He teases people with it. Makes bullshit promises. That's the way he convinces you into doing his dirty work. *You* do the work, *he* collects, then offers spit and gets surprised when you complain."

They stood at the curb and waited at a light. A row of buses passed by. "You mean his coming on to the women? Looking to find ways for sex?"

Veronica began to say something, hesitated, and kept quiet.

"Look Veronica, I understand your reluctance. You need to be open with me. I'm not a cop. You don't have to worry about anything you divulge. Really, I'm just trying to get to the bottom of what happened that made him so angry to fire you like that. I had the impression he liked you from what you told me when we first met. Is he on a tear because of Fiona's death, or somehow taking it out on you because you and Fiona were friends?" She put her hand to Veronica's arm and held it. "Please help me out. Figure the truth." As she spoke Cora had a tingling feeling at the back of her neck. She looked over her shoulder briefly, wondering if she was being followed again, or was it merely her uneasiness?

"I'd like to help you, Mrs. Gus. But there are lots of things going on under the surface at La Luna. It's difficult to explain."

"Try. Please."

"I would but I'm afraid. I've told you that." Fear was palpable in Veronica's eyes.

"Afraid of what? Of Enzo? I realize he has the leverage to intimidate, but he can be handled, believe me. I've dealt with successful men in my life far more powerful than him. There are lots of other places needing employees."

Veronica blew out air. "It's like a Coney Island hall of mirrors, no one trusts no anyone. Everybody walks around on eggshells. Tiptoes. Frightened."

Cora seemed confused. "Why? Enzo's an expert on making people feel good. I know he's a phony, that it's all a front to keep wealthy customers happy, but whatever he thinks inside his head he plays village idiot outside…"

"No, no, Mrs. Gus. You don't understand."

The light changed and they crossed the street. "Then help me understand. Explain it to me. I'll make it worth your while. Find you a good spot to work, get you some decent money. Make me get it. I need to know. I need answers to find out what really happened to Fiona."

The two women stopped walking and looked at each other. Veronica weighed the possibility of opening a dangerous can of worms vs. keeping her mouth shut. Of confirming Enzo's nasty accusations against her vs. continued unemployment. She studied Cora's face for a long minute. Cora seemed open and honest. And had a reputation for getting results. Veronica took a deep breath and decided to gamble.

"You guarantee I can really trust you, Mrs. Gus?"

"I do. You have my word. Whatever it takes. What has Enzo done?"

"It's not Enzo, Mrs. Gus. Don't you get it…?"

"Not Enzo? So, what are we talking about?"

"I'm talking about Mrs. D'Amico. I'm talking about Vera."

"You're telling me Vera's the one running the show at La Luna? She makes all the tough decisions? That's no surprise. I could see that."

"She does way more than that. She's the real go-to for money." Here Veronica paused again, ready to go all in with Cora, but anxious about the outcome.

Cora pressed her. "Are we talking about money La Luna brings in, or are we really talking about something else? Something more than that?"

"*Shit.*" Veronica hissed with distain. "How do you think the place remains so successful? It's a small, out of the way of any major avenues…"

"But it serves quality food and sells lots of booze. Top dollar," Cora pointed out.

"Yeah, they have a great cash flow. Money comes in, money goes out. Enzo spends, everybody knows that. Big house in Westchester County, his private little hideaway, lots of new suits, clothes, puts away bundles of cash." Here she chuckled. "I've even caught him swiping some money left for tips, the asshole. But it's more than that, Mrs. Gus."

"He pampers himself, sure. But that's not what you're hinting, is it?"

"No, it's not." Veronica swallowed, her mouth dry. She stood shaking her head. "I can't. I just can't. I'm sorry." She turned away, ready to leave. Cora reached out to stop her. "What's wrong? Why did you stop confiding in me?"

"Simple. Fear, Mrs. Gus. You don't realize, you don't know them like me."

"So make me understand, Veronica. If you're being threatened, if they're holding something over your head, I'll protect you. I have the ability to keep you safe, but you have to trust me…"

"Can you guarantee that my name will never be mentioned, huh? Change my address and phone number and keep it secret except for you?"

"Yes. We can find you a new place. I gave my word, and I'll give it every time. If there's something criminal or unlawful going on I need to hear about it." Cora was chomping at the bit to learn what the waitress was hiding, but she already had a fitting idea of what might be coming next.

It took long moments for Veronica to regain her composure. They walked over to a quiet storefront, a flower shop, out of the way of passing pedestrians.

"A couple of times a month Vera and Enzo receive a package. Unique packages not delivered by food trucks or UPS. Some creepy guy will slip in before opening or just before closing. Enzo goes to his office, gets loads of cash in plain envelopes. Cash Vera likely hands him because we all know she doesn't trust her husband. The money is passed on to the carrier who quickly leaves. Hardly a word spoken…"

Hearing this gave Cora chills. Was it possible? Would the owners of such a respected and beloved restaurant prove to be no more than petty drug distributors? Callously making their real money from the miseries of sick and dying crack, fentanyl, and heroin druggies? "Go on."

"You know how these games are played, Mrs. Gus. Nothing illegal is sold inside La Luna. The place is spanking clean. They're not stupid or begging for trouble. Consider them like low-level wholesalers. The packages exchange fast from wherever they came. No questions asked. Cartels, who knows? Then it all gets sent to obscure networks of dealers who sell poisons on the streets where more hard cash changes hands. No credit. Their cut of profit gets directed to Enzo, or should I say Vera? He takes it, turns everything over to her, I'm sure."

Cora narrowed her gaze. "How do you know all this?"

"Because there are a couple of fools who work at La Luna who sometimes acted as messenger boys, delivering."

"And should I assume from time to time you've been one of those fools?"

Her laugh had no humor. "We don't ask or care what's inside. If you want a fast few hundred dollars ask no questions, and you'll get no lies." She gestured as though she was washing her hands. "Go back to the restaurant, pass along a fat envelope, go home after your shift. Easy as that. One, two, three."

"But why you, Veronica? Why did you agree to do this?"
She looked down, avoiding Cora's stare. "I feel shame, Mrs. Gus. I know I've degraded myself. But I'm alone with my kids. One has ADHD. Bills, meds, food, rent, I can barely cover it in the best of times. Don't judge me, Mrs. Gus. Please…" Her plaintive voice was like a small, lamenting cry.

Cora felt like a door had opened and bathed a dark room with bright light. Answers that fit—finally. Drugs. Cocaine, maybe heroin, fentanyl too. Maybe all three and more. La Luna served as an agent for contraband cartels operating down to the street. Vera's handiwork, Cora speculated, realizing the cash flow that ten dinner tables generated mightn't be enough to keep up their lifestyle with today's inflated prices. Vera assigned Enzo to be the charming public face, playing the role of smart moneymaking restaurant boss. Lauded by customers for his menu, admired by leading members of the local Chamber of Commerce. Cora certainly wasn't shocked at that, but the thought of all this trafficking secretly occurring at a restaurant with such a respected reputation made her feel revulsion.

"Now do you get the picture, Mrs. Gus?"

"Oh yeah." It was no revelation that Enzo was a pretentious prick. It fit. However, something else nagged deeply. She now had to ask an even more difficult question, one which she wasn't looking forward to hearing the answer.

"The truth, Veronica. Don't pull back now. I have to know. Was Fiona...was she ever involved in this sordid business? Did she ever operate as a mule?"

Veronica grew more uncomfortable. She hesitated, biting her lower lip. "Here and there they coaxed her to make extra money. She was always broke, ya know? Always needed more no matter how good the tips. I think she gave the cash to her shithead boyfriend, helping him pay his debts and gamble more."

That realization left a stench that wouldn't go away. An ugly reassessment of the girl who's life had finally turned around and was pictured as an example of starting a new life. "Who else was involved, Veronica?"

"Me and a few people who'd already quit. I don't want to name names, okay? Enzo, Vera, carefully chose several individuals they felt could be trusted, or who were needy enough to do as told. Sometimes we all need extra money, right? Remember, I have a sick kid to take care of. Medical care cost money."

"I hear you," Cora murmured as soothingly as she could manage. Yet her body remained stiff, her fists clenched, imagining a different side to Fiona. Exposing this to Hunter could put her own investigation at risk. Once she told him, the world would turn topsy-turvy, everything beyond her control. Still, he must be informed, and be able to swiftly get these horrid dealers off the street by shutting the doors and hopefully saving some lives. It came down to a matter of her sharing this.

"As I promised, your name will be totally kept out of this. Protected."

The waitress put her hands to her face and burst into tears. "I've been so scared for so long from all this." Tears streamed down her otherwise pretty features. "I despise Enzo, but I hate Vera more. She's a heartless bitch. Sadistic. You don't know what she's capable of."

"Like what?"

"There was this young busboy a couple of years back, a nice kid with ambition. He refused to be treated like shit by Vera's constant demands. He not only spoke up, but when she cursed him he spit at her. Sure, he was fired. We understand that. But a few months later he was found dead. Shot up with drugs, the tv news said, another sad, tragic overdose. Only the kid wasn't a druggie. He was clean, didn't use, but the coroner said his body was riddled with opioids. I think *they* did it, Mrs. Gus. I think they had him killed. Oh God, the poor kid was found at dawn in Forest Park, laying across a bike path.

Ruled an overdose, but I know better." Her eyes were wide and wet as she looked at Cora. "Do you get a bigger picture now?"

Cora nodded, hiding revulsion, softly replying, "Yes, Veronica, I believe I do." Opioid deaths were an ongoing and worsening crisis in America, and what better way to get rid of someone than shoot them up with fentanyl.

Veronica added, shuddering, "I pray for him like I pray for Fiona. Understand?" The tears turned to sobs as Cora held her in her arms on the street, passersby turning their heads to look at the two embracing women.

"We'll find out the truth, I promise. We'll find out everything and deal with it." Looking over Veronica's shoulder, Cora wondered whether Robbie's debt collectors still had anything to do with what happened to Fiona. Her death might have come from a totally different direction.

On her way back to the diner Cora struggled to unscramble the knots of scattered facts into a coherent stream of thought. La Luna had achieved an outstanding reputation for quality food and service, given a hundred four-and-five stars on restaurant review sites. Why would they lower themselves? Was any amount of money worth it?

She shook herself from these depressing meditations. She was sweaty, weary, and felt a raging headache coming on. This newly gained knowledge left her feeling dirty, desiring intensely to soak in a hot bath and remove the grime. But was it possible this new information wasn't true? Was Veronica making it up? Cora's gut told her that was unlikely, but a small part of her wanted to believe.

It was likely fact, and Cora knew it. The D'Amico's wouldn't be the first nor the last businesspeople seeking an easy road to affluence. And what better than not needing to ship these deadly substances themselves, keeping their own hands clean. Better fashioning a devilish pact to receive and move it along to a coterie of gangland pushers, covertly selling on corners and alleys. Let their crews hawk in the streets for addicts needing to be juiced.

Indeed, clean hands for Vera and Enzo.

Cora shuddered with the notion. There was no going back. Everything regarding Fiona's life had to be rethought. So many what ifs.

Thankfully everything at the diner was running well. Eddie worked his magic to keep the place operating smoothly. Sara covered the register and acted as hostess, happy to be back, keeping busy and not drowning in self-pity. Allison, Ronaldo, and Stavros had their hands full waiting tables, while in the kitchen Chef Claude, slicing and dicing vegetables was berating the new dishwasher, Carlos, while keeping an eye both on incoming orders and also line cook Diego, sweating over the big stove where chickens were baking, bacon was sizzling, and pots were boiling.

As Cora she came in she told Eddie, "I need to work in the office, but if necessary out here, come and get me."

She pulled her chair in front of her small desk and scanned the camera screens. All looked well. Relieved, she opened her laptop to review last month's staff records. She went over the diner's workforce with a discerning eye. Eddie Coltrane, Chef Claude, Stavros, Sara, she felt confident about. Even Diego, Leo, and Anna Pulido, a cousin of Sergeant Molina who worked long hours on weekends Cora skipped over. That left a handful of others. Suzie Grazer, a longtime part-timer, Faye Dominga, another stalwart, with good experience who came to the Athena as needs demanded. Holidays, summertime when schools were closed and the like. Alison Zoran, a regular who began about the same time as Stavros, proved a good worker. A handful of subs came next. Again, these were also experienced people Cora had known for a long time. Ashley Cribb, a divorced mother of three always needing extra spending money. Tony Faro, a student whose school schedule determined how much he was available to work. She liked Tony. She'd miss him when he finally earned his law degree. Busboy Leo was dependable, too.

Cora pushed her chair back and sighed deeply. There were a couple of others who came and went. Incidental staff, sometimes available, sometimes not. Line cooks seeking experience and ready to leave for higher-paying jobs elsewhere. Same with busboys and delivery people. No one seemed a likely suspect.

The list was as solid as she could hope. The Athena wasn't La Luna, she reminded herself. Don't compare. Still, she felt troubled. Veronica's admissions had shaken her to the core. A good workforce was appreciated, and Cora felt lucky to have them and luckier to keep them. Her own willingness to pitch in whenever needed, every job from cook to manager and janitor, helped instill a sense of loyalty among her staff. She worried what might happen to all of them if someone like Ursula's bosses were ever to take over.

The recollection of meeting with Ursula made her yearn for fresh air. She knew she'd be hearing from the European currency peddler soon enough. Meanwhile there were other concerns to deal with. She reached for her phone.

"Hunter," came the familiar voice.

"It's me. I need to talk again."

"No news. I'm still waiting for Enzo's DNA results."

"Not that. Nothing we can discuss over the phone. You have time to meet?"

"Okay. At the pocket park in an hour?"

"I'll make it work. An hour."

Sara Sweeney appeared stronger and abler than she had since the news of Fiona's death. She was trying hard to seek a little normalcy in life again, and returning to work was a healthy beginning. Cora was pleased to see it.

She glanced at Eddie Coltrane, and he understood Cora was leaving again. He nodded, giving a thumbs up. Everything was under control.

Again, Detective Jonah Hunter had arrived before Cora. She smiled, seeing him bending over, tossing handfuls of breadcrumbs to an assembly of pigeons. Some crumbs fell beneath a tree and other birds came swooping as if out of nowhere. Grinning, he reached in his pocket and tossed some more. It seemed so out of character Cora felt a chuckle infiltrate her cheerless mood.

"Getting ready for your retirement?"

He saw her and laughed sheepishly. "We always keep scraps and birdseed handy at the precinct. Weather's good, so I stuffed my pocket…"

"I didn't know you're a bird lover."

"We all have hobbies and escapes. I bet you're carrying one of those Greek philosophy books you love? In the original Greek no less." He chided her with a lopsided smirk. She smiled, sat beside him, yawning as he wiped his hands clean, not bothering to mention there was indeed a philosophy book in her shoulder bag.

"Aristophanes mostly wrote about ancient life through satire," she retorted dryly. "I pick up good wisdom from our ancestors. Including how to handle difficult situations, dealing with adversity, and why we make so many wrong choices. They're my best teachers."

Hunter wished he'd paid more attention to studies of the ancient world at school. Although he enjoyed teasing Cora he was impressed with her background and knowledge, plus the ability of reading these ancient philosophers in their original tongue. "So, talk to me. What have you come across you need to discuss?"

"Well, earlier I had an especially upsetting chat with someone who worked at La Luna. Someone who recently left. I promised not to use her name."

"I'm listening. Tell me more."

She faced him evenly, pushing away a small tangle of hair. "It's serious. It's also given me a troubling feeling regarding Fiona Sweeney. That perhaps..." She faltered. "Look, I promised my source in no way would her name be involved, alright? She has a sick kid and didn't have to tell me any of this."

"Whoa. Back up, Cora. I can't promise immunity without all the facts. I see you're uptight. Just relax. I'm a friend, remember?"

She lowered her gaze. "You're right. I'm feeling like I'm holding a lit stick of dynamite at arm's length." She drew a deep breath, counted to five the way her yoga teacher instructed, and blew it out at the count of seven. "I have it on good authority that both Enzo and his wife traffic drugs out of La Luna."

"Oh? You saying Enzo likes to snort a little coke?"

"Take this seriously. Big amounts. Bundles delivered, then covertly dispatched to assorted street contacts. This could be a bigger operation that I ever would have dreamed."

Hunter's face grew sober. "Give me a few more details. I can advise the Drug Enforcement Task Force. They have more manpower to investigate and—"

"No." Cora was emphatic. "Not yet. There's more." She took a tissue and blew her nose. "Listen...I'm also troubled that Fiona

Sweeney may have had some unexpected role in this. Possibly only a small part...It's all unverified at this point." She fidgeted, fretting over what she was about to share. "First, let me say I fully believe the person who admitted this to me. She's had plenty of experience. It appears that the D'Amico's have been functioning as an underworld go between for some time, accepting cartel shipments, quietly delivering to whichever gangs rule the streets at the time."

Hunter listened intently. He understood more about the hierarchies of drug crews than Cora realized. "Any particular names of gangs that distribute and sell?"

"No, none. I can try to find out more. This woman is savvy, although I'd guess for her own safety she purposely doesn't want to know specific names."

"They're all ruthless. M13, Crips, Bloods. Wherever, whenever."

"Hunter, what I need to tell is upsetting. I've done some soul-searching, and not liking what I find. It's possible, maybe likely, Fiona Sweeny was closer to these people than I'd ever imagined possible. That she may have played some part in running drugs to local dealers."

The detective shut his eyes, scratching at his chin. "Well," he uttered, "we know she needed quick cash. That would give her what she needed."

"Money probably turned over to Rob Perry to feed his gambling debts. I'm concerned the bigger his debts grew the more she took on risks—until she found herself over her head. Throw that into the mix."

He blew air out of his mouth. He recollected his lengthy interview with Robbie, simultaneously aware of his spurious charm, plus the list of names he provided that were suitable for investigation. Robbie obviously cared about Fiona, but his devotion coexisted with dangerous needs and fear of reprisal. Possibly creating an explosive, unpredictable combination. In his present state of emotional instability there was no predicting how he might react to this. Robbie was quite capable of doing something perilous without thought. While he sat evaluating the situation, Cora continued her own train of thought.

"Apparently the D'Amico's have been functioning like a well-oiled machine for a long time. And they've sucked into their whirlpool who knows how many others."

"For the moment let's stick with what your source told you."

"She claims that Vera plays the central role in trafficking and dealing, while he's up front, smiling and running restaurant business and looking good—"

"I need some proof to take this further, helpful corroboration." Here he stopped. "As for our wild card, Mr. Perry, I have no grounds to hold him, so he remains on the loose looking for trouble. He gave me no indication about drug dealing at La Luna. He's fixated on finding her killer. You think he knew about Fiona's complicity in any of this? Or she purposely kept him uninformed?"

"Don't know, but after Robbie left the precinct some thug from somewhere found him. Gave him a bad beating. Knocked him around pretty good without breaking bones."

"What? When was this?"

"He showed up at my door virtually on his knees, doubled over in pain. He's young, healing well, but a couple of broken teeth spoil his winsome good looks."

"Robbie's staying at your place?"

"For the past day so far. He needs somewhere to heal."

"Keep a careful eye out, Cora. He's erratic to the extreme."

"I've had Stavros coming in and out while I'm working. Sara Sweeney is staying with me, too. Between us he's under control. But I know the minute he feels he can manage he'll sprint out again."

"Back into the streets."

"Like you, my gut says he's going to seek payback for Fiona. Looking for his own clues, talking with some of former buddies. He's smart but blows up without thinking. If he gets any hint of who may have pushed Fiona he'll find some kind of righteous temptation to act. He thinks he's got justification for revenge and a perverted strategy to accomplish it. Right now he's remained focused on these jokers who do Troy Finlay's bidding."

"That's my presumption, too. But these things may have changed if he does know about the trafficking, and what I learned an hour ago."

"Learned what?"

Jonah Hunter took his time, debating if this was appropriate to share it with Cora now. She could easily see his doubts and vacillation. "Tell me, please."

He spoke low in a gravelly, grim tone. "The DNA report came back at last. Assuming the napkin sample you gave me is actually Enzo D'Amico's, then it's a match. Fiona Sweeney's baby is his."

The blood drained from Cora's face.

NINETEEN

Rubbing at a purple bruise that was turning green, Robbie limped to the kitchen. He poured a cup of coffee from a pot Sara had prepared that morning. Experimentally, he tested his shoulders. The left one still ached from his fall after the blow to his stomach. His body was sore all over, but he was able to move between rooms and no longer feeling like a cripple. The attacker's fist had marred his face, leaving scabs and contusions, making it impossible to shave. He hated looking in the mirror. While swollen and discolored, he could tell at least his nose hadn't been broken as he feared. Today he could breathe properly through both nostrils, which was an improvement. The sharp edges of the two broken teeth cut into the inside of his tender mouth when he spoke. He felt like a prize fighter who didn't make it past the third round. However, he was improving. The long days and nights of agony in the guestroom bed had passed. He was by no means healed yet, but strength was beginning to return. He was eager to leave this place ASAP even though he had to admit everyone from Mrs. Gus to her friends had been good to him and for him.

The whispering at night agitated him. He was aware that Cora Drakos, Sara and sometimes Stavros were having lengthy talks about Fiona, the police investigation, and whatever else. He recognized he was deliberately excluded, considered part of the problem rather than part of the solution. It was frustrating because his deep desire to help bring her killers to justice was being discounted and dismissed. He couldn't wait to get away and prowl on his own.

"You're jumping to conclusions," Cora had told him firmly. "It does look like she was pushed, but there's no solid evidence yet. Let these police specialists do their jobs examining the security cameras."

Robbie felt certain that Troy Finlay or one of his paid enforcers had done it to make an example of him by harming Fiona, demonstrating to others owing big debts what could happen if they didn't pay.

Sara Sweeney didn't want to hear any of it. She shut her ears to Robbie's annoying voice and theories even though she was quite well aware it could have happened exactly that way.

When Cora returned early from the diner that evening, she was in no mood to be confronted by her unwanted guest. "You think you have all the answers," she snapped as Robbie began to repeat his argument. "What if you're wrong? What if it wasn't someone taking revenge over your debts?" He had not been told the news of the DNA match with Enzo. In the current atmosphere Cora was concerned that giving him this information would immediately set off Robbie's explosive temper.

"I need to get outta here," he grumbled, gingerly scratching his scabby sore knee, wondering if in another day or two he could be on his way.

"You only think about yourself!" Sara yelled at him. Robbie looked startled. Weary of his constant theories and tirades, she had reached her limit.

Aware of the ongoing tension in her home, Cora sat on the couch and tried to diffuse the growing antagonisms.

"For the hundredth time, let the cops do their job. Analyzing video is difficult, you know that. If they need to, they can request FBI assistance. They have the best tech for retrieving images. Fiona's case is time sensitive. We know that, too. The NYPD lab is looking at every pixel. I've told you that a hand is seen on the CCTV video, appearing from behind, seemingly showing Fiona being shoved as the bus pulled in. Now let them go ahead and prove it."

"Yeah, okay. But *whose* hand? Who's doing the pushing? I need to find out."

"What's *your* plan, bigshot?" said Sara, again barging in and stirring Robbie up more.

Robbie was too frantic to heed the pang in his stomach when he realized that he had no real plan. He decided to revisit haunts and places he'd so often frequented, find some of the very people who names he provided to Hunter, people who'd been friends. Get ahold of anyone who'd heard anything, push, probe, even threaten. One way or another he'd be his own detective. There were scores to settle. He felt a compulsion to act now, whatever the cost.

Their conflict could ignite at any moment. Cora gently spun the argument in a less volatile direction. In her softest adult voice, she turned sideways and painstakingly asked without hinting anything regarding drugs to Robbie, "What did Fiona tell you about the people working with her at La Luna?"

"Lots of things. She worked there for a few years, remember? She told me about how her boss Enzo was such a schmuck. How he liked chasing his women employees, how he played around on his wife, Vera. And what a piece of work this Vera is. She cooks the books, uses double billing tricks, watches both the money and her husband like a hawk. Lots of cash flows through that place. Open bar, expensive booze, celebratory diners with guests to impress. All that kind of stuff."

"Any friends there? Anyone who didn't like Fiona or got out of line?"

He rubbed at the left side of his face where a healing cut itched. He hardly hid a grin. "Wow. I don't know where to start. There was jealousy. She had good shifts. Sure, she had some friends, but when it came to tips it was everyone out for themselves. Everybody vying for the best tables, best hours, biggest bar bills. You know this stuff, Mrs. Gus. You run a restaurant."

Cora didn't know if he was being cautious in his answers or just didn't have any insight into Fiona's world.

Leaning forward, trying to appear casual and curious, "This boss, this Enzo, didn't Fiona talk much about him?"

"When she was new at La Luna, yeah he tried to get into her pants. I knew that. Typical for that type of guy. Made promises, gave a small bonus for good work, told her she was so lovely," he frowned, not appearing too troubled by what he was relating. "She laughed him off, just another drooling idiot. You know how Fiona is, she hears the come-on lines and answers with a joke, keeps these creeps away."

"She never did any special favors for him?"

He shrugged, saying with special emphasis, "She loved *me*. I loved *her*. Still do, no matter how much she screamed and how many times she threw me out. It was my own fault, I know that. She was only protecting herself."

Cora became more cautious, asking, "All this extra cash she gave you. You were running up debts almost every week…"

"That's not true," he huffed. "I won sometimes. And sometimes I managed to pay her back."

"Oh bullshit!" Sara cried. "You lying bastard. She worked her ass off to help you out. Prevented you from getting killed by your buddies at the card table."

With a protest of innocence, he repeated, "I *loved* her."

Sara snorted in disgust.

"Your kind of love killed her," Sara spit out shrilly. Robbie glared back and retaliated, "But how would you know? Your husband's always away, working as far away from you as he can get."

Sara blew up. "When Mrs. Gus took you in you looked and smelled like a cigar butt in a spittoon." She was shaking. Cora realized both of them were out of control. "Go make some tea for all of us, Sara." Her gaze told the girl she meant do it immediately. "And take your time in the kitchen."

Without a word Sara stood up, mouth tight and fists tightened, and stiffly walked away.

"Shit. I can't wait 'til I can get the hell outta here," Robbie muttered, rubbing his hands over his face.

"You'll be better off waiting a day or two more, 'till you have some place to go," Cora replied calmly. "Your choice. I don't care. But look, I spent some time scrutinizing people at La Luna myself these past few days. Are you really oblivious as to how things operate there? Or you just don't want to talk about it?"

They could hear Sara in the kitchen, obviously pissed off, clanking a pot on the gas stove. Robbie looked evenly at Cora. "I'm not stupid. I don't like talking about it, especially in front of *her*." He looked sideways toward the kitchen.

Cora felt so sick of stepping gingerly around her unwanted guest. "If you really want to find out the cause of Fiona's death, tell me what you know. It'll help me sort out the mess."

"Look, I know what Enzo is, okay? I know how he followed Fiona like a puppy when no one was looking. Or at least when his freaking wife wasn't there. Fiona was so angry at that prick that sometimes she wanted to quit. But tips were so good, you know? I mean the place was like a goldmine."

"You think all that cash came from tips?"

"What are you insinuating?"

Cora heaved a long sigh. "You tell me, Mr. Perry." Robbie stood up unsteadily and silently limped around the living room. After a time, he delicately lowered himself into an armchair opposite Cora, and said firmly, "No, I don't think Enzo could be making all that money from his restaurant. Neither did Fiona."

"So, what did she say about it?"

"She mistrusted Enzo and Vera. She figured they were skimming money from everyone. Her, the waiters, the busboys, the kitchen. The suppliers, the customers, the tax man. Anywhere and everywhere."

"Any other sources?"

"Like what?"

Cora decided to confront him bluntly. "I think there were additional schemes going on."

There was no immediate answer. Robbie was clearly trying to find the safest way to respond. "Okay. Drugs are everywhere. I'm not gonna lie. I snorted some coke at card games when they passed it around. Me and Fiona would share weed from time to time. It's become a way of life. Human behavior. You know it too, Mrs. Gus. Why not ask Miss Goodie-Two-Shoes here if she's ever indulged?"

Robbie was trying to deflect, Cora recognized. Saying yes without saying yes. Direct confrontation was needed now, she decided, no matter what the cost. "I'll say this once, Robbie. Don't try to confuse me with your glib mouth and the excuses you give most people. At La Luna, Enzo, Vera, did Fiona ever tell you about their role in delivery of the hard stuff? A mule who carries it to the final destination. Good cash for prompt distribution. You know what I'm talking about? Don't even consider lying to me." Sara was standing at the kitchen door, a tray with steaming mugs of tea in hand. She stood frozen and nervous. "If you try to con me I'll have Hunter's people here as fast as this." Cora snapped her fingers.

Robbie's eyes grew wide, and he swallowed hard.

"Well?"

He stammered, out of character. "Fiona knew there were…shady, shady things going on. Some waitress, I think her name was Ronnie or Veronica, was said to be used as a courier, you know, a mule. Someone to minimize Enzo or Vera's risk of getting caught themselves. Carried stuff to some secret people at some secret address. It's a pickup and deliver thing."

"And what about Fiona?" said Cora.

Robbie looked over his shoulder at Sara. "You want inside information? Why haven't you asked Miss Innocent over here? Come on, ask Sara. *Ask* her!"

Cora watched as Sara shakily placed the laden tray down on the coffee table. "Shall I pour?" she said.

"I'll take care of it. Sit back down. Tell me the truth, Sara. Does Robbie know some things you've been keeping from me?"

"Like what?" She asked uneasily, avoiding the direct gazes from both Cora and Robbie.

"Go ahead," Robbie dared. "Spill it. All of it."

"Talk to me, Sara. Are there things I should know? Things that may change the picture of working at La Luna?" Cora purposely avoided using her sister's name.

It took long moments before Sara could say anything. Cora felt she could almost see the wheels turning in Sara's mind, seeking for the easiest way to explain or defend against Robbie's unspoken accusations.

"There were drugs, yes," she said in a low, tentative voice. "I was told it had been going on there for a long time."

"And where did you learn about this?"

"My sister told me."

"And how did she learn it?"

Sara shrugged with discomfort and guilt. She felt Robbie's eyes were like burning lasers on her. "She mentioned...Yes, Fiona knew..."

While she fumbled for words, Robbie interjected, "Fiona admitted to me she was informed where the real income came from. Cartel money. That Vera D'Amico had approached her about becoming a mule if she needed quick cash. And she admitted to me she spoke with Sara about it. Wanting Sara's opinion if it was worth the risks. If you didn't approve, you didn't stop her, did you? You were aware of it all, Sara. From the beginning. Don't play pure and surprised."

"I didn't know!"

"You did!"

Again, Cora interfered. "Sara, if you value me, not just as an employer, but as your *friend*, you'll tell me the truth. Now. All of it, understand?"

"Alright," Sara admitted. "Fiona was offered. But isn't it obvious she was coerced, can't you understand that? They knew all about Fiona's troubles in the past. Drug use, booze. Her rehab. They threatened her, okay?"

Cora narrowed her eyes with a hard and sharp interest. "Threatened her over what?"

"Him! This bastard sitting right there." She pointed a forefinger directly at Robbie, biting her lip and holding back tears. "Some time ago Sara said she needed to get her hands on fifteen hundred dollars. So, she went and asked for an advance. She went directly to Vera, who refused outright. Vera never liked or trusted my sister. No loans, no advances. Period. And you know why. So, then she quietly went to Enzo and asked him. He told her maybe he could get it, but she had to play along, make herself available to do things for him."

Robbie started to speak but Cora stopped him. "Go on, Sara."

"The cash, the fifteen hundred, Fiona needed it for her boyfriend. Robbie was in another of his messes, and one of the card players loaned it to him with strings attached. So, Robbie borrowed, played more, then lost it all in the same fucking game! He was in deep, and he knew it. That money was due. Robbie practically begged Fiona for help. Could she get it from her mother? Some friend? So, Fiona did what she had to, understand? She did Enzo's bidding for the cash. Robbie took the money without even a thank you. Ran out, paid off the guy who threatened to put him in the hospital, got high with his friends, and didn't bother to come home for days. Fiona was devastated." She turned toward Robbie. "Remember that episode, you motherfucker?"

Robbie kept his eyes lowered, staring at his feet.

"She did it all for him. And now she's *dead*!" Sara broke into heaving wails. Cora got up and kneeled beside her, hugging as tight as she could. It was true, Cora realized. The whole wretched heap. Her glare at Robbie warned him not to say a word. He remained silent. At length, Sara wilted into her chair, exhausted. Cora seized the abandoned tea mugs and distributed them around. They sipped the lukewarm brew, searching for the strength to face their predicament.

Cora made herself loosen up her body and minimize muscle tension. She knew that tonight might be the last conversation she could have with Rob Perry before he ran off half-cocked in search of vengeance. While he had been emotionally abusive to Fiona, she believed he'd had genuine strong feelings. Unfortunately, his macho pretensions could inspire him to do something dramatic and even dangerous if given the chance. He could self-destruct and take others with him.

"Can we all speak a little more calmly now?" she asked.

Robbie bobbed his head. He kept his lips together, covering the broken teeth. Sara dipped her head slightly.

"Robbie, do you realize how self-destructive you are? You're clever, street smart, charming and good looking. You'll even be handsome again after you get to a dentist for those broken teeth. I know so little about your background, but I do realize it wasn't good.

After so much trouble you found a friend and lover in Fiona, and you know how she twisted herself inside out to take care of you and keep you safe." Robbie had begun to relax, but as Cora continued, his insides started to squirm, wondering if there was another shoe about to drop.

"You don't know anything about my life," he protested.

"I know there were a bunch of things that soured. Loss of your biological dad, stepfathers who didn't give a damn. You have no place to live, no car to sleep in, debts everywhere, and worst of all by far Fiona's gone." Cora paused to draw a breath, and Robbie leaned forward to respond. "No, Robbie, don't speak yet. We, you, me, Sara too, we have to decide if we're on the same side, working together as a team to find out the truth. Or are we going to continue infighting, yelling at each other, blaming each other. Think about it."

"Well, I suppose you have a point. You and Sara, have been good to me, helping me recover. And I do want to be part of finding out who was responsible."

"Hey, take that chip off your shoulder, okay? I'm looking at a whole series of events needing investigation. You blame everything or someone or something without any facts. Shooting from the hip will get us nowhere."

"I hear you," he replied, looking first to Cora then to a subdued Sara.

"You may not believe this," Cora continued, "but there was a time…A time when my life was torn apart. My own partner murdered by terrorists. I went off the walls looking for vengeance. And I found it. Nothing could stop me. I fed the hunger that ate at me, tore me apart. And the results were bad. Stupid—on my part…"

Robbie's eyes widened. Mrs. Gus had a reputation, he knew. And now she was letting in a little light.

"I took responsibility for my actions. Spent years filled with remorse. I still pay a price, understand?"

His jaw slackened. "What do you want me to do?"

"Be careful. That's what I want. Don't get stupid with these street thugs. I know you'll get the hell out of here the moment you can, and I do understand your need for it. I got it for you." She tossed it to him, and he caught it easily.

"Your reflexes are coming back. Good. Now you'll remain in control, right? Search and talk to anyone you like. All responsibility is on your head, not mine."

"You have good skills, Mrs. Gus. I owe you."

"But I want a promise. I want you to keep in touch. Let me know what you find and bring it to me before you take any action."

She reached deep inside her bag and felt around for a moment, pulling out a cheap phone. "Here, it's a burner. Prepaid time." He put the phone carefully away. "Thank you for this."

She nodded. "Don't make the same mistakes I did. History has a nasty habit of repeating itself.

TWENTY

"Hello, Cora. This is Ursula."

"I've been expecting your call."

"I'm glad. Your time is up, my wealthy friends say."

"Oh really?" Her laugh was purposely sarcastic and uninhibited. "Don't be dismissive, Cora. One final meeting."

"One *final* meeting," Cora responded, intending to irritate.

This verbal sparring seemed to be setting the mood for the upcoming face-to-face showdown. Cora planned to win. Ursula was fighting dirty for a business deal, status, money or whatever. Cora was fighting for the life she had built, the people she cared about, and for her there was no option but winning. Night after sleepless night she had gamed scenarios for winning against this hydra monster of unknown proportions. Though she was tempted to contact Solerno to see if he had unearthed any information about Ursula's backers, she decided not to disturb him yet. He would undoubtedly take his time, painstakingly checking with his numerous contacts, old and new, legitimate, and criminal, he'd gathered over a lifetime. Once he had solid information on whichever cartel or organization was behind the hostile takeover of her diner, he would be there to judiciously explain his information and share his best ideas on how to handle it.

Cora headed out early to the appointed meeting place to scope out a table where morning daylight would glare into Ursula's eyes. When Ursula arrived, her magnetic presence drew virtually every masculine eye in the café. As she stood in line at the coffee bar queue, many female eyes were drawn to her elegant dress and aristocratic posture. Cora sneered, thinking, *She's wearing her best armor, doesn't that show me she's scared?* She wondered what the consequences would be if Ursula didn't return to her bosses with Cora's capitulation. What would be their next step? Burn the whole Athena to the ground? Cora promptly leaned back in her chair in as a relaxed, laidback posture as she could muster. Ursula placed down her coffee, saying "Good morning, Ms. Drakos." Cora waited until she adjusted her chair to turn slightly away from the light before offering a taciturn, "Morning, Ursula. I trust you're well this morning."

"Excellent, thank you. Ready to do business."

They sat wordlessly for short time, both blowing on and sipping from their steaming paper cups, once more sizing each other up for battle.

"Today I brought you the final offer my friends are willing to pay," Ursula said at last, not bothering to make taxing small talk. Yet again she pulled a folded piece of paper from her leather bag and slid it across the newly cleaned table.

"Ah. For me?"

"I do hope you have come to your senses about the generous offer we propose," Ursula ventured in her unmistakable accent, which Cora still couldn't quite place. She took her time in taking the paper, unfolding it, and peering. "I see," Cora said as she momentarily scanned the amount. Her poker face exhibited no emotion, depriving her opponent of clues to her reaction.

"Unfortunately, the offer has diminished slightly again," Ursula said impassively. "I asked my colleagues to reconsider, but they feel your obstinacy created unnecessary delays and slowed their suitable strategies. Creating cause for displeasure. That happens in business, I'm sure you understand."

Stone-faced, the reply was, "Although this offer is meant to be generous, your bosses are wasting their time as well as mine."

"Wait, Cora. You are aware the streak of bad luck you've been experiencing may not be over. Things happen. As with any businessperson, you run the risk of some unanticipated additional misfortune. I forget, how much inopportune ill luck have you experienced lately?"

Cora remained impassive. "You seem to know quite a bit about damage incurred at the Athena. Are you claiming responsibility for our losses? If so, I'm sure my insurer and the police would like to know," Cora added coolly.

"We keep current with events both positive and negative, and we pride ourselves on being a reputable consortium of international investors. Nor do we involve ourselves in petty illegalities. Nor, for that matter, do we dirty our hands." Ursula spoke emphatically, gazing directly into Cora's eyes. Then she dabbed the corners of her own eyes with a paper napkin. Cora took note of her actions, pleased that Ursula seemed to be experiencing a degree of discomfort. Cora decided to press the point.

"Have your investors ever given inducements to sellers of property or businesses to encourage them to sell? Study what will work and what won't?"

"We like to keep our ducks in a row. However, our definitions of 'inducement' likely differ." Ursula forced a wide smile exposing her perfect teeth. She wiped the sides of her mouth with her napkin again. "I will be sorry to inform my friends of this decision. May I say I believe it unwise on your part? There will be a considerable disappointment on both sides very soon. Allow me to add that I think you're being shortsighted under the current circumstances."

"Oh really? I apologize if this outcome frustrates your bosses," and here Cora leaned forward with candid cynicism adding, "And I do trust you won't find these colleagues displeased with you due to your total failure. As you've pointed out, the outcome of business deals can be unpredictable, and I wouldn't want to find out you also experienced some sudden unexpected misfortune."

With that, Cora pushed back her chair, got up and left, leaving Ursula by herself, startled, and unsettled.

Cora walked down the throughfare, relieved the meeting ended on her terms and feeling a little smug. However, once again she had the uneasy feeling of being followed.

The further Cora got from the coffee shop the more drained she felt. She looked over her shoulder several times but saw nothing untoward. She bent down to tie her nonexistent shoelaces, carefully scanning the crowd of pedestrians behind her. A couple of times she zigzagged to the opposite side of the street but couldn't detect anyone one pursuing her. Cora concluded that she must be overtired and perhaps also feeling a bit paranoid. It was time to get down to the real business of her life, the Athena Diner.

She was relieved to enter the restaurant's front door. The hum of conversation, the aromas of meals cooking, even the sight of Harry Benzel sitting at the far counter drinking one of his free coffees made her feel secure and at home. Harry saw her come in, raised his coffee cup high in greeting, and grinned with a big hello. She was home.

Sara was manning the cash register and serving as hostess, Stavros and Alison waiting on tables with their typical good manners. Cora entered the noisy kitchen to find that Chef and Diego had everything well under control. Claude had no trouble in reading the exhaustion on her face. With a snap of the finger, he had Diego ladle a bowl of comforting avgolemono chicken and lemon soup at a nearby table for one. Cora gave him a wan smile of thanks and sat to eat before retreating into her small office.

Hands to her head, breathing deeply, she went over the morning's events. Somehow she felt sure she hadn't seen the last of Ursula.

The first problem needing to be tackled was security. Ursula's repeated veiled threats of more 'bad luck' reverberated in her mind. She might be through with Ursula in person, but her backers were certainly not done playing their game to take the diner over. Securing the diner twenty-four hours a day was an impossible task. From here on out Cora felt she was at war. She considered hiring full time armed security, but not only would that prove extravagantly expensive, but signal to customers that something strange at best and dangerous at worst was going on.

She needed luck and she needed to be smart. She expected that whoever was behind the effort to expropriate the Athena would now intensify their efforts. Make things even worse. But when? How? She could protect the diner day and night, but at what cost both financially and physically? And what if the next round was personal? Coming after her either through some random act of violence or psychological hostility?

Cora again thought of calling Solerno but decided on holding off. And Hunter could not and would not take any action against a nonexistent hazard. Not to mention Solerno's unwillingness to work with police in any way whatsoever, and Hunter's refusal to be a part of anything regarding standing members or former members of organized crime.

Her office door opened slightly. She looked up to find Eddie Coltrane sticking his head inside. "*Ma gwaan*? he said in his Jamaican patois, one of the few phrases which he retained since coming to America forty years earlier. "How are you doing?"

Cora offered a washed-out smile, not answering his question. "Everything okay up front?"

"All good, boss." He dropped his own smile. "May I come in for a minute?"

She gestured. "Of course. Please."

Eddie slid the door quietly behind, his eyes asking if he could take a seat. Cora nodded without hesitation, trying to resume her professional appearance. "How can I help you?"

"Not help me, Cora," he said, dropping the 'Mrs. Gus' title everyone used during work hours. "Help *you*." He reverted to the proper American English he employed when dealing with customers.

She was taken aback. She stammered, starting to say she didn't understand. He held up his strong right hand, the years of thick callouses easy to see. "It's not hard for those of us with eyes, ears, and caring to see something bad is happening. I saw—we all saw—the dumpster fires, then that damn hanging dead rat. Listen, you've been bearing the brunt yourself, which is admirable, maybe, but not wise. I know you need some help. A team to support you with whatever the hell is going on."

"Eddie, I'm so grateful to hear you offer—"

He cut her off. "I may work with my hands, Cora, but stupid I'm not. Someone, some people are playing rough games out there. I see it in your face. Nearly every time I look at you I can tell you're hurting." He leaned in, fingers drumming on the desk. He met her wide eyes. "Talk to me. Tell me what's been going on. It feels like bad things are being done to us on purpose. I think maybe you have some enemy trying to put us out of business?"

"Eddie, we've worked together for almost two decades, years before Gus passed on. I trust you more than anyone else. But I…I need your word, your oath, that what I'm going to confide to you is strictly between us, understand? No one else knows any of this or must know…"

He made the sign of the cross. "My oath. Cora. Confide in me. Let me be your friend. You know how my life was before, in Kingston. The troubles. Bad trouble. I almost lost my life by fooling with that gang. When I fled to New York in desperation I looked for work. An all-night dishwasher for a year, then a janitor, mopping floors. Looking down on me like dog shit on their shoes. It was you and Gus at this diner who gave me a chance, who were there for me. You showed faith in me, said everyone deserves a second chance. You showed me the different jobs I could have if I worked hard, didn't steal, didn't fight, didn't make trouble. Busboy to waiter, then assistant and assistant manager. You even made it possible for me to ask Shantelle to marry me. To have our children. To make a good life. None of this would have been possible without you. I owe you more than I can tell. Now permit me to help you. To do whatever needs to be done."

Cora was filled with rising emotion. She sighed deeply and tried not to let him see welling tears. "Oh Eddie…" She held her arms around her midriff and let out a small whimper. "It was *you* who turned your life around. We only gave an opportunity. You proved your value long ago. The Athena wouldn't run without you." Then she reached out and squeezed his calloused hand. You're right on the money. There is someone out there trying to take the Athena away. For pennies on the dollar. Trying to steal it from me, from us all."

"Take over the *Athena*? How can anyone force you to sell? This is your home, your life."

She took offered tissues from a box on the table, sniffed and blew her nose. "Let me bottom line it for you. Some weeks ago, I started getting these calls on my personal phone. I don't even know how they got the number. Someone on the line told me they wanted to buy this place. At first I laughed it off. Some joker, a clown. Then a few more phone calls. Warnings. And then we had that fire."

He whistled. "I suspected someone, or something was behind the blaze."

"Right. We were advised to install cameras, new smart locks. Police promised that squad cars would take careful notice at night on patrol." She took a drink from an open bottle of water. "Then came another call, another threat. Not overt, just telling me time was running out. I had already contacted friends who knew the right people to check things out. It doesn't matter who. And they promised to learn all they could about who was doing this damage…"

"But it didn't stop," Eddie protested.

"No, it didn't. More calls, threats. Then that hanging rat." She looked up in disgust at the memory. "Next, our power failure. That couldn't have been accidental. It's being investigated. I don't know who or how, but I think it was sabotage."

"*Sabotage?*" Eddie was aghast. "The police need to get involved. What about your detective friend?"

"He wants to help, but right now we still have no idea who could have gained entry and not been seen by the cameras. I've checked and checked. Gone over every minute from every angle. And matters are getting worse. I met with someone claiming to represent these so-called buyers. They're trying to frighten me out of business. But then they don't know me." She threw her head back and hissed, "I've dealt with trouble in my life too. I'll find a way handle them."

"You may be putting yourself in danger, Cora. Ruthless people. Let me help."

"I think maybe so. And I've also had this feeling of being followed for the past week." She hunched her shoulders. "Maybe I'm being paranoid, I don't know. But I'm going to fight back. Fight with everything I have. Find my way, expose these criminals for what they are."

"Then let me assist. Just this one time. Please, Cora."

She nodded. "I need you like never before, Eddie. But most of all I need you to be here. To watch over the diner carefully. Everyone and everything. Customers, delivery truckers, even the staff…"

"Alright, if you let me watch over you, too."

"I need time, Eddie. Trust me on this. I need to feel free to use my own methods while not worrying that the Athena isn't in good hands, the best care. But I also worry for you. These characters *are* dangerous. I don't want you to risk getting hurt. Especially now you have that family you're so proud of."

"I'll do whatever you ask or need. But remember, the bigger your enemy the more they think they can get away with anything. We have a saying back home in Jamaica: *Di hiya di monkey climb, di more dem expose.*" She didn't understand the patois, so he repeated it in plain English. "The higher the monkey climb, the more he exposes himself."

Cora smiled through a rising tear. She stood up, leaned over and kissed Eddie Coltrane. "Then when this monkey finally climbs his highest limb I'll cut that branch and finish him for good."

With Eddie now temporarily taking charge, the Athena would run without a hitch. Cora felt an immediate weight lifted from her shoulders. All her time was now her own. She unlocked the bottom drawer of her desk and took out the Smith & Wesson .38 Special hidden under a pile of folders. The gun was legal, and she hadn't fired a single shot since that repellant event so long ago in Athens. She'd sworn to never fire a shot again, but times had changed, and she felt the need for essential self-defense. She carefully opened a small box of Black Hills Honey Badger cartridges and loaded it. The gun was placed at the bottom of her leather-strapped shoulder bag, the ammunition box she returned to the locked draw.

Cora closed her eyes and recited the Greek prayer of protection.

God Almighty, Lord of heaven and earth and of all creation both visible and invisible, look upon us who have gathered in your name. Be our helper and defender...

She got up decisively from her desk, slung the bag over her shoulder and left the diner with determination.

TWENTY-ONE

"What if they called a war and nobody came?" Cora wryly recalled a historic poster she'd once seen; it matched her mood. For the first time in weeks, she was free to fight all forces arrayed against her, and yet she felt at loose ends. Where to start? What did she know and what did she need to know? Robbie had gone, as expected, seeking some way to right the wrongs of his own doing, uncaring of any dangers he was facing. And Sara was back at work full time in the diner, struggling to regain a modicum of normalcy. Cora decided that home was the best place for her to sit still, reflect and consider her next moves. It felt like finding herself lost in a thicket, an unfamiliar briar patch, safe while standing still but a move in any direction would get her pricked by merciless thorns.

Intelligence first, she thought, chin resting on her hands, staring at the dregs of her coffee. Hunter and his group were dealing with the investigation of Fiona's death and his team had the resources to deal with the drug distribution network emanating from Enzo D'Amico's restaurant. But the escalating threat to the diner puzzled her still. Who was this Ursula really, this would-be aristocrat who appeared out of nowhere and presented bids and perils? Most importantly, who were the racketeers behind her?

Solerno's call that afternoon came as a welcome surprise. Daylight was fading when they met on a corner where construction of a high-rise was beginning. The site had recently been a row of half a dozen modest townhouses that had been bought out by investors and rapidly demolished.

Cora looked at the huge, fenced hole in the ground and shook her head. The new edifice certainly seemed out of place amid the older neighborhood surrounding of small homes and retail shops leading away from the busy Boulevard and its heavy traffic.

"Why did you bring me here?" Cora wondered aloud.

Solerno stood beside her and also peeked through a hole in the surrounding security fence. It was a tangle of rubble below, bulldozers amid heaps of brownish red brick gathered into mountains, and surrounded with huge dumpsters crammed with more debris of rocks, steel and broken glass. White and brown powdery dust covered everything.

"I've been busy making enquiries for you. Including lots of connections from the old days." He stretched his neck and spread out his arms, flexing his hands and reminiscing. "I try to keep my muscles firm and my body in shape. It gets harder as the clock moves faster." There was no humor in the small smile he gave, but Cora saw that for a man his age he looked quite fit and trim. "But it ain't the same," he went on. "So many of my old pals are gone. Guys I worked with, even a few who used to be on opposite sides. Those animosities change with time. If you live to retire it no longer pays to have enemies. After all, one hand washes the other…"

Cora listened, unsure where he was going with his small talk, and a bit afraid to ask. He had phoned her to meet so he must have news, but she wasn't going to interrupt him. Solerno put his hands on his hips, shook his head from side to side looking upward toward the sky, wondering how tall this new luxury condo residence was planned to be. "I gotta thank you for asking me to follow the money trail, Cora. It's been really interesting. And I got to talk to some of the guys I haven't seen for a long while. They've got new ways to launder money around the world, but the basics don't change. Get the cash, move it, switch currencies, launder and invest it somewhere safe in legit businesses. Sit back and collect fat income living happily ever after. And then do it all over again." He laughed loudly at the truth of how the more the world changes, the more it stays the same.

He noticed her rubbing at her arms. The temperature had dropped as the sun went down. "So, Cora, I asked. Where's all the new loot coming from? Is it coming outta South America, Central America? Drugs are always in transit. Is embezzled money still pouring in from Eastern Europe, fat Russian oligarchs eagerly obscuring their fortunes? Or is it from the war in Ukraine? Heaps of money pilfered, laundered, and pocketed? China's another hot place spending big, thousands of billions they move and conceal now, integrating into the financial systems of the world, making it look like it came from legitimate sources."

He paused, scratching at the stubble on his jutting chin. "Maybe the more important question is, where is all the money *going*? All of this cash has to land somewhere, right? Wind up buying everything anywhere and everywhere all over with these dummy shell corporations masquerading as legitimate. Oh, there's been lots of debating who's doing what. I was told about new ventures pouring into the Middle East. Look at those Saudis. Damn, some of these kingdoms are swimming in more cash than oil. Impressive when you can tell America off, no?"

Cora listened intently, not sure where Solerno was leading.

"Drugs go on forever, of course, but the cartels, they're a lot smarter now, too. Layering, it's called. Money shuffled around. Almost like playing Monopoly, isn't it. Buy a hotel in China? Mexico? How about the UAE? Working to buying up legal properties and businesses. Just as my old Mafia learned to do here decades ago. Now cybercurrency manipulation, that's a worldwide play, don't you think? Who knows how many billions are thrown like fastballs into it every minute. World events create havoc all day long, so anywhere can suddenly become the latest hot place to bury cash. Funny thing, though. All this capital, treasure troves of currencies hustling, no one sees it especially splashing around here..." He halted briefly to cough up some phlegm. "Damn cigarettes," he muttered after spitting on the dusty pavement.

When he cleared his lungs, Cora said, "Isn't there a trail of some kind out here? Who's straining to buy up in the outer boroughs beyond Manhattan and Brooklyn?"

He thought through how to answer best. "Unfortunately, there's no word on the street. I'd know if it came from the big cartels floating offers. And nothing I hear says it's coming from these so-called oligarchs. My contacts know of various muscle moves going on, but not that kind of big loads being lobbed around here. It ain't them, Cora. It's something else."

"But someone is funding this effort…"

He laughed. "Oh, you bet they are."

"Look, I've been prodded into meeting with this woman who calls herself Ursula. Blond, blue-blooded European aristocratic type. Has an accent, speaks fluent English with British pronunciation. She passes along these lowball, diminishing offers."

"An old school tactic. Ignore it. Tell me more about this woman."

"She phoned me out of the blue. Said she needed to discuss important business matters. I realized she was a front for these people trying to buy me out. We met at Starbucks. She was polite but no nonsense. She informed me her so-called 'friends' like to buy properties that appeal to them, and it's in my best interest to cash out. I stood my ground and walked away. A few days later, after the power outage, she called again requesting a 'final' meeting. So we met, and again I refused. This time I walked away leaving her flat."

"So, where does it stand after your final summit with Ms. Europe?"

"It's a waiting game, I suppose. I don't know what they'll do next. Maybe come after me?"

Solerno didn't like that. "You need protection, Cora? I can arrange something."

"I'm armed, Solerno. I know how to use a gun."

"I know you do." he said dryly. "Keep your eyes open. My guess is that they'll come after the diner again, but you never know. Stay vigilant."

She nodded grimly, aware of her vulnerability. "What now?"

He glanced around at the new construction site. It was more extensive than he would have expected for this lower middleclass neighborhood. He looked at the sign providing the builder's name. Something didn't jive.

"Listen, what I'm gonna tell you doesn't go anywhere else, ok?"

"My word, Solerno."

"I know I can trust you, Cora. There are these rumors humming these days. Nothing definite. Maybe total bullshit, I don't know. But this new construction location has made me curious…"

"I'm not following you."

"Let's walk. It's getting chilly. Here." He took off his army fatigue jacket and gave it to Cora. "Put this on."

She refused it with a wave of the hand.

"Put it on. It's getting windy. Too cold for that thin blouse you're wearing."

She took it and thanked him. Solerno never liked being turned down. Some things never change. He smiled as she pulled up the collar. It was clearly too large for her, yet somehow she looked good in it. Very feminine. It made him wish he were about twenty plus years younger again.

They walked slowly, strolling, looking almost like a man together with his daughter. The streets were dark except for street lighting and passing car headlights.

Solerno made note of the small two and four floor apartment buildings on the block. All of them built well over three quarters of a century ago, looking worn but well-kept, inhabited now by the latest waves of immigrants. Largely Spanish-speaking, plus Asian and Russian, with a mix of leftover old timers from European heritages. There were several bodegas on street corners as they walked, he noted, plus a Dollar Store. Cora could tell he was deep in thought, looking around and deliberating, nodding here and there, making mental notes.

"Any of places ever go up for sale?" he asked.

"Not too often. I think a family from India bought a place on the next block about a year ago." She shrugged. "It's not deemed a very desirable area. But squad cars patrol pretty often at night, so it's considered safe."

"Safe and cheap to buy," he speculated.

"Sounds about right. The Athena is on the fringe of this district, just off Jamaica Avenue, near the El train. The station is right there."

"Hmm. That station gets really busy, too. You have a good location."

She looked at him askance, saying, "You interested in buying my diner also?"

His laugh was loud. "Maybe thirty years ago I would. Not now. I'm just trying to piece some things together. Trying to guess what Ms. Europe's bosses really want."

The next block over a group of young people were gathered around a stoop smoking weed. Now that it was legal in New York the slow-passing patrol car didn't even bother to look over.

"Quiet area, too," Solerno muttered. "Also, not too far from the 59th Street Bridge to the city, is it?"

"Just a few stops on the express train. The local takes a little longer."

"Express buses to Manhattan run this way too, right?"

"Yeah. I heard there's an interest to expand the expresses. They're more expensive but reach Manhattan fast. What's on your mind? Thinking of investing?"

"Naw, not me. I'm just an old pensioner. I keep my own cash nice and safe."

They waited for a light to turn green and crossed over, passing the pocket park where Cora had met Hunter. The police precinct was also close by, but she didn't mention it.

"So, maybe a few of these loose rumors could pan out," he said.

"Tell me. What rumors have you heard?"

"There's a lot of chatter among my trusted contacts. Some hush-hush deal the governor is supposedly involved in. Right now, said to be a top-secret thing."

"Can't be very secret if you know all about it," Cora pointed out.

"You're really a clever smart ass, Cora. Okay, we, I mean all of us, just follow the money. No different than the fucking FBI, see? But I'm serious about this being pretty undisclosed stuff. A sly surprise waiting for us all, maybe."

"How about you stop beating around the bush?"

Solerno cast his view down and then looked at his companion with mutual respect, something not usual for him. "This is more than gossip, I think. And walking around here now confirms it, at least for me. See, our wonderful governor, together with our equally wonderful mayor, well, they have plans in the works. Big plans, I hear. Talk among my people say some biggie technology companies, maybe Meta, maybe Microsoft, even could be Apple, are interested in New York again. Being offered some huge tax incentives, and big promises. Forget that last fiasco that happened, the one with Amazon turning tail. This one—they say—has legs, real legs."

Cora felt a chill, and not from the wind. "This area. It's still pretty cheap. Off the beaten track to some, but potentially perfect. Is that what you're hinting?"

"Let's say that if your dad were still running his business in Athens, have him buy up some things around here."

"He's retired. But you're telling me what? Bigshots want to scoop up some properties in this neck of the woods in case this deal is real?"

He held her by both shoulders. "Pay attention. It's real estate, Cora. If these tales are true, values around here are going to hit the roof. If Big Tech were to move in, this whole part of the city is likely going to turn to gold."

She didn't answer at first. Her heart was beginning to beat faster. Solerno was making sense. Was it possible? "Cartels don't need to invest here. Eastern European oligarchs didn't need to bring illicit money here. They'd have no way of knowing anyway what the city officials may be contemplating…"

"You haven't lost your edge, have you, Cora? Come on, who would benefit the most? I mean right now, if some word has leaked, if someone on the inside of these secret talks spilled a few silent hints and winks…"

"Tons of money could be made fast."

"Real fast," he snorted with distain. "And big real estate builders would have hungry tongues hanging out like mangy dogs. The sneaky bastards. Buying and buying, then selling and selling, back to the city for a profit, back to the eager tech giants thinking of moving in. Someone in the know could clean up a bundle in the process. A new Las Vegas Boulevard has come to Queens. Get rid of the scummy low class locals while they're at it, see. Toss the jerks a few scrawny bones…"

"And break any laws to get what they want."

"Exactly. How can anyone fight these giant real estate companies? As Yogi Berra said, 'It's déjà vu all over again.' Did you know Columbia University is the biggest private landowner in New York? They're not the only ones. It's called 'scarcity in action'."

"So we have a new set of robber barons in the making."

"Twenty-First Century Agency owns this property here. Sort of new kids on the block. Been pushing their way in for about twenty years or so, but more in recent times. I noticed their sign at the site where we met up. They want to compete with the bigger boys. Get into the biggest games on the ground floor. And maybe they don't care how they do it."

A silence of agreement and understanding prevailed between the retired mafioso and the Greek owner of the esteemed Athena Diner as they ambled down the block.

Was it possible a colossal developer like the one Solerno named, or another, might by vying to rapidly acquire as much local real estate in anticipation of such an enormous venture? Why not? Capitalism was all about taking chances, wasn't it? From the invention of the steamboat to the airplane. Railroads to rockets.

"Do you see the scenario?" Solerno said, eager to hear what Cora thought of his spontaneous guess.

"Your instincts are always good," she told him. "If this company benefitted by prior notice of the project, they'd pull out all the stops. My obscure piece of land might be an essential piece of some master plan we don't know anything about."

"Right. A superior locality. Like a small Grand Central Station because of subway access. First you sell, then piece by piece everything around gets bought up. Pizza places, bodegas, insurance agents, whatever, retail and residential. Paving the way for office towers followed by high-rise condos. A good spot for those wanting a piece of the action in a trendy new neighborhood. Nothing illegal about that. We've all seen this game before. Call it insider trading. But…"

"But if one stubborn business in a crucial location doesn't want to play, it could create a delay or throw a curve ball into a rigid planning schedule."

"They play hardball. They'd kick this slowdown out of the way. A little fire here, a verbal threat there. Any small business would become alarmed."

"As in thinking drug lords or organized crime gangsters are involved. What have they got to lose? Bullying, intimidation. Do what you gotta do."

"Bingo, Cora. This is all speculation. No proof of anything—yet. But you've had three warnings, the last temporarily putting you out of business. You told me the cops are investigating, but it could take years to prove with the bureaucratic nonsense involved. You can't afford to sit around and wait. And you shouldn't. Tell me again about the power outage that almost ruined you."

Cora went into slow detail, finishing off by saying, "Someone, somehow must have slipped into the diner before closing. Hid nearby, then after the staff was gone manually pulled all the right switches."

"Wouldn't it be possible for somebody to hide away inside the Athena? A bathroom, a closet? You think of that?"

"Bathrooms are mopped and cleaned every night. No exceptions. My little office gets locked tight without exception. As for closets?" Here she hesitated and acknowledged vulnerability. "Our few closets are mostly jammed with stuff. Shelves loaded with canned foods, extra cutlery, boxes of industrial cleaner. You know what every restaurant needs."

"Got a coat closet?"

"Pocket-sized, mostly used by staff. But lately the weather's been warmer, not so much." She rubbed knuckles against the side of her cheeks, pondering. "If someone crawled under our lowest shelf of extra aprons in a closet they might be able to hide. It's not a big or very deep space…"

"Could a man fit into it?"

"I doubt it. These are big guys I work with. Young men like Stavros, tall and muscular. My chef is even taller, his assistant no, but bulky round the gut. I don't see it. Besides, I trust these guys. They've worked for me for so long. Stavros is newer, but I know his family well. Unlikely, Solerno. No."

"Then what about a woman?"

Cora paused thoughtfully. "A woman might fit. But it would be uncomfortable."

"Well, what if the woman didn't come in as a customer?"

"Then it has to be staff."

Solerno nodded dolefully. "Get back to the diner," he advised. "Look around carefully. Check over the staff roster, current personnel as well as those who maybe left recently for one reason or another. Someone who knows the diner layout well, who's also aware of who stays late, and maybe how to keep out of sight at the right time." He stopped abruptly with a memory of his own. "You know, my Family had an informer once. He was with us for maybe a decade. Good guy, too, we thought. Took orders and seriously carried them out. Then one day we found out he betrayed our boss for a few worthless promises from another Family. Such a shame. Monumental mistake. I don't need to go into detail, let's just say that his own personal family never saw him again."

"I get the warning. Thank you." Cora stood up slightly on her toes and kissed him on his bony cheek. "You give better advice than a priest, Solerno. I'll be in touch."

The time weathered ex-hood stood with a contented grin as Cora removed the fatigue jacket he'd lent her and walked briskly in the direction of the Athena, waving behind with her hand in the air.

Not bad for an old mafioso, Solerno though cheerfully to himself, slinging the jacket over his shoulder and walking in the opposite direction.

Cora couldn't wait to dig into the fresh ideas Solerno provided. She headed to the diner with an extra bounce in her step. At last some of the crazy events and disasters that had befallen the Athena during these past few weeks began to make sense. If she could find some underlying pattern, identify a likely culprit or culprits, she could plan a counterattack.

Eddie confronted Cora as soon as she passed the cashier's station just inside the diner.

"Hey, Mrs. Gus. I thought you were taking some time off. What are you doing back here tonight?"

"Nothing big, Eddie, I just wanted to check on some back orders I forgot about. I'll work in my office for a while. You're still running the show." Eddie listened, nodding. Cora did what Cora thought was necessary. She greeted the various staffers with smiles and waves and disappeared into her office. The door was left partially open. Eddie heard her computer power up.

Cora deftly pulled up staff rosters for the last few weeks, trying to narrow down likely perpetrators for sabotage. Glancing over some scribbled notes she saw that Eddie was planning to visit family in Kingston for two weeks of vacation; he had new nieces to meet and his two teenage kids to show off. Suzie, the likable part-timer, was hoping for five days to spend at Atlantic City, enjoying the casinos and beaches. Stavros already delayed his own plans to go skiing in New Hampshire this winter and was set to go as soon as the resorts reopened.

As Cora perused the upcoming schedule she could hear the banter coming from the staff outside her door. Business was all but done for the night, and staff were relaxing, sitting at the counter, snacking, drinking soft drinks and coffee, and chatting. She smiled a little as she could hear Stavros flirting with Allison. It was obvious to all he liked the appealing slender waitress who had one of the nicest smiles Cora had ever encountered.

"Skiing is one of my favorite things in the whole world," Stavros was saying. "I'm already saving up. If you like, maybe we can go together next year."

Allison ignored the offer. Her dream vacation was Hawaii, she answered, adding, "But not the overcrowded beaches on Honolulu. No way. When I go I want to see *natural* Hawaii, maybe even that huge volcano Haleakala on Maui, or maybe the falls and rainbows at Hana on Kawai."

Impressed with her knowledge, Stavros said, "Sounds great, also. It's sure on my bucket list. How do you know so much about it? Been reading travel books?"

She laughed innocently. "Of course! Doesn't everyone?"

Cora kept her smile as she heard every word. Oh-oh, she thought. Stavros is smitten.

"My husband is taking me, too, one day," Sara called from the cashier's booth. "Allison, I envy you. I want to hear more."

There was general laughter all around. Eddie chimed in. "I've always wanted to go…"

"Who hasn't?"

Showing off, Allison said, "Did you know Hawaii is the best place in the world to see rainbows?"

"Really?" said Stavros.

Cora had listened to the staff's conversation flowing gently past her ears, almost like some light music playing in the background.

"Come on," Stavros urged, "Is that really *true*?"

"It is," chimed Allison, repeating the phrase, "It's definitely the best place to see rainbows in the world!"

Something about hearing that caused Cora to stop her work mid-sentence. She'd heard that exact phrase recently. Where? She cudgeled her brain but couldn't quite place it.

Clear and uninhibited laughter broke out among the staff, now preparing to clean up for tomorrow's shifts. Cora pushed back in her swivel chair, moving tendrils of hair away from her eyes as she rubbed at a stiffness in her neck. She dropped her pen with a devastating realization. It was Ursula who had mentioned Hawaii and rainbows.

Getting up slowly, she sauntered from her office door and forced a hint of a smile. She beckoned to Allison. "Can I see you for a moment?"

Allison slid off her stool. "Of course, Mrs. Gus."

She came into the office cheerfully, surprised when the door closed.

"I overheard you talking about Hawaii a moment ago."

The young woman's eyes widened brightly. "Oh, yeah. I'm just dying to take a trip. I hear so much about it."

Cora relaxed by sitting on the edge of her desk. "Where did you hear that expression about the rainbows?"

"Oh that." Allison laughed with a big smile. "I hear it a lot. My mother's been there. She says it all the time. I think she uses it like an icebreaker when she meets new people."

"Colorful phrase," Cora muttered. "Well, maybe I can do some adjusting on your schedule. Let me see." She took hold of her laptop and put it on her lap. A finger ran down the list of names." There you are. Allison Zoran, right?"

"Right, Mrs. Gus."

"Interesting surname. European, like mine. Drakos is Greek, you know. What's the background of Zoran?"

"Serbian. My parents came from there a long time ago."

"Both your mom and dad?"

Here Allison frowned. "Only my mom now, Mrs. Gus."

"Oh, I'm sorry to hear that. What happened?"

"He and my mom divorced a long time ago. He died back there. She came here and went to work to support us."

"What does your mother do? For a living, I mean."

"Well," and here Allison became a bit reserved. "She's done a lot of things. Her work takes her away much of the time."

"What kind of work?"

"Real Estate mostly. She's a specialist…" She looked at Cora quizzically. "Why all these questions, Mrs. Gus?"

Cora didn't answer. She looked again at the schedules. "The phone number I have, that's your cell phone, right?"

"Yes. I gave you mine. And you've called me a bunch of times when you were short-handed, remember?"

Cora nodded. "You're right. I remember now."

"Yes, um, why all the questions?" Allison asked again uneasily.

"Oh, don't mind me. I always like to get to know my employees better. Am I being nosy? I don't mean to. But look, I don't have any emergency numbers for you. Everyone needs to give me one. Just in case. Please, give me your mother's number to keep here. It's my policy."

"No problem." She gave the number, Cora noticing a slight hint of suspicion on her face, so she smiled fully and closed her laptop.

"Okay, great. Come on, I'll help you guys with cleanup so you can get outta here a little early."

TWENTY-TWO

The closet shelves were cluttered as expected, jammed with emergency canned foods, peanut butter, jams, and more. There was a large box of extra placemats and napkins on the top shelf side by side with boxes of paper cups and take-out boxes. Then there was a shelf of new cups, saucers, and plates. Cutlery, a toolbox, various condiments, salt, and pepper.

Cora bent down and examined the space available under the last shelf. Could she fit under it? Maybe crouching with her knees up, arms wrapped around them. She tried to squirm herself into the darkness. It was a tight squeeze, but she could do it. How long would someone have to hide after the staff finished cleaning and left? If the diner's late staff that night had finished and gone home before eleven or so, maybe someone could remain an hour. Then about midnight crawl out, sneak over to the fuse boxes, and interfere with the power. Shut the diner down completely.

Cora was tall and limber, and she mused that a younger, thinner person might have an easier time remaining scrunched for longer than an hour if necessary.

She edged out and went back to the scheduling to double check what she already knew and suspected. Allison was working a shift that could have allowed her to slink out of sight into the bathroom while the final touches were finished. Then slip toward the kitchen, while Eddie, or herself or Stavros were locking up and remain hidden in the closet as long as needed. Allison was barely twenty, shorter, well-built but supple. It would be possible for her.

The idea of it filled Cora with fury. The waste of food, the damage, the costs of repair, the people she called friends thrown out of work, not to mention the price tag of losing days of business and customers stoked her anger.

Stay cool, she told herself, thinking what both Hunter and Solerno would be advising now. Opportunity to commit a crime wasn't proof. An outsider might yet have been responsible. Perhaps a teenager pulling it off for kicks. Perhaps a kid with a grudge or gangland initiation.

Start with what you know, she told herself. She put her feet up on the desk, squirming restlessly to get comfortable. She punched a number into a new burner phone she had tucked away in her desk.

"Yes?" came the voice on the other end. An accented voice.

"Hello, Ursula," Cora said in a strong timbre.

"Who's this?"

Cora gently clicked off the phone. A solid lead. A moment of exhilaration, followed by a cry of deep despair. Cora dropped her face into her hands, weeping silently. Sweet-faced, energetic, happy-go-lucky Allison Zoran was Ursula's daughter. Was Allison a plant from the beginning, seeking work at the Athena so she could learn how to undermine it? Spying from day one, or did that come later? Could Alison have been used by her mother and the unknown people behind the effort to take over the diner?

Betrayal. Cora felt crushed. At this moment, more than anything she missed her mother's soothing voice whispering words of comfort, assuring her everything would eventually turn out well. She longed for the reassurances that had given her hope back then, although she never learned the reason for the death of her partner and lover, Dirk Bonneau. That with time Cora would begin to heal. She would build a new life. Cora hadn't believed it possible then, but in fact her mother's assurances had proved prophetic. America awaited, a new world, which indeed provided Cora with a new life.

Now that was in jeopardy. Because of some individual's greed, all her years of work, her vows to Gus to keep the Athena alive, might be for naught. This little restaurant in a quiet older neighborhood of Queens had been his own life and soul, and now it was Cora's too. And at this moment, she didn't know how to keep it from dying.

*

Robbie pulled back his hood and sat at a table near the edge of the bar's pool table. Dim lighting and shadows helped hide the healing bruises on his face. His stomach muscles ached. He was gaining strength, he could feel it. He kept his mouth closed, his tongue feeling the tender gums and sharp broken teeth. The bulky man sitting opposite regarded him with reservation. Though his poker partner appeared calm and collected, Andre DuPont knew Robbie well and was fully aware how volatile he could be. Andre crossed his designer clad IGGY lambskin jeans and Loubitin shod feet. He was prepared to deal with Rob Perry if necessary. Andre sipped at his beer bottle, then folded his arms and waited. "Your lip is scabbed, man," Andre said at length.

"I'm grateful you agreed to meet me," Robbie countered, twirling his own beer bottle slowly on the table, ignoring the comment. The vibe of the bar was like a throwback from a movie, he thought, looking from Andre to the dark booths, the small hanging lights over the dark teak wooden tables. Fans spun lazily from the ceiling. Only a few other people were there in the midafternoon, a man and a woman huddled at a far booth chatting softly. The smell of alcohol pervaded the room. The bartender was sorting something unseen with his hands below the bar, unconcerned with his few customers. A young waitress sat on a stool near him studying her fingernails.

Robbie leaned forward, focusing intently on his interlocutor's eyes. Andre leaned back in his chair. "You know I've had bad trouble with Marcus and Troy lately," he said through gritted teeth. "I don't have a rich family to turn to like you or Stuart. Or Devin from the Hamptons."

"Hey man, nobody forced you to play these all-nighters with us. You were glad—eager—to meet guys like me and them. You were drooling to hang with us, be like us, slobber over the sizzling hot ladies we party with, so don't come crying to me about it now."

"How do I make you understand? I loved Fiona. I'm scared. She was on her way to *school*." His voice cracked, and Andre felt a pang of sadness. He'd never met Fiona, didn't know anything about her, but dying the way she did, that was bad.

"Yeah, I heard about it," he said with a dour frown. "Everybody's heard. It was all over the news. Rob Perry's angel who paid his debts, a shame."

Clenching his teeth, Robbie tried to hold back his impulse to grab Andre Dupont by the collar and yank him closer and spit in his smug face.

Andre saw Robbie's eyebrows knit, his mouth tighten and his fists clench. He realized that Robbie was about to erupt. Instinctively Andre leaned further back, relaxed his face and hands, and lifted his beer to his lips. Several swigs later, he emitted a small, almost polite belch. "Chill, man," he said. "You asked me here to see if I help you".

He gave Robbie plenty of time. Robbie eased himself, grabbed his bottle, tried to settle in for a quiet talk. "Sorry, man."

Andre studied Robbie's face, like a professional assessing damage. Robbie squirmed but resisted the urge to cover his discolored mouth. Recovering his cool, he said, "So, you know the score, and I admit I fucked up. The reason I asked you to meet today wasn't for sympathy. It's about information. You heard what happened, you said. She was killed in some freakish bus accident during that bad storm. Maybe pushed. I gotta know if it happened because of me, because of the losses I ran out on."

"Whoa, that's a pretty big leap, Rob. You owe twenty-five large, right? All on a single fucking football game by taking the spread?" He held up his palms, making Robbie feel really stupid.

"You don't understand the circumstances, Andre. It was a desperate move to cover my losses. Okay, I dug myself into a deep, deep hole. But then I heard about Fiona from her sister. I was terrified but anxious for answers. I blamed myself and came hurrying back. I wondered if her death may have been a result of my trying to hide. Absurd? Maybe, but I wasn't thinking straight."

"Still a pretty dumb thing to do, Rob. But if you're asking if anyone might have targeted her because of it, I don't think so. You're worth more alive than dead to Troy, right?"

"That was my thinking, but Andre, I just don't know anymore. Everything's become so damn confusing. Troy was threatening me, you know that. I mean in ways like I'd never heard before. Sending that ape Marcus to track me down. I had to get away fast. Get as far as I could. Even Fiona told me to run."

Andre shook his head slowly. "She must have really, really loved you, man. Nobody was surprised with all the I.O.U's you have around town. But then for Troy or some goon to go after your girlfriend like that? *Push her in front of a bus?* Shove her, risk killing her? That would be *something*. You thinks these guys would jeopardize themselves being caught for a murder? Wow. And now, after the stunt you pulled with getting Troy arrested, everyone in the world is keeping heads down until the cops lose interest."

"Hey, I didn't pull any stunts. I had to find Troy so I could try to placate him. And maybe learn if there was some weird connection with Fiona. I needed to find out, I still do. I'm so sick over it…"

"You're dreaming if you expected Troy to admit to anything like that."

Robbie realized he wasn't talking logic to his poker buddy. "Also, I brought some jewelry with me. I stole it and wanted him to accept it as a down payment. Better than nothing, no? Troy himself picked out the place to meet up and I agreed. His choice, not mine. The minute we met the police showed up. But I have no idea how these cops appeared out of nowhere, or how they were alerted. Whatever went on, that's not on me."

Andre Dupont shrugged. "Whatever went down. I'm just repeating what people are saying. Troy Finlay being shoved into a cop car in broad daylight. Wow." He whistled and chuckled at the notion of the sight.

Gruffly, Robbie said, "Maybe I'm a lot of things, but I'm *not* a rat. I give my word the arrest had nothing to do with me. The police took me and interrogated me too."

Andre listened, held up his hands, fingers spread wide. "Hey, okay. I'm just saying. And if you don't already know it, listen, Troy Finley got released on minimal bail for inconsequential old charges. As usual, none of the shit really stuck to the wall. He's a crafty pro, back free as a bird, taking all the new bets he can handle. You really had your ass handed to you. In spades. That's a good start from them. Doesn't mean someone won't come after you some more, this time break a few bones, just that maybe you've got a little time to deal with this girlfriend thing. Hell, you owe me seventy-five hundred not counting the vig for late payment, and I'm sitting here in this dump still talking to you. The truth, Robbie, I haven't heard a single word about your girl being on anybody's list. That's a stretch. I think you're barking up the wrong tree. Maybe feeling paranoid after what happened? Nobody's talking that way, and nobody's bragging. Nada." He looked Robbie straight in the puffy eye. "There's other fish for them to fry. Think Troy or Marcus or any of those slimy animals would chance life in prison over your twenty-five k? I don't. They *wanna* scare you, man. Freak you out every which way. That's what they do. And it looks to me like they've done a real good job."

"But I don't believe in coincidences," Robbie protested.

"Okay, don't. But I think it's bullshit. My advice is to keep ducking while you do your looking for answers." He held his bottle high, lifted his head and drank in loud gulps.

Robbie slumped dejectedly. "Thanks, Andre. I believe you. I still consider you a friend, and I owe you."

"You sure do," Andre said with a touch of irony. "Seventy-five hundred. And I want it in cash. I don't do jewelry. Now let's get the hell outta here."

Robbie hunched his shoulders and walked down the block. He was baffled and worried. Was Andre playing him, or could it be that Troy and his enforcers didn't have a role in Fiona's dying. An accidental tragedy? But *someone* pushed her...

He knew very well that when needed Fiona had acted as a mule for her boss. A secret kept between them and never discussed. He acted as though he had no inkling about it, but he knew it was true. He also knew that the money was good and that more than once she had given it to him, helping to keep him out of trouble. Was it possible that someone at La Luna had it in for her? Why would they? It made no sense. No way was she a snitch. The very thought was ludicrous. She was making good money with every delivery. Why would anyone there turn on her?

He took the remaining cash he had from his pocket. Sixty bucks. Nowhere to go. No one to borrow from, no friends to call. Everyone had cut him off. He was alone and broke in New York. Maybe he could spend a night or two in a shelter. Get a few free meals from charities. Then what? Call his mother, beg her to let him come back? Listen to her berate him for stealing jewelry on top of everything else. She had already saved his ass, lying to the police, telling the detective who called that she indeed did give it to him to hock. If not for that he'd be facing theft charges, rotting in a cell with no one to ask for bail money. It was a real mess, he knew it.

Robbie recalled Cora's plea to keep in touch, and although normally he would ignore requests, he also recognized that the diner owner was smart. Deemed a credible investigator in her own right. And at this moment, her opinion carried weight.

"I need to talk to you, Mrs. Gus."

His voice was high-pitched, hesitant, and somewhat frantic. "I spoke with a friend, things may not be what we thought. Listen to me—"

"Slow down, Robbie," Cora said.

"I...I've been trying to work things out in my mind. Fiona...It may not have been the guys after me. It could have been something to do with La Luna, those people, see?"

"I hear you, Robbie. Slow down."

"You asked me to keep in touch, right? I'm trying to explain what I've been up to. This friend, this poker buddy, we met up. He says it wouldn't be any bookie lowlifes who went after her. People have been talking. But I know some things about what goes on at La Luna. I think they could have played a role. We need to talk."

"I follow you. I probably think some of the same things. You need to pull back for a while. It's all a jumble of facts mixed with fiction. I'm working on it, I promise you. So are the cops. I need you to stay away from it for the moment. There are things you don't understand."

"I gotta find that guy Enzo. Have a talk. It's real important."

"No, you gotta keep away," Cora angrily responded. "Robbie, listen. The best thing you can do for Fiona now, for yourself, is to settle down. We'll talk, okay. Keep away from La Luna, understand?"

Robbie protested. "Keep away? I don't think you get it. These fucking people..."

"I get it fine, Robbie. Where are you now?"

"Some street in Elmhurst where I met this poker guy...I have no place to go. I slept in the subway last night."

"First, go get something to eat. Then you can go to Fiona's apartment for a few days. The cops have finished with it, rent's paid till the end of the month. There'll be a key under the mat."

"But Sara told me to keep away—"

"I want you to go there and stay there. I'll deal with Sara. Just do what I ask. Get some rest. Sleep. You're in no condition to tackle anything now."

"I...I don't want to go there. Too many memories. I'll find some shelter."

"I need to know where you are, Robbie. Fiona's place is safe. Go. I can meet you there after you get some food and rest. Okay? We have a deal?"

Grudgingly, Robbie, said, "Okay. I'll head there now."

"Good. See you later." Cora hung up and took a series of deep breaths. She needed time, and time was at a premium.

Although supposedly taking time off Cora found herself locked in her tiny office while the business of the diner buzzed around her. Events were moving faster, she knew. And she had to get a handle on it all.

She set her laptop close and stared at the screen. She typed in the name Twenty-First Century Agency, eagerly looking over the names of its chief officers. C.E.O., C.F.O, Corporate International President, and others. It was a private company, not required to report its undertakings and actions the way public companies do. She took a screenshot. As Solerno had hinted, this was a new and aggressive company with headquarters in New York. However, she found it interesting that among the long list of executives a large number had Eastern European names. One she even recognized as having been involved with a Greek corporation. None of the others stood out but she jotted a few notes for later research. She was tempted to phone Ursula and try and pepper her with questions.

A knock on the interrupted her. "Yes?"

Stavros looked perturbed. "Sorry for another interruption, Mrs. Gus. Eddie told me to knock. There's this woman here who says she has too see you. A waitress I believe. I told her you weren't interviewing now but she said it's not about a job. She claims she knows you. She said she's got to see you. Something important."

Cora waved a hand in the air. "I'm really busy. Next week. Take her name."

"She asked me to tell you her name. It's Veronica Labrano."

Cora did a double take. "*Veronica*?" she repeated. She closed the laptop. "I'll see her now."

"You sure? You didn't want to be interrupted…"

"It's all right. Send her in."

Looking sheepish and disheveled Veronica came in, standing in front of the desk.

"Forgive me if I'm intruding. Your manager was about to toss me out. I kept trying to explain. Finally, he said he'd have someone check if you were in."

"Please, sit down, Veronica. Eddie protects me when I'm tied up with things and doesn't want me to get sidetracked. He's just doing his job. I'm surprised to see you, but not upset."

Veronica crossed her legs, pushed strings of hair away from her freckled face. Her eyes were downcast, breath uneven, lower lip thrust out. It was obvious she was distraught. She seemed anything but warm, safe, and untroubled.

"What's up? Did something bad happen? Did Enzo or Vera threaten you?" Her tone became almost motherly. "I see you're agitated. It's safe here, I promise. Take your time, we can chat." Cora pulled out a chair for her, then asked the kitchen for coffee and cookies.

Veronica assembled her scattered senses. "Thank you for seeing me. I've been angry with myself ever since we walked and talked. I held back some things that were too difficult to talk about. And I was too scared to tell you." Large, anxious eyes regarded Cora.

"It's not that I told you any lies. I didn't. What I said was the truth, my hand to God." She held up her right hand, palm forward.

"I'm not accusing you of anything. In fact, I'm grateful for alerting me to some realities at La Luna."

"Yes, but not all the realities," Veronica's voice quivered with pain and guilt.

"Slow down, breathe and then tell me any way you can."

"The pregnancy. Because of the pregnancy."

Cora tilted her head, her interest piqued. "Go on."

"It changed everything, ya know? When Fiona first told me I was shocked. But she said she has a plan to make something good come out of it. I saw her smile. A bright, beautiful smile." She cleared her throat. "It all went down just days before the bus accident. See, that's what bothers me the most. It makes me wonder…" Veronica halted again.

Sensing something serious, Cora said, "Take your time. I'd like to hear exactly what happened." Having been a waitress herself, Cora had an inside perspective on what staff actually saw on the job. Families arguing, couples breaking up, affairs, abuse, the best and the worst. She felt certain nothing would surprise her.

"Fiona told Enzo about his baby and demanded a hundred thousand dollars."

"*What?*" Cora was stunned.

Veronica Labrano flinched and began sobbing.

Cora sat silent, in disbelief, but believing each word. This could explain so many things. So many.

A long silence hung in the heavy air. One woman fractured with emotion, the other stupefied and resisting its truth.

TWENTY-THREE

Cora passed Hunter his favorite gyro wrapped in a pita, along with a short stack of napkins. With a thermos full of coffee, the sunny afternoon gave their meeting the feeling of an impromptu picnic. The pocket-park hosted a group of mothers and their toddlers, as well as a pair of bundled-up elderly women taking in the warmth, chatting. Hunter and Cora munched their lunch in companiable silence. When Cora began to pack up the detritus of the meal, Hunter drank coffee, ready to begin the business at hand.

Cora glanced at the trees, leaves in full bloom, the rich green of the grass still damp from overnight rain. It all seemed so pretty, innocent and pastoral, so different from the world it shared with human beings and their ongoing intrigues and scheming. "Hunter, I can't explain how dumbfounded I was when she told me. It felt like being hit in the gut, betrayed somehow."

He gently squeezed her hand. "We all find ourselves let down by the realities of human nature. I learned that in this job long ago. Fiona Sweeney was human, she wasn't a saint. She saw an opportunity and tried to take advantage of it."

"Veronica said Fiona was going to use the money for a down payment on a little luncheonette for sale. She asked Veronica to become her partner. They'd have their own business and be their own bosses. She'd learned her lesson. Robbie was out of her life, and they could escape from dirtbags like Enzo or that conniving bitch Vera."

He pulled a face. "Yeah, but how did Enzo like being blackmailed?"

"Fiona told Veronica he was shocked, beside himself, stuttering like an idiot. Like he was frightened of Vera finding out."

"She thought Enzo could find a hundred grand lying around? Just agree to pay her off? As long as Fiona had an abortion, of course."

"We don't know what Fiona was planning, do we? Possibly she'd have the baby," Cora thought about it, biting her lower lip. "Or maybe not. I've never been so confused about a case."

"People are strange and their motives stranger. We're taking a good look at both Enzo and his wife. Poking around. Undercover work. Slow and tedious, but I want to get this right. And I hope your friend Rob Perry never gets word of what Veronica told you. He's a loose cannon. No knowing what irrational things he'd do."

"I've thought about that. Despite everything, I think he did love Fiona. I think he still does. You should have heard him at my house. All he wanted was to find out who hurt her. And to get some kind of revenge. I warned him. I told him he was putting himself in danger. Now more than ever."

"I have nothing to arrest or hold him on. Otherwise, I would, if only to keep him in the precinct cooler for a few days. He hasn't committed any crime, as far as I know."

"No, he hasn't—*yet*." Cora corrected. "Hunter, does it make any sense that despite everything I sort of liked him?"

He grinned. "Everyone says he's charming and fun to be around."

Cora made a face. "Are you being sarcastic? Look, he could have remained in North Carolina. Stayed away forever, maybe worked out some money deal with his mother. She sounds like a real winner. He didn't have to come back after he learned Fiona had died in some bizarre bus accident."

"Don't go social worker on me, Cora. She clearly made stupid mistakes, especially with Robbie's father. And she certainly was lacking as a mother, but she worked hard and made her money honestly. She's not the one in trouble or looking for it."

That was true enough. Nearby a little boy began to cry as his mother scolded him for some infraction. The mother rose up from the bench, clearly annoyed, and taking the crying boy by the hand, left the park. Cora's eyes followed as they crossed the street and disappeared in the pedestrian crowd. Would that kid grow up angry and mixed up like Robbie, she wondered. Would he be looking to take on the world, seeking fast money, or join some revolution promising salvation for humanity? Or would this kid do the opposite, study hard, find a good career, maybe make a name for himself. Become a father, doctor, lawyer. Maybe make some breathtaking science discovery?

"The Lab downtown has finished its investigation of the camera's video," Hunter said, breaking into her musings. "They're feeling pretty certain that the hand seen in the far corner is most likely a strong shove, not an accidental brush against Fiona Sweeney. Therefore, we're ruling out some accidental misadventure. They enhanced the

CCTV as best as possible, but still couldn't determine whether the hand belonged to a male or female."

"What happens next?" Cora sipped some coffee, looking hopefully at her companion.

"NYPD drug enforcement is aware and getting involved. Remember, we obtained Enzo D'Amico's DNA without permission. We collected it on the QT. And it'll pay off. Meanwhile, we need proof of what's going on in that restaurant. Then we can try to piece together whether Fiona's demise has a direct relationship."

Cora sat quietly, aware that self-absorbed Rob Perry had missed the wider picture. He was grateful to take monies Fiona offered without realizing how deeply she had become entwined with the dark world of La Luna. How long had she been secretly sleeping with Enzo? Was it a one-off? Done out of anger at Robbie as payback for his lies and unfaithfulness? Could she possibly have played a larger role in the drug distribution network more than even Veronica knew, and with that knew far more about their drug operation? Could that have played some role in her death?

She knew that Hunter had been thinking about the same questions. If Fiona had indeed played a hidden role she'd have been arrested right along with the D'Amico's and anyone else involved with trafficking drugs at La Luna.

Hunter cut off her thoughts. "I'll need to talk with Veronica Labrano at some point," he said.

"I promised to keep her safe," Cora objected. "I gave my word."

"I can hold off until we get ready to make arrests. Right now, all we have are allegations. If we catch any of them it the act we won't have much need for your friend's cooperation. We'll implement immediate action. Shut that place down with Enzo D'Amico and his wife Vera taken away in handcuffs. But I might need a written statement and substantiation for the D.A.'s office. Testimony for a Grand Jury from Veronica."

"She lives alone with her kids. You could put her in danger—"

"When the time comes we can offer good witness protection."

She pulled her hand away, feeling like an informer. "I want your word, Hunter. She'll be kept out of it unless absolutely necessary. Without her confiding in me, none of us would know anything about their dealings."

They locked eyes. "You have my word now, Cora. I recognize Veronica took significant chances."

He thought about ways to change the topic and approached it carefully. "Before you leave, please tell me how things are going with the problems at the Athena. You've been able to get things under control? I know all about the power outage investigation. It's good it's being taken seriously." He sidestepped the matter of Solerno and the advice she'd been getting.

"It's been rough," she admitted. "I met with someone purporting to be speaking for my eager buyers. A woman claiming to represent big money. I don't know how great her role really is. I do have a suspicion how the power got shut down—sabotage. An inside job. But I'm not ready to act on it yet."

He listened and nodded sternly. "Be careful, Cora." The deep apprehension in his face was real, she knew. Cora continued, "There's another thing. Sometimes I feel like I'm being followed. Eyes on me, you know? This woman, the people she represents, maybe they're keeping watch…Or maybe all this situation has me feeling paranoid."

He took both her hands and locked fingers with hers. "Just stay on your toes, okay? I'm here for you, remember that."

He meant it she knew. She leaned forward to kiss his cheek. With the slightest turn of his head, he kissed her lips. Gently, tenderly.

"I'm sorry if I was too hard on you, Cora. You know I care."

Her eyes became watery. "I know you do. I care about you, too."

For the first time they both realized a new step had been taken in their relationship.

An important one with the potential to deeply affect both their lives and worlds.

"I have to go," she said softly.

He nodded. "Me too. Keep me posted."

"I will. I promise."

Hunter watched her leave the park, straight and tall, ready for whatever was coming next.

*

Robbie cased the street. Dry cleaners, an insurance storefront, a pizza place, two small shops for rent. At the end of the block, opposite the darkened glass windows of La Luna was a physical therapist, and a small pharmacy next door. A few apartments topped the two-story brick buildings. He was nervous, keeping a constant eye over his shoulder, as he watched the people coming and going from the restaurant. Daylight was waning, he was chilly in his thin jacket and Yankee baseball cap he wore pulled low. His stomach growled. He allowed himself to buy a single slice of pizza and a hot coffee. He sat at the counter, close to the front window so he could still keep his eyes on La Luna's entrance. The muted hues of the logo indicated a formal, pricy establishment. He had been inside a couple of times to pick up Fiona during the past two years. The atmosphere was warm, friendly, and inviting. No peeling paint there. It was classy, Fiona was right about that. The single time she had introduced him to Enzo he felt the owner's eyes casting unflattering looks at his clothes, unimpressed with jeans and tee shirts. Enzo said hello at Fiona's introduction but kept his right hand in his pocket, declining to shake hands. Likewise, Robbie had looked at her boss with disapproval. A smiling, well-tanned simian wearing an expensive suit, he thought. Gold ring, gold link chain around his neck. King of the hill. He wanted to rip off the chain and stuff it up Enzo's ass.

A delivery man came out with a number of orders, put them in the trunk of a small sedan and drove away. Shortly after came a family, a middle-aged man with a paunch, his well-dressed wife, and a couple of teenage kids. Robbie paid little attention until he saw the well-dressed individual with the cigar come out to smoke. His face was hidden by shadow but there was no doubt it was Enzo. A waiter smoking a cigarette followed and the two stood chatting for several minutes. Robbie studied Enzo carefully, his dress, his polished brown shoes, the way he gestured with his hands while he talked, the way he shifted from one foot to the other. Know your enemy, he thought. Don't get surprised.

When Enzo returned to La Luna, Robbie slipped out of the pizza shop, head low, walking along the shadows on his way back to Fiona's apartment. He was getting stronger, his legs carrying him swiftly on his mission to study the comings and goings at the popular Italian restaurant.

Cora had lost track of time. Stavros knocked, opened the door to see Cora half asleep in her chair, a small notebook and pen on her lap, the computer screen saver illuminating her tired face in the dim light. "We're closing," he said in a soft voice.

She opened her eyes. "Oh. Sorry." A cup of cold coffee stood near the edge of her desk. As she studied the permits applied for by several real estate developers in the broader neighborhood, she had come across a small gold mine of information. Twenty First Century, the private property company Solerno had pinpointed, had applied for a large number of permits in her neighborhood and nearby. What caught her attention was the of inordinate number of applications compared to other companies, even far larger ones. Did they expect the city to authorize building a list of properties like this?

"You go home," she told Stavros. "I'll finish here in a few minutes and shut for the night."

"Sure, you don't want me to hang around a while?"

"No, thanks. You go home. I'll get out of here soon. See you in the morning."

"Okay, boss." He gave a military salute, laughing as he caught the pencil she tossed at him.

Alone now, Cora drew a series of deep breaths. She would phone Solerno tomorrow to report her discovery. She was eager to hear his opinion about the private equity Twenty-First Century Agency. So many certification requests. What were they planning, some mad scheme to take over most of Queens one day? It wasn't unusual for corporations to be aggressive, but this was outsized enough to garner attention. Weren't they biting off more than they could chew?

She had carefully written down each of the listed officers from CEO on down, intent on doing searches of each name, one by one, checking backgrounds and experience.

High margin. Attractive to institutional players. Were they really in position to raise cash like this? These were big moves. Who were these backers? Involuntarily shivering, Cora could only speculate at the reasoning behind it. She recalled again what Solerno had told her, —rumors of secret negotiations underway. The state and the city were always seeking prospects for urban renewal, more jobs, and innovative sources of revenue. Everything and anything could be up for grabs in some undisclosed hush-hush negotiation.

She needed sleep. Badly. It felt like too much to deal with at once. The differing lines of inquiry felt blurred. Danger to the Athena, fires, probable sabotage resulting in perilous power outages. Fiona Sweeney likely pushed to her death, drug running at La Luna, Enzo proven the father of Fiona's baby. Robbie was still deep in debt, running loose and crazed for some unknown revenge that no one could prevent. Hunter's cautions, Solerno's warnings. Ursula's threats. It was a dizzying array of goings-on at once.

Get a grip, Cora told herself. *Get a grip.*

She set the alarm and locked the diner door behind her. The walk home was a welcome respite allowing her to unwind and then go directly to bed. New York City streets are rarely empty, but there were few people about, and the refreshing spring breezes blew soothingly over her face. She had her apartment to herself tonight, and thankfully she wouldn't need to be speaking a single word to anyone.

She turned into the side street nearest her home. A figure emerged from the nearby alleyway. Standing near the streetlight some six feet in front of her was a man. A formidable looking man with a scowl etched across a wide, ruddy face. He was tall with broad shoulders and menacing.

Cora stood still. Squinting, it took barely a moment for her to view his face.

It took everything she could muster to outwardly appear steady and calm while inside her chest her heart was pounding madly. A small piece of her mind castigated herself for not realizing that something like this might happen at any time. How often lately had she felt she was being followed?

"Hello, Cora." The man said in a deep but casual tone as if they were neighbors. "I've been waiting for you." He had a thick accent. Russian?

Her voice was disparaging. "Well, I'm here," she answered with false bravery.

A quick glance around told her there wasn't anyone close by to help. *Stall for time,* she told herself. She began to inch backward toward the main street.

"I'm sorry it's come to this tonight, Cora," he added dryly. "This is really your own fault, you know. If you'd listened to reason in the beginning, yes? I think you could have been flying away tonight to some lovely resort, drinking cocktails, instead of finding yourself helpless here in this crummy street." He pulled a face even as he spoke in a matter-of-fact tone without threat or anger. "You were given three offers, I was told. Three. Fair offers. You were a fool." He spit on the pavement.

"Who are you?" she demanded as she continued to inch backward. He shook his head and waved a finger at her. "You won't reach the main street. Stop trying. You're not fooling anyone. But don't worry. This will be all over in a couple of minutes." She looked at his hands. If he was holding something there was no evident sign of it.

Focus, Cora, focus. She shifted her shoulder to try to bring her bag closer to her hand. Her gun was at the bottom. It would long seconds to reach it, pull it out, shoot if needed.

She heard footsteps behind her. A second man stepped out of shadows, halting on Cora's far side, looking to his companion for direction.

"It's a shame you were so stubborn. Not realizing you were outclassed from the beginning. These people we deal with, they don't like bargaining with anyone unreasonable, yes? Especially one who can't recognize generosity. You could have spared yourself this," he continued reproachfully, as though he were a schoolteacher and she some feckless student.

Russian, yes Russian! She was quite familiar with it from her days at the embassy.

In her peripheral vision Cora could see the first enforcer pulling a small plastic bag from his pocket. It was filled with pills of some sort. Things started to become clear to her. She was going to be poisoned with drugs. That was the plan. Left to die on the street or be dragged into the nearby alleyway.

Quickly assessing her situation, she reached her right hand ever so slowly inside her handbag. She felt her fingertips touch the cold metal of her .38. The second man shoved her hard from behind. She stumbled toward the pavement, still able to keep her hand firmly inside the purse. Her fingers closed around the handle of her gun, instinctively pointing her bag upward toward him. "Stop right there!

Tell your friend to back up. I can put a bullet in your gut faster than your friend can jump. Step back now!"

Her voice was rock steady. She had one knee down on the ground. She saw the perplexed look on the enforcer's face, debating whether she was bluffing about having a gun. He shot a glance toward his friend, indicating for him to hold still.

"It's not worth your life to test me. Don't try."

The lurking assailant took advantage of Cora's focus on his partner and hurtled forward. She swung around to fire. The first enforcer vaulted, knocking Cora's arm upward. His strong, hairy hand closed tightly, painfully over her wrist. She cried out. The second attacker jerked the handbag from her numb fingers, tossed it aside, too far for her free hand to reach.

Cora thought desperately, aware that within a minute she might be dead. To her astonishment, the first man stepped back against the flat brick wall of the building behind him, pulling her up with him. He immobilized her by crossing her arms around her midriff and pulling each wrist tightly behind, making the hold feel like a straitjacket.

It hurt. Cora shouted out. "Help! Someone help!" as loud as her breathless lungs could manage. The second assailant pulled out a damp sponge from his pocket and tried to force it into her mouth. She kicked wildly, hitting ineffectively. Cora bit down hard on the hand holding the sponge, drawing blood. He abruptly drew back in pain, then drew back a fist to retaliate. Neck taut, the first enforcer barked at him, "Dima, no marks! No marks on her."

Cora kicked, striving to head butt the man behind her, to break free. She was overpowered. Seconds later she was subdued and gagging from the sponge. The first enforcer sucked the blood from his fingers, and took an extra measure of sadistic joy, saying, "See this tiny little pill in my hand, eh? It might kill you, you fucking slut. It's a delicious mix of heroin, plus meth, and laced with fentanyl." He squeezed her cheeks hard with his hand. Cora moaned with the pain.

"Don't worry," he hissed. "Soon you'll be feeling good. Really good. Flying high into heaven until maybe your heart stops ..." He grinned.

Her eyes grew wide with fear. Her arms were still held back, as she wrenched her shoulders trying to break loose. She could barely budge. She attempted to spit at him but the choking sponge being stuffed into her prevented it. He wiped the feeble spray off his face with a hint of a smile and slapped her face with the back of his hand. She twisted as the pain struck her and blood trickled from her cut lip.

"Your diner will be sold for pennies on the dollar after you're gone. And your fine reputation will be smeared with mud and shit. Surprise, eh? Your fancy friends will see you've been a druggie all along. Look at her, she died of an overdose crawling in the streets."

She thrashed her legs backward against his shin. The man holding her took the hit and laughed.

"Say goodbye to my friend, Dima," said the man holding the bag of pills. He took one with a cursory glance, making sure it was intact, and lifted his hand to force it into her mouth. Cora clenched her teeth as hard as she could, shook her head violently from side to side. She felt her mouth being forced open. With every bit of remaining energy, she continued struggling to break free. She was frantic. Kicking, fighting back with all she had left. Fear intermingled with flowing tears.

Is this the way my life ends?

"Police!" came the loud voice in the night. "On the ground! Now!"

The first enforcer spun instantly, confused by the voice.

"On the ground, fucker!" It was a female voice. A woman in a raincoat ten feet away was holding a gun with both hands.

He sprang forward toward the unknown figure.

A single shot fired, and he dropped the pill, hands grasping his stomach as he doubled over, falling to his knees with a groan. Blood poured from his wound like a fountain. The second man instantly released Cora, his thick hands lifting high into the air. "Don't shoot! Don't shoot!"

"You too, on the ground!"

He released Cora and she flung herself away, shaking, trying to stand without falling over. She gasped struggling to regain her breath.

The woman with the gun said told her, "You're safe now. You're safe, Cora."

Cora held out her arms and staggered to reach her before she fell. Her hands were clammy and cold, alternately painful, and numb.

She heard whine of sirens filling the air. Spinning colors and flashing lights. More voices. Men's voices. An arm took hold of her, keeping her from falling over. "It's alright. It's all right. We got to you in time."

Amid her fog, it sounded like the voice of Sargent Molina she thought as she passed out into his strong arms.

*

When Cora finally opened her eyes she saw a window, light curtains, and bright sunlight streaking inside. Groggy, she said, "Is it morning?"

"No. Soon the sun is going to start setting."

She blinked several times, her eyes clearing from sleep. At the side of the bed sat Hunter, holding her hand, leaning forward, looking at her face, with its swollen lip.

She moved her free hand to wipe away eye crust, lifting her head slightly higher above a large comfortable pillow. "Where am I?"

"Queens General hospital. Don't be alarmed. You're alive and well."

"Huh? The hospital?" She ran her tongue over her lips. "I have this awful taste in my mouth." Cora was puzzled by it.

"That sponge they tried to stuff into your mouth. It was soaked with different brands of booze. They were trying to make it look like you'd been drinking as well as taking drugs. Your blouse and jacket were soaked with it."

At the mention of drugs, she pulled back slightly. "I…I remember. Two of them. These two sinister guys appeared out of the dark…"

"It's all over, Cora. There's nothing to be afraid of. It's all taken care of."

She looked directly into his eyes. "I had this feeling I was being followed recently. I told you about it, didn't I?"

"Yes, you did."

"My instinct was right."

"Well, don't worry about that now. It'll all get explained. It's good to see you awake and talking." There was a lump in his throat, worry in his eyes dissolving. "You made it. Got through in flying colors."

"It's good to see you too, Detective."

She tried to move closer toward him. She grimaced. Her ribs hurt. She put a hand under the blanket to feel her side. It was bandaged. "Ow," she said, becoming aware of an antiseptic smell, and medical equipment surrounding her.

"Nothing too serious, I promise. Ribs bruised from getting knocked around, thrown to the sidewalk. A few other bruises plus your split lip. They kept you here as a precaution. Ordinary stuff for you." As he smiled Cora saw the dark shadows on the sides of his face. "You didn't shave," she scolded mockingly.

"I haven't shaved for two days," he replied with a grumble in his voice.

Just then a young nurse came into the room. She looked at Cora with bright eyes and a small smile. "Oops, am I interrupting?"

"No, no," they both said.

"I knew you'd be waking, Ms. Drakos. Making my rounds, so don't mind me." She pulled the curtains wider, checked a few vital signs. The oximeter on her finger read ninety-eight. "Good." She sat on the edge of the bed and checked Cora's blood pressure. "One-thirteen over seventy-two. Excellent." Her hand waved a laser-like thermometer at her forehead like a wand. "Ninety-seven even."

"I always run a little low, nurse."

"Call me Jill. It's perfect." She turned towards Hunter. "They'll be collecting the menus for dinner soon." Then to Cora, "You must be hungry. I'll be back in a while." Jill closed the door softly and left.

Food. She hadn't given food any thought at all. She didn't know when the last time was she had eaten anything. Hunter handed her the menu to look over. "How long have I been here?"

"Since sometime after last midnight, more or less."

"And how long have I been sleeping?"

"They put you out right after you arrived by ambulance and the docs checked you over. My guess is you've been sleeping around fourteen hours."

"*Fourteen?*" She managed to sit up straighter. "I never sleep that long."

"You did last night and all day today. I think they gave you a little something extra to help."

She stretched out her arms wide and returned her hand to Hunter's. "And you've been here how long?"

"Me?" He stared from the window. Shadows were forming, the sun was lowering behind nearby high-rises. "Just a while. Since I got the call they brought you here. I drove over as quickly as I could. I'd say I've been here since about two."

"Two in the afternoon?"

The room door opened. "Two in the morning, he means," the newcomer said in a cheerful voice.

Hunter was momentarily startled by the new entrant, then relaxed. "I thought you'd be stopping by at some point."

The woman came over to the other side of the bed and held out her hand. She was in her early thirties, Cora guessed. Flawless soft skin. Dressed in a blue blouse and dark gray skirt, low heels, her blue eyes exposed a few shadows. She was holding a light raincoat over one arm.

"You do look familiar," Cora said. "I think we've met?"

"I've seen you a couple of times at the precinct. When you've come by to meet with my boss."

"She's a valuable member of my team," Hunter quickly added.

"My name is Kasey. Kasey Cosgrove. Detective Third Class. New on the squad with Detective Hunter."

"That's the only place I've seen you?" Cora asked questioningly.

Hunter and Kasey shared a look that had a history.

"What is it?" asked Cora.

Kasey hesitated before answering. Hunter shrugged, saying, "Go ahead, tell her. She might as well hear everything from you."

"For the last ten days or so, Ms. Drakos…"

"Call me Cora, please."

"Cora, then. Let's say I've been assigned special duty. You see, my boss, Detective Hunter, directed me to trail you. He knew you were becoming heavily involved in the Fiona Sweeney case, and conceivably in danger from whoever set the diner fires. He wanted to keep you safe. So, he instructed me to watch you, from a distance."

Cora's mouth opened. She glanced at the familiar looking raincoat. "*You're* the one who's been following me. It was *you*."

"It was my assignment."

"She was told not to interfere with you in any way," Hunter interjected. "Only in case of emergency."

"I was in my car near your building when I heard your scream. I hit the gas and saw you being attacked. I'd have done the same for any citizen in imminent danger."

"You saved my life, Kasey."

Kasey smiled with a nod. "If I did, you can thank my boss. He's the one who gave me the assignment." Looking over at Hunter, she said, "I'm officially off duty, sir. If you don't need me I'm going home to rest." She smiled adding, "My overtime time sheet is waiting to be signed."

"I'll look it over in the morning. And congratulations on a job well done."

"Thank you, sir."

Cora sat speechless as Kasey Cosgrove left the room. For a long minute she collected her thoughts, the memory of the previous night surfacing in fragments. She trembled at the realization of how close she might have come to dying.

"Those animals last night…"

"One's in critical condition, under full-time police watch. He'll live. The other quickly gave himself up. He was questioned all night and was willing to talk. You'll be glad to know we learned a great deal."

"Who were they?"

"Thugs." She curled her lip. With distain. "East European types, we think had been mercenaries. Reached here illegally and put themselves out for hire. Their plan was to drug you, leave you lying in the gutter."

"Who sent them? Do we know who they work for yet?"

"Here's where it gets interesting. For the past few months the guy who wasn't shot claims they both worked as part of a security team for a wealthy Russian immigrant who calls himself a legitimate businessman. Someone who fled to America claiming amnesty, his life being in danger back home. Colorful tale."

Cora listened with interest, making mental notes.

"Naturally this businessman for the past decade has spread money all over to smooth the way. Parking millions in real estate, owning a number of these ostentatious mansions we see springing up all over

Queens, Brooklyn, and a few suburbs. Turns out the FBI has him under investigation. We're waiting for release of their files. Suspicion of money laundering, conspiracy to defraud…"

"Defraud?"

Hunter nodded grimly. "It's a complicated affair, being studied and unraveled. It appears this guy's also a silent partner in a large enterprise in the city involved with commercial real estate. Office towers and the like. We're talking serious bucks. His lawyers claim he denies any knowledge of who your assailants are, and that's likely true. He keeps a low profile, avoids limelight. He wouldn't get his hands soiled with lowlife scum like them. He has layers of underlings to do that for him."

Cora understood there must be multilayered fraud going on. "So, someone lower down in his organization ordered them to go after me? Why? I'm not important to bigshots like that."

Hunter sighed, biting his lower lip, trying to piece together himself the disparate bits of information he had. "There's no proven evidence now. However, my FBI liaison hinted at some notable confidential dealings happening at City Hall these past weeks. We're following it up. Possibly it could have connections to this guy or his business partners. All under wraps. Nothing's clear, at least yet. But someone's leaked bits of info is out. Of course, the mayor's office has no comment on any kind of special deals or current negotiations. Hush-hush stuff." He sneered, recalling how many of the city's promised deals had fallen apart.

Cora took it all in with a growing feeling that she could help Hunter find that missing connection.

"Would this businessman's company name happen to be Twenty First Century Agency?"

Hunter's eyebrows rose in astonishment. "How in hell did you know that?"

Cora chortled, wincing as last night's bruises protested.

"Don't make me laugh. It hurts." Hunter helped her settle back against the pillows.

"You never fail to astonish me, Cora. Explain," he demanded.

She told him about her own recent research into local building permits applied for in and around the neighborhood, and the vast number of recent applications that staggered her.

"So, this Twenty First Century Agency has been working on buying up properties far in excess of any competing real estate company in Queens. Many more. As if they're aware of something that no one else is."

"And maybe they are, maybe they do." He let go of her hand, standing and taking out his phone. "I'm going to check on something. Excuse me for a minute," he said, holding up an index finger and leaving the room. He remained in several intense, lengthy conversations before he returned.

Cora felt a sweeping feeling of relief come over her. Her examination of public records was paying off. Solerno had hinted at it, and she took it from there. Things no longer appeared as the senseless hodgepodge they had yesterday.

Putting two and two together, she wondered if it was likely Ursula also worked for this same company? And anyway, what was so special about her diner that would make it such a coveted target? Surely not the good food and service. Any restaurant planning to remain in business for more than a year offered that. Location? The streets on either side of the train tracks were lined with ordinary retail shops. It wasn't for the menu. Greek food was tasty, but hardly exclusive. The Athena stands close to the Jamaica Avenue train stop on the El, but such a premium for that? No, she didn't think so.

Nothing in particular was remarkable about the diner. Nor did anything seem unique about all the specific properties Twenty First Century Agency was likely targeting. Nothing special at all.

Hunter was still active on his phone as another possibility came to mind. The remaining prospect was that Twenty First Century had knowledge about some critical dealings no one else had. Advance facts and data. Call it some secret awareness. Vital for Ursula and her bosses to learn and give them decisive advantage over all competitors. And it appears to have something to do with the local neighborhood.

She signaled to Hunter to come back as he was finishing up his calls.

"You mentioned some secret things going on at City Hall, right?"

"Yeah. Negotiations of some kind possibly worth billions. Nothing I'm privy to, or anything I could share even if I had knowledge."

She left her hand on top of his. "Whatever it is, I'll bet this real estate group and their lawyers have some knowledge. Insider knowledge. And that would explain all these applications for a neighborhood offering nothing special." Her eyes brightened. "Unless these 'worthless' areas are being considered for something really big. Something that would make valuations skyrocket."

He squeezed her hand. "Ouch!" Cora withdrew her bruised fingers. Hunter winced and apologized.

"You make a good point, Cora. If there are secret talks underway with City Hall and maybe the state, and *if* this organization has gotten leaked info…"

"This neighborhood, maybe this whole area is going to pop overnight. Double, triple in value. Wouldn't unscrupulous brokers be willing to take illegal actions to get their bids approved? Anything necessary, including unethical or criminal measures?"

Their eye met again. The answer was obvious. "Look, I've got to go, Cora. This is potentially too critical to sit on."

"Can you help get me outta here, too?" she pleaded. "I'm fit to leave."

"Your doctor will authorize your checkout shortly. I spoke with him before. Needless to say you were quite lucky. Things could have gone much worse."

"I know it. Please tell them at the nurse's station on your way out. I need to get home right away. And I need to go after the scum that's been burning me out of business."

TWENTY-FOUR

The best cure was work, Cora knew. The day after being released from the hospital she wasted no time. Shortly after Eddie opened the diner she got up from bed, pulled on stretchy slacks, gingerly donned a patterned knitted sweater and headed off. She came into the Athena finding a number of customers plus Stavros standing in front of the television.

The breaking news headline flashed across the screen. The TV anchor looked directly at the camera's eye as the attention-grabbing music faded. "Moments ago," he intoned sincerely, "City Hall confirmed persistent speculation that multi-billion-dollar discussions have indeed been ongoing between New York City, the Governor's office, and several as yet unnamed world-renowned high-tech companies. While these negotiations have been going on in secrecy, unspecified real estate companies and possibly some banks have apparently been receiving confidential information of the talks by some clandestine means to give themselves an illicit advantage over proper public bidding. For weeks now these rumors had been hotly denied by both the Mayor's Office and the Gubernatorial Communications Office in Albany…"

Stavros nudged Cora gently and smiled, glad to see her. Then they both stood watching the monitor placed at the far side of the counter. The sound had been low, subtitles on. "Make it a little louder," Cora said. Stavros played with the remote. Several diners in nearby booths stopped their conversations and turned to look.

"This is a developing news story yet to be properly unfolded," the anchor continued in a direct communicative way. Wasting no time, he turned to a colleague sitting opposite. "Susan Warner, our financial expert on these matters, has been digging deeply into this story in recent days." He looked at the smiling, glamorous brunette.

"Thank you, Douglas. First let me say that currently there is as yet no proof of these allegations. However, my sources have spoken to numerous individuals who have worked in similar situations over many years."

"Isn't it true that the city has been trying to lure tech companies like these for years? Offering long-term tax abatements, transit improvements, and the like?"

Susan Warner agreed. "Definitely, Doug. It's a fact that in the years since the Covid pandemic the city has suffered losses in jobs and population, especially among the middle and upper classes. Taxes, crime, and air quality have all played a role."

"So, what makes this particular discourse different?"

She smiled briefly. "Accusations of improper, if not illegal, advance knowledge, Doug."

"What sort of accusations?"

"Again we are reporting on scant, unconfirmed details. It's complicated. It takes a lot of work to dig out all the facts, and we're just scratching the surface. All we know for sure is that a possible scandal is brewing regarding the City, top-secret negotiations and deal making with some of the country's and the world's largest organizations, and as of now unnamed real estate corporations and banks using their intelligence to buy or take over unknowing businesses and real estate. An advantage possibly worth many billions of dollars."

The broadcaster dog whistled in amazement. "Can we expect this story to soon be made public?"

"Of course. We're merely reporting unconfirmed information at this point but hope to have much deeper coverage as soon as possible. Needless to say, this could turn out to be a major piece of news affecting all of the city's residents."

"Thank you, Susan. We'll keep our viewers informed on this more as information becomes available." He signed off, and the station resumed its regular broadcasting.

Cora and Stavros exchanged serious looks. Something was looming, she suspected. Something that might have ramifications for the efforts to take over the Athena. Hunter had disclosed information he'd heard. Now it seemed to be on the verge of going public.

Inwardly Cora also thought of Solerno and mentally thanked him. Was it possible he already had known more than he let on, she wondered. Solerno had asked her to meet him at a huge building site on purpose, presuming she would take the hint. Which she did, recalling her hours of online research of this new real estate goliath Where had he received his information? Former mafia friends, or perhaps someone at City Hall? An insider. Likely an unknown faceless bureaucrat who had a conscience and a way of learning the best kept of secrets. Was this somehow part of the breaking news story?

Stavros lowered the volume, everyone went about their business.

"Is Allison Zoran on the schedule for today?"

Stavros nodded. "Yes. She's working the lunch and dinner shifts today. Due anytime."

"Good. I'll be busy in my office all day. But when she comes in have her see me, okay?"

"Sure. But are you sure you're not overdoing work after…after the other night?"

"I'm good, thanks Stavros. My ribs throb a bit, but working is the best therapy for me. Besides, I'm planning to just be on the computer."

A small hot pot of coffee was waiting on her desk alongside a grilled cheese and mustard sandwich on rye bread. Cora ran through a number of tasks she hoped to achieve, starting with a review of the online information available on this intriguing Twenty-First Century Agency. She poured a cup of the waiting coffee, leaned back, and sipped as she went over events of recent days. Propping her chin in her hands she was about to switch search engines to see if there were other sites popping up regarding the company she hadn't seen before.

A soft knock, Stavros saying quietly, "She's here. Hanging up her coat. Want me to send her in now?"

"Yes, please."

The young woman knocked before entering. "You wanted to see me, Mrs. Gus?"

"Hi, come on in," she said gesturing with the sandwich in one hand. She took a single bite. "Close the door."

Allison stood meekly in front of the desk. She seemed a bit uneasy, Cora noticed. She certainly looked prim and proper in her black and white uniform, her smooth hair shiny and neatly brushed, not a single split end showing. A very pretty girl, with a delightful smile. Now, waiting to learn why her boss wanted to see her again, she wasn't smiling. Hands at her side, standing straight and tall, she appeared almost like a soldier at attention. That was good.

Cora chewed a single bite, swallowed, and said, "Please sit down, Allison. Don't mind my eating. I had no time for breakfast." She wiped her mouth with a napkin.

"I heard about what happened," Allison said. "Oh, Mrs. Gus, I'm so sorry. It must have been scary for you. Do they know who your attackers are?"

"Thugs." She shrugged, unwilling to give more information, and wondering what, if anything, Allison might add. The girl only shook her head in sympathy, her eyes looking downward."

"They're going to need me up front soon, Mrs. Gus. Was there something in particular you wanted to talk about today?"

"Unfortunately, yes. I'm also trying to deal with the scary and dangerous things that have been happening right here these past few weeks."

Allison met Cora's gaze and her eyes swam with tears. "I know. I…I wish things were different. That this awful stuff hadn't been happening. First those fires in the alley. Then that disgusting hanging dead rat, now the costly power outage."

"That's part of why I called you in."

Allison shifted in her seat. She showed no emotion, but Cora wondered if she was starting to feel uncomfortable, or perhaps even guilty for her part in these events as Cora suspected.

"I've been dealing continuously with all these mundane, tiring matters. You know, our insurance, allocating for our deductibles, what's covered and what isn't. That sort of thing. Then there are the cops," she noticed Allison flinch at the word. "It's been pretty ugly in their eyes. You do know the police believe that these things weren't coincidences."

"Some local punks thinking causing trouble is funny, I assume."

Cora purposely frowned. "Maybe. But there are at least a few other possibilities lingering we need to resolve."

Allison's brows rose. "Really?"

"Yeah, but never mind that now." She waved her hand and continued to munch on her sandwich. If Allison was beginning to feel awkward she was still concealing it.

"The dumpsters and the rat seemed like warnings, know what I mean?"

"I don't think so, Mrs. Gus…"

Here Cora regarded her directly. "But those power outage. There are serious questions. The police think it was an inside job. The investigative reports claim it couldn't have started after we shut for the night unless someone inside the diner played with the breakers."

"Maybe someone broke in after we shut…?"

"Ruled out." Cora shook her head with a finality that told the girl not to bother bringing the possibility up.

"Why? Couldn't someone outside been waiting for everyone to go home?" It was evident she was exploring ways to avoid being mistrusted.

"We've been consulting with our insurance company investigators and the police about these various episodes. Some of the damage, like the fire in the dumpster or the rat on the back door, could have been executed by outsiders. However, the electrical fire is another story. How did that happen? To have successfully shut us down required someone with access to our breakers." She allowed that to linger. Then quietly, she went on, "Do you have anything to tell me about that, Allison?"

"Why would I know anything?" Her voice was defensive and cautious.

"Okay," Cora said, blowing out breath and putting down the leftovers of her sandwich. "You've only been working at the Athena for a short time. So you really don't know me very well. I don't like playing games." Under Allison's bewildered gaze, Cora's demeanor morphed from relaxed boss into an imposing authority figure. "Thorough review and scrutiny of that night and the ensuing days. Confirming shifts, duties, employees. I was there together with

Stavros and Eddie. You had switched to a late shift, as I recall. You said you needed some time for a dental appointment. Do I have that right?"

Allison swallowed. "Yes, that's right."

"Then after you arrived you were among the last to leave. You did some cleanup, then prepared tables for the morning along with Stavros."

"Yes. Stavros will verify that, I'm sure."

"No need for that. I noticed. Mopping up, taking care of the kitchen. Everything necessary was done. Eddie needed to get home, so he was eager to close, I recall. I saw him with the keys, Stavros rushing out still holding his jacket. I was right behind. But where were you? I didn't see you. I asked the others. Seems like no one saw you clock out or leave. No goodnights, no waving as you went."

Allison stammered, straining to defend herself.

Cora held up a hand and stopped her. "Why don't we try and get to the bottom of all this, okay?"

"The bottom of what?" Allison was indignant. "What are you implying?"

"I spent a lot of time surveying the premises. The storage closet door wasn't shut. I went in, carefully checking and measuring space. I tried to squeeze myself inside the open area below the bottom shelf alongside all those boxes. It was tough cramming, but I managed, and I'm taller than you are. But there was just enough space for someone to fit. A smaller person might do better, maybe a shorter female able to hide below the lower shelves for an extended time. Say, for an hour or more. Anything to say about that?"

"I really don't know what you're implying." she said resentfully.

"You don't? All right, let me bottom line this for you. I have reason to think that the power outage that night was your work. You had the dexterity to hide away. And only a handful of people were aware how to disable the secondary circuits for the freezers. Ruining and spoiling everything. And I repeat, *no one saw you leave* when the doors were locked."

"All the lights were already turned off," she protested. "It was nearly midnight, everyone was exhausted." Allison looked to the door as if she wanted to bolt. She hadn't expected her explanations to be questioned. "Maybe I'd already left, and no one noticed."

Cora dismissed this out of hand. "Not likely. By the way, remember I recently overheard you chatting with Stavros. You were discussing the best places for vacations. Telling him that Hawaii was known to have the best rainbows in the world. Remember that?"

She shrugged. "I guess. I mean, Sure. Hawaii's known for that."

"Interesting, because I'd never heard that expression before. Not until I was told it in the same off-handed way to me just a day or two before."

Shifting uncomfortably, Allison said, "So? I don't understand."

"So that was my first hint, Allison. You'd both quoted that exact statement about Hawaii. Coincidence? I'd met with this person a few times. She also represents big money, she said. Overseas money. Also works for people who desired to buy this very diner. In fact, she gave me a written offer and cautioned me to accept it, even though I'd told her that the Athena wasn't for sale." Cora leaned in closer, her hands pressed down on the desk.

Allison sat immobile but her knuckles were white with tension. "I'm confused, Mrs. Gus...Why are you telling me all this?"

Cora let a moment of silence pass, letting her stew before springing new facts onto the worried girl.

"You told me your mother is also a real estate specialist working for a big real estate company. Dealing with properties all over the world, no? Representing some large corporation with interests right here now. Ursula. I suspected it then, and now I'm sure. Ursula is your mother, isn't she?"

Allison swallowed and nodded. "Yes."

"I expect you knew that I'd been meeting with her, didn't you?"

"You don't understand, Mrs. Gus. Please. It isn't the way you think..."

"What isn't?"

"My...My mother," Allison blurted, barely holding back tears. "She has no choice in what she does." She was striving to keep her composure, while picturing Cora phoning her police buddies and demanding she be arrested immediately.

"No choice? Go on, explain," said Cora sternly. "This time no bullshit, no games."

"How we came to America is a little different than I told you. Back home, my father was considered a well-connected man. He worked top security level for several minor government oligarchs. He was an expert at accomplishing whatever was required regarding their safety. But there were other duties. Sometimes arresting illegal armaments buyers during the revolution or capturing political opponents. Sometimes committing whatever considered necessary to obtain information they required. It was a dreadful job. Working with human trafficking when ordered. Doing business with agents from Russia, Ukraine sometimes, Albania and more. He was a good man with few options. Everything he did depended on immediate political circumstances." She wiped away bourgeoning tears, hoping Cora realized she was speaking the truth.

"And he loved my mother. She wanted us to flee, to seek asylum somewhere in the West. He refused, saying it wasn't safe, but promising when the proper time came we would leave. But running now would mark him. I was still a small child. My mother knew he meant well but was naive. Without him knowing she went to the top man in his ministry to ask for his help. He listened and agreed. He could intervene and provide safety. He could help her. But there would be a price."

"What sort of price?" asked Cora.

Allison's face reddened with embarrassment. "My mother was a very good-looking woman. She was educated and smart. This man saw we were desperate and life back then in Serbia was cheap. He made her an offer. He and others had use for someone with her skills. There was money, foreign cash, that needed to be laundered quickly. This corrupt minister offered her protection for her work."

Cora knew that in recent years many tens of thousands of Russians had fled to Serbia after the Ukraine invasion began. They'd been and still were seeking safe places to invest. In search of legitimate properties to acquire, hiding embezzled currencies and gold.

"She agreed to his offer," Allison went on, "and this ministerial man did keep his word. Meanwhile my father was sent on special assignments outside of Serbia. Sent to work in a dangerous task of assisting smuggled wealthy people out of Russia and other places during their ongoing upheavals. He believed his days were numbered, and sooner or later someone would betray him. But as a good ministerial officer he did as required."

Cora knew much of this was true. Since the day of Russia's brutal attack on Ukraine all of Europe, especially Eastern Europe had been shaken with ongoing turmoil. "And then what happened with your mother?"

"She was told what was expected. Finding safe havens abroad, they first chose London. This was dirty cash that came from drugs or theft or black market. No matter. She was sent to London with me. My mother was fluent in English and presented herself as a special envoy on behalf of certain new enterprises, and a translator for the powerful back home. She understood the rules of this game she was playing. In time they would eventually own her. They will always own her. If she acted as told then life could be good, even if she was being handed from local boss to boss. If she has success they pay her more. Enough for a decent life, but under their thumb. Always under their thumb. That was the price for our freedom."

Cora was well aware of the numerous international cartels that flourished throughout the world and the huge amounts of monies involved. They flourished everywhere. Now with China's rise and world intervention all the more the need to find safety had only increased.

"I have a good grasp. Go on, please."

Allison sighed deeply. "My mother wanted to try to sneak my father away from Belgrade quickly. He distrusted the plan, but eventually he agreed. Before anything could be done, he was given new instructions. Again involving Eastern Europe, Bulgaria, and Romania. He was sent on a new supposedly secret mission. While promised protection, he was murdered. Killed we were told by rival traffickers in Belarus, but who knows the truth? It might have been these very men he worked for no longer needing or trusting him. Someone, my mother was certain, wanted him gone."

As Cora listened she became aware of similarities between the death of Allison's father and her own fiancé in Athens, Dirk Bonneau, who had worked on assignment for the American Embassy. Dangerous missions only growing worse.

Allison gathered herself and continued. "My mother didn't learn of it for some time. Thinking all was well she scouted out several properties in London which these bosses purchased using local brokers and lawyers. These proved to be excellent investments, and my mother was rewarded, as promised. But they desired more. She travelled for them. South Korea, Hong Kong. Few questions were ever asked. She scouted out the best that met their requirements and made reasonable offers in cash. Next we came here to America, to New York. It was here she finally received word of my father's death. She was trapped and knew it. Now a widow and with me to support, she agreed to continue working unofficially. We've remained here since. A few devious representatives within the ministry from Serbia fled when a new government was elected. They found innumerable ways to bring their riches with them and became well-heeled investors. Valued entrepreneurs in this city of endless growth and wealth. Substantial stakeholders, and investors in a newer private corporation that had vast ambitions. It's for these people she still works. To betray them would be suicide. As I told you, she was trapped."

"And they continue to seek out areas presenting some kind of promise?"

"Yes. They pay well for information not yet identified to the public. They have a number of advance people who scout likely possibilities. For some reason this location, I think this whole area, was chosen. How many businesses they want to take over, I don't know. But they told my mother to learn as much as she could about this diner. I was instructed to look for a job locally. You hired me."

"With the intention of looking and learning everything you could, I assume?"

Allison nodded. "That was what I was told."

"And you agreed?"

"Yes. For my mother. She is getting older, her beauty has begun to fade. Charming unsuspecting sellers has become more difficult. She needs me. She's been a good mother, although I suppose it's hard for you to believe that."

"I can believe it. Life is hard everywhere, but much harder where you came from. But tell me, you've avoided giving the name of the company your mother works for. Is it the Twenty-First Century Agency real estate corporation? Are they connected to these would-be buyers?"

"They are."

Cora kept her lips tightly closed, fiddled with her coffee, straightening her computer, deciding how best to deal with the unfolding situation. "Are you ready to admit you cut the power off?"

Allison replied, "If I do, are you going to call the police now? Accuse me of purposely shutting down the diner?"

"I'm not sure yet. But like everything else in this world there will be a price. In the meantime you can go home. I'll cut a check for the hours you worked this past week. Go on, go." She avoided Allison's gaze.

As the door closed behind, Cora sat with her elbows on the desk, hands folded under her chin. If Allison admitted causing the outage and received a criminal sentence in court, what good would it do? What purpose would her serving hard time accomplish? With her ribs still hurting and her psyche still dealing with her near brush with death, she decided to put this dilemma aside for the moment.

TWENTY-FIVE

Robbie waited again. He didn't feel cold. He didn't feel warm. All he felt was antagonism. La Luna had a good night. A local business had booked a party of twenty to celebrate gaining several new, large clients. There were a number of regular diners mixed with younger couples crowding the small tables for two. Enzo was pleased, eagerly looking forward to summer when outdoor dining would begin adding another eight tables.

The bar was full, more than a few customers sipping cocktails while waiting for tables to become available. It was going to be a late night. A very late night. Vera had already received her obligatory phone call at home that her husband would be staying over in his small apartment tonight. His mind was busy adding up guesstimates of both income at the bar as well as the food, possibly setting record for a late spring evening. Again, he wished La Luna could expand. The restaurant had certainly outgrown its capacity as the increase in diners was a sure sign people from other areas had traveled to sample the lauded cuisine. A favorable review in a city newspaper had only added to the interest.

He rubbed his hands together with delight. Tonight, his smiles didn't need to be fake. His mood was elevated, and his pleasure showed with his hearty greetings and backslapping. The long-tiring shift would certainly pay off in every respect. Vera had always cautioned regarding leaving the neighborhood and the regulars that provided the backbone of their living. Perhaps tonight's receipts might convince her another spot might be worth renewed consideration.

Close to midnight the last diners were lingering, the weary staff quietly presenting the checks and no longer doting or suggesting new desserts or drinks. The bartenders were cleaning the counter, the dim lights became slightly brighter. Everyone was tired to the bone, eager to count their tips, looking forward to getting off their feet.

Enzo couldn't complain, not tonight.

One by one the customers departed, then there was a hurry to clean up. Floors, counters, and tables were wiped down, scrubbed to a shine. The kitchen staff finished their chores also in exceptionally rapid time. The dishwashers and line cooks left first, followed by most of the wait staff. Except for Enzo, a bartender, and a couple of others, the place was all but empty. After the night's receipts were tallied the lights were turned off.

Robbie sat up straight. He had made himself comfortable sitting in the recessed doorway of a two-story apartment building on the opposite side of the street affording a clear view of La Luna. He flexed his muscles, stretched out his arms and legs. It had been a long night for him too. He felt the remaining aches from his beating healing more fully. The swellings on his face were all but gone. He was even becoming used to the broken teeth that rubbed and irritated the insides of his mouth. He was pleased with the rapid improvements.

Cars pulled out from parking spaces along the street. A police cruiser drove by. Robbie saw it coming and pressed himself into the doorway shadows.

He had rehearsed this scene over and over these past few days, but now that the time was here he found himself uncertain, making modifications, eager to make maximum impact with the first sentence he'd utter. Enzo D'Amico wouldn't forget it—ever.

The sky clouded over. Robbie stood straight against the wall when he saw the owner and bartender leave and lock up. Robbie had counted on Enzo being alone. Dealing with two men would certainly complicate things. He saw the two men stop to chat, both gesticulating with their hands. Enzo patted his companion on the back, and to Robbie's relief watched as they started walking in opposite directions. Much taller than his boss, the bartender walked faster, taking long strides while Enzo strolled along, clearly in a pleased mood.

Shifting from foot to foot, he decided to make his move. He stepped out of the doorway into the dimness of the street. Crossing at an angle, he stepped onto the opposite sidewalk, landing directly in front of Enzo. The restauranteur stopped abruptly and looked at the shabbily dressed youth. He moved to one side, intending to sidestep the annoying intruder. Robbie mimicked his movement, remaining at the same distance apart. The glow from an overhead streetlight allowed each of them to clearly view the other.

Who was this punk, Enzo thought? The street was deserted except for a little kitten scurrying away. He felt for the small knife he kept in his pocket, straightening his shoulders, trying to appear bigger and taller.

"Move out of my way," he growled. With his opened collar Enzo became aware of the thick gold chain he wore around his neck. The hoodlum likely was looking to grab it and run. No way was he going to let that happen.

"Don't you recognize me?"

"Huh?" Enzo squinted. Who was this kid? Somebody he'd turned down for a job? A neighborhood creep who hustled weed near La Luna and had been chased away? He didn't answer the stranger's question. He tried moving the other way. The peculiar kid again mirrored him.

"What do you want, punk?"

"Don't you remember me, Enzo?"

"What? How the hell do you know my name? Who are you?"

"I know all about you, Mr. Restaurant Man. Your place, your staff, your trying to hump every woman you meet."

"Move, you little shit. I'll have the cops here in less than a minute."

"I could do you a lot of damage in less than a minute, Mr. D'Amico."

"How do you know my name?"

Robbie faked a laugh. "Everybody knows *your* name. Enzo the stud. The restaurant Romeo. The lady-killer."

Enzo wrestled to keep his cool. This punk deserved a good beating. "Shove off. Get the fuck out of my way. *Move!*"

Robbie held his ground, remaining immobile, shifting easily from foot to foot, legs apart. He reached into his jacket pocket and pulled out a large chefs knife. The wide steel blade glimmered in the rays of the streetlight.

"Oh, you planning to cut me up, kid?"

There was no reply. Robbie held the knife in front of his face. "See this nice blade, Enzo? It's good for cutting up meats in the kitchen. Steaks, poultry. You know the score. You have a nice kitchen in La Luna. In fact you like feeling up all the waitresses there. Touch some tits, feel an ass. Everyone laughs at you behind your back."

Enzo felt anger rise, but with it a feeling of caution. How would this little prick know this stuff? "Listen, who the fuck are you?" He voice grew louder.

"You still don't have a clue? Look at the knife. Know where I got it?"

"I don't know or care."

"It's from a smaller kitchen than yours. Much smaller. *Now look at it!*"

This kid was certified crazy, not just a street punk looking for someone to rob. Enzo stepped backwards, feeling for his phone to call 911.

"I see you reaching for you fancy phone. The latest iPhone, isn't it? You only got it a few weeks back, right? Vera ordered it for you."

At the mention of his wife's name Enzo felt his stomach churn. How did this kid know so much? It sent a chill up his spine. "I asked you a question," he said, trying to hang onto his tough guy exterior. "Who the fuck are you?"

"I'll let you guess. This knife. It belonged to my girlfriend."

"*What*? What the fuck are you talking about?"

Robbie smiled widely, not caring that his broken teeth would show. "Big hint. It's Fiona's. Fiona's knife. She swiped it from your kitchen."

"Oh, now I know who you are. You're that boyfriend. The bigshot gambler. Yes, I have seen you before."

Robbie nodded. "Fiona introduced me to you more than a year ago. I came to pick her up one night. You acted like a real gentleman, not exposing how much you wanted to fuck her."

In the past Enzo had a few confrontations with angry husbands, and he knew how to handle them, keep things under control. This bizarre kid could likely also be dealt with as soon as he let go of that lethal knife.

"No big deal, fella. Fiona was a good-looking girl, and she knew it. A lot of guys liked her. But she knew how to handle herself. No harm, no foul. Relax." The instruction to relax had its usual paradoxical effect. It infuriated Robbie.

"Relax? What the fuck, man? Fiona's dead because of you."

"Because of *me*? I had nothing to do with what happened to her. It's a terrible tragedy."

Beginning to feel drained, Robbie said, "Bullshit. Fiona told me everything, you bastard. How you used her. How she became your little pastime. Don't think I don't know. And after you got your rocks off and bored you offered her money to help with your fucking drug operations."

At that Enzo froze. "I have no idea—"

"Don't bullshit me, Enzo. Those days are over. She became one of your mules. You and your slob pig of a wife. The shit comes in and the shit goes out. Not so very top secret now? That's where you make your real money. Loads of in hidden away."

"You don't know what you're talking about. Just beat it!"

He continued taunting Enzo, keeping him on the defensive. "Vera gives you an allowance, doesn't she? Like a little kid mommy doesn't trust. Turns the other way while you fuck waitresses at your nearby pad. Your little love nest." He grinned, looking at Enzo's paled face with unblinking eyes. "And now, after you saw Fiona was out of the way, you've moved on, seduced new girls, convincing them to also become mules."

"You're nuts. You think I had something to do with her death?"

"Yes, I do." He peered closer. "Or maybe Vera put you up to it. We all know she hated Fiona, didn't she? *Didn't she?*"

Enzo's eyes darted to the left, then to the right. The street remained deserted. He could try to outrun his assailant or start yelling for help. With luck someone in the nearby homes would hear and call the cops, or better still maybe that patrolling police cruiser would come by again.

He put his arm out. "Listen kid, you have things all confused. I have nothing to do with any drugs or Fiona's death. I'm just a businessman. I run a restaurant. Yes, I liked Fiona Sweeney. She was an excellent worker. I paid her top dollar—"

"Top dollar because you fucked her!" He brandished the knife.

"No, wait! Listen, she told me about you, too. Losing every dime you ever had at poker. How she had to continuously bail you out, then finally kick you out. Toss you out of her life for good. Nothing that happened between her and me was without her full consent—ever. Understand that? I never forced Fiona or anybody else, ever."

"Liar." A peculiar expression came over Robbie's twisted face. He was genuinely pained, Enzo saw. Emotionally suffering and crying out. Enzo thought fast how to best use this to his advantage. He held his hands up. "Maybe I can help you, Robbie? That is your name, right? Fiona talked about you all the time. There's gotta be a way you and me can work things out. You short on money, Robbie? I think I could give you a few bucks to tide you over…"

"I don't need your dirty drug money. I'll take my payment in different ways. Cut you up a bit. Make you hurt like you hurt Fiona."

"She's gone, Robbie. Dead." He spoke with genuine emotion. "I cared about her also. Please believe that. Put down that knife. Let me try and work this out, alright?"

"Did you know my girl was pregnant? Carrying a baby." Robbie wiped tears as he spoke, sniffing, shifting the knife from hand to hand.

"Yes," Enzo said grimly. "I did know that."

"When she died she was carrying my child. Maybe a son. *My* son. And you ended both their lives."

"No, no. She wasn't. You're wrong."

"Her sister Sara told me the truth. There was no mistake. Fiona was definitely pregnant."

"You stupid fool. She didn't care about you anymore. I know she threw you out on your ass. Everybody knew it, and everybody was glad. The child, the baby. It wasn't yours, Robbie. See? Not yours, understand? She broke the news to me herself only days before the accident."

"Fiona told you what?"

"That her baby was *mine*."

"*Your*s? Are you fucking crazy?"

"It's true. Your innocent sweetheart even barged in on Vera and told her. She demanded money. Payment. Blackmail. Get the story now? A hundred grand payday to keep her mouth shut."

"That's a lie! Fiona would never do that."

Enzo laughed in his face. "You really didn't know her, did you? Sure, Vera hated her. She saw right through her from the very beginning. Told me to get rid of her a long time ago. But you're right, I didn't. I kept her. Paid her. She never turned down money. Money she likely gave to you."

Robbie listened, baffled by what he was hearing. "I...I don't believe you..."

Enzo sneered. "You don't? *I* suggested we pay her off. Vera refused. Not a dime, she told me. She said Fiona had to be dealt with. The pregnancy pushed Vera over the top. She swore that if I didn't do something fast, she'd take care of it herself."

"You're telling me Vera wanted Fiona dead?"

"Vera wanted Fiona gone, period. Whatever way. You follow what I'm saying? No pregnancy, no baby, one way or another. Whatever it would take."

Robbie shook his head, refusing to believe. "No, no. *You* were the one that used her and abused her."

"I was the only one trying to help Fiona. You weren't there, were you? You were running around like the loser you are. She'd been counting on me, get it? Excited to be having a child and looking to find a way to start a life of her own. But trying to blackmail me and Vera was the wrong thing to do. She came into the office and made demands. Veiled extortion that angered Vera all the more. Threats to expose La Luna. Vera wasn't going to listen to that. She was livid. And Fiona's ultimatum pushed Vera over the edge. She told Fiona to get the hell out and never come back. Vera screamed, blaming me. I walked out. Then, without me knowing, I think she could have planned carefully. I wondered if *she* followed Fiona that stormy morning to the bus stop. I don't know. She didn't care if Fiona lived or died. There wasn't going to be any child. Period. It's possible she's the one who pushed her into the street when the bus came rushing to a stop in the rain."

Robbie's face contorted at the revelation. The reality closed in on him; Fiona's death really did have nothing to do with him, his debts or Troy's grimy collectors. Nor was it an accident. It was premeditated. "Your *wife* killed her?"

"I can't say for sure, you dumb fuck. But you don't know what Vera's capable of."

Rage mixed with horror and disbelief. "No! that can't be. You're lying, trying to throw blame on someone else."

Enzo glared with scorn. "I'm telling you the way things are. You idiot. Fiona would tell you I was trying to help her, not harm her. And she also would have told you that I'm the baby's father."

Disoriented, frantically trying to take in Enzo's version of what had happened, Robbie howled with anguish. The cry of a wounded animal, loud and tortured. A heartbreaking whine that relayed and echoed, trumpeting down the street.

He clutched his knife and charged like a gored bull.

Enzo veered sideways, trying to protect himself with his arms raised. The weight of Robbie's hurling body knocked them both off balance. Robbie's arm swung out. The blade slashed with homicidal velocity straight across Enzo's throat. Enzo froze, eyes growing ever wider with fright, sputum dribbling from the sides of his wide-open mouth. He stood motionless for brief seconds as thick blood spurted from his neck, soaking his shirt, spraying over Robbie, and splashing on his feet.

Staggering, he tried to emit some sound while Robbie stared, then clumsily he dropped, tumbling to the ground, falling on his back, head hitting the sidewalk with a sickening thud.

Robbie kneeled down beside him, dropping the blood-soaked knife.

Enzo's eyes grew glassy as he stared upward toward the cloudy sky. He gurgled and struggled for breath to utter final words. His fingertips were trembling slightly. He mouthed something that might have been the word my, or mine. Then his eyes grew vacant.

Robbie's face dripped with sweat and splattered blood as he watched Enzo's life ebb away. With his head hung low, and not knowing what to do, he began shaking uncontrollably. "No!" he wailed loudly. "This isn't what I wanted!" He pounded onto Enzo's lifeless chest as if somehow he might revive him in a grotesque imitation of CPR.

Light came on from a window "Call the police!" someone shouted in horror at the scene below.

Robbie looked over his shoulder at a woman staring from an open window above. Other lights along the block turned on. He stood shakily, turned around in a frenzy. What had he done? He fled as fast as he could, not knowing or caring in which direction. His bruised ribs ached, his thoughts fragmented. What had happened? Was it real or imaginary? His heart was beating wildly. And somewhere deep within he realized the truth. He had taken Enzo D'Amico's life.

TWENTY-SIX

Cora used her thumb and index finger to wipe gunk from her eyes. She'd been in a deep sleep, dreaming of her youth in Athens, her parents, sister Lyra, the lovely views of the sea from their country villa terrace. Looking at the ringing iPhone she saw the time was just before 3AM.

"Yes," she said, clearing her throat.

"So sorry, Cora. This can't wait."

"Huh?" She sat up. It was Hunter. "Are you okay? Everything all right?"

"I'm good. Listen, Cora. I just received a call at my house from the precinct. A body was found outside of La Luna. It's been identified. Enzo D'Amico is dead. Stabbed to death with a large kitchen knife."

Cora sat up straight, pushing flowing hair from her face. "Oh my God. Enzo? Was it Rob Perry?"

"Don't know anything yet. I wanted to check with you. The killer got away but there's blood all over the place. There'll be lots of DNA. Have you seen or spoken to Robbie last night or yesterday?"

"Not a word. Not since he split from my house three or four days ago."

Hunter hesitated. She heard him sigh. "An all-points bulletin is out on him. The APB was placed because he's the number one suspect. Listen, he may try to get in touch with you. You're his only contact here now. He may still be armed, we don't know. But I do know that if any squad cars find him they'll be having guns at the ready..."

"And Robbie's crazy enough to try and fight with them."

"They'll shoot him dead if he does, Cora. You gave him a burner phone, right? Hopefully he'll get in touch. If he does, warn him. We want him alive."

"I did try calling. But he may have tossed the burner already."

"Or bought another. Enzo's wallet was still in his pocket, although some cash might have been taken. He may be trying to get out of New York as we speak. We've got alerts at trains and buses and airports already. I'm concerned for him. You and I know he's not a killer."

"He's not, Hunter," Cora agreed. "He's an emotional wreck since Fiona's death. Won't listen to reason, let the police take charge. He didn't listen when I told him I was following leads. He's been determined to find out who did it by himself, no matter what."

"Well, it wasn't Enzo. I can guarantee that. Hal Capps had been watching La Luna with a few plainclothes officers setting up surveillance. The other night they followed a suspected mule from La Luna and hit pay dirt. We collected evidence, enough for arrests. Now there's already a court order drawn up against La Luna and its owners. Both Enzo and his wife Vera were set to be arrested."

"That's wonderful news."

"Yeah. But this complication throws a wrench into everything. We expected to close the damn place down—until this nightmare."

"If Robbie gets in touch I'll try and get him to meet me. Promise he'll get some protection, anything I can think of to try and keep him calm. But he likely won't listen. And now…"

"And now that he's taken a life he'll be even more terrified."

"Is there any chance that this was a street fight? That Robbie may have killed Enzo in some kind of self-defense?"

"Doesn't look that way, Cora. Enzo was a first-class sleaze, for sure. But more than twice Robbie's age and not nearly as big. It doesn't look good."

"I'll do everything I can think of. Even try to get Sara Sweeny involved to help me find him."

"Good. She can be a help. I'll be getting up and driving into the precinct now. Sorry to have called like this. I felt you needed to know."

"I'm glad you did, Hunter. Thank you. I'm getting up too. I'll be in touch."

She put down the phone and hauled herself to the bathroom. She took a cool shower and forced herself awake, her brain working overtime to think clearly and attempt to put together some sort of a coherent plan.

Cora grimly opened the Athena an hour before dawn. In the bleak morning she stared at the street outside. As expected, there was no answer on Robbie's burner phone, though she had tried numerous times. He'd either tossed it or was purposely not answering. Whichever, she had no way of reaching him.

Sunup was close when she put on the local news. Nothing was said about a killing. She left on the television for background noise to fill the depressing silence. Her ears picked up when the newscaster mentioned the mayor's office. "... Stay tuned for an important statement from City Hall at 9AM".

It broke her concentration on Rob Perry, if only for the moment. The television anchor yesterday had hinted at some kind of important news breaking, and she wondered if this was it. Tiredly she picked up her third cup of coffee and took a cold sip. Ugh. She pushed it away.

A key turned in the back door lock. Eddie called out a cheery good morning, followed shortly by Claude and Stavros. The morning bustle of the diner helped Cora concentrate on something other than her worry about Robbie. By 7AM, locals were arriving for their breakfasts, and commuters for coffees to go.

"Can I bring you something else?" asked Sara, with a morning greeting smile.

"Fresh coffee when you have time."

"We have time. Eddie already called Andrew and Maggie for extra help."

Good old Eddie, Cora thought. *Ma Gwann*? She muttered to herself in Eddie's Jamaican patois. What are you doing?

Back to research. The home page for Twenty-First Century Agency LLC popped up. Colorful and packed with information of their wish to build a better New York for everyone. She chuckled at the hackneyed motto. Used a thousand times.

Real Estate. We build. We Lease. We Rent. Cora mouthed the title standout words. Highlighted were a number of photographs of successfully built and sold high-rise properties both in Queens and Brooklyn. Hundreds of thousands of square feet the ad boasted, built to improve neighborhoods across all the five boroughs. Arguably the most competitive place in the world. The list was impressive, Cora had to concede. Clearly the worth amounted to many tens of millions if not more.

The professional PR went on to discuss how they were relative newcomers on the block but were here to make their mark. That their staff was top quality, made up of experts from virtually all over the world.

Again she searched the names and photos of its top officers, several of which had been brought over from rival corporations, two Asian board members, plus several European. Nothing unusual, nothing to catch attention. The single name of Greek heritage had no meaning for her. A clever bunch, she surmised, with a fresh, clean image. Numerous brokers and agents followed, names, years of experience. Oh, to be a fly on the wall during a corporate meeting, she mused. People who could afford such mega-deals are typically only handled by the city's top firms. What role did someone like Ursula really play?

Sara brought in a fresh pot of strong Greek coffee. Cora wiped her eyes with her hand and poured herself a cup.

Stavros knocked and came in for a moment. "Everything's good," he said. "Breakfast business is brisk. Your friend Harry Benzel is here, enjoying his free coffee you promised."

She laughed. "He's worth every cup. Keep his mug full to the top." Then added, "Oh, and also, Stav, there's supposed to be some high-powered announcement coming out of city hall at 9AM. Keep the television on a twenty-four-hour news station, okay?"

"You got it, Mrs. Gus." He gave his usual mock salute and left. Cora sat enjoying her fresh brew. It was eight-thirty when Hunter rang. "What's up? News on Robbie?"

"Something else, Cora. The secret deal I was telling you about currently going on at city hall. Recall that?"

"I do. Any news about it?"

"I received this phone call from a lawyer I know who works at the Office of the Chief Council to the Mayor and City Council…"

"Fancy title," Cora said, fascinated. "Can you tell me why the lawyer called?"

"I can, just a little. She and I go way back. I once helped her with some personal matters. Since then she's always kept me in the loop on important things. Her name's O'Malley. Anne O'Malley. Sometimes she's appeared on TV as a mayoral spokesperson when needed. Anyway, this time O'Malley alerted me. There's a very important statement being released from the city…"

"I heard something about it. 9AM, right?"

"Exactly. What they have to report this morning may have wide-ranging repercussions."

"Affecting me?"

"Could be, and maybe explain a lot of the crazy shit that's been going on. I only know it involves some heavy-duty real estate negotiations underway."

"I'll be watching for sure, thanks."

"Gotta go." The phone clicked.

Cora continued sipping her coffee, wondering, speculating about events that warranted such an extraordinary civic pronouncement.

Harry Benzel sat at the end of the counter at his usual seat. He saw Cora leave her office and waved his hand to catch her attention.

"Getting your coffee the way you like?"

He lifted the cup and grinned. "You betcha, Mrs. Gus."

"Great. Any complaints just let me know. I'll fire anyone who gives you a hard time." She slipped by Stavros as he was taking breakfast orders from diners.

"It's good to see you up and around so fast," said Sara, working as the cashier, putting aside several receipts, giving Cora a sweet smile.

Cora ran a finger by her swollen lip. "This look bad?"

"Naw. Just slightly discolored. Hardly noticeable. Your lipstick covers it well."

"My ribs feel sore but otherwise I'm fine. I know things could have been worse."

"We heard about those pigs. The cops should have killed them both." Glancing at the wall clock she saw it was nearly time for the expected press conference.

The television station switched live to New York's City Hall. There were dozens of microphones set at a slender podium up at the top of the wide concrete steps. TV journalists, radio and online press people were gathering around in a wide semicircle. Two or three were busy checking their mikes and sound systems when the local commentator appeared. "We're eagerly awaiting for this morning's announcement to begin. Hopefully they'll be on time."

The tv journalist poked her microphone toward a round-faced man standing beside her. He had thinning hair, wore an expensive suit. Cora didn't know his name, but he was a recognizable pundit, often seen on local television. "Have you received any advance word on what we're about to hear?" she asked him. He shook his head dourly, eyes squarely facing the camera. "Not a word so far, Susan. But this is highly unusual, seemingly coming out of nowhere with no advance information."

Cora avoided the ongoing chit chat and kept herself busy going around tables and booths, speaking with customers, making sure everyone was being well taken care of in the diner.

Within moments a handful of people came through the doors and approached the podium on the television. A tall, attractive, youthful woman wearing a trendy Scanlan Theodore dark designer suit took the center, with another man and woman standing with serious expressions on either side. She was carrying a handful of written papers containing her notes for impromptu remarks. She tapped the microphone, making sure the feed was live. One of the males at her side whispered a few things in her ear and she nodded, turning her attention to her audience, aware she'd be able to view almost everyone and answer as few questions as necessary.

Within seconds the hum and murmurs of news people ceased, and the crowd huddled and waited.

"Good morning everyone, nice to see so many here on this warm, sunny day." she began with a smile, her hair neatly pulled back away from her forehead. She wore a minimum of makeup, a lightweight concealer hiding several barely noticeable blemishes, and a tinted moisturizer which enhanced her features in a minimal way. If she was apprehensive it didn't show.

Cora moved closer to the television, Stavros standing directly behind her. This woman was a pro, Cora thought. Knew precisely how to straddle the line between looking natural and professional in public. The mayor obviously had chosen his spokesperson well.

"My name is Anne O'Malley," she began, "and I'm the Deputy Chief Council to the Mayor and also to our City Council. Today I have several significant announcements to make, and then I'll answer a few questions. My time is limited so I'll not keep any of you here longer than necessary."

Professional cameras snapped ceaselessly, photographers straining from every conceivable angle to get the best shots.

Anne O'Malley's astute eyes glanced down to the papers she had placed before her, then back to her audience. "For some time now the City of New York's Mayor, with the full knowledge and input from our Governor, has been negotiating a highly sensitive and private series of meetings with one of America's and the world's largest and most famous technology corporations." She waited for that statement to sink in.

"Needless to say, these previously undisclosed discussions were completely confidential. Our city had been approached with a credible and worthy business offer. For certain inducements, including extensive tax breaks, various other incentives and the like, this corporation, and possibly others, had been interested in constructing and opening an entirely new innovative campus of executive offices, artificial intelligence lab facilities, plus a gradual introduction of several new operation centers. Of course, this project was welcomed not only because it would bring an influx of billions of dollars of new income into our city, but also incalculable positive exposure. A world-class endeavor." Here she paused again.

"The location of the anticipated campus and its multiple additional facilities had been carefully drawn out, both by the tech corporation, and by the city itself in an effort to maximize available capacity to accommodate the space required, as well as the huge numbers of newly created jobs. The city was determined to accommodate and win this offered financial bid through challenging and intense *undisclosed* negotiations."

Before she could draw in a breath to continue, a number of reporters began calling out questions.

"Which company is negotiating to build its campus, Ms. O'Malley?"

"How much money is the city being offered?"

"What localities, and what kind of tax abatements and incentives are offered?"

She ignored the shouts. Drawing in air, she continued with a small frown and knitted brows.

"The Mayor's office and this particular business venture had implemented maximum security to safeguard confidentiality and proprietary information..." She halted briefly. "Yet, to our great vexation, we have become aware of ongoing rumors and speculation stemming from leaks of these talks. Initially, we were determined to seek out the disseminators of these trickles of possible information, certain our discussions could continue unabated. And for some months we succeeded."

The crowd now held a collective breath in anticipation of the next revelation.

"However, during this past week it came to our attention that several of the individuals peripherally involved with our complex negotiations had leaked information regarding possible locations of the areas on which this corporation planned to build. For obvious reasons, these were areas with easy access to both of New York's major airports, John F. Kennedy International, and LaGuardia International."

With word of possible leaks numerous reporters shouted out multiple questions simultaneously that grew into an unintelligible roar.

"One at a time!" O'Malley skillfully restored order by pointing to specific reporters. "Yes? You can go ahead."

"Will it be located in Queens, Ms. O'Malley? Or Brooklyn?"

"Both," she said in a quiet, even tone. Then she permitted her voice to grow louder and sharper. "Unfortunately, our mayor has received credible reports that these leaks were genuine. It appears that proprietary information was secretly provided to both individuals and unnamed real estate corporations. Our own investigation was swift and decisive." She waited again to deliver the bombshell.

"As I am speaking now, law enforcement of the NYPD, in conjunction with the F.B.I., are arresting several executive officers of one of the city's largest and most well-known industrial builders, as well as a handful of lesser associates."

A near-pandemonium erupted. Additional shouts ensued, all were ignored.

"Please quiet down, O'Malley demanded. "Equally critical," she continued after a brief hiatus, "a middle-ranking assistant to the Deputy Mayor has been placed under arrest with criminal charges pending for conspiracy with the unnamed real estate company involved. This individual's identity will also be released shortly.

Arrests of some other city officers and employees are currently pending."

This latest revelation caused near pandemonium.

Cora's mouth opened wide. *Oh My God,* she whispered. Solerno was right. He'd recognized the corruption involved, and possible coercion regarding city neighborhoods.

"Name the company, Ms. O'Malley! What are the charges?"

Anne O'Malley lifted her arms and called again for quiet. "In addition, because of this unfortunate discovery, this grave embarrassment to our great city, the technology company involved has today informed both the Mayor's Office and the Governor's Office, that they are rescinding their bid immediately. All negotiations are permanently ended, and their decision is final. They say they cannot and will not continue under circumstances of unlawful practices that could discredit their name and reputation…"

The crown hushed.

"Let me emphasize, due to the actions of these individuals and companies, New York City has lost a major opportunity. This is an appalling and traumatizing blow for both our city's future and its now-blemished reputation."

The flurry of activity and the cacophony among the reporters and journalists swelled to greater heights, shouts, demands, cries for further information. Which famous corporation was pulling out of the talks? Was it Microsoft? Apple? Meta? Maybe a dominant Chinese AI corporation?

Cora's eyes grew wide, as she listened. Her heart was beating wildly. She felt certain the locations requested for the technology campus undoubtedly included this and nearby neighborhoods. The Athena's location might have been a strategic prize, she realized, with close proximity to all major highways to airports, easy subway, and bus access into Manhattan. No wonder these would-be buyers regarded the Athena Diner as something of a vital position in the area. And how many other businesses in nearby areas may have also been quietly threatened or intimidated? The ensuing boom in local available land value would have proven enormous once contracts with the unnamed tech company were finalized. And the unique character of these neighborhoods would have changed forever. Vanished amid a vast new landscape of expensive, cookie-cutter, high-rise construction.

How close that had come to happening.

The city had lost a premier corporation's newest regional headquarters offering jobs and massive tax revenues. Cora felt badly about how much the city may have lost, but inside she rejoiced that the Athena was no longer a target on anyone's wish list.

And she didn't regret for a moment that her stubborn refusals had hindered this project, and maybe she'd therefore played a small part in a demise of Twenty-First Century Agency.

Of course, sheer greed was the root cause of this conflict. It had proved to be an irresistible temptation for the criminally inclined to get in on the action. Now, because negotiations were ended, everything surrounding the affair was terminated. Other local businesses were saved from experiencing their own intimidation and threats, and perhaps worse. This area, in all its shabby urban glory, was saved by human avarice.

Ann O'Malley next spoke of upcoming updates, new details, then thanked the crowd and walked quietly and calmly back into City Hall.

The plethora of talking heads on the local television stations took over with a vengeance. Another major New York scandal to be trumpeted online and in newspaper headlines. This time it was fortunately nipped in the bud, but still left the city humiliated. The jokes, satires, editorials and social media would hum for months with the shame of the city's gain and loss of potential billions of dollars in a New York minute.

Cora answered her phone. It was Hunter sounding excited. "Did you hear it?"

"I heard it. Yes, I heard it all. Is it what I think? This Twenty-First Century Agency has been caught?" She crossed her fingers.

"No one is named yet, but that's my guess. Indictments from bribery to kickbacks, intimidation, payoffs, fraud, plus violating federal banking rules, and perhaps we can include attempted murder."

Cora needed to sit, some time to absorb all the news. She took a seat at the counter, next to Harry Benzel. "Did this business have anything to do with your problems here, Mrs. Gus?"

She smiled at him. "Yes, Harry. I think it does."

It wasn't time for celebration, though. Right now she was exhausted from the trials of recent days. At least the broadcast gave her hope.

Sara Sweeney also let out a deep sigh of relief. She hugged Cora, tears in her eyes, and told her she loved her, and she was the best friend Sara had ever had. It was an anodyne to the grief that would always be part of her life.

"I'll bring you some lunch in your office," said Eddie, recognizing how drained Cora was after these last few days. Cora agreed, eager to unwind. But as soon as she sat down, her mind began to churn with questions. She wondered what might be happening with Ursula. Was she one of the brokers scheduled to be arrested and indicted? And what to do about Allison? That was one decision she dreaded having to make. Cora was stuck between sympathy for her loyalty to her mother and outrage at Allison's betrayal. Her youth was a factor as well. The course of Allison's adult life could be determined by Cora's choices. Should she bring charges against Allison for the power outages? Did the police require Allison to be interrogated about her mother's actions as well as her own?

Claude had cooked a small Greek moussaka for Cora, and rumbles of hunger growled in her stomach when Stavros delivered it on a tray. The last full meal she recalled eating was dinner in the hospital before being released. This was a concoction of mincemeat, eggplant, slices of potatoes fried separately before being layered in a frying pan and topped with a bechamel sauce.

Although a small portion, it tasted like a banquet and provided a spark of vitality. An early celebration for her and the Athena itself, assuming that today's stunning news reports were accurate. Later she was sure Hunter would be calling again, and perhaps they could plan to have a real dinner for two.

When the phone rang it wasn't the head of the detective squad.

"Mrs. Gus?" asked the quaking voice.

"Yes."

"It's me. Veronica. Veronica Labrano. Please can I speak with you? It's important and I'm scared…"

Cora was well aware that Veronica had admitted to being a mule in the past for La Luna's illicit drug operations. "Veronica, listen, if this is about your past dealings, you'll have to turn yourself in and speak with the cops."

"I know," she said, on the verge of deep sobs. "But there's more. Please. I heard about Enzo. I heard what happened described on TV."

"No one is coming after you, Veronica. You're safe. Enzo's death had nothing to do with you."

"It'…it's more than that. Can't you find me a little time? I'll explain everything. *Everything.*" The way she emphasized the last word made Cora curious.

"Where are you?"

"With my three-year-old. Outside, walking. I'm afraid to go home."

"Bring your son with you here. I'll meet you in front. We'll talk alone in my car. It's in the parking lot. How long before you get here?"

"I'll be in front in half an hour."

Cora had been taken aback by the call. Clearly Veronica was terrified. Of course the police investigation would name her in the drug operation both Enzo and Vera D'Amico had carefully set up years before. But it seemed there was more. How she might be able to help Veronica was puzzling. Undoubtedly, there would be arrests coming, and there was little chance of Veronica not being among those charged. How many more were involved she had no idea, but it struck her that if Fiona were alive she also would be facing charges. A sad requiem for a young woman with a bright future waiting.

Veronica Labrano saw Cora beckon from the open driver's seat window in the parking lot. There was only room for half a dozen cars, and she made her way between several. Cora waved her into the front seat next to her, and her son climbed into the back. As Cora shook hands with the little boy and gave him a lollipop, she couldn't miss noting Veronica's red and swollen eyes. It looked like she'd been crying for a long time.

"Thank you for meeting me," she said, blowing her nose into a bunch of tissues bunched in her right hand. Cora passed her a small unopened bottle of water which was gratefully taken. Then she passed it back to her son.

"I know I look a mess, Mrs. Gus."

"I think it's understandable under the circumstances."

"Poor Enzo. You know how I felt about him, but he didn't deserve to die. Not like that, lying on the street. I saw headlines. They said he was stabbed…"

"The details aren't clear yet. I suppose you've also heard about the investigations into La Luna's drug trafficking?"

"I…I had a call from another former employee. She's scared too. She'd also done some running for Enzo and Vera. How am I going to deal with this? I know the police will be looking to talk to me."

"I won't lie to you. They'll want to speak with anyone and everyone who had dealings with La Luna. From busboys to suppliers. In my view, the best thing you can do is be honest. Seek a plea deal. Give evidence if you have to."

She hung her head, hair untied, sagging lifelessly at the sides of her drawn face, skin looking stretched to the bone. Cora noticed more gray hair at the roots than she'd expected. Veronica was likely older than she had thought.

"They'll send me to prison, I know it. I know it."

"If you volunteer to be a witness, admit your part, they'll cut a deal. Maybe even offer immunity. It depends."

"Vera. You don't know Vera." She shuddered and burst into more tears. Cora did her best trying to pacify her with a squeeze of the hand.

"I know you're worried about your kids…"

Clearing her throat, Veronica said, "Not so much my older Jerry. He's almost eighteen and wants to join the army. He's a tough kid. He'll be fine. It's my three-year-old, Eric. They'll grab him from me and throw him into the system. I know how it works. An unwanted foster kid handed from family to family." She shut her eyes and bent her head upward as if praying.

"What about his father? Won't he step in? Or his family? Somebody should be willing to help."

Veronica looked deep into Cora's eyes without blinking. "His father...Eric has no father."

Cora shuddered. Something occurred to her that hadn't until now, and she was hoping against hope she was wrong. "Your son, Eric. Tell me the truth. If you really want me to try and help, I need to understand everything that's happened in your life. *Everything*."

"I wanted to tell you that day in the library. But I just couldn't. You knew that I'd been working at La Luna much longer than Fiona. I told you Enzo used to come on to me. Appraising me like admiring a horse. Making offers and bullshit promises. You know the deal. Trying to get me to go to his place and have sex. Back then *I* was his dream of a woman." She laughed without humor.

"I get it. Enzo pressured you and you finally agreed. Tell me all, Veronica. You wouldn't be the first employee to be abused. Eric is a beautiful boy. *Your* boy conceived with...?"

"Yes, Mrs. Gus. You must have guessed the truth. Eric is Enzo's child."

Cora took in the potency of her words without showing emotion. Inside she was appalled and dismayed. "And you never told anyone?"

"Enzo, of course. He slipped me a little cash to keep my mouth shut, but he wasn't going to lift a finger. He denied any responsibility, snubbed me, and threatened my job if I dared make a fuss about it. I was also scared to death if his wife found out. She has no heart, no conscience. My son Jerry was fifteen then and still needed me. What was I to do? My own family was in no position…alcoholic dad. No mother."

"You're telling me *nobody* was aware?"

"I lied to people, made up a fake boyfriend who was in the navy, based in Seattle. It wasn't hard to do. Fiona hadn't begun working at La Luna yet."

"You said Fiona became like a sister, though. That you shared so much. Fiona didn't know? I find that difficult to believe under the circumstances."

After a brief silence Veronica exhaled out of her mouth, and said, "Yes. I did tell her my secret. She swore she wouldn't tell anyone. Said she could totally understand. Especially with Enzo chasing her like a sick puppy."

"When did she learn the truth?"

Veronica shrugged. "I think when Eric got sick a year ago. He'd had regular shots but caught what the emergency room doctor called RSV. A respiratory thing."

"I know what it is. So then what?"

"Fiona helped me out a little. Traded some shifts, bought groceries for Jerry and me, things like that. She was a real friend."

Cora nodded. "I see that. So that's why she felt comfortable talking to you about her own situation. And not just about her boyfriend's gambling."

"We talked so much. During quiet times at work. Sometimes we met someplace for lunch. Occasionally meet at my apartment or hers. I understood all the pressure she was going through with Enzo and his mean-spirited, spiteful wife. Even why Fiona felt she needed to do some of these drug drop-offs. We were like two sides of the same coin, ya know?"

"What did you suggest she do regarding Enzo?"

"Between her and Enzo it was the total opposite. Me he fucked and tossed aside. Old and used like a rag. Fiona was a different deal. He fell for her, see? More than just getting into her pants. We talked about it. Even with the pregnancy. Enzo was determined to help her. The money. That hundred grand she was going to get."

"And make you a partner in her new business, correct?"

Veronica frowned with annoyance. "She said that, yes. But it still hurt. I tried to get something too. Not for me. Money for Eric. Enzo already had a son--*my* son. But he didn't care about that. Now Fiona, that was *different*. He'd find her money without his wife knowing, he said. Imagine." Tears streamed down her wet face. "I told Fiona it wasn't fair. But she was in another world now. She was concerned about her kid. At first she planned to get an abortion. But something changed her mind. I don't know what exactly. I told her to do it, avoid endless problems with Robbie or Vera, not to have to deal with Enzo having any rights."

"You really think Enzo cared about the baby?"

"He told Fiona it was good by him. Ha. Bastard. My kid was worthless, ya know? Eric was a nothing, a nobody. That's why Fiona had that fight with me."

"Oh? What fight? You never told me that."

Veronica stumbled for words. "We, I thought I'd said…" She turned around and smiled at Eric. "Are you all right, sweetie? We'll be leaving soon." The child seemed calm enough, hearing his mother and licking his lollipop.

Cora instinctively returned to her question. "What fight, Veronica? What fight? Talk to me."

"She…Fiona decided to keep her baby. That's all, really. It wasn't such a big deal."

"I don't believe you. You asked for my help. I don't need to give it. If you don't tell me exactly what happened you can get out of the car now, okay?"

Veronica was shaken by the threat. She had nowhere else to turn. Taking a few very deep breaths, she closed her eyes and put her head back against the headrest, finding it hard to speak. "When Fiona changed her mind I thought it was a big mistake. A kid was the last thing she needed the way things were."

"Maybe, but it was her decision, wasn't it? Why were you so opposed?"

"Because she was ready to throw everything away. She had a good life going for her compared to me. Back at school. Finally rid of that no-good boyfriend. Making top money with the schedules and tips Enzo gave her. I told you, he really had a thing for her."

Cora narrowed her gaze. "You were jealous of Fiona, weren't you?"

Hearing that threw Veronica off guard. "No! I mean we were close. Like a sister to me. I only wanted what was best for her…"

"On your own you decided she shouldn't have the baby?" Cora felt her heart sinking.

"She didn't need a kid, did she? What for? So Enzo would slobber even more over her? Maybe even toss more breaks her way. Time for her to take care of his child? More money to make sure the kid had good food, good care?"

Cora dug in further, sensing something different going on with Veronica. Something telling her Veronica wasn't quite the friend she made herself out to be.

"Sounds like it really bothered you, huh? Enzo quietly being daddy, caring about his new child. Actually willing to go an extra mile. Not like with your baby."

"Damn right! Fucker didn't give a damn when Eric was born. Told me if I said anything to Vera he'd see I was blacklisted from every restaurant in Queens. Tossed from La Luna with a bad reputation, and I know he could do it. He called me a slut, lucky to be working. Think I would let him get away with treating me like a dirtbag? No fucking way, Mrs. Gus. No fucking way!"

"You resented it. You and Eric were just trash to him."

"And Fiona was a queen. Oh what a lady! That wasn't right, you know? I'm not *trash*. I'm no less than *anybody* else. Fiona knew it wasn't right."

"So how were you going to deal with it? Enzo didn't care one iota about your feelings…"

"Really. Well, I was going to show him. I told Fiona, that the money, that hundred thousand he was going to pay, I wanted half. I deserved half. I told her that. When he pays you, I'm entitled to my share."

"And what did Fiona tell you?"

"She said she'd make me a partner in her new business she wanted to open. Put me to work with her. What kind of shitty deal is that? I told her no way. That wouldn't do. She got angry with me, like all this was my fault." Veronica started to quiver as she talked. Her eyes blinked incessantly. "Go get the abortion, I told her. The kid is bad luck for all of us, see? Bad for her, bad for me, bad even for Enzo. Guess what? She all but laughed in my face. That money was hers, she'd help me. *Help* me, like I was some beggar. I told her, and I warned her not to fuck with me."

"Your anger kept growing, didn't it?" Cora's mind kicked into overdrive. "You decided to take action."

"Of course! I'm not stupid. This baby was changing everything. You see that? It wasn't right. I kept pleading with Fiona to recognize that. No one wins if she has this kid."

Cora stared through the windshield, feeling a malevolent new shadow slinking into the bottomless depths of this affair. She thought she had foreseen every contingency, but this was something more. She checked her sudden impulse to shake Veronica by the shoulders. "And you couldn't stand it, could you? You felt cheated, embittered, screwed first by Enzo, and now turned on by your best friend. You were determined to do something about it." It was a statement not a question.

"What a fool she was being, Mrs. Gus. Anyone could tell. If Robbie found out what do you think he'd do? Learning Fiona was having Enzo's kid? With his temper he'd likely kill them both. I told that to Fiona. She brushed me off. Said I was being rash and hysterical. Said Robbie was a good person inside. Kind and caring. He couldn't help his gambling addiction. She'd admit the truth and he'd sooner or later come to terms with it."

"And that made you what? Even more infuriated?"

"I just wanted Fiona to see what was so obvious. Trouble ahead. Big trouble all the way round for everyone." She clenched her teeth. Tears flowed, several dripping from her chin. "She needed to get the abortion. If not, then she needed to somehow lose the baby. An accidental miscarriage, understand?"

Cora gasped, trying to appear as nonjudgmental as she could. But she knew and feared what was coming. Softly she managed to say, "What did you do, Veronica? You need to be honest and the truth if I'm to help you."

"I wanted her to not be pregnant. For things return to normal. If I needed to see to that, I decided I would."

Cora knew she needed to be cautioned in her words, but Veronica also needed to speak the whole truth. She took hold of both of Veronica's cold hands in her own, her face next to hers. "What did you do, Veronica?"

"I...I made up my mind. Fiona needed to have some kind of accident. Fall over at work, maybe slip while carrying some heavy trays, or trip over something in the street. I don't know, and it didn't much matter. Nothing too hurtful, okay? Just to have an accident. Miscarry. It happens all the time, all the time."

"But she didn't fall at the restaurant or in the street, did she?"

"No, she didn't."

"Then what?"

"Then...Then I had this idea." She put her hands to her face and sobbed like a frightened child. "Oh, God! I...I thought I could make it happen myself. I mean, not hurt her. Not really hurt her." She snorted back some of the mucous that ran down her face. "If she wasn't going to fall, maybe a push would do it. A sharp shove, see? So I decided in my mind. I wasn't sure how or when." Her crying became frantic, and Cora put an arm tightly around her. "It's okay,

Veronica. It's all going to be all right. Let it out. It's time to stop holding back."

Young Eric leaned forward, touching her shoulder with his chubby hand. "Don't cry, Mommy," he echoed. That made Veronica bawl even harder.

"Take your time," said Cora, "but we need to understand everything."

After deep breaths, she managed to speak in a low grueling tone, "God forgive me. I followed her that morning in the rain. I waited until I saw her leave her building. I had my umbrella covering me. She had no idea I was walking close behind. All I truly wanted was for Fiona to slip on the sidewalk, ya know? Fall just hard enough over something. A soda can, a piece of broken concrete. Rain was pouring into the sewers, so easy to stumble in water. So slippery. It shouldn't be hard, right? In that driving rain, that awful wind. We made it to the bus stop, me a handful of steps behind. I could have done it then, but there were so many people, all gathered and waiting. I elbowed myself closer to the front. Just a little at a time. Bit by bit. Fiona was already up front, standing by the curb. If she fell there, over the edge and into the street, it might work. It could happen to any woman, couldn't it? An unfortunate accident."

"But Fiona didn't slip in the rain, did she?"

Veronica shook her head, eyes wide like a helpless child's. "No. Damn it, *damn it*! So I did what I needed to do. I saw the bus coming. The wind was howling and so strong. Umbrellas were turning inside out. People were staggering, jostling, pushing ahead. So I held my breath. Then with just one hand I pushed her. I shoved Fiona. She fell headlong, awkward, and stiff into the wind. Real hard. And then that fucking bus came so fast, slamming its screeching brakes... I heard Fiona scream. I saw her falling, yes. The bus pulled by the curb, tossing her into the air. It wasn't supposed to hit her! It wasn't supposed to." Breathless, Veronica coughed as though she was going to vomit.

"But it did hit her," Cora said softly. "It struck before she had a chance to turn."

"Yes. And Fiona cried out. I heard her wail. I saw her tumble to the floor by the fender and big tires. I wanted to grab her and pull her back. This wasn't the way I planned. No, not like this. It wasn't supposed to *harm* her. Her scream ran right through me. Understand? It gave me chills."

"Yes, Veronica. I understand."

"I...I'll never forget it. Don't you know I hear it every night as I try to sleep. Over and over I hear her cry out, her scream for help. But the damn bus crashed right into her." Veronica pulled at Cora's sweater, her face inches away. "Every night I relive that day. I hear it. I hear Fiona. I can even hear her now." Veronica bawled with the desperation of a hungry infant. In the back seat Eric was now crying too.

"Trust me, if you want me to help. You'll admit what happened. Offer to testify against Vera D'Amico for her role in pushing drugs.

Then I'll do everything possible, so you don't lose Eric. Help find him a good home while you're away. Right now he's your number one care."

Veronica took the boy in her arms and hugged him so tightly he was nearly smothered. "I'll try to do as you ask, Mrs. Gus. Promise me. I need you."

"I promise to do everything I can."

Shaken badly herself, Cora tried to comfort them both in her car. But there was no comfort for anyone.

TWENTY-SEVEN

Solerno winked.

"So, you showed up today for a visit?" Cora said, strolling to the small table in the back where Solerno positioned himself relaxedly with a large latte and a croissant, showing off a pair of nicely shined pricey brown shoes.

"I did. After the mind-blowing news on television I thought it was time. Can you find a few minutes to join me for a while?"

Cora glanced over her shoulder to see Eddie looking and smiling widely and with his thumb pointing up.

"I won't be long."

"Take your time, Mrs. Gus. You're supposed to be taking time off, remember?"

She nodded and sat. Her companion offered her his croissant. She broke off a piece and chewed. "It's good."

"This is a good place to eat."

"So I've been told."

Solerno stared at the silky layer of foam topping his latte. "How many shots of espresso is in this cup?"

"Two. We always put two. One third espresso, two thirds steamed milk. Hot steamed milk."

He nodded approvingly. "So that's how they do it. It's good." Picking up his head, looking closely at Cora's still slightly bruised face, he said. "I'd have killed them both. On the spot."

"They'll serve time. Hopefully get thrown out of the country after they serve. Deported. Plus they'll testify against whoever hired them to cop some kind of leniency."

He scowled. "I saw two of the Twenty-First Century executives get busted on tv. Trying to cover their faces, cops and FBI pushing pressing a heap of media out of the way."

"You knew all along that company was shady. That they were behind having businesses strong-armed."

With a shrug, he replied, "It wasn't a slam dunk. Friends of friends had heard a few things. I passed it on to you, that's all."

"Yet you led me right there. Right to one of their building sites, with their name splashed all over the signs. Couldn't miss it. Made me curious to investigate."

"I knew it would peak your interest. Rattle your cage. Lord knows they played extra hard to get at you and the Athena." He leaned in closer, lowering his voice. "What about that elegant woman handing you the offers? Cunning little—"

"Ursula Zoran. Don't know where she is, at least yet. She's on a wanted list. Airports are on alert."

He waved a hand. "If she was smart she fled the country before arrests were made. Maybe drove to Canada and flew from there back to where she came from. Maybe even has several passports with different identities. Who knows? These folks ran a pretty slick operation, I have to admit. Lasted almost a decade. If it wasn't for that assistant to the deputy mayor getting greedy and stupid the whole arrangement might have worked successfully for years." He chuckled at the irony of the FBI investigating various NYC officials instead of the mafia.

"Tip of the iceberg, I'll bet. He won't be the last city official arrested, will he?"

Solerno smiled widely. "Won't he? Ask our beloved tough-on-crime mayor. Elections are coming up. His ass is fried. Staff at City Hall will fall like dominoes, more inquiry committees will be formed, media calls for new leadership. Our beloved Governor will proclaim no knowledge whatsoever of any of this. The tech company that was negotiating with the city will run away as fast as a jack rabbit out of town. Denial, denial. Our deals with everyone are transparent and legal. Yada, yada. History repeats itself, doesn't it?"

Cora agreed, recalling other recent scandals. "Everyone will blame everyone else. It'll be fun watching matters play out though. Maybe I'll throw a popcorn party to celebrate."

"Hey, your hands are clean. You're a victim of their crimes, maybe more than anyone else. You might even be able to sue the city. Think about it. They'll be hundreds of lawsuits against the real estate company plus their brokers. And the deputy mayor's complicit assistant? Fuckin' disaster. Go and get yourself a good lawyer."

"I have one." She smiled.

"Well, I'm clean in this business, too. A citizen bystander." He winked again and thought for a moment. "But what happened with that girl who shut your power down for them?"

"Allison Zoran. Ursula's daughter. I was told she'll be pulled in for questioning. Small potatoes, but so far they haven't even been able to locate her. My guess is that she fled together with her mother."

"Good riddance."

Cora sighed. "Luckily my customers are pretty loyal, so the damage she caused didn't affect things except for a few days. I took a money hit for fresh supplies and the like, but fortunately we were up and running fast."

"You're too nice, Cora." He bit into his croissant. He chewed slowly and carefully, enjoying the sweet buttery taste. After he swallowed, he said, "Maybe she got out of the country with her mother."

"That occurred to me. We'll find out. But the Athena is safe. And you played a large role in keeping it that way."

Growing serious again, Solerno asked, "And, er, that other matter still hanging?"

"Nothing yet. Enzo D'Amico's killer is still on the loose."

Solerno pretended to spit. "Enzo was a jerk. I knew him from way back. No man is gonna make it if he can't keep his dick in his pants."

Cora kept quiet, not wanting to explain about Robbie, and her hope she would hear from him before the police found him.

"Another latte and croissant on the house, old friend?"

"I can deal with that." Cora got up and kissed him lightly. "Don't be a stranger."

"And good luck with that cop friend yours." He was smiling, not bearing any ill will toward Hunter.

*

Cora and Hunter ambled away from the Japanese restaurant on the boulevard. It was one of the newer restaurants that had opened up in recent months along this stretch of condominiums near the Queens Center. He had miso soup and chicken teriyaki. She had the soup and a salmon teriyaki. Red bean ice cream for dessert. They looked into each other's eyes, Cora feeling rested and comfortable as they ate, talking about almost anything rather than events of the past few days. Hunter discussed his ordeals after returning from his army tour in Afghanistan, how his alcohol addiction and PTSD played such a damaging role in causing his divorce. Now after years of AA and therapy, he recognized his own responsibility in the failure of his marriage. The rupture between him and his two children he was still a work in progress. Some of this Cora already knew, but never had Hunter been so open and frank, nor appeared so vulnerable.

In return she shared more of her own past in Athens. She told stories from her privileged childhood, her family, her adventures as a student and career as a translator at the American Embassy. She spoke of the terrorists who caused the death of the American she expected to marry, and the painful ramifications that followed. What she was not yet ready to talk about was the terrible thing she had done afterward, caused by her rage, her demand for revenge, and her own deep sense of guilt. Just as her own view of herself had shifted drastically after these events, she feared that Hunter would see her differently if he knew. That she would lose this developing relationship. So she held back. Hunter, an experienced interrogator, noticed when she changed the subject. But his feelings for her had grown. Now it was obvious. He even admitted that colleagues like Kasey Cosgrove and Hal Capps regularly teased him, and she conceded that everyone at the Athena from Eddie Coltrane to Stavros, to Sara Sweeney, and others could see through her denials of attractions to him. So they shared a laugh and walked on.

Their closeness and smiles spoke of a budding future.

It was a pleasant warm night. Stars were visible through the urban haze. Reluctantly, she brought up the matter of La Luna. "So what's the latest?"

"Well, Vera's going to be booked on drug trafficking. She can try to blame Enzo, but that won't work. We've already got witnesses from some staff prepared to give testimony to cop a plea. They had so many mules over the years. Hopefully we'll put this one to bed. But we know it's less than a tip of the iceberg."

Cora's phone sang and vibrated urgently. She shared a fretful look with Hunter, hoping to keep the evening positive.

"Yes?"

"Mrs. Gus, it's me, Robbie."

Her heart thumped. "Robbie, where are you?"

A pause. "That doesn't matter."

"It does matter. We need to talk. Can you come over to my apartment?"

"I can't, Mrs. Gus. No."

"It's urgent, Robbie. We need to talk about what's happened…"

"There's nothing to discuss. It's over. Done."

Hunter bent over, his ear near the phone. "Keep him talking," he mouthed to Cora, hoping to hear a sound that might identify Robbie's location so he might be taken safely into custody.

"The police need to speak with you, Robbie. You do know—"

"About Enzo?" He sounded like he was about to cry. "It was me."

"Oh Lord, Robbie. Tell me what happened." Hunter could hear Cora's effort to bond with him, keep him talking.

"I guess I just lost it, Mrs. Gus. You don't know. He taunted me, tried to make me feel worthless. And how he talked about Fiona. He said awful things. And he laughed. I don't care what he said about me, but not these awful things about Fiona. I couldn't stand it. I just had to shut his filthy mouth."

"He must have been scared. He tried to shock you."

"He did that, Mrs. Gus. He talked trash. He said Fiona's baby wasn't mine."

"Listen, Robbie. Things were complicated."

"I know you mean well. But telling me that pushed me over the edge. I only meant to scare him with that knife. I knew he had fucked her. I knew Fiona did it out of anger at me. But when he told me my kid wasn't mine...I lost it. I came after him like a crazed bull. It took just seconds. Next thing I knew I was leaning over him, watching him die, and I was crying. He gasped for breath. I pounded on his chest. I told him I didn't mean to take his life."

She could hear the anguish in his voice. "But who's going to believe that? No one. I know I fucked up bad."

"Robbie, hear me out, please. You're so young. What happened, it could be called a crime of passion. He...he'd abused Fiona. You know he did. A jury will see it, too."

"You don't get it, Mrs. Gus. There's no life for me. Not now."

"I can help you get a good lawyer. A top trial lawyer. You and Enzo had a street fight. His death was an accident. It's *not* murder, Robbie. At worst they'd call it manslaughter. You didn't mean to kill. He provoked you."

"I'm a wanted man. Not just the cops. Those thugs are still looking for me. You know how they beat me. That was just a taste of the torture they inflict."

"We can deal with that too, Robbie. Give yourself up. I have friends in the police. They'll keep you safe. I promise." Cora's voice quavered. She squeezed the phone as she fought back her tears. "Fiona would want you to live. To have a fair trial and start a new life."

"Murder one for what I did. That's the law. If cops find me I know they'll lock me in solitary. I know how it works. And then what? A trial? Prison. Prison for life? I'm better off dead."

"You'll get a fair shake, Robbie. Second degree manslaughter could see you free in five years. And if you'll go to the local precinct I guarantee my friend Detective Hunter will take charge and protect you. Give yourself up, please. *Give yourself up now.*"

"It's too late. You've been real nice to me, Mrs. Gus. I appreciate everything more than you know. You became my only friend."

"I'm still your friend! Just think about what I'm asking." Hunter was holding her tightly. Cora was speaking from the depths of her heart and Robbie couldn't see that. And she was right; a good lawyer might plead him down to a minimum sentence. "Can I talk to him?" Hunter whispered.

"Let my detective friend tell you, Robbie. He'll tell you how he can help."

"No, Mrs. Gus. I just wanted to let you know what really happened. Straight from me. This way is better."

"I understand how lost you feel. You know my own life hasn't been as easy as it seems to others…"

"Then tell me. Tell me the truth. Did Enzo lie? Was that his kid or mine?"

"Enzo raped her. That's all you need to know. He was a dog. A pig."

There was silence on the other end.

"Robbie, you there?"

"Are you telling me Enzo *was* the father?"

"I'm telling you that Fiona loved you with all her heart until her last breath. You were the love of her life…"

"And she was mine. That's why I have to go now."

"Robbie, no. Go where? If you run from the cops they may shoot you."

"That won't happen. I'll be gone."

Hunter regarded Cora with a gloomy countenance. He shook his head slowly, indicating there was nothing more to say or do. Rob Perry was going to do whatever he'd already decided.

"Think about what you're saying, Robbie…"

"I have, Mrs. Gus. Believe me, I have. Goodbye."

"Please, don't hang up yet…" Cora implored with a tremble.

The last words Robbie said were, "I have to go. Fiona's waiting for me."

Hunter held her hand tightly. "There's nothing you can do, Cora. It's all up to him to decide."

She nodded. "Of course you're right, but I think I know what's going to happen." Hunter put his arm around her, saying, "Can I come home with you tonight?

She looked at him with wet eyes and a smile. "Yes, Detective, this is our time."

The following morning Cora came into the diner and kept herself busy. She greeted Eddie with a big hug, as well as Sara. Stavros brought her a tray with Greek coffee and an English muffin.

"I think you need to eat," he said, aware that Cora's smiles and hugs were a front for the way she was really feeling.

"Ah, perfect," she said, sitting at the counter, close to Harry Benzel's stool. He'd be coming in any time now she knew, ready for another cup of free coffee. "Do me a favor, put the television on," she told the busboy.

"You usually don't like having the noise begin so early."

She shrugged. "I'm curious about the headlines on the local news." Her toasted muffin dripped with butter. It crunched as she chewed. The coffee was strong and good.

"Hey, Mrs. Gus."

"Hey, Harry. Pull up a stool." She greeted him like an old friend she hadn't seen for a long time. Having her close by made him smile. Cora looked around and felt secure, surrounded by friends, people she genuinely loved. It was a good feeling.

The local news began at the top of the hour.

"Good morning New York," the female anchor said in a cheery voice. "It looks like today is going to be a beautiful one. We'll have the full weather report coming up in just a few minutes. Meanwhile, in a sad story, it was reported that shortly after dawn, a young man was witnessed crossing Queens Blvd. during the early morning rush. Witnesses claimed he purposely stopped and stood still in the middle of this major roadway. He was struck by a grocery truck on its way to make morning deliveries. According to EMS and local police, he was killed instantly. An eyewitness told officials he seemed to purposely want to be hit. We'll have more information on this story as soon as it comes in…"

Cora shuddered and looked away. Stavros stood behind her. Sara came over with her mouth agape. "Robbie," she muttered.

Stavros met her gaze. "How do you know?" he asked.

Cora looked at him. "Sara's right. I think it's Robbie, too." In the heartbreak of recent days the story unfolded with the inevitability of a Greek tragedy, Cora thought.

"Eggs over easy," Anna called from behind the counter to the kitchen.

Cora wiped away welling tears with a napkin. None of this had to happen, she knew. Fiona's death, Enzo's death, Robbie's death.

Maybe Robbie, was right. Who knows? Maybe he and Fiona now were really back together again, at least that's what she wanted to believe.

She reached into her handbag and pulled out a well-worn book of Stoic philosophy.

Life goes on, she told herself. Life goes on. She looked at the book with a heavy heart. If ever there was a time for wisdom, that time was now.

Other Books by Graham Diamond

1- The Haven

2- Diner of Lost Souls

3- Maybe You will Survive

4- Samarkand

5- Lady of the Haven

6- Captain Sinbad

7- Cinnebar

8- Samarkand Dawn

9- The Thief of Kalimar

10- Black Midnight

11- Cry for Freedom

12- Forest Wars

13- Dungeons of Kuba

14- The Falcon of Eden

15- The Beasts of Hades

16- Outcasts

17- Chocolate Lenin

18- Marrakesh Nights

19- Habitats

20- Tears of Passion Tears of Shame

21- The Empire Princess Omnibus Books 1-4

22- Daring New Tales of the Arabian Nights

Made in United States
North Haven, CT
23 June 2023